RUST: HARVEST OF THE HIDDEN

BY SCOTT TAYLOR

RUST: Harvest of the Hidden

Copyright © 2025 by Scott Taylor, All rights reserved.

No part of this publication may be reproduced, distributed, or transmitted in any form or by any means, including photocopying, recording, or other electronic or mechanical methods, without the prior written permission of the publisher. For permission requests, contact the author at scotttaylor.uk.

The story, all names, characters, and incidents portrayed in this production are fictitious. No identification with actual persons (living or deceased), places, buildings, and products is intended or should be inferred.

Cover Design by GetCovers.

Chapter One
    The Hills Have Eyes   3
Chapter Two
    The Funeral   10
Chapter Three
    Auld Mary   16
Chapter Four
    The Secret Ingredient   27
Chapter Five
    Mr Biscuits   36
Chapter Six
    Welcome to RUST   45
Chapter Seven
    The Shuynd   58
Chapter Eight
    Sons of the Owl   63
Chapter Nine
    A Short Drive   76
Chapter Ten
    Thorne   81
Chapter Eleven
    Rescued   89
Chapter Twelve
    Haggvar   100
Chapter Thirteen
    The Gift   105
Chapter Fourteen
    Guest at the Hotel   113
Chapter Fifteen

The Mighty Kah'Baj	119
Chapter Sixteen	
A Fathers Betrayal	128
Chapter Seventeen	
Kiss From A Rose	132
Chapter Eighteen	
An Old Friend For Dinner	145
Chapter Nineteen	
Hammer & Nails	155
Chapter Twenty	
You Can't Say No	162
Chapter Twenty One	
Infiltration	167
Chapter Twenty Two	
Unrepentant	173
Chapter Twenty Three	
Crash	179
Chapter Twenty Four	
We Are Lost	182
Chapter Twenty Five	
Equilibrium	188
Epilogue	
The End.	193
Acknowledgements	

Scott Taylor

Chapter One

The Hills Have Eyes

"Jeez mate, calm down! Let me get my ruddy bag out the... WILL YOU BLOODY STOP YA BUGGER! I know you're angry mate, just let me heave this out of the back... OI! YA NEARLY RAN OVER MY RUDDY FOOT THERE!" Dean scrambled with the catch on the rusted car's rear door, pulling it open and dragging free his rucksack just as the heavily abused motor spluttered a quick protest of black smoke from the exhaust, the door slamming itself closed as it lumbered slowly down the dirt road.

"Thurso is a few miles THAT way!" shouted the angry taxi driver, his head bouncing off the window frame of his barely legal Ford Escort as he trundled away over the patchy road.

"And I hope yer eaten by midges 'afore ye get there too, ya prick!"

Dean stood in a daze, watching the car trundle back down toward the main road, the driver continued shouting obscenities out the window and waving various digits, clearly showing that the red-nosed cabbie had no problem at all using his fingers to count to the number two.

As he planted his rucksack on the grassy mound beside him to use as a makeshift seat, Dean sat himself down and looked over the moorland in front of him, making a mental note that it may be a bad idea to ask an overweight alcohol-soaked taxi driver if he was wearing a skirt because it was comfier on his tackle when driving for extended periods. Sadly nobody had thought to include in the travel brochure that he had picked up before leaving his home in Adelaide that playfully insulting a Highlanders kilt was pretty much up there with trying to eat a house brick. People are going to look at you like you're a madman, and inevitably you're walking away missing more than a few teeth.

Closing his eyes and taking a deep breath, Dean exhaled slowly as he swept his gaze over the scenery, bathed now in the soft light of the setting sun behind him. There was no point in worrying about where fate (*or angry taxi drivers*) had led him this time. This was it, this was what justified him taking a large lump of savings, and on a whim paying for the flights that took him here from the other side of the world.

All his days he had dreamed about visiting Scotland and seeing firsthand the rolling countryside and almost liquid sunlight that bathed this part of the planet. He had spent years with his face buried in books about the Highlands, fascinated with page after page of dramatic battles, snow-capped mountains, and men in kilts hoisting swords that were almost taller than they were. He would dream of riding horseback alongside a warrior princess, her long red hair flowing like fire behind her as she took steady aim with her bow to take down the deer they had spent hours chasing over the moors.

And he would lose himself in tales of myth and legend, of creatures that would steal cattle and crops from unwary farmers, of sea monsters that roamed free in the deep peat-filled lochs, ready to snap up any livestock that drank from the nearby banks or to appear in grainy black and white photos taken by tartan bonnet wearing tourists filling the decks of tour boats.

Dean pulled off his large mud-stained hiking boots one after the other, rubbing his feet through the heavy-duty woollen socks his mother had packed for his trip. He smiled as he remembered her panic when he had told her of his plans. As far as 'Mama Mayes' was concerned, the only thing she knew about Scotland was what she had seen in the film Braveheart. She had then spent the next two weeks buying every piece of warm, tartan clothing she could find so that her little boy wouldn't look out of place when he got to that 'backward, mud-covered hell hole' that he was insisting against her educated advice on visiting, and gave him a stern warning that should he meet anyone with one of those 'melty, lumpy faces like that bugger in the film', he needed to get himself on the first plane back home and into a warm anti-bacterial laced shower.

It was a calm and wind-free evening, and Dean sat enjoying the light as it slowly dimmed over the horizon. He had rarely felt more at peace, or more at home than he did at that moment. His job as a full-time nurse back home meant he was spending upwards of fourteen hours a day running around jabbing people with needles, cleaning bedpans, and shaving fat peoples' privates. To have this time to truly relax and not worry about the pager on your hip vibrating every two minutes was one of the most fulfilling times of Deans' life.

Slowly he pulled his boots back on, lacing them tightly before standing and heaving his large blue rucksack onto his back. Dean realized that he had spent longer here than he really should have, as the light was now failing quickly and he still had miles to go before he arrived at the hotel room he had booked in nearby Thurso.

Dean could see the main road down the hill from where he had been kicked out of the taxi, its muddy track marks still showing on the dry tarmac where it had rejoined the road and sped off.

Pulling out his smartphone he launched the in-built maps application, plotting out exactly where he was in relation to the warm hotel bed that suddenly seemed to be calling him, as the temperature around him started to dip. According to the app, he could follow the road and be there in about an hour and a half. Or if he were willing to risk going as the crow flies, he'd be there in just under the hour. Dean looked ahead into the fading light. The terrain seemed relatively flat between here and Thurso from what he could see, apart from a couple of hills and some small groups of trees that blocked his view of the town ahead. The main problem was the small gorse bushes that smothered the way forward which might make some of the going difficult, but Dean didn't feel that they would put up too much of a challenge against his new, top-of-the-range hiking boots. Hell, they'd been on that television commercial climbing a bloody mountain. How much resistance is some rolling hillside covered in flimsy bushes going to do to them?

Dean opened his rucksack, pulled out his water canteen, and took a large drink. He'd half-decided what he was going to do. He could follow the sensible option and follow the road, maybe thumb a lift on the way to the town. Or he could do what he bloody well came here to do, and spend some time hiking through the Scottish highlands. What would the flame-haired warrior princess have said to him had he decided to take the easy option?

No, he was in the Highlands now, and by proxy a Highlander he would bloody be. If clans of men could cover this terrain in bloody skirts and mud-stained cloth wrapped around their manky feet, then he could do it in his designer hiking trousers and boots. Pulling out his head torch from a zip pouch at the front of his bag, he fastened it above his brow and set off in the direction of Thurso.

The going was slower than expected, the thick knee-high bushes proving to be more difficult to work through as the light continued to fade around him. Eventually, he was forced to take off the head torch and keep it held pointing down toward his feet, looking out for the rabbit holes or rocks that had already tripped him up on more than one occasion. After around thirty minutes of fighting with the terrain and making slow progress, Dean stopped and set down his rucksack, digging out his smartphone again as he sat down, to check he was still moving in the right direction.

As the screen lit up in front of him he heard what sounded like a sharp intake of breath behind him. He spun around, his torchlight splashing itself over the landscape as he searched for the source of the noise, but there was nothing nearby he could see that could explain the sound nor where it may have come from.

"Probably just the bloody wind, stop being a bloody idiot" Dean scolded himself, resettling himself upon the makeshift rucksack seat and turning his attention back to his phone and the map that illuminated its screen, reminding himself that he was the only person out here, and there were no dangerous wild animals that could threaten him this close to the town, whose lights he could just make out ahead through the nearby treeline.

He could feel his blood thumping through his body, as he strained to listen in on his surroundings while he stared at the screen in front of him, paying no attention to the small map it presented. He couldn't stay calm, he was sure it was a human sigh or intake of breath that he had heard so close to him moments before, even though reason suggested that couldn't be the case. As he stood back up and needlessly fiddled with the straps of his bag he searched out of the corner of his eye for anything around him that could be a threat.

"It's maybe another walker or a domestic dog? Ah, it could be one of them wild cats or something, too bloody scared to get too close I bet. I SAID YOU'RE TOO RUDDY SCARED TO COME CLOSE, AREN'T YA!" Dean bellowed into the darkness, raising his arms as a way of threatening the stillness and calm around him, determined to show whatever had rattled his thoughts that he wasn't to be bloody messed with.

From somewhere behind he heard a soft, menacing chuckle.

He swung his torch around, defiant to the night and whatever it contained, before a flash of four or five sets of eyes were caught in the beam as it swept over a crop of nearby rocks. They were only there a heartbeat before they were gone, but that was enough to throw Dean into a panic. Scrabbling toward his rucksack as he held the light up ahead of himself defensively, he managed to hook his hand onto one of the shoulder straps and haul the heavily laden backpack up into the nook of his right arm before half sprinting toward the town lights that glinted faintly through the nearby trees.

His breath came in short gulps as fear drove him through the rough bushes as fast as he could manage, the short ankle-length branches he powered through tearing at his trousers and scoring his legs with welts. The lights ahead were getting brighter now, it wouldn't be long he thought before he made it to the outskirts of the town and to safety from whatever was stalking him.

Struggling to maintain balance whilst trying to support the awkward unbalanced load of his rucksack, his foot dipped into a rabbit hole and he flew forward into his chest, his face crunching through one of the low-level gorse bushes and sliding off a sharp rock hidden amongst its leaves. He lay stunned, his bag had fallen off to one side and he couldn't see it in the moonlight. The torch was of no use, as it had flown from his hand as he fell and had landed facing down in the dirt a good few feet away from where he lay.

Dean lay in the dark, his chest heaving up and down gasping for breath as his wide eyes scanned left and right for whoever was tracking him. He felt something wet roll down into his right eye and lifted his hand to his head, tracing a small split to the skin above his eyebrow that he must have picked up from the rock.

Scrabbling to his knees he braced himself against the rock with his left hand, dizziness sweeping through him as he tried to remain upright and focused on what was around him. Despite his fear, he was also enraged. If whoever was out there thought he was going down without a fight, they'd have another think coming! If he could survive fifteen hours of work in an Accident and Emergency department, he'd survive some backward, skirt-wearing local, out scaring tourists to get his jollies.

"WHY DON'T YOU BLOODY WELL SHOW YOURSELF AY? C'MON, COME HERE AND LET ME PLANT A BOOT IN YER BLOODY ROCKS!" He'd managed to get unsteadily to his feet now, his left eye scanning back and forth while the right contended with his brow swelling from the bash it had taken and the blood still seeping down his face.

Pulling his t-shirt out from under his jacket, Dean tore at the dark fabric until he had pulled away a good length of the bottom seam. Standing defiantly with one foot braced against the rock, he tied the torn material around his head to stem the blood flow from the cut on his brow while he looked around for the torch.

It was gone, or perhaps the battery had died? Either way, he couldn't see any light coming from the place where he thought it had landed before. Maybe it had taken as big a knock as he had? Well, there was no point worrying about it now, he needed a light source to get his bearings, find his rucksack, and try to make it to the town before whatever was following him made a move.

The phone! He could use the screen as a light source, at least as much as the screen would allow so that he could get the hell out of here. His head throbbed as he pulled the phone from his pocket, and a fresh wave of dizziness hit him as he dropped again to his knees, doing his best to stay upright as he lifted the phone, turned the screen on, and pointed the light outward ahead of him.

Eyes. All around where he stood, eyes stared back at him, all from just below the height he was now kneeling at. He fell back onto his backside, his hand shaking as he scanned the phone around from left to right, illuminating more and more sets of eyes all staring at him as he started to scream.

The phone tumbled from his hand in his panic, his hands scrambling in the bush below him to drag it back up and shine it outward to the eyes all staring at him, unblinking. There were at least twenty or more pairs of eyes around him. Small, dark bodies moved closer to him now than they had been moments before. He scrambled backwards with his free hand, shuffling along backwards on his ass through the rough bushes that scratched and tore at his palm. As he moved backwards his hand slipped into another hole and he fell, jarring his back and banging the back of his head on the ground.

His phone flew into the air and landed just behind his head in the dirt, the light blinking off as it struck the ground. He twisted himself round and reached back, his hand thumping against the dirt trying to find his phone. He froze as the screen lit up, in the hands of... Something. The creature's red-smeared face was lit up by the screen, which now cast a blue-tinted glow over the wide, unnatural eyes that were glued to the smartphone held in its small claws. It turned its face slowly toward Dean, now lying frozen in fear at what he was seeing, and smiled, showing off rows of small, jagged teeth.

Before Dean could react, a roaring sound broke the silence around him. Two screaming trucks were racing toward him with rows of headlights lighting up the whole hillside, horns blaring, and voices shouting over the roar of the massive tyres crashing through the trees ahead.

Dean swung his eyes back to the thing holding his phone, but whatever it was had disappeared. He scrambled onto his knees as the two trucks screeched to a halt facing him and looked around to see where the thing had gone. He could make out no sign of the smiling, wide-eyed creature nearby. Only the rustling of the low-level bushes as whatever 'things' had been there now took off across the moors around him, or he assumed dived down the rabbit holes that peppered the ground.

"A'right pal! Haha, what a bloody state ye are! Have you been on the Drams already? You're lookin' a right bloody shambles! Aww wait, that's a bloomin' Iron Maiden t-shirt you've wrecked there man, I'm sure there's a law against that kinda disrespect. Honestly, some folk have nae appreciation for the classics.."

"Focus Gunnar, the poor man's hurt. Get out and help him into the truck."

"Aye, okay, keep yer knickers on. Jeez man, I'm just saying. Ach, dammit, I've caught my braces in the bloody seat belt again. Right pal, let's get ye sorted! Ooft, look at the buggerin' state of yo- WHOAH! That's a bloomin' tour shirt too! Ye'll no replace that easy ye fecking eejit." The man continued to grumble as he leapt down from the truck and made his way toward Dean, picking up his rucksack and hefting it up into the flatbed.

"Let's get ye back to our place and sort ye out, and we'll have a wee chat about what you DIDNAE SEE tonight eh? Dinna worry pal, it's nae far and we have scones!"

Scott Taylor

Chapter Two

The Funeral

As I desperately scrabbled with the inner pocket of my suit jacket, I instantly learned three important life lessons. Firstly, never buy a jacket with an inner pocket that's over an inch smaller in width than the diameter of your hairy hand, unless you enjoy getting your knuckles jammed in the velour lining and then pulling the whole thing inside out like a prolapsing anus. Secondly, never let your recent ex-partner have access to your phone when you're in the heart of the breakup unless you want her to set your ringtone to be loud sex noises with the volume set to full.

And finally, not one single person amongst the large congregation of mourners standing around at your uncle's funeral will offer to help you or your now orgasmic shouting trapped hand as you struggle to remove the infernal mobile phone from your pocket.

"I'M SO VERY SORRY!" I screamed as my hand finally came free with the phone, accompanied by a tearing sound as the internal pocket detached itself and came along for the ride. "That's not my usual ringtone I swear! Let me just.. Where's the damned mute button.. That's it!" I held up the now silent and pocket-lining wrapped phone triumphantly for all to see before stuffing it into my trouser pocket, shuffling backwards to try and melt into the crowd around me, or preferably the ground below me.

The minister having regained his composure, re-flattened his substantial comb over against the howling Highland gale that was battering the gathered mourners and once more began extolling the virtues of my late uncle Huey. I couldn't help but smile at hearing the minister call him that. It wasn't his real name after all, just a nickname that he'd picked up in his younger days and had stuck with him throughout his days. It didn't bother me to hear it being used, in fact, it made things feel a bit more personal as we all stood there in the freezing wind staring at the dark wooden box that held him.

His birth certificate branded him as Alan Stewart, however, he'd earned the nickname Huey courtesy of the Thurso Police Force, who spent a night listening to him shouting that name into the police cell toilet. He'd been locked up after he'd spent eight hours drinking peach schnapps in the nearby Royal Hotel, then lost a drunken bet that he could eat a whole 'Winter Spice' scented candle before Coronation Street came back from its commercial break on the telly over the bar.

He'd got as far as the 'mulled wine' layer before his stomach turned, and he projectile vomited a rainbow of waxy peach-scented evil over poor old Isla McPhee, who had been sitting quietly at the next table minding her own business excavating boogers from her lumpy nose and wiping them discreetly under her velour chair.

I only paid half attention to the Minister as he droned on, telling the gathered mourners about how Huey was a wonderful, caring man who would drive out to the Minister's croft at least twice a month to help with restocking the peat stack and chase off any foxes that came to bother the old Ministers hens. I couldn't help but chuckle to myself, passing it off quickly as a cough after my Aunt Cathy shot me a look that let you know your arse had been marked for a wallop with her brolly at a later, more convenient time of her choosing.

Chasing off foxes! What a load of pish! I couldn't help but smile as I kicked away an empty Cheesy Puffs packet that had blown against the leg of my freshly paid-for black suit trousers. Everyone who mattered knew that the only reason that Huey went out to the Minister's croft was that he was stealing eggs from the hen house, attaching bicycle clips to the bottom of his trousers, and then piling as many eggs down the legs of his plus fours as he could. He only stopped after the minister one day noticed his lumpy legs from the kitchen window as Huey waddled back to his car.

The minister had hurried to the door and shouted after him, asking if he'd seen a doctor yet about the shape of his hips. Huey, taking a fright upon hearing the Right Honourable croft dweller roar at him from the open door, tripped over his brogues and landed awkwardly on the cobbled driveway, mashing a good dozen eggs into his 'meat and two veg' before jumping into the front seat of his battered Mini Clubman, mouthing apologies through the closed car window as he sped off along the single track road back to Thurso. It took a week of scrubbing to get the egg out of his car seats, and a month of sleeping on the sofa when Aunt Maggie saw Huey's trousers with the crotch stained in white, gooey fluid hanging out of the laundry basket.

"We've all suffered a terrible loss this day," said the minister, the comb-over now standing perfectly upright above his left ear as the wind howled through the headstones surrounding us, "losing our good friend and family member Huey has left a hole in all of our hearts, but I have faith that our community is strong, that we'll pull together and offer our love and support to the Stewart family during this dreadful time."

I nearly jumped out of my skin as someone grabbed at my hand, drawing a good few extra black looks from the seemingly professional mourners around me. I yanked my arm away when I realised that it was my other aunt Maggie, who'd worked her way through the mourners with an almost CIA-trained combination of stealthy elbows directed into ribcages, and the odd polished shoe getting the point of her walking stick right in the pinky toe to shift the more stubborn graveside mourners out of her path.

"We need to talk Angus, it's important." Maggie glared at me straight in the eye whilst simultaneously rearranging her knickers.

"Come to the house tomorrow afternoon, make it about twelve." Another dig at the twisted elastic of her undercrackers, "Once you've got yourself settled and done the rounds of the people you need to see first of course."

Maggie had a way of letting you know that she was giving you the option of doing other things first because she was all nice and caring like that. But something about her inflexion also suggested that if you didn't make her request a priority, your kneecaps would be seeing the business end of her heaviest soup ladle. The big one too that she stole from the Salvation Army, after ramming it into her wheeled tartan shopping trolley during one of their free lunch days for the senior citizens.

"Okay, okay.. I'll make sure I'm there tomorrow" I slowly shuffled backwards unconsciously to keep myself out of headbutting or biting range. Aunt Maggie was lovely, but ever since she'd had that nasty fall at the Post Office counter she was prone to having a swing at you for ill-perceived slights, or even if she just 'felt it in her pish'.

"Right then, that's settled." with one last heave at her crotch she turned to walk away, looking slowly over her shoulder back at me.

"Your uncle Huey loved you you know, broke his bloody heart when you took off to Aberdeen all those years ago without a bloody word of goodbye." Maggie set off toward the grave, "He's left you things too, a wee box at the hotel. Couple of other matters too needing yer attention before ye piss off back south, but we'll talk about that tomorrow."

She turned back toward the grave as the minister was winding his eulogy up, whilst desperately holding down his wayward hair with the heavy bible he took everywhere. With one final blown kiss toward the casket, Maggie turned and walked back to me, taking my arm before setting off along the path back toward the car park.

"Anyway Gussy my boy, enough bloody grieving for today, aye? Let's get ourselves down to the Legion before the Minister." Maggie gave my hand a reassuring squeeze, while a grin broke out across her face at my grimace at being called 'Gussy'.

"I hear his missus has taken to her bed with a dose of the skitters, so you know he's nae touched her homemade scones this morning before coming here." Her pace suddenly quickened, "If we don't get to the bloody Legion Hall in time, the hungry bugger will have worked his way through a' the bloomin' ham and pickle sandwiches before I can get a bloody look in!"

We made our way into the car park, jostling towards the steamed-up Fiesta that was going to be Maggie's lift to the wake, It struck me that this was the first time in years that the majority of our large family had been together in one place. Looking around the small car parking area I saw cousins climbing into people carriers with small kids arguing about which seat was lava and which one was safe. I saw aunts hugging uncles, hurriedly smoking rolled-up cigarettes against the cemetery wall before the wind tore it out of their mouths, and friends of the family heading back to their cars, a sea of black ties waving in the wind as they ducked into their condensation covered vehicles before setting off on the short journey back into town.

I stood for a minute watching the cars pull out, waving at my cousin's kid who was giving me the finger out the back window of their battered Audi. I pulled my collar up against the wind and jogged a few steps to catch up with Maggie, whilst fumbling through my remaining intact pockets for my keys as another car of mourners passed, staring blank-eyed at me as they drove away toward the town.

I couldn't help but feel a wee bit like an intruder. Like I was somehow faking being a member of this grieving family who were all now heading on their way back to the British Legion hall in a procession of crappy, half-rusted cars that they probably paid a Highland motor dealer an arm, a leg and at least one testicle for.

These were family who'd never really left the boundaries of Caithness, and if they had it would have been little more than a day trip to Inverness where they would spend the day panicking about the traffic and head straight to Mcdonald's, buying ten Big Mac meals from the surprised counter staff. Enough to feed themselves and the rest to bring home for the relatives with waiting microwaves, eager for a reheated taste of big city living.

I however had moved completely away to a new life in Aberdeen and had rarely ever come back. A world of fancy burgers, bendy buses, and 24-hour garages was now second nature to me. Coming home to Thurso was a relief, a chance to get away from the noise for a while and breathe.

But still, I felt like an outsider when I arrived at the family gatherings like I was tainted by the bigger world and they were just doing their best to accommodate me until I flew away south again. A quick strike in the shin from Maggie's stick broke me from my daydream, snapping me right back to throbbing-legged reality.

"Wake up halfwit! What the hell are you doing?" I quickly stepped back as she rearranged her grip on the stick, fully expecting a possible whack in the baby maker, "Honestly, I'm sure your mother held you under the bath water for a bitty too long when you were a kid.."

She swung open the car door and waited with a glower for me to hurry the hell up and give her a hand. Without another word, I was soon lowering her into the passenger seat and helping her buckle in as she complained about my head being full of 'tattie water and nonsense'.

"Now mind, be sure and come tomorrow. And while I'm thinking of it, best if you wear that suit again too, but give it a tickle with a good brush first eh?" She struggled against the seat belt while pulling her bunched-up dress out of her lady garden with the complete lack of discretion that becomes your birthright after you hit the age of sixty, "And bring some Rich Teas too, I'm all out and I'm not having you gobble your way through all my bloody Hob Nobs."

I stood and waved as the car took off toward the exit to the car park, my wonderful Aunt giving me the finger through the steamed-up glass as the car swung around past the caretaker's shed.

I couldn't help but laugh to myself as I watched the car pull out onto the main road and disappear, before pulling my keys out of my trouser pocket and taking the few short steps that led to my crappy motor. I stopped with my key halfway to the car, suddenly feeling the heckles on the back of my neck rising. If I had any form of 'Spider-Sense', it would be bouncing around my head screaming for me to turn around.

"Surprised you made it today 'Gussy', I didn't think you'd deem us worthy enough of your almighty presence."

Only one person in the family other than Maggie called me Gussy, it had been one of those nicknames that as a kid seemed hilarious to the bullies, before they realised it was just bloody stupid and gave up on it. But there was always one brain-numbed halfwit who couldn't see why it had stopped being funny and would continue the mocking until the day they inevitably died alone in a smelly flat, covered in empty crisp wrappers. In my case, it had to be a family member.

"Hey Paul, long time no see. You're still looking well." I turned slowly around to see my sneering cousin standing grinning in front of me. I was flat-out lying, and as I leaned against the damp door frame of my nearly dead Mondeo, I couldn't help but stare at the state this man had let himself get into.

Paul was a large, overweight man with a permanent sneer raking itself across his oily, spot-filled face. Not so fat that he had to wash with any kind of sponge duct-taped to a long stick, but enough that if he was faced with more than three sets of staircases in a row he'd give up and go for a seat and a jammy doughnut instead. What was more disconcerting about Paul were his eyes. Not that they were any kind of unusual shade compared to anyone else, but that they were just that dark and far enough apart that you couldn't help but wonder if at some point in time one of his early ancestors had maybe played 'Naked Twister' with at least one or two domesticated farm animals.

"Are you coming to the Legion for the wake? You don't have to you know. You could easily just jump in your car and head due south instead. Get yourself back to the big city, eh?" Paul produced a swift chocolate bar from what I could only assume was a hidden pouch in his sleeve, "I'm pretty sure they're missing you down there and I'll just tell people that you had an important call on your 'Sexy' phone". Paul chuckled to himself, his jowl quivering above his black shirt and rainbow-coloured tie as he shoved the entire bar of nutty chocolate into his face. If I'm honest, I was unconvinced he'd fully taken off the wrapper first.

I smiled, mainly to stop myself from scowling at the cocoa-stained sneer on the tubby bastard's face. I hated Paul, always have done, ever since we were kids together and Paul had used a cigarette lighter on at least fifteen of my prized Smurf collection. Poor Smurfette had gone from looking like the chirpiest, happiest Smurf that had ever Smurfed, to looking like a prop from the classic horror movie, 'The Thing'.

He had a thing for fire all through his childhood too. Always armed with a pocket full of stolen lighters he'd gathered over time, stolen from passed-out relatives who'd had one too many supermarket-own-brand vodkas at the latest family drunken gathering. Paul had been spotted a few times by worried neighbours hanging around the scene of various burnt-out wheelie bins, staring glassy-eyed and ecstatic as the pyre of flaming nappies and burning chip wrappers would blow smoke all over the street. He'd also been chased out of at least two gardens by nearby residents for standing staring at their brand-new wooden sheds whilst casually flicking a disposable lighter by his jacket pocket.

"You know Paul, today isn't the day for this. Let's just play nice for a while, eh? At least for the next twenty-four hours, please." I turned and opened the car, stepping around the silver door as it swung open. "Today's not about you, and it's not about your stupid attention-seeking tie or whatever bloody problem you have with me these days", I dropped into the driver seat, stuck my key in the ignition, and started the engine, "God damn it man, It's about your father, who we just bloody watched get lowered into the ground. So can we please just act like normal flippin' people for today of all days?" I turned the key and started the engine, "Anyway, if I was you I would be less worried about me today and more about the bird shit all down your crotch."

With the sleight of hand speed of a young Paul Daniels, I quickly shoved the car into gear and pulled away, watching Paul in the rearview mirror trying his best to wipe his crotch furiously with the large, bogie-covered handkerchief he'd been clutching since I first saw him on his arrival at the cemetery. There was nothing on Paul's crotch for him to wipe away, but with Paul's massive stomach obstructing any view south since he was fifteen years old, there'd be no way for him to properly check until he waddled himself in front of a full-sized mirror. Winding up Paul like that would just cause more problems, especially with Maggie when Paul inevitably moaned and complained about what a horribly disrespectful shitbag I was. I just hoped that for once in his life Paul could take a wind up on the chins, and no more would come of it.

Chapter Three

Auld Mary

As I pulled out onto the main road and accelerated, turning the volume of the radio down to hide the sounds of the latest talent show winner screeching their way to the top of the festive charts, I considered turning around and apologizing to Paul for the joke I'd played, perhaps be the better man and offer him a lift back to the wake.

I kept thinking this as I sped up toward the town and the nearby Mount Vernon flats and realised that no, there was a reason that everyone had sprinted, hobbled, and fought their way to their cars before Paul could waddle himself away from the graveside. Having that brute in your car not only would cause serious structural issues with your heavily strained suspension and brakes, but also because Pauls' obsession with eating anything that was coated in, or had even been in the vicinity of cheese within its shelf life meant that his 'movements' were a thing of horrendous legend amongst the pub regulars around the town.

Many a man had risked sprinting out of a bar into fast-moving traffic than dared to hang around nursing their lager while Paul waddled towards the toilets complaining that his pub lunch 'just wasn't sitting right'. One of the local bars even had to call in a drain man to clear the lines after one of Paul's visits, requesting that the poor guy maybe best bring his most secure haz-mat suit, at least two priests, (*young and old*) and some kind of flamethrower apparatus to help tackle the demonic entity Paul had left behind.

No, it was probably best I left Paul to make his way back and avoid any more contact with him if possible, especially since I wasn't planning a long stay in the Highlands at all. I'd told my Sergeant when I left that I would be back to work by Friday at the latest, that being up north was merely a formality and a chance to quickly 'show face' out of respect for an uncle I had loved, but had long fallen out of touch with. I didn't mention however that alongside coming to pay my respects, the details of Huey's death just didn't sit right with me, and I wanted to do a little prodding around to see if everything was correct.

As I listened to the cars' fans trying feebly to blow hot air against the steamed-up windscreen, I worried that I may come across as a bit cold toward my family when I'd mentioned to them earlier that I was planning on heading south as soon as possible, that perhaps that was why I was getting cold looks from those who had passed me on their way out of the graveyard's car park.

It wasn't that I didn't care about the family who still called this far northern town home, but between my work shifts with the Police demanding most of my waking hours and my somewhat unhinged ex-girlfriend doing pretty much the same, I just didn't have time to get into family small talk and idle chatter. I had to get myself back south to keep the proverbial boat from tipping over and taking on water, and judging by the number of brown envelopes with red ink writing that were piling up behind my front door, it would have to be sooner rather than later.

I was confident that the family would all understand that I was a busy man with responsibilities and that there was no chance I'd be able to hang around and take part in the many whisky-soaked wakes that would pepper the next fortnight or more of mourning. Plus, the thought of having to face a drunk Paul at some point left a sour taste in my mouth. No, it would be better if I left as soon as possible. Less stress for everyone that way. I'd hang around to see Maggie in the morning and maybe an extra day to visit some of the other family members and ask some questions before heading back south.

The traffic lights ahead shone red through the thin sheet of rain that had started to pepper the Mondeo's windscreen, the light pitter-patter punctuated by the occasional thump of the intermittent wiper blades as they cleared the screen. I was lost in thought and completely on autopilot, my body doing the necessary driving work while my brain drifted off toward old memories of the times I had spent with Huey.

My own parents were deadbeats, my father had taken off down south when I was only a small boy, leaving behind a trail of infidelity and broken hearts, while my mother became reclusive and spiteful, only finding solace in the bottom of a deep whisky bottle. When she looked at her son after the divorce all she saw was his father smiling nervously back at her, so a large portion of my childhood was spent avoiding her sudden, drunken rages or the obvious disdain she had for me, leading me to hide out at friends houses until the storm had passed and it was safe to go home.

Uncle Huey had always been around after his brother, my father, had deserted his family and took off with his tail between his legs. Huey would make a point of taking me out on 'wee adventures' each weekend, where we would go down to the river and fish for a while with whittled-down tree branches and bits of string dragged out of one of the many pockets that covered Huey's trousers until the gamekeeper chased them off under a string of obscenities and threatened shotgun pellets. Or we would jump in Huey's old truck and handbrake turn through some nearby fields for a while until the day that is when I got a little bit too excited and vomited up my entire lunch of cheese spread crackers all over Huey's dashboard. The offroading adventures after that were always a bit more subdued, and nearly always happened before lunchtime.

Huey would pull up outside my mother's house to drop me off, promising that the next weekend there would be an even bigger adventure to be had. And as my mother sank deeper and deeper into her misery and hatred of the cards she had been dealt by the world in general, our adventures would happen more regularly as Huey stole me from the dark, clutter-filled house as often as he could.

Realising where I was, I swung the car into The Regent Hotel car park and turned off the ever-complaining motor. I picked this hotel partly because it was close to the British Legion building and the town centre, but also because I'd gotten horribly drunk there once in their public bar during my younger, wilder days and they'd graciously put me into one of the rooms to sleep it off overnight free of charge. While I slept, they also managed to recover my missing torn trousers and underpants from the end of the flagpole that hung out over the main street. After that, I kind of felt obliged to make sure they had my business whenever I was north visiting.

After unfolding myself from the most uncomfortable seat that Ford had ever designed, I pulled my bags out of the back of the car, slammed the boot lid down, and dragged myself through the rain around the building to the main entrance. I didn't mind getting wet, it was a given when you were a Highlander that you were going to spend most of your waking moments perpetually soggy due to the temperamental nature of the northern weather system.

It wasn't uncommon to see locals dressing for all weather conditions, their top halves draped in waterproof jackets and hoods while their bottom halves sported garish shorts and white sports socks pulled up to the thigh, with their feet jammed into open-toed 'Flip Flops' in case the sun appeared for more than a few glorious minutes.

Shaking the loose water off my jacket, I stepped into the ancient revolving door that had stood at the front of the old hotel since time began, designed ingeniously to be just that inch too narrow to accommodate an average-sized person with more than one bag in tow. After a good couple of minutes of swearing, breathing in, and cursing out whoever's job it was to oil the bloody hinges, I burst out into the reception area of the hotel and stumbled to a stop. For a second I was glued to the spot, taking in the decor around me and how absolutely nothing had changed in the past eight years since I'd left the town. Well, that wasn't strictly true, they had replaced a couple of the small tables that crowded around the large ornate fireplace in the reception area. Word had it that the last ones had been 'badly damaged' after a recent McPhee wedding reception had got a bit out of control, and ended up with the drunken newlyweds taking bets on which of them could headbutt their way through a table the quickest. Seemingly the bride had just edged into the lead before fainting into her pint of lager and bowl of mixed nuts.

"Angus!! ANGUUSSS!! OVER HERE! Ach, get oot my road wi' that stupid wee bag. What? LOOK AT ME AGAIN LIKE THAT SUNSHINE, AND IT'LL BE MORE THAN YOUR EGGS THAT'LL BE GETTING SCRAMBLED IN THE MORNING!" A very round, small woman had crashed out from behind the reception desk and was plunging through the assembled queuing backpackers, kicking bags and shins out of the way as she steamed in a straight line toward me.

"MY BOY! How the hell are ye! I've been waiting all day for you to arrive, been excited since I saw your name on the booking sheet!" Before I could say a word she was pressed against me, hugging the life out of my legs and hips whilst her bosom snuggled in just close enough to my 'Gentlemans Sausage' to make me feel really uncomfortable.

I wasn't surprised to see that Mary Gunn was still working at the Regent Hotel, and as I wriggled myself free of her bear hug I couldn't help but grin as she pinched my cheek and hugged me again. I was sure that Mary was ages with my grandmother, yet was still impressed by how quickly she could move through a crowded reception area, almost like a greased-up Russian gymnast as she dragged me by the arm toward the main desk.

"Damn, it's good to see you Angus, When was the last time you were here? Ach, it's that bloody rare that I forget!" She shot me a mischievous look as she sprinted behind the desk, forcing a worried-looking manager type in a suit to leap out of her way and apologise profusely while she grabbed a key from the nearby rack. She'd worked at The Regent Hotel since she was a young girl, and despite being nothing more than a glorified reception desk operator, it was pretty much understood that she ran the whole place with an iron fist[1].

"Right, got your keys here! C'mon loon, let's get you up to your room." She bustled out from behind the desk and motioned for me to follow her past the line of people waiting for their turn checking in, all glowering silently with very British indignation that I had skipped past the queue.

"This way! Ach, and I got you a damned fine room too, one of the ones with the new toilets that dinna fling yer wee brown soldiers right back up at you. Oh, and it's double glazed too, so you'll no' hear the people spewing up their cheap vodka outside the pub next door in the early hours!" She took off up the stairs two at a time, her little legs thundering against the carpeted steps as she waved me on to follow her. I did my best to keep pace, trying to get the image of a sprinting Orangutan out of my head as I watched her power up the staircase.

"It's this one over here! It's a good bit of the hotel this one, and the old boy in the next room is as deaf as a post, so he'll no' hear a thing if you happen to be, 'entertaining' while you're here!" She hammered on the door, "I SAY YOU'RE DEAF AS A BLOODY POST JIMMY! HAHA!" She stormed on while I quickly followed, swearing that I heard a quiet crash coming from poor Jimmy's room[2] as she fumbled the key into Angus' door.

---

[1] Over the years several managers had been hired from some of the big cities, and had moved north with grand dreams of remoulding The Regent Hotel into their own image and to show these country bumpkins a thing or two about management, only to find themselves less than six months later humbly asking Mary if it was okay to go out for a cigarette break and apologising profusely for serving her morning cup of tea to her at anything but her exact preferred temperature

[2] Jimmy was spotted in the hotel's public bar two hours later, his shirt on inside out as his shaking hands spilled most of his pint down his trousers, telling anyone who'd listen that he'd managed to avoid being snatched by the SS troops who'd tried kicking his door in earlier that evening by sticking an upturned bowl over his head then standing by the bed for over an hour completely still, pretending he was a lamp.

Mary swung the hotel room door wide and pulled me into the room. Once inside, she leaned back out to the hallway, looked back and forth for what seemed an age then closed the door and snibbed it before relaxing and leaning herself against the nearby table.

"Aww son, you have to know how sorry I am that your uncle is gone" She waddled over to the small chair beside the bathroom and slumped down into it. "I know that he wasn't your dad, but he always tried to be like one for you. He talked about you all the time you know, Hah! At least when he wasn't lying passed oot on the bar floor or eating a bloody candle for a dare." She pulled a small handkerchief from her bosom and dabbed at her eyes, seeming to be lost for words as she blew what sounded for all intents and purposes like a good pound and a half of snot into the soggy cotton bundle. Ramming the sticky ball back into her top, she stood and stared at me, her mouth slowly moving as if her brain was working out what to say next.

"Can I get you some water or something Mary?" I stood and walked over to the tabletop beside the bed, lifting the water jug and heading toward the bathroom taps.

"No my boy, I'm fine. It's just.. It's no' easy you know, you've no idea what that man meant to us, what he did for me and my bairns." Her bosom heaved gently as she let out a small sob, "But you'll learn. There's so much about him you should know. When are you speaking to Maggie?"

I sat down on the edge of the bed, "She's pretty much ordered me to hers for tomorrow afternoon, so I'll probably head over the bridge around twelve". Mary stood up and brushed herself down, readjusting the chemical warfare-riddled hankie in her top before brushing down her blouse top.

"Right then! That's good! You're going to learn a lot of new things my boy, a lot of things. And things that may confuse you. But know this, what your uncle did day to day helped us. It helped us all, and without people like him, life here would be a helluva lot different." She moved toward the door and pulled it open, stepping out into the tartan-carpeted hallway.

"Huey stayed here a lot you know. When his work kept him in the town or he'd pissed off Maggie enough that she'd boot his arse oot for the night. He would come here and stay in this room, we always kept it empty for him.." Another sob set her bosom away in a slow jiggling motion. "He used to keep a small locker for all his stuff down in our staff room, so I gave it a wee clear oot and put everything from it in that box down there beside the bed." She turned away, staring at the floor and sighing heavily.

"I spoke to Maggie about it in case Paul might want it, but there's nothing in there he can sell, eat or set on fire, so he doesn't give a shite about it. But Maggie made a good point, Huey would have wanted you to have it." Mary fished out the hankie and gave it another toxic load of boogers, "I can't tell you everything your uncle did for me Angus, I'm no' allowed to. But there's a letter in there he sent me that will explain a lot. Or at least make a bit o' sense after what Maggie shows you tomorrow". She turned to walk down the hallway and flashed a quick smile back over her shoulder.

"He was a good man, I can see a lot of him in you too even though you never come to bloody visit anymore!" Mary rubbed her face and straightened her shoulders, "Now, get yer shite sorted oot and I'll go get the cook to make you up a feed for when you're ready". And with that, she closed the door and waddled off back down the hallway. *BANG BANG BANG* "EH JIMMY, YOU AULD DEAF HALFWIT! CANNA HEAR A BLOODY THING! HAHAH!"

I stood up and walked around the bottom of the bed, and saw the large box down on the floor beside the nearby window. Picking it up, I turned around and set it down on the bed before sitting myself down to look at it. It was nothing fancy by any means, an empty salt and vinegar crisps box that Mary had taken from the hotel bar.

I shifted the box around, flipping it onto each side and over onto its lid, struggling to find a way past the layers upon layers of tape that cocooned every square inch of the cardboard. I imagined whilst looking over the sellotape mummified box that probably she had wanted to make sure the contents stayed safe and secure. Another more cynical part of me however also believed that Mary was one of those monsters who loved to watch their grandkids break fingernails and have emotional breakdowns whilst spending hours trying to get into their Christmas presents, while she got a chance to sit with a large sherry and hurl insults at the telly during the Queen's speech.

Finally, after a good ten minutes of heaving, swearing, and employing the use of a now badly bent teaspoon from the nearby complimentary coffee tray, the lid of the cardboard box lay open. I stood up, staring at the open box lying on the bed. Slowly I reached forward and lifted out the familiar dark brown leather jacket that was neatly folded on top of his uncles possessions. It was Huey's favourite jacket, the very same jacket he had worn for nearly all of my childhood. The same jacket that he had refused to replace despite much protest from Maggie, who was sick of patching it up all the time when Huey would come back from a hard day at work.

Opening it up, I gave it a couple of shakes and swung it over my shoulders, remembering as I slid my arms into the sleeves how Huey had once saved it from Aunt Maggie throwing it into the wheelie bin after he'd come home with it covered in cow shit.

I turned and looked at myself in the full-length mirror on the cupboard door. It wasn't a bad fit at all. Hell, I'd have gone so far as to say I looked pretty damned good with it on as I strutted around the hotel room like I was on a Paris catwalk. It was just the right amount of scuffed and worn so that it had the 'distressed' look that people paid over the odds for in darkened, exclusive retail shops populated by beautiful, dimwitted staff.

As I ran my hands down the front of the jacket I felt the rough outline of the faded patch that was stitched over the left breast pocket. Pulling the jacket off I sat back down on the bed, laying the patch upright to get a closer look at it. It still looked the same as I remembered from my childhood, with faded red lettering over a black and grey square background, spelling out the word 'RUST'. I remembered asking Huey several times what it meant, and each time I would get a different answer, ranging from "Ah, it's describing what my knee joints are made of!" to, "It's what your auntie stirs into her morning coffee to help make her extra cranky.."

I grinned at the memory. It probably didn't mean a thing, maybe just one of those generic labels that manufacturers put on clothes to make them seem quirky. Either way, I was delighted that the jacket had found its way to my hands since Paul had made it clear that it meant nothing to him. I slipped the coat back on, hung my suit jacket up in the mirrored closet, and turned my attention back to the box lying open on the bed.

There were some old local newspapers in there, red marker either underlining or circling different articles ranging from accident reports to wild cat sightings. I pushed them aside meaning to look at them later. I had never believed the rumours of large wild cats roaming the Caithness wilderness, nor the talk of 'beasties' that came into town late at night and made off with your freshly washed knickers that you'd forgotten to take off the line before you went to bed. Anyway, I was pretty sure most of the panties thievery was down to that strange wee lad Michael who I used to live next door to up in High Ormlie. He was forever making superhero capes out of stolen bedsheets, and I was pretty sure that the little fucker had made off with a pair of my favourite Bart Simpson pants that had been out on the line to make himself a badly fitting Ninja Turtles mask.

I set the newspapers down on the floor and turned back to the box. There was a little toy troll in there with purple hair and the name 'Maggie' scratched into the leg, I set that aside too, smiling as I wondered if it was supposed to be a cute memento or a sly dig at Huey's long-suffering wife.

Digging further, I lifted a bundle of old photos from the box held together with a couple of thick rubber bands. The top photo in the pile was a Polaroid of Huey standing alongside a group of people that I didn't recognise, many of whom wearing jackets with the same 'RUST' badges as Huey's. So this wasn't a fashion thing then? Maybe some kind of club he was involved with? Deciding to go talk to Maggie about it to see if she knew more, I shoved the bundle in the top pouch of my suitcase and turned back to the last item at the bottom of the box. It was an envelope addressed to 'Mary G'.

Realising this must be the letter that Mary had told me about, I opened the envelope and pulled out the folded sheet of paper inside. Leaning over to turn on the bedside lamp, I lay back on the heavily starched bedsheets and read the letter.

"Dear Mary, I know you've been through hell these last few days, and I wish I could tell you more about what happened with the boys, but please let it be enough that they're home safe and sound, and seemingly none the wiser about what was going on around them. I know that over the years through your network of grey-haired or blue-rinsed spies, you've learned more about

what our group does than anybody else in the county, and you more than anybody knows what we are dealing with out here. But you must understand that despite what you and the boys have gone through, some things just can't be made public knowledge, more for the safety of those 'others' than ours. Please know that your sons were never in any danger, they're smart kids and knew how to behave around the Maulagg clan. You've taught them well, and it's largely down to your guidance that they're home safe and sound, and less to do with what we did to get them home. Please don't worry, new boundaries have been set and stricter monitoring of the Maulaggs movement is in place. Gunnar and Crash are taking great delight in hoonin' around in their new off-road truck doing boundary checks!

And please don't worry about me or my injuries. A wee scratch on my side is a small price to pay to make sure your boys are home safe and sound. If anything it's taught me not to trust a grinning Maulagg with a pointy stick! Lots of love to you and yours Mary. As always, if you need anything from us then speak to Maggie. I swear there's little that wonderful wee wife of mine doesn't know, she's like a walking encyclopedia... If only I could legally bind her in leather and stick her on a shelf out of the way.

Take care, Huey."

I sat up and set the letter aside, staring out the window facing the now-darkening sky. What the hell was Huey involved with? An agency? But he worked all his days as a gamekeeper. Walking into the bathroom I turned on the shower, letting the steam build up as I leaned on the sink and stared into the mirror.

A scratch to his side? I remember my uncle being hospitalised when he was younger, but he fell down an embankment while working and got impaled by a tree branch. Damn near killed him too, they had to fly a surgeon up from Aberdeen especially. Stripping down I climbed into the shower, wondering what the hell all those things in the letter meant. Who the heck were the Maulagg clan? I didn't know any family that went by that surname and was pretty sure I'd remember hearing that name before, being as it was so unusual.

And Huey's death, it just didn't feel like something that would have happened. I'd managed to access the official report through my work, and the cause was put down to being struck by falling rocks whilst out rock climbing, splitting his head and killing him instantly.

This just didn't ring true to me. Huey never climbed for fun, he was scared of heights. And if he ever did have to climb while game-keeping, he made sure that he wore every single bit of expensive PPE that he could get his hands on. The thought that a rock split his head when he was climbing just seemed wrong, especially considering there was very little in the way of climbing gear, nor a helmet of any kind found with him when the body was discovered. I needed to find out more, maybe asking Maggie about this 'Rust' thing might lead me to someone who could shine some light on it.

I dried myself off with a disgustingly lime green towel and headed back through to the room, folding my suit away and placing it in the closet beside the bed. I didn't feel bad that I'd chosen to miss the wake, I'd driven all morning after leaving Aberdeen first thing without having time to clean up properly before jumping in the car, having been up late the night before dealing with my house phone constantly ringing while my enraged ex-girlfriend Stacey stood outside my house banging on my door demanding an audience.

In hindsight, I wished I'd had my mobile on 'ring' rather than 'silent', at least then I would have been prewarned about the inappropriate ringtone long before the funeral.

My ex got the attention she craved pretty quickly when the police rolled up in a van at 3am, especially from the short blonde haired police woman who Stacey had spat at in fury when she had been politely asked to move along. I was pretty sure as I watched things unfold from the gap between my bedroom curtains that the human body shouldn't really be able to fold that way without the help of industrial equipment.

It had been her that set my phone off ringing during the funeral after I'd stupidly left it on loud rather than silent, and as I looked down at the screen of my currently silenced smartphone the eighty-three missed calls and thirty text messages told me she was out the cells and wanting to have a wee 'pow-wow'. She'd have to wait though, I'd enough on my plate dealing with my family, and with how mad I was at her for pulling this shit even after I'd told her I was going to the burial of the man who I loved like a father.

If I'm honest, I was worried about what I might say to her while my blood was still boiling, so best to keep ignoring the calls and texts for now and make her wait until I was back south before lighting that particular fuse.

Dressing in a pair of jeans and a loose-fitting checked shirt I threw on Huey's jacket, turned and grabbed the door handle to the room, and stepped out into the hallway.

Making my way downstairs I debated with myself whether or not to question Mary about what was in the letter. She had seemed pretty upset when she gave me the box, maybe it was for the best to leave it until after speaking to Maggie tomorrow when I had more information about what was going on.

As I came to the bottom of the stairs, I remembered that Mary was going to sort out dinner for me. I headed for the reception desk, maybe a hot meal would settle my stomach a bit and help me get some energy back after a long day.

A young woman sat behind the counter, her feet perched on another chair beside her as she reclined back with her face buried in one of those generic gossip magazines.

"Is Mary about? Was hoping to catch her before I head out". The woman turned slowly toward me, her hair so harshly pulled back in the tightest ponytail I'd ever seen that I wasn't sure if she was deliberately squinting at me, or she was suffering the consequences of damn near bulldog-clipping her ears together at the back of her head.

"Aye, she's through in the dining room. I wouldnae bother her though" pausing briefly to pile another full Twix into her face, "One of the guest's catheters exploded after the porter ran intae him with the coffee trolley. Pish everywhere, It's made a right mess o' the complimentary nuts, I'll tell you that much.." Strangely that kind of put the kabosh on whatever appetite I may have had.

I left the young lady with the 'council face-lift' to her gossip rag and mouthful of saliva and caramel biscuit, and set off out the revolving door onto the darkening main street of Thurso. It had been at least a couple of years since I'd last visited the town, having last come north to attend a friend's wedding function. That one had ended up in fine Caithness fashion, with the bride being carried to her room drunk after having one too many blue coloured bottles of cheap vodka mixers and for the best man getting himself into such a drunken state that he ended up vomiting into the Mother of the Bride's handbag.

"Wouldn't have been so bad if she hadn't been keeping her stupid wee dog in there.. " I laughed to myself as I headed across the road toward the town square, heading through the iron gate and up to the old fountain that sat in the middle of the gated square of greenery.

Perching myself on the edge of the fountain I pulled out my mobile phone and checked the display. More missed calls from the ex that I quickly deleted, and a text message from Finn.

Finnlay and I had been friends since we were kids, almost glued together at the hip until we hit our late teens. Whereas I chose to seek my fortune down in the big city, Finnlay chose to stay in Thurso and start his own business as a local brewery. Business had been booming too, and I often saw bottles of his beer appearing in some of the bigger stores down south. Finn also had the honour of producing the most alcoholic beer in Europe, so potent that one drinker famously appeared in a popular YouTube video reviewing the stuff, then woke up the next day wondering where his trousers had got to and why on earth there were two chickens kicking off in his bathroom shower stall.

'Alrighty Gusalicious, drop me a call when you're free of the funeral and fancy a catch-up. I'm free all night, and I've got some new brews here needing to be tested. - F'

My finger hovered over the call button. Common sense said that I should just head back to the hotel and get something to eat, maybe have an early night before seeing Maggie in the morning then getting sorted for the journey back down south. That was it, be sensible and tell Finn that I wasn't free tonight, and what about we meet tomorrow instead for a quick lunch. Nothing worse than having to drive south for nearly five hours with a sore head.

I hit the call button.

Chapter Four

The Secret Ingredient

I woke up with a start.

"Wha.. Where the hell.. Wha, where am I? Finn? FINN! Jesus, my heid.. FINN! What did you call that stuff again? It's gon, gone and messed with gravity Finn, I dunno but my right side seems a lot heavier than my left side man.. Aww jeez, what if I'm having a seizure? FINN! CALL AN AMMBELL.. AMUBUL... AMBULE.. Uh, CALL ME A FECKING NEE-NAW DOCTOR CAR THING! Unng, I can feel pressure all down my right side. Is that the heart attack side? I'VE FORGOTTEN WHICH SIDE IS THE HEART ATTACK SIDE FINN!"

    I dragged my arm out from under the massive dog that had fallen asleep on top of me, shuffled backwards and tumbled off the edge of the sofa I'd passed out on. The dismount from the sofa caused me to spin round and land on my chest, the hard wooden floor knocking the wind out of me whilst the contents of a discarded and half consumed late night purchase of fish and chips cushioned my face from slamming too hard into the laminate flooring.

"Uuuuurrrrgh.." I'd lost the ability to form any kind of coherent speech as the wind was knocked out of me, whilst the cold salt and vinegar coated haddock soaked into my face and pickled my eyes. Struggling to draw breath, I wiped my face on the cushion from the sofa and looked around. I was definitely in Finn's house, nobody else would waste as much money buying a six foot tall Batman statue to stand behind their telly.

"FINN! I swear I'll plant my foot in your arse right up to the kneecap if you don't get through here now!" A loud crashing sound came from the bedroom as I lay back on the floor, doing my best to stop the room from spinning whilst feebly fending off the large Alsatian now licking the cold haddock off my face.

"ANGUS! You're still here? I thought you left ages ago! And why you laying on the floor snogging my dog?" Finn shoved an empty kebab box off the armchair and slumped down, his dressing gown hanging wide open showing off his Bugs Bunny underpants.

"Jeez, my heid is ringing today.. How many of those Mazaroonis did we have?"

Empty bottles lay scattered all across the floor. Finn picked one up that was still half full, wiped the lip on his dressing gown and gulped down the stale contents.

"Christ, it feels like I've used the cat's litter tray as a mouthwash. How you feeling pal? Good beer isn't it!" Froth dripped through his rough stubble and down onto his dressing gown as he grinned wildly,

"This recipe was my gran's idea you know. If there are two things she knows about, it's John Wayne movies and how to get pished like a 1940's miner!"

While my eyelids did their best to keep my throbbing eyes in my head and after a few exploratory rocks back and forth, I rolled onto my front and tried to push myself up to my knees. Partly to try and shield my eyes from the daylight streaming through the blinds, but mostly to escape the probing tongue of Charlie the Alsatian, which had last been felt a good few soggy inches down my ear canal.

"Finn.. Man, What in the hell was I thinking?" I picked a loose piece of fried chip out of my collar and threw it at the Batman statue, "I'm supposed to be driving south today.. I can't drive like this! I've got work to catch up on and I'm.. I'm not even sure these are my shoes."

Pushing myself up off the floor, I sat back on my knees and rubbed my face with my hands, trying desperately to rub away the fog in my head and the dried sauce on my cheek.

"I've got things needing to be sorted out. Christ, and Stacey. She's probably round at my place right now kicking the crap out of the place."

I pulled myself delicately up onto the sofa, "And I need to get back to work! Christ, I've got a bloody performance review in a couple of days to get ready for!"

"Ach, don't stress it man!" After three attempts Finn got to his feet, stretching his arms out over his head whilst giving me a full frontal shot of Bugs Bunny with far too wide a smile. "Everything will be peachy dude! How often do you get a chance to let your hair down? Hell, last time we had a drink together was back when we visited Tattie in hospital, right after he got his new arsehole fitted!"

I stared at the now wildly grinning Finn, "New arsehole? He had to get a stoma for Christ's sake, not a transplanted pooping chute!" After three attempts I managed to rock myself off the sofa and onto my feet, then suffered instant regret as the walls danced around me, forcing me back down onto the suspiciously damp sofa.

"Ungh.. And, I still don't think he's properly forgiven us for you taking homebrew into the ward and passing it around the nursing station. I don't know what you put in that stuff, but I'm pretty sure at least two of them got sent home with the wobbles."

Reaching down I dug my shoes out from the side of the sofa, my bladder protesting furiously as I leaned forward to tie them onto my feet,

"Look, I had a great time last night Finn, I really appreciate you doing this.", I straightened back up, delighted that I'd managed to fasten both shoes and not urinate all down my trouser leg,

"My head's been mince since Huey passed, I needed this break from the stress probably more than I thought. Thank you brother." Wobbling to my feet, I stepped across the empty beer cans and grabbed Finn in a bear hug,

"I know we live in different parts of the country now, but you're still my closest friend. If you need me for anything, you just call."

Snatching Huey's old jacket from the pile of coats laying over the hallway table, I flung it over my shoulders and staggered toward the front door.

"But right now I need to piss off back to the hotel and get washed up before going to see Maggie. Speak to you later, and brush that dogs teeth! He's left my face smelling like a rig workers crotch.."

Now you can generally judge the level of a friendship through the offensiveness of the greeting or goodbye that passes between them. When you're in the workplace you'll generally greet the colleagues you marginally like with a 'Good Morning!' or a thumbs up when you're passing, showing that these are people you wouldn't invite along on a night out to end up drunk in your flat at 3am singing Katy Perry songs. But people who are close will usually be horribly offensive to each other as they meet or greet, sometimes to the concern of others around them who will hover their finger over the emergency services number on their mobiles expecting a fight to break out.

And usually the closer the people are, the more abusive and horrible they become to each other, as proven when I turned back to the house to give Finn the one finger salute, only to be faced with a milky white ass pressed up against the window, Bugs Bunny pants riding low around the knees and a hand on each ass cheek making Finn's back end wink as I quickly strode away staring at the ground pretending I had no idea who this maniac flasher was.

"OH AYE! Oot all night were we! Hahah, you dirty wee bugger, who was the lucky lady then!" Mary bellowed from behind the hotel's reception desk, dragging herself up against the counter and nearly over the shoulders of a nervous looking backpacking couple in matching winter jackets.

"'You better go and wash your hands you clatty bugger, I'm no' letting you touch my breakfast scones 'til you've bleached yourself raw in a hot shower!" I smiled awkwardly at the carpet as I made a dash for the stairs, Mary bellowing laughter behind me while the backpackers second guessed their holiday accommodation arrangements.

After a strong shower to purge away the foggy beer demons, I pulled out my suit, white shirt and tie and gave them all in turn the 'bachelors iron', which involved vigorously shaking each item out in the hope that the creases will magically disappear with some faith and a bit of wind.

Hurriedly getting dressed I smoothed my hair down and flung my tie around my neck to tie in place. After making a half arsed attempt at a decent knot, I leant over and picked up the suit jacket and threw one arm into a sleeve. I paused, forgetting that I'd torn out the interior pocket at the funeral the previous day. Second guessing if I could get away with wearing it or not, Huey's jacket caught my eye from the bed where I'd flung it down a short while before.

It wouldn't be inappropriate to wear that instead, would it? Slowly pulling the creased suit jacket off and placing it back on the hanger, I thought about having to go downstairs to speak to Auld Mary to borrow a steamer or an iron, and as much as I wanted to look smart I didn't want to spend the next half hour or so fending off sexual innuendo laced questions about why I'd been out all night.

No, it was decided. I picked up Huey's jacket and threw it on, quickly straightening my tie in the mirror before zipping up the tan coat and taking off out the door to go and see Maggie.

Managing to dodge the ever-watchful eye of Mary who it seemed was stuck in the middle of a full-on fistfight with the hotel reception printer, I stepped onto the pavement outside the hotel, debating the quickest way to get to Maggie's house.

There was no way I could drive due to Finn's newest brew still bullying its way through my system. Gone were the days when the local bobby would shake your hand and tell you to go 'straight up the road now' if he caught you driving home after a few afternoon pints, then come join you at the house to help you finish off a bottle of single malt. Nope, it was either a taxi from outside the chippers, or I could just man up and hike it over the bridge to Springpark. As a sudden 'beer spin' made me grab the nearby railing for support, it was decided that maybe a brisk walk would sort me right out before I got to Maggie's house. And worse case was if I felt sick, I could lean over the side of the bridge and give the fish below a somewhat hop flavoured breakfast.

Twenty minutes later of shaky legged marching, I reached Oldfield Terrace and was outside Maggie's door. I paused to straighten my jacket before ringing the bell when a loud banging from the living room window beside me made me leap backwards and fall into the garden behind.

"WHY ARE YOU BLOODY SUNBATHING IN MY FLOWERS YE BIG EEJIT? GET YOUR BONEY BACK END IN HERE RIGHT NOW BOY!" Maggie's face was pressed up against the glass, making her look like the cartoon cat Tom after he's sprinted round a corner chasing Jerry, only to be met with a swiftly swung garden shovel to the face.

Maggie's voice sounded muffled as she turned away from the window, her voice still rattling through the clearly ineffective double glazing,

"Honestly, I tell the bugger to get here sharp and smart, and here he is pissin' aboot in my geraniums.. AWW SHITE!" There was a loud clatter as Maggie suddenly went wide eyed and shot downwards out of view.

Panicked that she'd fallen and hurt herself, I clambered out of the now crushed flowerbed, pulled open the front door and ran into the hallway beyond, turning sharply into the living room before stopping dead in my tracks.

Standing over my aunt with his hands wrapped around her shoulders was the largest, most multicoloured-clad man I had ever seen. Wearing a bright orange and red coloured pair of tartan trews and a jacket that would have made Joseph throw aside his technicoloured windbreaker in envy, the behemoth kicked aside the tipped-over-footstool that Maggie always used to nose out the window at the neighbours, lifted her into the air then set her down gently on the sofa before turning toward me, a wide grin breaking through the mass of ginger beard that engulfed most of his face.

"Alrighty laddie! I hear good things about you from wee Maggie here!" The widely grinning brute blocked out most of the light from the window as he stared at me, massive hands resting on his hips while his head bumped off the tassles hanging from the garish lightshade above, "So don't spoil that and put doon' that wee stick before I take it off you and we all have a horrible afternoon eh?"

Looking down, I realised that I'd backed myself against the fireplace and had subconsciously picked up the old bent metal poker that hung beside the coal bucket. Pulling my hand away sharply, the poker clattered against the rug below as I stumbled backwards and sat down hard on the chair behind me.

"There we go! See, we're all still friends! Name's 'Gunnar' by the way." within two quick steps the huge man was looming over me, grabbing my hand in a handshake that nearly loosened my shoulder from the socket.

"Well, since we're all bestie pals now, who's fancying a cheeky wee coffee?' Gunnar pulled up his sleeves and turned to Maggie, "And as a special treat since you've had a wee tumble wifey, I'll put in a teeny splash from the hip flask eh? That'll sort us all oot!"

The Technicolour Man-Beast took off toward the kitchen, "Now, come wi' me Angus lad, you're on milk duty. I always put in a bitty too much according to your aunt, and then she gets awfa' shouty."

Transfixed, I followed the huge ginger-headed bear into the kitchen, keeping one eye on the exit in case this seemingly nice man suddenly decided he would like to rip me into squidgy bits, then insert those into my other squidgy bits.

I couldn't help but wonder if some part of me was still in dreamland. As I dutifully pulled the milk out the fridge and gave it the customary sniff to make sure it wasn't honking, I tried to work out the chances that I was still laying on Finn's floor somehow, and this was all some kind of IPA fuelled hallucination.

"Go and throw some sugars in these laddie, while I sort out the secret ingredient!" The huge man reached into his jacket and pulled out the biggest hip flask I'd ever seen, screwing open the top and with a wink, pouring a generous portion into the three mugs. I moved my hand to try and stop the sharp smelling spirit from going into my cup, but it was pushed aside by a monstrous pinky.

"I'm sure you'll benefit from a wee hair of the dog laddie. You look like a bag of smashed arseholes right now, a wee nip of the good stuff should sort you right out." Bigfoot put the flask back into his jacket, "Plus, you'll need a wee 'pick me up' today loon, I've got a feeling in my pish that it's going to be a long one for you."

We made our way back into the living room, where Maggie had seemingly recovered from her fall and was now hanging the bent poker back up beside the fireplace.

"Buckled that thing over Huey's kneecaps you know!" She sat back on the sofa and took the cup from the large man's hands, "The bugger came home one night after a skin full, lay on that sofa and sharted all down the back of my new Royal Wedding commemorative cushion.. I just dinna have the heart to throw it out now the auld bugger's gone."

Maggie fished a suspiciously crispy tissue from her sleeve and wiped her eyes before taking a big gulp of tea from the mug in her lap. She froze, her eyes went wider than the china dinner plates that filled the standing unit against the nearby wall before she pulled the tissue out and wiped them again.

"Bloody hell Gunny, how much o' that stuff did you put in this? I can barely feel my tongue!"

Gunnar sat back on the dangerously wobbly stool he had pulled through with him from the kitchen, and belly laughed while Maggie wiped tears from her face.

"Ach, it's only a wee bitty lass! It's a new batch though, the wee critters have been working extra hard this last while to come up with that. It'll put hair on your chest that one!"

Lifting his mug to his face, Bigfoot downed the contents in two big gulps, wiped the back of his hand over his mouth and with a slight glaze in his eyes he winked at Maggie, who was gripping the armrests on her chair with white knuckles in case she drunkenly fell off her chair. Judging by the pinkness of her cheeks, I was pretty sure this wasn't Maggie's first doctored tea of the day. But judging by the smile she was flashing at the large rainbow clad man beside me, (*whose beard was suspiciously sizzling in places where the coffee had dripped*) I wasn't going to mention it.

This strange multi-coloured man who I'd found in my aunt's house had clearly been helping take her mind of things, and I found myself relaxing back into the chair as my aunt and Gunnar chatted, laughed and threw insults back and forth. I smiled to himself, and took a big drink from my cooling cup of coffee.

Everything suddenly blared into sharp focus, like someone had spun the contrast dial far to the right. Fireworks blew their loads behind my eyeballs, throwing all the colours in the room spinning around me like a tornado. I turned to look at the widely grinning Gunnar, whose trousers alone were throwing off reds and greens like someone had set off a stick of dynamite in a Christmas shop.

"Hahah! It's good stuff, eh laddie! That'll put a fire in your belly, and a foot in your arse for sure!" Gunnar grabbed his sides as his face went scarlet with laughing, I found it hard to notice, as I was too busy between giggles trying to make sure my feet stayed on the carpet and didn't take off toward the roof like a Soviet-era rocket.

"You'll be fine laddie, it's always a bitty strong when you first try it." Gunnar slowly got to his feet, placed a massive hand on each of my shoulders and gently pressed me back down onto the chair before turning toward Maggie.

"I've no idea really how the critters make this stuff, but I'm nae gonna try to stop them. Hell, if only they'd let me sell this at the Farmers Market I'd make a bloody fortune.."

"Aye, and you'd have the few farmers susceptible to it waking up after a moothfull wondering why the hell they're trying to milk the dog!" Maggie climbed out of her chair and walked over to where I was vibrating,

"Dinna worry my boy, you'll feel just grand in a few seconds. It's nae a long burning stuff this." She bent down and stroked my face, pushing my hair back over my ear, "It's some kind of mix of gin, bacardi, whisky and some bloody herb yon critters grow doon in their bunkers. Grand for clearing the heid and does a damn fine job of taking the plaque of the auld dentures!"

After a short while the world seemed to calm down around me. The colours that had been swirling around my head moments before returned to their original places, Gunnar's jacket and trousers in particular stopped acting like a cheap nightclub disco ball and calmed down to their normal, garish level. Surprisingly I felt fine. In fact, I felt fantastic, better than I had all morning. The beer-fueled fog from the night before had been completely burned away, leaving me feeling packed with energy. If it wasn't for the fact that both Maggie and her monstrous guest would think I had snapped, I'd have dropped to the floor and pumped out a good hundred or so press-ups to loosen himself off a bit.

"Pretty good stuff eh?" Gunnar returned to his stool, the wobbly leg groaning in protest as he levered his massive frame down onto the frilly cushioned seat.

"It's a strange stuff for sure, a wee sip sorts you right oot, but you have two or three nips of that and you'll wake up the next morning wondering why you're two hundred miles away and missing your shoes! That's only happened to me once by the way.." Gunnar blushed as Maggie playfully swatted him. 'Well, maybe four times. Costing me a fortune in custom made shoes this stuff.'

I jabbed my fingernails into my palm in an effort to stop myself from furiously nodding in agreement. If only I could get my hands on the recipe for this and rope in Fin with his brewing skills, we could make a bloody killing! That however was the least of my concerns for the moment, as I clenched my fists into the cushion below in an effort to stop myself from vibrating off the sofa and onto the floor.

"So how you feeling now son?" Asked Maggie, sitting forward in her chair and smiling, "You're not needing to be sick or anything? Nae needing a shite or feel like you have to rake yer eyes oot? I've got the loo roll sitting in the fridge if you need it, sometimes people have an awfa' burning reaction to Gunnar's Firewater.." Both Maggie and Bigfoot were staring at me now, huge grins breaking out on their faces while I continued to vibrate away quietly on the sofa.

"No no, I'm good.. I think." I could feel my vibrating back-end slowly start to return to normal, "I don't feel like I'm going to vibrate through the floor anymore.. What in the hell is that stuff?"

"THAT STUFF my boy is exactly what we were hoping for!" Gunnar unfolded himself from the proportionally tiny stool, stood up and straightened his jacket.

"Just like your uncle boy, I bloody knew it!" he said, as he turned and bent to kiss Maggie on the cheek. "I better be for the off lassie, The High Heid'yin will be wondering why I'm not back yet with his jammy biscuits." Turning toward me, he extended his massive bear claw out for another bone-loosening handshake.

"And you laddie, I'm looking forward to working alongside you! Huey's shoes are pretty big ones to fill though, but I'm sure you've got it in ye!" Before I could ask what he meant, Gunnar had made his way out to the hallway and opened the front door.

"Right Maggie, I'll see you both tonight, mind and bring your dancing shoes!" A huge grin split the massive ginger beard that ringed his head like a lion's mane, before he turned away and set off toward the town centre.

"Tonight? Maggie, is he expecting to see me tonight?" I followed her back into the living room and sat down, a brief feeling of regret that the special blend coffee cup was empty beside me.

"And what's he on about working beside him? I have to be off back down the road as soon as possible."

"You're going nowhere in a hurry my boy, you'll be coming with me tonight to see your uncle off properly with some people who really knew and loved him." Maggie slumped down into her chair, her body seeming to melt slightly into the backrest as she stared at the floor in front of her.

"Not like that pack o' pecking hens who showed up at the planting yesterday." With a small sigh she turned to look at me, her eyes damp as she smiled.

"Half o' them were only there to peck for more information about how he passed you know." Her knuckles again whitening as she gripped the armrest. "Always with their bloody noses twitching for gossip, it makes me sick so it does!"

Quickly I lifted myself off the sofa and moved across the room to kneel beside her, placing my hand over hers hoping to reassure her. "Maggie, I have to ask, Huey didn't just have an accident, did he?"

Her eyes widened as her other hand came over mine, squeezing as she stared at me for what felt like a long time before turning her attention to the poker by the fireplace.

"Paul was never interested you know." she ignored my question, seemingly distracted as she stroked the back of my hand, "He's my son and I love him with all my heart, but apart from yesterday I haven't seen him for weeks. He's got no interest in what happens to me or what happened to his poor father." A tear rolled down her cheek as she turned her gaze back toward the floor.

"If it doesn't benefit Paul, then he just doesn't care." Her hand again gripped mine as she turned back to face me.

"But you laddie, you were always Huey's boy. Oh, your own mither would bleat and blare about how nothing was her fault, she was doing her best and you were always her little boy, but she was wrong. She was too busy passing you round to family while she went oot and threw hersel' into the drinking. No son, you've always been Hueys bairn. While she consoled hersel' in the bottom of a vodka bottle we all could see from when you were just a wee toot that you and that auld brute shared a heart." Maggie pulled close and kissed me on the forehead.

"You were his boy Angus, he considered you his son. And though it'll probably have your mither spinning like a bloody top in her grave, you were always my wee boy too. And you'll know the truth as much as it is. Now, let's get tonight out the way first though eh?"

I sunk to the floor still clutching Maggie's hand, tears stung my eyes and a lump clogged up my throat while my aunt pulled me close and hugged my head into her chest.

Chapter Five

Mr Biscuits

Hours passed as we sat together in the old house where I'd spent most of my childhood. Tears of laughter rocked the room as we shared memories of Huey and the fun he brought into our lives, Maggie laughing so hard she nearly choked on a Digestive biscuit while she told the story about Huey getting his hands stuck in a VCR one day whilst trying to fish out a toy car I had allegedly stuck in the hatch. Four firefighters arrived at the house in the middle of the afternoon to find Huey trapped on the floor in his underpants until they freed his hand from the mechanism.

"He didn't even have the bloody sense to unplug it from the wall and go put some trousers on before they arrived!" I roared with laughter while Maggie coughed up more biscuit into her sugary cup of tea. The kettle was boiled repeatedly as more stories peppered our time together, while outside the sun started to dip below the houses on the other side of the road.

"Oh hell!' Maggie leapt from her chair and looked out the window, 'What bloody time is it? Six! Christ, I better go and sort my face oot!"

Moving round the chair faster than a woman her age should be able, she grabbed Huey's jacket from the back of the sofa and went to throw it toward me. She stopped short, realising what she was holding before it left her grip, her hands now cradling the tan leather as she lifted it to her face, losing herself in the memories the leather smell of Huey's old jacket brought back to her.

"I'm.. I'm glad you have this loon, he'd have wanted you to have it." Maggie paused, then tossed the coat over to me. "Now get it on and go lock up the back door, I'll be five minutes sorting myself oot and then we're for the off!"

With my orders received, I made my way to the back door and locked it up, stopping afterwards to quickly wash our cups in the kitchen sink and give the worktops a wipe down with a cloth before pulling my phone out of my pocket and sitting back down on the sofa. Did I really need to get back south so soon? The house was pretty secure after I'd changed the locks when Stacey wouldn't give her key back, and I was pretty confident that she wouldn't find a way in to the place. No, the least I could expect when I got back south was something horrible smeared over my windows or shoved through my letterbox for not answering her calls.

Work might be a problem. I had a performance review coming up soon and things weren't exactly rosy with my Sergeant as it was. There'd been an incident in the centre of Aberdeen that we had responded to that went wrong, and I still had questions to answer about it when I got back south. My shift partner had left me with a lot of mess to explain, and I was not looking forward to working my way through any of it.

Trying not to stress about what waited for me back south, I pulled the zipper up on Huey's jacket and walked outside to meet Maggie who was waiting to lock the front door behind us.

As I stepped outside I noticed a large, expensive black car with darkened windows sitting idling by the pavement. It looked like one of those upmarket ones you see being driven on TV by men wearing sunglasses and earpieces, ready to transport important men with bad hairdos away from aeroplanes.

"Well? Move yer hips lads, we've not got all night!" Maggie had dumped her keys in her bag while I was staring at the large car with the black windows, then rattled my shin with her stick as she hurried past me toward the back door of the vehicle, pulling it open and motioning for me to hurry up and get bloody in.

I jogged down the steps and climbed into the back of the car, shuffling across to make space for Maggie to get in behind me. It was one of those cars where the two rows of rear seats face each other, letting four people sit and chat, play cards or plan acts of industrial espionage. A black partition screen hid the driver away from view which I found a bit unnerving. I quickly looked round to see if I could find the button that lowered it so I could see exactly who was going to be transporting us, just as Maggie thumped in beside me and pulled a small package wrapped in a carrier bag from her handbag.

"Righto Mr Biscuits! That's us in and sorted. Get the foot down and this here full packet of Hob Nobs has got your name all over it".

The partition slid down slowly, revealing the back of a large, bald head as it slowly turned to look back at them. I felt the hair on the back of my neck dancing as the head turned almost unnaturally round to stare back through the partition. The face and head were clean shaven and unnaturally smooth, and large black sunglasses perched precariously on a long thin nose that looked not only the wrong shape and colour to match the head sporting it, but also seemed to be attached to the frame of the glasses with some sticky tape.

I tried not to stare in case I was being rude but I couldn't tear my eyes away from this unnatural-looking face poking through the small partition space between us. I could feel myself sweating through the white shirt I was wearing, and my heart was hammering in my chest under the watchful glare of those black sunglasses, and couldn't help but notice that the ears looked the same off-colour as the nose did compared to the milky paleness of the rest of the head. I started to turn to Maggie to ask what the hell was happening when the pale driver reached up and lowered his glasses.

Sure enough the ears and nose were attached to the darkened shades, detaching themselves from the pale head leaving only an overly large, sharp toothed mouth. I clung to the leather seat below me and tried desperately not to fear-piss all over myself while this 'thing' in a black suit smiled right at me. Just as I could feel a scream climbing up my throat the face suddenly turned toward Maggie, and a disproportionately long and pale thumb appeared through the partition in a 'thumbs up' gesture, just as the black glass climbed back up and hid it again from view.

My door was locked, and I figured the child lock was in place and was pretty secure too, considering it was holding up pretty well to me smashing the door with both feet. With this not working, I was just figuring out how much speed I would need to put my head right through the window to get out when Maggie grabbed my hand and yanked me around to face her.

I won't lie, the second she grabbed me I let out a yelp of terror that even made me stop and wonder where the hell it had come from. Maggie grabbed both my hands and shifted over to sit in the seat facing me, and also directly below the partition that hid away the nightmare who was currently occupied indicating past the junction at the bottom of Maggie's street.

"Look at me lad, look me right in the eyes and take some big deep breaths." Maggie moved her hands up to my face and cradled my cheeks,

"You're fine son. That feeling o' terror you're getting is no' your own doing. Focus on that, that you're no' really scared and this is all fine."

Her grip on my face tightened as she pulled my face toward hers, while my right hand still desperately worked the door handle hoping it would pop open and I could tuck and roll out of there.

"Mr Biscuits is doing this to you, but no' on purpose! Ach, a nicer soul you couldnae meet, he canna help that his pheromones cause this kind of reaction, but it's all chemical son! Keep that in yer heid, it's all chemical, you'll soon develop an immunity to it." I started to calm down as Maggie stroked my face, my heart however still threatened to punch its way out of my chest and make a break for freedom.

"He's a nice man honestly.. Well, not 'exactly' a man in the traditional sense, but he's a damned good driver and gardener. Oh, and he's bloody thorough wi' the filing systems!" I think Maggie sensed I was calming down as she let my face go slowly and leaned back in her chair.

"Bloody mad for biscuits though. Would paint yer hoose for a few packets of Jammy Dodgers if you gave him the chance, and you wouldnae have a problem with birds shiting over your satellite dish anymore after he'd been up on your roof, I can tell you." She smiled, which helped a lot toward calming me down. I still had no idea what the hell that thing currently driving us over the Toll Bridge toward the centre of town was, but Maggie being so relaxed about the whole situation took my mind away from my plan to headbutt my way through the window to sweet, non-terrifying freedom.

I was still shaking and staring at the partition when we pulled up outside the chip shop on Princes Street, the car gliding smoothly to a halt across the street from the line of taxis awaiting the drinkers pouring out of the bars and then then into the fast food shops directly beside their awaiting cars later that night. The door locks clicked, and realising I had a break for freedom in front of me I yanked the door handle and rolled out onto the road.

A nondescript red Peugeot full of acne-coated teens barreled past me by a few short inches, the car's tinny speakers blaring out the classic dance track 'Ebenezer Goode' as the crater-faced youths in the back seat gave me the finger when they passed.

I jumped up and jogged onto the pavement, huddling under the awning of the chip shop while I waited for Maggie. I may have felt like running for the hills and never looking back, but if I'd left Maggie alone without a word I'd have faced a far worse fate when I finally arrived back within reach of her walking stick.

She climbed out the car on the pavement side, gave me a reassuring smile then walked round to the drivers side window. I stood up and walked cautiously round to the front of the car to watch her, my gut was screaming at me to pull her away from the blank faced creature who had now wound down the window and was graciously accepting the carrier bag containing his prized biscuits. One long, thin arm snaked out from the window and wrapped itself around Maggie's shoulder, it's long fingers patting her back gently before the limb slid back into the car and waited for Maggie to make her way back safely to the pavement. With a grin and another terrifying thumbs up in my direction, the pale headed 'thing' indicated and slowly pulled away into the pitiful selection of 'boy racer' cars currently doing countless laps of the main streets of Thurso.

I stood staring wide-eyed at the large black car as it pulled away, wondering if I'd just gone fucking crazy and imagined what had just happened. Maybe the combination of last night's Mazarooni's with Finn along with whatever the hell concoction I'd been given by that big guy Gunnar earlier were combining to make me hallucinate, and leaving me sweating like Josef Fritzel on MTV Cribs.

"Will you get your arse in gear boy! We're running bloody late as it is!" While I was daydreaming, Maggie had set off at a swift pace toward the nearby St Peter's Church, and by the time I got moving she had already turned up onto East Church St and had disappeared out of sight. I jogged after her and caught her halfway along the road.

"Maggie, please, we need to talk about whatever the FUCK that thing was driving the car!" That earned me a rattle over the kneecap with her stick for my choice of language, before she stopped dead and looked up at me.

"Son, you need tae understand that no' everything is black and white in the world" She set off walking along the pavement again,
"There's a helluva lot of grey out there that people don't have a bloody clue about.." We reached the junction with Barrock Street, and she turned left to walk behind the church.

"Take Mr Biscuits there. To you he is something out of your nightmares, something that gie's you the heebie-jeebies while you're cowering under your duvet late at night. Something that people scribble down on a bitty o' paper when they're trying to scare their pals." She turned at the back of the church and crossed the road, heading straight toward the old public toilet building on the other side.

"And you know why? Because his scent causes terror in folk that get too close, so they think he's a monster. Because he's tall, thin and disnae have a face, do-gooder's think it's okay to hunt them down and chase them off." She stopped outside the toilet building and turned to look at me.

"His species used tae live all over North America, and did their damndest to integrate and make contact with humans as we expanded more and more intae their territories. Hell, they only wear the suits because they thought that it would make us feel more relaxed!"

Maggie set her cane against the wall beside her, and worked the snib holding the small grey gate closed leading to the building.

"And still they got chased off or killed, their bodies burned and buried by God fearing, Bible hammering Americans who saw them as demons, never to be talked about in case their words summoned more o' the creatures down upon them, until they were doon to near double digits in number."

Maggie finally got the gate open through a mixture of kicking at it, shaking it vigorously and a small splash of mumbled swearing. She pushed through and waved me along to follow her into the toilet building.

"But STILL Mr Biscuits and his people tried tae make peace, despite the near extinction of his people! It bloody sickens me so it does.. And Mr Biscuits case in particular is a sad one'" she pushed into a cubicle and grabbed my arm, pulling me in behind her. I hadn't been here for a while so I wasn't sure, but judging by the smell I was guessing that this facility wasn't facing a regular or thorough cleaning schedule.

Maggie pulled a key out of her pocket and slid it into a small hole in the toilet roll holder. With a quick twist I heard a clicking sound behind the wall, before a panel slid up to expose what looked like a tablet of some kind attached to the wall. Maggie pressed her hand against the device and it flashed green, a message popping up on the screen read; 'GREETING: WELCOME MARGARET STEWART, PREPARING TRANSPORT'.

Before I could ask what the hell was going on, Maggie started talking again.

"That poor critter was living by himself in some deep woodland in the heart of Wisconsin, nae bothering anybody and keeping himsel' to himsel' and oot of harms way." I was fascinated by the story Maggie was telling me, but also couldn't help but wonder what the hell we were doing jammed into a public toilet facility while the floor and the walls around us were starting to make faster clicking noises.

"So then some developer starts cutting into his woods and building luxury houses. Oh, you might want to hang on to the lavvy roll holder son"

Maggie sat down on the lid of the toilet and leaned back, a seat belt appeared out of nowhere and strapped her safely against the wall behind her,

"Just hold tight. You'll be fine, a sturdy strong loon like you.."

The floor started to drop, lowering Maggie, the toilet and my panicked expression down into the unknown. Between the encounter with Mr Biscuits and now this, my nethers were rumbling in a dangerous way. With the way my adrenaline filled stomach was growling, I kind of wished I'd been the one strapped to the toilet just in case.

"So here's poor Mr Biscuits suddenly got a bunch of middle class families appear uninvited on his doorstep and setting up shop. However being the nocturnal yet awfa' friendly bugger that he is, he was upbeat aboot the whole situation and went to try and make friends with his new neighbours."

The cubicle came to a halt, and looking up I could see a new one sliding into the space we'd left empty. Strip lighting came on in the cubicle walls, and a roof slid into place above us. Locking clamps clunked into place over the graffiti covered door, and as I leaned down to grab the sturdy toilet roll holder I was suddenly slammed face first into the wall as the small toilet stall hit 0-60 in three and a half seconds.

"You okay there boy?" I had no time to respond before she continued, "So here's Mr Biscuits in the woods at three in the morning, standing staring at the back of a family bungalow waiting to say hello tae the new neighbours.." I peeled my face off the wall and after making sure I hadn't broken anything or lost any teeth, I tightened my grip on the toilet roll holder as the lights outside the small gap at the base of the cubicle zoomed past faster and faster.

"Out comes two wee girls to investigate after seeing him hanging around the edge of the woods from their bedroom window, but we've learned since then that pre-pubescent kids process the fear-inducing pheromone he pumps oot a lot differently than adults do." Maggie shuffled her butt around so she could look at the digital tablet on the wall.

"Ach, we're nearly there loon.. Anyway, turns oot that bairns go a bit loopy on the auld fear juice he unwittingly pumps oot. Next thing you know the two poor kids are running aboot wi' knives telling everyone they're the disciples of the skinny man in the woods wearing a black suit and wi' nae face. Well, you can imagine that narrowed down the hitlist a bit for the bible-belt 'Sons' formed to deal wi' Demonic entities." Maggie scowled.

"And get this for a bloody cheek, 'Sons of the Owl' they call themselves. An American group backed by their big-money preachers to hunt doon and destroy things that dinna fit in with their perfect vision of the world. Bloody animals using their supposed faith to justify killing and torturing, when really it's all about taking what they can.." I could see Maggie's grip tighten on her walking stick held between her legs,

"But they couldnae catch Mr Biscuits! Hah! We got to him first and now here he is, in protective custody and a vital cog in the machine! Aww son, there's so much you need to lear.."

"GREETING; WELCOME MARGARET STEWART." The ridiculously loud and stunted computer voice cut Maggie off, booming through our small cubicle, which didn't help my poor bowels twitching fear reflex one single bit. "DECLARATION; IT HAS BEEN 83 DAYS SINCE YOUR LAST ACCESS TO RUST. WE HAD HOPED, CORRECTION: FEARED THAT YOU HAD KICKED THE BUCKET."

"SHUT IT! Bloody hell Ham, I was in the middle of a story there!" Maggie spun in her seat again and banged her fist against the small tablet in the wall, presumably attempting to give the computer a burst nose.

"APOLOGY; SORRY MARGARET STEWART, WHEESHT PROTOCOL ACTIVATED" And with a small beep the voice went silent. Maggie gave the screen another good thump for good measure.

"Did you just call the computer, 'Ham'?" Maggie looked at me like I was stupid.

"Aye! His name's HAMMER. Dinna ask me what it stands for, something stupid like, 'Highland Arsehole Mouthy.. Uh, Motor Excrement.. Um.. Rudeness' or some pish. Anyway! As I was saying before I was RUDELY interrupted by that technological bastard", another thump to the screen before she turned back to face me, "There's a helluva lot you're about to see and experience my boy, so I need you to pull up yer big boy knickers and be a brave lad now for your favourite Aunty when we arriv.."

"DECLARATION; WE HAVE ARRIVED AT BASE WILDCAT. PLEASE KEEP HANDS, FEET AND OLD LADY BLOUSES AWAY FROM GAPS UNTIL FULL STOP IS ACHIEVED"

I grabbed at Maggie's arm as she spun to drive the tip of her whacking stick into the tablet behind her, easing her arm down until the tip once again lay on the floor. The cubicle shook gently as it's forward motion came slowly to a full stop, and the clamps disappeared from the stall door as it swung open to show a dimly lit hallway.

Maggie was up and away as I steadied myself, trying to make out what was ahead of us through the subdued lighting. I was about to warn her to be careful and mind her step when a powerful overhead lamp suddenly came on, shining a spotlight just ahead of Maggie's determined pace.

"Well? Come on then, we've not got all bloody night!"

Maggie kept on forward as another overhead light shone down in front her to light the way. I hurried after her, just catching the circles of light on the dark floor blinking out as I stepped through them before reaching my aunt, who was pointing ahead with her stick at the dimly lit doorway ahead.

"Righto Gussy," Maggie came to a sudden stop, "Come stand here beside me and stand still for a wee minute, winna take lo.."

"GREETING: WELCOME BACK TO RUST MARGARET STEWART. PLEASE REMAIN STILL FOR VERIFICATION."

I could see Maggie's shoulders shaking with the bottled up rage at being interrupted again, her grip slowly changing on the walking stick to accommodate a more effective stabbing motion should the need arise.

Suddenly a green laser show burst out from a small round bulb above the doorway, running over us both from top to bottom like one of those really cheap laser kits they would fit into 90's nightclubs to distract the pill-filled youth from noticing the watered-down drinks.

"DECLARATION: SCAN OF MARGARET STEWART ONLY 86 PERCENT EFFECTIVE. HAVE YOU GAINED SOME BODY MASS RECENTLY PERHAPS AROUND THE HIPS?"

Just as Maggie was about to lay into the scanner above the door for subtly accusing her of getting fat, the door swung open and out stepped a widely grinning Gunnar, wearing a fitted black suit with a light tartan trim on the collar. A suit that size must have tested the very mettle of whichever gentleman's outfitter had been asked to make it, and I couldn't shake the image of a poor tailor in a bow tie somewhere with a tape measure draped around his neck, holding his ruined fingers in a sink of ice water whilst sobbing.

"Hoho, It's yersel! Just in time too, everyone's here and ready for you!" Maggie barged past him, muttering about going to the data room and pulling out all the important looking wires. Gunnar turned to me and draped one of his massive arms over my shoulder.

"Come on laddie, you'd be as well coming with me. If it's anything like the old days I think you're aunty is going to be busy for a wee while kicking lumps out of the server room security door." I had trouble keeping up with Gunnars long stride as he walked me through the door and into a shorter and narrower hallway. Bare red bricks lined the walls on either side of us, with long cables snaking their way along the corners of the roof toward the second, dark mahogany doorway ahead.

"We've 'officially' been here since 1952, or at least only recognised as being here by Churchill a year after he took office. Used to be a lot more o' these bases too, but cutbacks and a' that pish." Gunnars pace slowed, "But they'll no' get rid of us wee man! Too important a job here to be left unguarded, too many things tae watch over."

"What is this place Gunnar? I'm not seeing any straight answers here, and I just traveled here in a sarcastic toilet cubicle, so any information would be wonderful" Gunnar came to a stop right in front of the mahogany doors ahead.

"This place? This is the last stand wee man, where we plant the flag against the destruction of the unknown!" Gunnar's chest seemed to swell, threatening the buttons on his tailored waistcoat before he relaxed and let out a short laugh.

"Sorry lad, I like a bit of theatrics now and again! This place-" He swept his arms out wide and spun around, forcing me to duck before I received the back of his hairy bear paw in my mouth as he spun, "-Is where we make sure that the things that go bump in the night do so safely, where the natural order meets the supernatural order. We're the ones that make sure that when the tooth fairy comes to collect your teeth, she's nae coming with a claw hammer!" Gunnar boomed with laughter,

'Officially this is the Regulatory Unit of the Supernatural and Transmundane.' Gunnar spun on his heel and lifted his foot, planting his heel into the mahogany doors ahead and throwing them open.

'This, laddie.. This is R.U.S.T!'

Chapter Six

Welcome to RUST

The large wooden doors crashed open under the pressure of Gunnar's oversized and subtly sequined boot, showing a large white, almost clinical looking room with a white desk directly in front of them. The racket of the massive doors crashing against the frame on either side caused the woman sitting at the desk across from us to heave her latte a good ten feet into the air, splashing down all over herself and her half read copy of the local daily paper.

"AAAAGH! You big hairy-arsed bastard faced shite! How many bloody times have I told you.." She paused briefly to slam shut the pages of her soggy paper, throwing specks of caffeine laced foam onto her glasses, "NOT TO BATTER THOSE BLOODY DOORS OPEN!"

Gunnar sprinted across to the reception desk and pulled a patterned handkerchief from his breast pocket, doing his best to mop up the patches of coffee whilst apologising profusely for his behaviour.

"Aww jeez, I'm awfa sorry Joan, I just thought the new lad would like a bit of a dramatic entrance for his first day here." Gunnar stood now twisting his soggy handkerchief between his hands with worry, putting me in mind of Oliver Twist asking for more gruel while waiting for the heavy end of the big metal spoon from the irate Overseer.

"I mean, if ever a place needed a dramatic introduction when you first see it, it's this place.. RUST needs a bit of theatre!"

"THEATRE?" Joan leapt up from her chair, "I'll give you bloody theatre by planting my tap dancing boot in your hairy arse! Get the poor lad scanned and then get out of my bloody sight!"

Gunnar hustled over to where I was standing frozen in place, still dumbstruck from the whole situation, but also distracted by what looked like a plant in a large pot by the doorway that I was sure was giving me a shitty look. As Gunnar grabbed my hand and pulled me toward the desk, my suspicions were confirmed when the plant pot folded up some of its leaves and rearranged its branches so that it was, without doubt, giving me the finger.

"Right loon, just a wee formality here, be over in just a flash" A chair slid out from the end of the reception desk, and Gunnar quickly plonked me down in it. Before I could ask what the hell was going on, (*and what was up with the leafy prick by the doorway*) he spun me round to face the gleaming white worktop.

"Just face front laddie, this is usually pretty harmless enough. Just make no sudden movements and it'll aw' be fine!"

"No sudden movements?" I tried to twist round to face Gunnar but the two powerful hands on my shoulders made sure that was near impossible.

"What the hell is goinMMPH!" What felt like a large rubber hand sprang from the table and grabbed my face, holding my head in place while a small screen opened in front of my eyes, with the words 'DECLARATION: REMAIN CALM PLEASE' flashing in bright, neon colours over a smiling cartoon face that looked a bit like a teddy bear.

As I fought against it, Gunnars' hands grew tighter on my shoulders, and I could smell his flowery aftershave as he leaned over to talk into my ear.

"Honestly it's all fine! Ach, it'll all be over in a few seconds and we'll have a good laugh aboot it afterwards.." His voice took on a slightly more stressed tone.

"'Just dinna move your jaw too much for the last bitty lad, I'm no' wanting to explain to Maggie why I handed you back to her missing a couple of your sweetie-chewers!"

As the screen before me now flashed 'CALM REQUEST: OPEN WIDE' in sparkling pink Comic Sans, I felt something push into my mouth and run itself over the inside of my cheeks. 'Oh Christ, this is it' I thought, 'This is the bit where the thing goes down my throat and plants something in my chest that'll burst out covered in teeth and ribcage in a few days'.

I was in the full throws of panic as the device in my mouth suddenly retreated back into the rubbery claw and the screen turned green, flashing the words, 'STATEMENT: DATA GATHERING COMPLETE. HAVE A LOVELY DAY ANGUS STEWART.' The device spat my head backwards and retreated back into the desk.

I leapt up and pushed myself away from Gunnar, spun round on my heel and made a dash for the large Mahogany doors that led into this clinical walled hell hole. As I ran past Joan she paused in her attempts to wipe coffee out of her blouse top to look at me briefly, before rolling her eyes and returning to her task at hand. I ignored her and carried on toward the doors, making a point to give the still gesticulating plant pot the 'double-bird' as I ran past it before hitting the large mahogany entranceway.

Of course it was bloody locked. I was trapped in here with the monstrous Gunnar with the bejazzled handkerchief and the offensive plant pot that was now making a motion toward me with one of it's branches that indicated that I was an overly enthusiastic proponent of self pleasuring.

"Gunnar! Joan? Let me the FUCK out of here right now or I swear I'll.." I grabbed the stem of the offensive plant and pulled it up by the roots, "I'll launch this flippin' plant prick RIGHT into the ceiling fan, so help me I will!"

Gunnar and Joan stopped and stared at me, perhaps not taking in the seriousness of how mad I was since the plant pot was now gyrating against my arm, pretending to have carnal knowledge of my elbow. Gunnar stepped forward, his hands raised in front of him in a calming motion as he came toward me.

"Honestly loon, nothing here is trying to hurt you! This is all procedure, we've all gone through it!" He stopped and patted at his pockets,

"It's just the computer taking samples of your hair, a wee eye scan and a wee swab from yer mouth so that we know yer fit for duty!"

"Fit for duty? What BLOODY DUTY Gunnar?" I threw the gyrating plant back into his pot, noticing that he gave me a very good leafy version of the 'go fuck yourself' arm motion before re-rooting itself back into the soil below it.

"Nobody has told me why the hell I'm here, what THE hell this place truly is, why I had to get here in an UNDERGROUND RAILROAD TOILET and why that desk had to stick its.. 'proboscis' in my mouth!"

I slumped down on the floor and loosened my tie, feeling myself close to having a panic attack. Gunnar looked crestfallen, placing his hands in his pockets and shuffling nervously.

"Ach laddie, I've always said they should bin that claw and do the job instead with a cotton bud, a clipboard and a pair of scissors.." Joan stepped around the desk and placed a hand on Gunnar's chest before he could get any closer to me,

"Sit down big boy, I think you've put your oversized boot in this already up to the shin, I'll talk to the man." She walked over to me, knelt down and folded her arms over her knees.

"You're right son, they've gone about this all wrong," She put her hand on my hand and smiled, "I think what's happened here is that the boss has told Gunnar to get you inducted into our systems, and the big galoot has over-extended what could have been done with a keyboard and some patient typing."

She shot him a look that made him shrink a good few inches lower than his near seven foot in height would suggest.

"You've just lost your uncle, they didn't need to expose you to all this so soon after the funeral". She took my hand and pulled me to my feet, leading me slowly back to the desk before motioning that I take her chair.

"Sit there lad. Maggie will be here shortly and we'll get you through to the memorial hall. Once that's all done I'm sure this big idiot and his friends will fill you in more on what's happening here" Joan took my hand between both of hers and smiled gently. Her dark blonde and grey hair pulled back in a bun and her warm, blue eyes started to soften as tears began to form.

"This probably goes without saying, but your uncle was much loved and respected here. And if truth be told, if it wasn't for him this place would be in a far worse state than it is." Her hands fell back to her lap, a sullen look fell upon her face as her eyes lowered slowly to her lap.

"And I'm scared with him gone now, that's exactly what's going to happen."

"DECLARATION: MARGARET STEWART IS RETURNING TO THE RECEPTION AREA, NOW RELEASING CLAMPS ON BOTH DOORS TO ACCOMMODATE INCREASED MASS AROUND THE BUTTOCKS".

A howl of rage echoed forth from the double doors at the far side of reception, before both swing doors burst open and Maggie stormed into the room. Her cane rattled furiously against the floor as she stamped a path toward us, her face softened as she saw me sitting on the ground with Joan cradling my hand.

"What's going on here, are ye alright Gussy?" Her eyes darkened as her head turned to face Gunnar, who seemed to shrink another couple of feet under the powerful glare.

'You! What did you do?'

Gunnar dug his hands even deeper into his pockets,

"I thought we'd get it out the way while we were waiting for you to get done! I didnae think it would be a problem Maggie I swear." by the look of the way he was leaning back against the desk, I imagined he was hoping it would swallow him up to shield him from the darkening tide of anger flowing out of my aunt.

"I didnae think.."

Maggie lifted a finger and he stopped dead.

"No, you didnae bloody think, and that's the problem. Now is no' the time to talk about how we'd planned to do this a few days AFTER the ceremony, nor is it the time tae talk about how we were going to ease him into a' this slowly like."

'Honestly Maggie, I thought..' Maggie's knuckles tightened,

"AND NOW IS NAE THE TIME to discuss how far along yer lower intestinal tract my hob-nailed boot is going to travel once today is all over with!" She slowly straightened her jacket, brushed a small mote of imaginary fluff from her shoulder and took a deep breath before turning back to smile at me.

"No, now is the time to go and celebrate the life o' the man that's gone from our lives" She took my hand from Joan and waited until I climbed to my feet, then after a quick hug, Maggie took off back toward the double doors towing me beside her. "And Joan? Buzz us through please. And If I catch yon overgrown Dandelion by the door giving me THAT gesture again," The Plant suddenly froze in place, shivering slightly under the stern glare of Hughie's widow, "It'll be getting ripped oot by the roots and launched into the waste disposal before it can say Day of the bastarding Triffids!"

The double doors that Maggie had come through earlier swung open as we approached, Gunnar falling in to step quietly behind us as we entered a passageway much like the one we came through when we first arrived. Spotlights and dark patterned brickwork led us forward as we passed some generic office looking doors, before turning a corner and stopping before a beautifully carved, dark wood chapel-style doorway.

"Now mind lad", Maggie pulled me closer and took hold of both my hands. "Everything you see here tonight is safe, it's all for Huey." Her grip tightened.

"Most of all son remember, you are safe. No matter what you see remember you are in absolutely no danger here, everyone is here to celebrate that galoot that's left us."

She turned toward the large door and placed her hand against it.

"Oh, and Mr Biscuits has probably made it back in time too, so when you see him try not to act like a giant fanny again and pish all doon yourself!" And with a quick smile, she pushed the door open and we walked into the large room ahead.

I caught my breath as we walked into the large oval-shaped chamber. The same dark brickwork covered the walls, but with small alcoves interspersed randomly from roof to ceiling holding what looked like framed photographs, small candles burning beside them throwing light on the serious faces of the people they displayed.

Round the sides of the room sat long curved benches, all facing toward the middle of the room where a small podium stood, upon which stood a small table holding what looked like a golden bowl on a small metal frame with a small blue flame burning within. Beside this stood a man in an immaculately fitted black suit, his head bowed looking down upon the picture frame held tightly between his hands.

The only illumination in the room seemed to come from the subdued spotlight that lit up the man on the podium, and from the small candles that flickered in the various alcoves. This made it hard to see the people that sat around the room, but as Maggie led me across to a bench on the left I noticed other people in dark clothing sitting around us, all wearing sad smiles and holding small bits of cards of various bright colour.

I felt the heckles on the back of my neck rising slightly as I looked around and spotted Mr Biscuits sitting on a higher bench behind us, smiling down at me with a long thumb pointing enthusiastically up in the air. Because of the low height of the benches in relation to the floor, this caused Mr Biscuits long legs to fold up in front of him, nearly pushing his knees up as far as his chin which in turn was almost crushing the bundle of angered, ginger fur that he had clutched to his chest with his other hand, the furious face of a beleaguered cat poking out from between his fingers as it desperately tried to reach up and claw out his non-existent eyes.

He looked almost comical as I smiled back and gave him a thumbs up, which seemed to give him a start as his hand slowly lowered in front of him. Suddenly his face broke out in the widest, most terrifying grin I've ever seen in my life, his hands clapping enthusiastically in front of him which caused the now forgotten rage-cat to launch into the air. The shocked face of the suddenly airborne moggy spun over three benches before landing on its feet, where it took the brief opportunity to sprint at full speed for the nearest available exit. The poor cats plight aside, if it wasn't for the comical way he was sitting and Maggie's reassuring grip on my hand I'd have been seriously battling my terror weakened bladder control right there and then.

I caught Maggie watching the interaction between myself and Mr Biscuits, and she gave me a reassuring squeeze as she pulled me down to whisper in my ear.

"You've no idea how happy seeing that makes me." She pulled out a crusty looking tissue from her sleeve and dabbed at her eyes. "That poor wee kind soul just wants to be loved, to be accepted. You see how close he and Gunnars' cat Colin are?" I jumped suddenly as she blew her nose violently into the offending tissue, "Bless, he just wants to have friends!"

I smiled back at her, not wanting to admit that while Mr Biscuits was now enthusiastically waving at me, I was busy worrying that the fear-sweat would show through my white shirt. I zipped up Huey's jacket a little higher and looked around the room as more people entered.

It seemed that there were about twenty or so people there, despite the room clearly being built to accommodate much more if it had to. I was looking around trying to pick out faces, to see if there was anyone there that I maybe recognised, but so far nobody seemed familiar. As I looked across the room I noticed a smaller, much less grand door than the one we came through opening near the far side of the room, the room growing quieter as in walked two blue skinned men in dark shawls.

My eyes went wide as they almost glided across to a bench on the other side of the chamber and sat down stiffly, their gazes fixed on the podium and the man stood there, still unmoving with his head bowed. Maggie pulled me closer again to whisper in my ear.

"They're known as the Blue men of Minch." She scowled and almost spat the name out, "They used to only live in the water between the Isle of Lewis and the mainland, but these last few years they've taken over most of the coastline up tae the Pentland Firth. Nasty wee bastards attack the fishing boats and try and drown the crews." Her face darkened as their gaze fell upon us, small smiles on their faces that didn't reach their eyes.

"They're only here because of the damned treaty that RUST brokered. A treaty they've no bother ignoring when it bloody suits them. Huey would have been livid seeing those buggers here, acting like they're bloody civilised when they're little more than monsters!"

Maggie's voice had risen by this point, prompting Gunnar to lean over and place a hand on her shoulder.

"C'mon now lass, today's no' the day for this. They're here to show respect, let's take it as it's given and we'll hae' an argument about it later when there's less of an audience eh?"

Just as Maggie turned to give Gunnar another of her trademarked 'black looks', the far door opened again and in walked what looked like a large built man in a black suit, wearing what seemed to be in the dark light a wide brimmed hat over a heavily bearded face. It wasn't until he sat down and looked across at us, spotting Maggie and giving her a wave before lifting off his hat that I noticed it wasn't a beard at all, he had the head of a large wolf.

I was half out of my seat pointing when Gunnars hand swiftly plonked me down on my ass again. Later I suspected he had sat behind me as security against just such a reaction, and as I turned to ask him what the blue hell that furry thing was that was maintaining as big a space as possible away from the blue skinned water guys, Maggie cracked me on the kneecap with her stick.

"Now dinna you embarrass me in front of Georgie!" She hissed at me through clenched teeth, as she smiled and waved back at the wolf headed guy across the room who was now chuckling to himself as he turned and shot me a wink and a smile.

"He's a Wulver, originally fae Shetland, and a nicer damned man you couldnae meet if you tried! He's done a lot of good for the poorer families around this county, damned fine fisherman he is too, leaves all his catches on the doorsteps of the needy through the night so they dinna see him and get a fright." Maggie smiled sadly.

"Was best pals too with Huey. Lost count o' the times I caught the pair o' them wi' Gunnar sitting in my front room till all hours, hammering their way through a bottle or two of single malt and trying to sing 'Donald where's yer Troosers' at the top o' their lungs. I couldnae even be mad at the buggers for it."

She laughed and started coughing, pulling the manky handkerchief out of her sleeve to cover her mouth. "Have you ever heard someone wi' a wolf's mouth try and sing the Elvis part o' that song? Ach, I pished a few nighties laughing while they made damned fools o' themselves!" Maggie's hanky hadn't lowered from her face, and I could see she was holding it firmly against her nose as tears ran down her cheeks. Gunnar leaned forward with a big smile on his face and whispered in my other ear,

"And look at the faces on the Blue Men, they're nae that keen on auld Georgie that's for sure." Sure enough, the Blue Men were staring daggers at Georgie from along the bench, but whether or not he noticed this, Georgie paid it no attention as he looked around the room, waving at people and giving a thumbs up to Mr Biscuits, who was now almost vibrating off the bench with joy.

"Like your aunty says, he's a damned good fisherman who works out of their water. They've tried catching him and cowping his boat a few times, but he's too bloody quick for them." Gunnar chuckled to himself as Georgie gave the Blue Men a thumbs up. I suspected the only thing that was holding them back from jumping on the Wulver and ripping him apart was the solemn surroundings and how heavily outnumbered they were by stern faced onlookers in black suits.

Three loud taps echoed around the auditorium followed by a slight cough as a deep voice resonated from the podium and started talking to the room.

"It appears that everyone is here now, so if I may have your attention, I'd like to begin the ceremony" The man in the immaculate black suit leaned forward slightly and rested his hands on the podium, his voice clear and filling the room, despite having no microphone that I could see.

"I feel a heartfelt sorrow that we've all been called together here this day, to mourn the passing of a man we all loved and respected like no other."

I could feel Gunnar lean forward to whisper in my ear as the man on the stage panned his gaze over the assembled crowd.

"His name's Jonathan Cleaver lad, but we all call him by his codename 'Teacher'". Gunnar's massive hand patted my shoulder as he leaned back, "We'll get a chat with him later when all's said and done eh?"

I turned back to the podium as the lump of ham with fingers left my shoulder, and froze in my seat. Cleaver had turned toward us and was staring right at me.

I panicked, was I expected to say something here? I looked around in case it was something around me that had grabbed his attention and stopped his monologue, but that only made me aware that every other pair of eyes around me was looking toward me too. Maggie once more grabbed my hand as Cleaver continued.

"And as you've all been made aware, we've disregarded some long established security protocols today," His hand swept in the direction of the Blue Men and Georgie, "Thanks to the consent of our esteemed guests, an uninitiated member of Alex Stewart's family is in attendance."

A small grin broke on his face. "Under the ever vigilant guardianship of his beloved aunt, former RUST team leader and wife to the man whom we are gathered here today to honour, Maggie Stewart".

Maggie smiled, wiping her eyes with the increasingly biohazardous hankie as polite applause echoed around the room, before Cleaver turned his attention back to sweeping the room with his steely gaze.

"If only we had the time, I could stand here and talk to you all about the many ways that our beloved colleague and friend 'Huey' supported, taught and tormented me over the years I've spent running this unit, aha. "Instead I will leave that for the gathering later where I will be providing us all with several large drinks.' He smiled as he turned and held up the photo in his hands. Staring at it for a few seconds, he turned it round and held it high for the room to see.

"And since there's little more for me to say here, I'll be handing the podium over to a distinguished guest who has travelled here especially for this evening's remembrance, before we all set our thoughts to the flame."

Cleaver stepped down from the podium and made his way over to where we sat. Climbing the steps beside us, he made his way to the wall behind and stopped in front of one of the empty small alcoves. Pulling a lighter from his pocket, he lit the small candle that already sat in the hollow before placing Huey's photo down beside it. Suddenly the small alcoves made sense, these were all photos of those who had passed. It didn't escape me either that there were easily fifty or more photos dotted around the walls either side of me. Not all of them strictly human by the looks of things either.

Maggie stood up from her seat and walked to the wall to stand beside Cleaver, taking his hand as they both lowered their heads with respect. Around me the room started to clap, slowly at first while Cleaver and Maggie moved back through the benches and headed toward the podium. By the time they stepped up beside the golden bowl with the blue flame, the applause was rapturous, people stood all around me and turned to face Huey's picture as they cheered and clapped. I got to my feet, tears stinging my eyes and running down my face as I too turned to face Huey's picture, clapping proudly at this amazing display of affection toward the man who took me as his son.

"Ladies and Gentlemen, I respectfully request that you all remain standing to welcome our guest of honour, the Selkie."

A collective gasp could be heard from all around me as the far side doors opened once again and a tall slim woman in a long flowing white dress stepped through. My breath caught in my throat, she was easily the most beautiful woman I'd ever seen, and I had access to the internet.

I sat dumbstruck as she glided into the room and made a path toward the podium. She flowed past the Blue Men, their gaze fell to the floor and their hands tucked in between their legs.

Georgie however was a different story entirely. His tongue lolled out of his head and his left leg kicked like he was waiting for someone to throw a ball. Once he realised what he was doing he clamped both hands down on his wayward limb to control it, and pulled off his wide brimmed hat before holding it to his chest.

It took me a second to realise I hadn't breathed for a good thirty seconds or more as the Selkie smoothly climbed the podium step and stood before Cleaver and Maggie. I couldn't take my eyes off her as she knelt down and held her palms up to my aunt, offering what looked like a silver brooch on a black cord. Maggie reached down and picked it up, a smile spreading over face as she clutched the brooch tightly to her chest. I felt the huge hand of Gunnar come over my shoulder and clamp onto my chest to hold me in place. It seemed that while I was lost in the beauty of this woman in white I had leaned forward so far that Gunnar thought I was going to tip onto the floor face first.

the Selkie stood up, and as both Cleaver and Maggie knelt to return her respectful bow, she turned toward those of us standing around the hall, her hands now held out wide as she smiled softly at the audience.

She put me in mind of of an Elven queen, like the one's you see in those fantasy epics that dominated movie theatres for years, albeit with a slightly sharper face framed by long blonde hair. Stunningly beautiful, yet as I watched her eyes sweep defiantly over the room as she prepared to address the spellbound audience, something about the power she projected made me want to edge along the bench I sat on toward the nearest exit, just in case I needed to suddenly run very fast in her opposite direction.

I noticed then a small man standing beside her, seemingly appearing out of nowhere. He'd be lucky if he was four feet tall in a Cuban heel, dressed in a sharp black suit, white shirt and black tie, thick framed glasses framing his oversized bald head as he handed the Selkie a small white napkin. She took the napkin without looking in his direction, and he bowed swiftly before ducking his head and scurrying back to stand at the doorway the Selkie had stepped through moments before.

I guessed he was probably her personal assistant, but before my curiosity took the better of me as I turned to ask Gunnar, the Selkie cleared her throat, pressing the hankie gently against her mouth as she did so, then placed it softly on the podium as she lifted her head to address the audience.

"ALRIGHTY YA HORRIBLE SHOWER!"

I was dumbstruck, what the hell had just happened? This.. This couldn't be the voice of someone as perfect and wonderful as the Selkie? I started looking around for someone else who might have spoken in such a rough, cigarette coated, gravely voice and perhaps had fooled me into thinking it could poss..

"IF YE'VE GOT IT, GET IT OOT AND GET IT DOON YE!" The Selkie plunged a delicate hand down the cleavage of her beautiful white gown and started rummaging, bending over slightly so she could get in deep there and really rake about.

I didn't know where to look, still trying to process the fact that not only did she talk like a twenty-a-day smoker who worked shifts on a fishing trawler, but also that she had just pulled an impossibly sized hip flask out from the cleavage of her dress, had raised it high and then spun the top off and held it to her mouth as she threw her head back to gulp it down.

Nearly a full minute passed as we all sat in silence, watching the Selkie work her way through the contents of the oversized flask. Two lines of dark fluid leaked out from the seal her mouth made around the flask top and rolled down her chest, which I blatantly failed not to stare at until I caught Maggie looking at me with one of her disapproving looks.

The Selkie kept gulping as more of the dark liquid ran down her chin, staining the neckline of the immaculate gown and prompting her small suited aide to jump sharply and run toward her. Without opening her eyes or moving her head to look, the Selkie quickly raised a finger in his direction as he skidded to a stop, before wiping her mouth clean with the sleeve of her right arm and throwing the flask down on the small lectern.

"Righto! Now that we're all suitabl.. Excuse me.." The Selkie raised a hand to cover her mouth as she belched loudly, causing her solid metal flask to briefly vibrate on the table.

"Ooft, that was a belter eh!" She turned around laughing to look toward Cleaver and Maggie who stood in a lower step of the podium behind her, "I'm pretty sure that shook loose a couple of fillings.. Anywho!" She turned back toward the wide eyed audience around her and leaned forward on the lectern.

"I bet most of you are wondering why the hell I'm here eh?" She swept a hand and a very faint bow toward Cleaver and Maggie,

"I know, the Matriarch shouldn't be bothering her arse with the affairs of the Redbloods" Her noticeably sweaty aide took a nervous step toward her, raising his hand before being stopped again by a swiftly raised finger. "Sorry, I mean 'Humans' of course.. Got to be politically correct when it comes to speaking about you lot!" Her aide looked stricken as he hurriedly started writing in his folder, no doubt preparing a grovelling apology letter of sorts.

"But to hell with the traditions I say! A lot of dusty book pish that nobody REALLY cares about if we're being even halfway honest wi' ourselves." She leaned forward onto the lectern, hands clutching either side as her face darkened and she slowly scanned the crowd.

"I've decreed that all ongoing hostilities between factions are stalled" She shot a look toward the Blue Men who had the decency at least to look shocked, "And for two weeks, we will observe the peace that not only we've all craved for so long, but we'll work to maintain that peace, the peace that Huey Stewart worked so hard to support and grow over all these years." Pausing, her right hand crawled over the lectern and bunching up around the hankie.

"We will honour that man with remembrance, and respect for each other, and I'm sure if Maggie gets her way, with a skinful of Single Malt later this evening." Maggie smiled as the Selkie motioned toward her to join her at the lectern. Climbing the steps she took the Selkie's hand and faced the crowd,

"Aye, and the bottles are sitting right now through in the gathering hall!" Maggie grinned, "And I know it's the good stuff, because it's all come from Huey's secret haul I found under a wee hatch at the foot of the coal bunker."

The audience laughed as she continued, "I knew all that man's secrets! Bloody hiding whisky from me like I wouldn't guess that Georgie, Gunnar and himsel' were oot in that shed every Friday night sharing stories and getting pie-eyed!" Gunnar's booming laugh could be heard over the rest of the crowd, and Georgie stood on his chair and bowed theatrically to all those around him.

"I can think of nothing he'd want more than us all sitting together, Humans, The Seelie Court, The UnSeelie Court and if they would consider the invitation, even the Sluagh Sidhe[3] are welcome amongst us to celebrate the man who took care of me all these years.. Hell, took care of us all!"

Everyone got to their feet, cheering and applauding as the Selkie leaned over and hugged Maggie to her side with one arm. I noticed the Blue Men

---

[3] The Seelie Court are a collection of generally passive Fae, who are more inclined to seek peace with Humanity and the other factions. The Unseelie Court are the darker side, a collection of Fae that have no issue wirth causing problems for the other factions or testing how far they can push the peace initiatives. They're not evil as such, probably best described as morally ambiguous. the Sluagh Sidhe, or as they're also known, 'Malicious Host', are considered to be a manifestation of the Wild Hunt. The Sluagh consist of the unrestful spirits of the dead and are considered by many to be a disruptive and sometimes destructive force. The word Sluagh refers to a 'host', or perhaps a more applicable translation would be 'army'.

remained seated, and as those around them returned to their seats, I could see they leaned in together in what seemed to be furious discussion. I couldn't think what had happened that could have annoyed them, and as their eyes returned to the podium where my aunt still stood beside the Selkie, I could see that their faces were dark and shaded as the Selkie retook the lectern.

"As 'Auld Mither', I need to formally pass our collected condolences to Huey's family and friends, and to those of you here at RUST who worked alongside the man. He will be remembered and honoured for as long as I draw breath."

She smiled wickedly, "And considering I'm barely a bairn at two hundred and thirty-ish years old, he'll be remembered for a fecking long time to come!"

The lights in the room suddenly darkened, all the candles in the tiny alcoves dimming as every eye locked on to the woman in white who now seemed to shine on the brightly lit podium.

"And since we're throwing rule books oot the fucking window today, it seems only right that we share with you one more thing, something usually only reserved for the fallen amongst The Courts."

The Selkie turned and stared right at me, a small grin spreading slowly over her face. "Something I suspect our uninitiated guest here today will undoubtedy enjoy."

All eyes in the room turned toward me once more as something crashed against my leg from below the bench. As I looked down, something small and furry picked itself off the ground, turned up to look at me before sticking its tongue out and sprinting off below the bench ahead of me. I quickly pulled my feet up off the floor as more and more of these things seemed to spill across the ground below me, all running toward the centre of the room.

I was confused, I thought they were small dogs at first, but the one that stuck its tongue out at me seemed to have a very human-like face, I looked up to see everyone else had lifted their feet from the floor as more of these things spilled out from below their chairs, but nobody seemed concerned in the slightest that we were being invaded by what looked like flat-faced hounds, running upright like they were human and late for a bus.

I was now squatting on my toes on top of my seat, hugging my knees for balance as more and more of these things spilled out from below the benches, swarming around the legs of the Selkie and covering the podium, as they all turned to face outwards toward the audience.

Gunnar's hand once more placed itself on my shoulder, "It's okay laddie, nothing here is gonna hurt you." He leaned closer until he was right beside my ear. "At least not here today in front of the big boss lady! HAHAH! Ach, I'm joking lad, sit doon and relax and enjoy this." Gunnar's eyes seemed to gleam as I lowered myself from my squatting position on the bench and sat back down on my ass,

"You'll remember this until you're auld and pishing the bed boy, a rare honour indeed, especially on your first bloody day here!"

The Selkie coughed into her fist, putting an end to the rumble of voices that filled the benches, and the squeaking noises coming from the strange looking 'Man-Dog-Things' that bustled together around her feet.

"As is well known to us all, this mourning ceremony is normally only ever witnessed by the current Selkie, and by the direct family of the lost, usually on the seventh day" She turned to wave a hand toward Maggie, who was in the middle of trying to wrestle her cane back from one of the furry midget things that were covering the floor.

"However in this case we have moved away from this rule at the request of our beloved friend Mrs Stewart, who made it very loud and threateningly clear that Huey's family wasn't just blood or direct descendents, it was every single one of us who had the honour of sharing his life, his sorrow and his humour." She looked at me directly and smiled, making blood rush to my cheeks and other unmentionable places. "And of course, to help those of us new to this life see quite how important Huey was to this life we share."

The Selkie spread her arms wide and lifted her gaze high above our heads. The dog-things too, slowly lifted their arms outwards and raised their heads.

"Ladies and Gentlemen. Fae, Beasties and Bastards alike. I introduce the highest honour the Haggvar can offer to the lost, their ritual mourning song, The Shuynd."

And then in perfect unison, the creatures around her legs began to sing.

Chapter Seven

The Shuynd

What started as a low rumble became a flowing melody I could feel through the soles of my boots, pulsing and twisting as the creatures sung in one flowing harmony. I slumped back on the bench as the song filled the chamber, and whatever tension I had been holding in my back and shoulders seemed to slide away while the song ran over me.

Of course, my brain was still on red alert considering I was surrounded by what looked like a two foot tall furry Welsh choir, a half drunk werewolf, some miserable blue gentlemen and an enthusiastically clapping seven foot tall faceless biscuit lover in an immaculate black suit, but I couldn't stop the smile that spread over my face as I looked around to see everyone as lost in the music as I was, all there to celebrate the life of a man who not only meant the world to me, but also it seemed meant a whole lot to this hidden world around him.

I turned back to the podium in time to see a solitary 'Haggvar' step through its friends and stand at the front of the pack. Slightly larger than the rest of its kin and more grey in colour than the brown shades of the rest of the pack, it stood with its chest pushed forward and stared out at the watching crowd. With a smile and a small nod of its head it burst into song along with the rest of the Haggvar, its voice louder and deeper than the rest of the furry chorus who stood behind.

I could almost feel the bass in its voice flow through me, gently soothing my muscles as the Grey's voice led the singers on the podium. Still grinning, I looked around at Gunnar to ask what on earth these creatures were and why they hadn't recorded a soppy duet with Elton John yet, but

Gunnars eyes were clamped closed, a massive smile breaking though his huge ginger beard.

And as I looked around I realised it wasn't just Gunnar that was happily lost in the song. Most of the people around me were now swaying back and forth, eyes closed as they either laughed to themselves, or wiped tears from their cheeks. I looked across at Maggie just as Gunnar's hand fell once again on my shoulder.

"Close your eyes lad, and keep them closed. You really don't want to miss this.." Close my eyes? Surely I'd miss whatever was going to happen if my eyes were closed? However, this wasn't the strangest request or thing I'd come across today, and If I can deal with suit wearing nightmares driving cars, rude plant pots and singing Furbies, then the least I can do is close my damned eyes.

The moment I did I was faced with a kaleidoscope of colours. 'Kaleidoscope' seems a very overly dramatic way of describing what was happening to the inside of my eyelids, but if you remember those tube telescope things you used to get as a kid that were full of coloured beads and glass, and when you held it up to your eye and twisted it you saw a kaleidoscope of shapes and colour, it was pretty much the same as that, except with far less danger of your pal bashing the end and driving the whole thing into your eyeball for a laugh.

I opened my eyes and the colours went away, was I suffering some kind of brain incident here? I turned to ask Gunnar if they had a medical facility nearby only to be waved down and given a thumbs up, all while keeping his eyes closed and grinning like a bloody idiot.

I assumed Gunnar knew best, so I took a deep breath and closed my eyes again. Straight away the colours came back as the song continued around me, swirling into shapes and patterns almost in rhythm with the booming

RUST: Harvest of the Hidden

voice of the grey Furby still singing on the podium. I watched the colours dance in front of my eyeballs, keeping my fingers crossed that this wasn't the sign of some kind of brain hemorrhage and I hadn't just imagined everything that had happened during the last hour and a bit because my brain was going through its dying throes, when suddenly the colours stopped and started gathering together.

As I watched and the song around me continued, shapes starting forming until I saw an image of my uncle Huey, clear as day on the back of my eyelids sitting at a table laughing and spilling coffee all over himself. I wanted to open my eyes to turn and ask Gunnar what was happening, but I was afraid that if I did this picture of Huey would be gone. Seconds later, the colours flew apart and fell back into a kaleidoscope pattern. I kept watching as they gatherered together again, and for the next couple of minutes as the Haggvar sang, picture after picture of Huey appeared to me.

These were images of Huey I had never seen before, most of which had him wearing the same jacket I was wearing right then and usually laughing. In one he was holding one of the Haggvar in the air like a father would pick up a toddler, in another he was sitting at a table pouring from a hip flask into three mugs beside Gunnar and Georgie. Another image showed him seemingly wagging a finger with a stern face at a seal, which was laying on a rock and pointedly ignoring him, another yet showed a younger Huey, picking up a darker haired and more youthful Maggie in a big bear hug while she laughed.. What was I seeing here, photographs? Memories? Whatever they were, they were all taken from a low angle and were all pictures I had never seen before. As I was pondering this the Haggvar's song seemed to slow around me. The large Grey's voice seemed to get lower too, and the tune turned mournful. My face hurt from holding my eyes so tightly closed, I was sure now that somehow the singing and the pictures were related, and I didn't want to risk a single chance of not seeing more of my uncle before the music finally stopped.

And as the song turned more sorrowful, as did the pictures I started to see behind my eyelids. Here was Huey crying over a small gravestone, around his legs stood a large pack of Haggvar with their heads lowered. As I tried to read the stone the image changed again, and now Huey was on his knees with his hands open in front of him in front of a small stone throne, upon which sat a darker, more menacing dog-faced creature with a dark smile and a red slash of paint over its face. And as that image fell apart, the Haggvar's song seemed to suddenly grow louder and faster. The colours spun quicker and started to gather together as the song flew towards what sounded like a dramatic end. The colours crashed together and an image of Huey standing in front of a pack of Haggvar alongside an equally bedraggled Gunnar, their clothes torn and bloody as they each held up large metal poles defensively against whatever was outside of the image heading toward them. And with one final and solitary howl, a brief flash of Huey laying on the ground unmoving, surrounded by these small creatures as the Haggvar's song stopped, and the colours behind my eyes danced away..

I spun round as everyone around stood and cheered, climbing up onto my bench so I could look the monstrous Gunnar square in the eye behind me.

"Gunnar, I've seen some crazy shit today so far, and I think I'm really doing a good job of not having a mental fit and letting my brain pour out of my fucking ears, so kindly tell me what the hell just happened before I completely lose my damned mind?"

Gunnar stepped over my bench and sat down beside me.

"It's the song laddie. The wee beastie's song is their way of sharing memories together." He waved at the Haggvar as they trooped off the podium and ran back under the seats to whatever doorways they had out of the room under the benches. "They canna communicate too well with the spoken word, so they store memories which they can share wi' their song." He sat down hard on the bench, sighing deeply.

"And what they shared today has rarely ever been seen before. The big grey one? He's their chief and their master of memory. He's like a walkin' Haggvar library that one, stores all their stories in his heid to pass on to the next generations. And they're nae usually that keen on us seeing those memories either. But aye, in their minds Huey was one o' theirs, despite nae being able to grow the right amount of body hair."

Even though the creatures had disappeared I noticed that the larger Grey one remained, and moved to stand beside the Selkie as she returned to the podium to address the crowd.

"Gunnar, at the end there I saw Huey laying on the ground. I think he was dead, and those things were all around him. Could they know what really happened to my uncle?"

Gunnar frowned, looking down at his hands as he spoke. "Son, you're not the only one that needs answers to those questions." I was about to push for more when the Selkie's voice boomed out behind me.

"Well, was that nae a wee bit special eh?" She reached down and took the offered paw of the large grey by her side. "Ye may never see the like again folks! Hold what happened here as close tae yer heart as you do the memory of the man we lost."

She smiled, once more lifting the unreasonably large hip flask and raised it above her head. "TO HUEY! Ye'll be missed ye bugger, you were a good foil when we clashed heads, and a grand laugh when we didn't."

She swept a smile over the audience around her before resting her gaze on me. I'd never experienced someone undressing me with their gaze so I had no point of reference, but I couldn't shake the feeling that her eyes were at least fiddling with the top button of my now clammy shirt.

"Now, I'm sure neither Maggie nor her very handsome nephew will mind me saying that we've spent enough bloody time in this dusty auld hall being miserable, so let's all make our way through tae the bar and properly say goodbye to our lost friend."

The Selkie stepped down from the lectern alongside the Grey and fell into step behind Maggie and Teacher as they walked toward the doorway on the opposite side of the room. I loosened my collar as I watched them walk away, realising that I'd been holding my breath the whole time the Selkie stared at me, which made me wholly aware that my shirt was now soaked with nervous sweat. I zipped up Huey's jacket a little higher as the procession left the room, and everyone around me stood up to follow.

"Stick close to me lad, easy to get lost in this place" Gunnar laid a hand on my shoulder as we stood waiting for our turn to step forward and follow the people now filtering out past the bowl with the blue flame, in turn placing their paper sheets within, with what I assume were notes or memories of my uncle, before bowing before the flame and then making their way out of the hall.

Gunnar passed me a small paper and pencil, urging me to write something that I could commit to the flame before we left.

I couldn't think of something on the fly, people kept moving forward and now that we were caught in the queue of people I had little time to think. During a pause in the movement, it struck me, and I bent down to use my thigh to place the paper to write on.

'Rest well Huey. Thank you for being my dad.'.

I folded up the paper, waiting my turn to pass the bowl on the podium, and committed it to the fire, watching it sail briefly into the air through the tears in my eyes as the fire quickly consumed it.

The giant was once again by my side, placing his own paper into the bowl before bowing slightly, and then turning with me toward the exit door and away from the podium.

"Come on son, let's go find where where Colin ran off to, and then we'll head for the bar and get a dram of Huey's favourite whisky to remember him. Oh, and maybe stick close by when we get to the bar too, I saw the way the Selkie was eyeing you up like a slab of fresh meat." I was about to protest that I totally didn't notice when Gunnar lifted his hand to stop me.

"Nae false modesty here lad, she's a beautiful creature for sure and you're a handsome young buck. It's only natural the two of you would be making googly bloody eyes back and forth." Gunnar leaned down and shot me a serious look.

"But remember wee man, she's generations older than you. She's nae daft and she usually gets what she wants, I suppose that's why they made her the bloody matriarch."

We stepped through the large doorway and out into the red brickwork-covered hallway beyond.

"But there's a lot more layers to her than that flimsy one you keep staring at that's barely covering her lady bits. I know, I know, you 'didnae even notice' that!" Gunnar rolled his eyes and chuckled, "But do me a favour eh? If you do get tangled up in her net, just make sure that you've always got a big knife on you to cut your way out when it fastens up around you." Gunnar stopped us both just outside the doorway leading into the brightly lit bar ahead.

"And in the name of the big man, don't tell Maggie! Now, where's that bloody cat got to."

Chapter Eight

Sons of the Owl

After a quick look around the hall for Gunnars' ballistic cat Colin, who'd clearly taken to the air vents to escape Biscuits cuddles, we shuffled along the corridor amongst the procession of bodies all heading for the bar, everyone engaging in quiet small talk with the people beside them whilst also keeping an eye glued to the floor in case they accidentally stood on one of the Haggvar that occasionally darted between our legs.

"I'm just saying, maybe Huey wouldnae want ye to hand oot the secret whisky stash for his wake." Georgie had pushed through the crowd to walk beside Maggie ahead of us, "Maybe, now hear me oot, MAYBE he'd have been happier knowing that his bestest pals were in that shed later getting pie-eyed in his honour!"

Maggie shot him 'The Look'[4], and he took a quick step back out of walking stick range.

"Listen Furball, dinna tell me you'd rather be stuffed in that cold shed with that big copper-headed galoot, sitting on an old oil drum and getting pie-eyed than be here watching a'body sharing Hueys' drams and swapping stories?" Maggie stepped forward toward the door ahead of us and moved to shove it open with her stick, only to stumble forward as it automatically swung open in front of her. Georgie and I quickly grabbed an elbow each before she face-planted the floor, and tried to get her to stand straight while she furiously gave the bird to the computer terminal

---

[4] 'The Look' is taught to every woman before they have their first child, usually at the knee of their own mother. It's said that 'The Look' has the power to instantly freeze the average toddler in place as they waddle toward your expensive telly with handfuls of nappy cream, or stop a fully grown man agreeing to his friends on the phone that he'll come to the pub, because he's suddenly realised that he'd rather sit through another few episodes of that period drama he's been told that he really likes.

camera watching us from above. I looked round to see if Gunnar was going to help, but he was busy looking under any desks or furniture we happened to pass, making those strange "t,t,t,t," noises that people make with their tongue pressed against their teeth when they're trying to get an uninterested cat to come over and get thoroughly petted.

"Aye, that's EXACTLY what I'm telling you!" Georgie pulled her forward through the door before the point of her cane could make contact with the computer screen on the wall beside us, "Look, the Blue-Heid's want to gut me like a trout, the Selkie is still mad at me for accidentally pulling her dad out of the Pentland Firth in a net and I'm pretty sure she's also still pissed that I had a wee, 'liaison' with the new Goblin ambassador and maybe gave him a dose of the fleas." He turned a pleading face toward her.

"I've got paws woman, PAWS! Do you know how hard it is to scratch your own flea-bitten arse without fully formed opposable thumbs? Don't take away what little joy I have left in my life!" Georgie's eyes went wide, clearly trying to impersonate the 'sad puppy' look that you normally see in cartoons, instead ending up looking like he was suffering some kind of constipation incident.

Handing me her cane, Maggie reached up and cradled Georgie's long jawline between her hands, before pulling him down and placing her forehead against his.

"Don't fret you auld mangy bugger, the key for the shed is still where it's always been, and I've nae touched a thing inside." She pulled his face up so they were eye to eye, "And if I dinna see you and Gunnar in there every so often getting drunk and murdering perfectly good songs between ye, I'll be VERY annoyed. Especially since I've restocked the badly hidden drink crate wi' some new bottles ye haven't tried yet."

Maggie's face lit up in a grin as Georgie's eyes went as wide as plates. He dashed forward and stood by the entrance to the bar, bowing dramatically before her as we walked on through.

"I'll tell you this Maggie Stewart, If your man hadn't just passed and I was in any way interested in the fairer sex, I'd be slapping the biggest bloody smooch on ye right about now!" Georgie swept across behind Maggie and swept her up in his arms.

"Now c'mere and give this auld hound dog a bloody big hug!"

"ACH, SET ME DOON YE DAMNED FUR FACED ARSEHOLE!" Maggie wriggled free and dropped to the ground, and from what I could see she was doing her very best to keep the smile off her face, yet failing miserably.

"Enough o' this 'feelings' pish! We've had a horrible few days, let's get in this bar and hae a good time. Gussy? Away ye go to the bar and get your poor aunty a wee nip o' brandy will ye? They know what kind!" And with that she was off into the hustle of bodies that crowded around the doorway to the bar.

I followed her into a large, rectangular room covered in panels of dark wood, with seating booths tucked together against the walls surrounding a large 'island' in the middle where the drinks were served. As I walked down the three steps leading down to the serving area I couldn't help but think it looked a hell of a lot like that famous American bar where everybody knows your name, how big your bar tab is, and how often the barman has tried to unsuccessfully get into the new owner's knickers.

I leant against the bar and waited my turn beside the others stood around me, watching the large barman dart back and forth from side to side handing out drinks. He caught my eye as he swung past, sliding to a halt and turned toward me.

"You're Maggie's lad ain't ya?" His accent was hard to pin down but sounded a bit Cockney mixed with a mouth full of wheel bolts. And his eyes seemed to sit just that fraction too far apart, enough that I couldn't help but wonder if he was also one of these 'Fae' people that I'd heard mentioned already.

"Oi! You gonna stare with yer mouth hanging open catching flies for a bit longer, or you gonna answer my bloody question?"

"Uh, yeah, sorry! I'm her nephew Angus. Sorry, I wasn't meaning to be rude, this is just all so new to me!" He smiled and leaned foward over the bar, his two massive fists pressing down into the collection of soggy beer mats that littered the bar top.

"Don't worry son, I understand what yer going through, this place is a lot to take in for anyone, let alone someone fresh out the wrapper." His grin slipped a bit as he stood back and wiped his hands down the front of his beer stained apron.

"Yer uncle was a topper and no mistake, he's a huge loss to us all, and as his boy yer always welcome in this bar." He wiped his hand on a small towel that he pulled from his shoulder before reaching across to shake my hand. "Name's Koba, and this is my pub! Now, I'm guessing Maggie sent you here to get her drink for her? Well, it's already sorted." He waved across toward the seating behind me where Maggie was holding court in one of the booths, waving her drink around her head emphatically as she no doubt told her small audience the same old story again about Huey stealing the minister's chicken eggs.

Suddenly everyone within a ten-foot radius stopped to stare at me, as the sounds of vigorous, orgasmic screams could be heard bellowing out from my pocket. I fumbled for my phone and quickly killed the sex noises, kicking myself for not changing out the ringtone that my ex had set before I had left Aberdeen. It was my work trying to call me, in particular my direct sergeant. I dismissed the call, noticing that there were several messages too from her asking that I get in touch immediately. I put the phone on silent and shoved it back into my jacket pocket, making a mental note to call her back for a probable bollocking once I got out of this. Whatever this place was.

As I turned back to ask for a drink for myself, the barman had already dumped a pint of lager in front of me, and a small shot of something that didn't look like a regulation measure.

"The lady herself has arranged all the drinks for you and your aunt, so the pair of ya won't be short of a top-up the whole night-" He leaned forward with what I hoped was a friendly grin, "-and I intend to have you leave here with your back teeth floating!"

The large barman waved his hand across the bar and pointed toward the raised seating at the very back, where the Selkie sat at a table dead in the center of a group of attendants. Even though she clearly sat on one of the alcohol and grime stained velveteen couches, she made it look like she was seated upon a throne and the whole room before her was little more than a court full of little people begging for her attention. The only thing that seemed to spoil the scene was Gunnar stumbling into view, grinning from ear to ear and clutching the ginger cat I'd seen Mr Biscuits with before to his chest.

"Found the little bugger!" Gunnar squeezed into the bar beside me and plonked the frazzled looking feline on the bar top in front of us, "He'd got himself in amongst the Haggvar again. Hah! Those little buggers love getting a chase around from old C4 here!" As I looked into the scar covered face of 'Colin' glaring at me from atop the bar while Gunnar fussed over him, I struggled to imagine that any chasing of the Haggvar was in any way consensual or 'loved' on their part.

"This is my wee boy! Say hello to 'Colin the Fourth'." Gunnar beamed as the ginger monstrosity rubbed against him, the cat never taking his malevolent gaze far from my face while his owner fussed over him, pulling lumps of cobwebs and what looked like other animal fur out of his coat. I suspected that there were a few of the Haggvar somewhere that were missing a clump or two of their pelt after having 'fun' with Colin.

"He's an absolute wee angel." Gunnar beamed as he waved to Koba for a drink, "Absolute Daddy's boy so he is, the fourth member of his family to live here at RUST." Koba arrived and thumped down a large, frothing glass in front of Gunnar, being very cautious it seemed not to attract Colin's attention which was still fixed on me.

Koba turned toward me still side-eyeing Colin as he spoke, "We call him 'C4' around these parts." His voice hushed slightly as he moved away from both Colin and Gunnar, "On account of him being somewhat, 'explosive' if you look at him funny.. Or breathe near him. Or, you know, exist near him." Colin, or 'C4', suddenly twisted round and stared at Koba, forcing the large intimidating barman to stumble backwards and pretend to clean an imaginary glass before dashing off to the other side of the bar to do something less dangerous.

"Is he... friendly at all?" I asked, setting my glass down slowly as C4 turned his attention back toward me, his hairy arse sliding across the bar top whilst Gunnar vigorously petted him.

"He's a wee softie so he is, best pals with everyone here!" Gunnar boasted, as Koba from a safe distance away shot me a wide-eyed look, "He's the fourth Colin we've had here at Rust. The first three all just disappeared over time, but Colin here, he's a survivor!". Judging by Koba's reaction as he walked away to the other side of the bar, I guessed that maybe C4 was a prime suspect in the case of the missing Colins. I was about to pick up the shot glass that Koba had given me, when I noticed that it had somehow moved across the bar top and was in the clutches of the ginger-hand grenade sitting purring in Gunnars' grip. I contemplated reaching for it, but my sixth sense told me that I should value having a full hand of working digits, so instead I picked up my empty lager and pretended that I was content.

"Mine. This is mine."

I looked around, expecting someone right behind me whispering in my ear. I could have sworn I'd heard someone speak to me, really closely too, but nobody around me was paying any attention to me. The only thing paying me any regard was the cat on the bar top, currently licking his non-existent testicles with one rear leg fully extended in the air, eyes still locked onto my face throughout. I won't lie, it's a little disconcerting trying to drink from an empty pint glass when a cat is grooming its empty knacker bag and maintaining eye contact, so I politely, and slowly moved a couple more seats away and stared across the bar, trying very hard not further interest the fourth Colin.

I looked across the bar to Koba, waving my empty glass in hopes of a top-up, my eyes drawn to the beautiful Selkie holding court with a group of the most diverse people I'd ever seen outside of a fantasy book cover when her head suddenly snapped round to stare directly across at me.

I fought the urge to drop to a knee as she stared at me with that cat-like grin she had shown me earlier in the remembrance hall, instead raising my glass toward her and bowing my head, hoping that this was suitably respectful toward someone who not only represented some kind of royalty here but whose gaze was causing more than a little stirring in my unmentionables.

She raised her glass in return, her smile widening as her attendants around her looked over to see what had caught their mistress' attention. I tried to appear nonplussed, leaning on the bar on one elbow in what I hoped was a 'cool' effort, despite the edge of the bar digging into my ribs and my elbow slowly soaking up whatever spilled liquid had been left unattended by the hefty barman.

"Another beer there son?" A full glass of lager and another shot glass of something was dropped down in front of me as Koba suddenly moved in front of the Selkies' gaze. "I'm hearing word we might be seeing more of you around here from now on? I'll get a tab set up for you when you next pop in." And with a wink he was gone to the other side of the bar where a woman with a massive forehead was complaining that someone had mine-swept her wine spritzer.

I picked up my drinks and moved away from the bar, spotting an empty booth near the doorway that nobody had claimed yet. It was also conveniently on the opposite side of the room from the Selkie, whose eyes I could feel burning a hole in my back as I spilled drink all over my hands walking over to the small booth table. I set my drinks down and collapsed into the chair, the air whooshing out the cushioned seat below me releasing a smell that I wasn't entirely sure was down to the usual mix of farts and spilled beverages.

I picked up my beer and downed it almost in one go, then for good measure I threw back the shot glass in one go. It tasted like someone had soaked bacon in toffee apples, but I barely noticed as I waved to the passing waitress to please refill both glasses. If my tab was being covered by the beautiful woman at the far side of the bar who looked at me in a way that you only see in really professionally made adult production, then I was going to abuse the privilege and get myself as horrendously drunk as was feasibly possible.

What in the hell had I gotten myself into? It seemed like only moments ago I was standing with family lowering my uncle into the wind-battered ground of Thurso graveyard, and now I was stuck in some kind of underground structure full of beasties and wolfmen, a scary bastard thing with no face that likes Hob-Nobs and an aunt who was determined to pick a fight with a disembodied computer voice.

I'm sure I was shell shocked, and how could this have been Huey's life, and Maggies, for so long and I never knew a thing about it? Surely at some point, a family member is going to pull you aside and say,

"Hey little man, you know how you're kinda freaked out about there being a monster in your cupboard when you go to bed? Well those things are real, and like to sit in an underground pub with other beasties and drink fortified wine until they can't feel their legs or tentacles."

I stared down at my clenched hands on the table in front of me, while new drinks were placed down by the smiling waitress as she skimmed past. I couldn't look up, knowing that the beautiful woman in white was watching my every movement from across the room. If I looked, I'd be hard pushed not to blush like a lighthouse beacon or pull out one of those goofy smiles you see when a comedian on TV is pretend-orgasming, making myself look even more of an idiot than how I already felt.

Here I was, trapped in a subterranean drinking den populated by grinning demons and ginger-headed giants, and all I could think of was how many casual glances at the Selkie I could get away with before I was accused of being a pervert on some idiots social media page.

I threw my head back in frustration and caught her eye across the room, watching as she stood up slowly and started to walk toward me. She flowed through the crowd at the bar, who began to separate into a pathway for her when they realised where she was heading.

It took me a second to realise that I was now standing as well, and was squirming my way around the table toward her. I took one step forward before something slammed into my chest and knocked me out of my daze. It was Maggie's cane.

"Come along, sunshine!" Maggie looked nervous as she glanced behind her toward the Selkie. "Put your eyes back in the sockets and out your pants son, you and I are away to hae a word with Teacher here!"

I turned and saw the man they called Teacher standing beside me, as he placed his hand on my elbow and motioned me toward a nearby fire escape door.

"If you'd be so kind Mr Stewart, my office is just through here, I shouldn't keep you too long, have you enjoyed your visit so far?" with an elbow each, Maggie and Teacher bustled me forward toward the exit door while I craned my head back to catch a glimpse of the Selkie, who slowly raised a hand to her mouth and blew me a kiss, before gliding backward toward her impromptu throne at the back of the bar.

"I understand this is your first time learning about the 'Others' who make up our community?" Teacher pushed the fire door open and led me through a long corridor with plain concrete walls flanking us on either side.

"I do apologise for the method and timing of your exposure to this new world you've been dragged into young man, sadly Gunnar isn't the most delicate when it comes to integrating unsuspecting people into this facility, aha" Stopping before a plain blue door, he took out a long gold key from his pocket just as Maggie caught up behind us puffing for breath.

"I have asked him repeatedly to attend sensitivity training if he wants to stay in the greeting committee, but he always seems to have a 'get out' clause." the key slid into the lock and the door swung open just as I was pushed through into the harsh halogen lit room.

"I believe the last excuse was his grandmother had sadly passed." Teacher strode into the barren-looking office and motioned me to sit in a stiff-looking chair in front of a very basic desk.

I couldn't help but wonder if he was called 'Teacher' because this room looked like the foreboding headmaster's office you would dread being called to in primary school.

Teacher sat down at his desk, straightened his waistcoat with a tug, and leaned back to cross his legs,

"Poor woman she is, I believe this is the fourth time she's passed away in the last six months. The first time she was swallowed whole in a shark attack, which I suppose is at least one blessing. Not very common an occurrence in the Pentland Firth I'm led to believe, aha. Tea anyone?"

I must have nodded yes, as moments later the waitress who had delivered drinks to my table in the bar came into the room carrying a tray with three delicate-looking china cups full of steaming tea, placing each in turn in front of us all before gliding back out and quietly closing the blue door behind her. I turned to look at Maggie, only to catch her discreetly pulling her small silver hip flask out of her pocket and adding some 'colour' to her decidedly fancy cup of Earl Grey.

"Again, let me apologise profusely for the situation you find yourself in this evening. To have all of this new information thrust upon you during our gathering of remembrance in your uncle's honour, must be absolutely overwhelming." Teacher leaned forward, his elbows planted on the desk and his fingers steepled together before him.

"But please know that despite everything you've seen and learned so far, you could be in no safer place than you are right now." The moment of serious reflection following this statement from both myself and the smartly dressed man who sat in front of me was shattered by loud coughing from the side of the room, where Maggie had just discovered the illicit supplementation of her tea had perhaps been a little too much on the generous side.

"Oh Jeer Desus[5], I think I just astral projected my liver into oblivion wi' that one!" Maggie stumbled to her feet and took off toward the door, "If you'll excuse me Gentlemen, I'm awa to lay down in a closet for an hour or two until I regain some kind of feeling in my nipples."

Maggie stumbled out of the room, noticeably turning back in the direction of the bar and the half-full glass she'd left abandoned and unloved behind her.

"Now that we're alone Mr Stewart, I wonder if you'd afford me more of your time so that I may explain exactly what we're about, and why you in particular have been afforded access to this facility?" Teacher rose from his unadorned desk and walked over to a small roll-top cabinet, slid it open, and pulled out a large decanter. "Might I interest you in a small libation while we talk business?"

I nodded as he poured out two glasses of the dark liquid, walked back to the desk, and placed one in front of me beside my untouched cup of tea, before sitting back down in his chair.

"I tend not to offer the more expensive whisky while your aunt is around. With all respect to that wonderful woman, I've lost more than one single malt to the darkened recesses of her handbag. Aha!" Teacher tugged at his cuffs before settling back into his seat.

"First of all, I would ask you to keep an open mind about everything you're about to hear, and bear in mind that already you've witnessed the unbelievable become believable. In fact, you've held yourself together with quite a strong decree of decorum if I may say so! aha." A brief smile flashed over Teacher's face.

---

[5] Despite generally having the well oiled vocabulary of a rum drunk sailor, Maggie never took the lord's name in vain. Not because of any fear of eternal damnation, but more that she worried about the vicar overhearing her and cutting her off from the homemade caramel shortbread that he liked to hand out to his parishioners.

"Not many people do you know." He took a sip from his glass, briefly smiling at the quality of the contents,

"Why, I believe our last recruit stayed for three days before handing in his notice, placed his humble abode on the market and moved south to Dundee to live a quiet life with his parents, where I believe he now spends his time sleeping with the lights on and helping his father catalogue pressed flower collections, aha."

I wasn't sure, but it sounded like he'd attempted a laugh at the end there, but his face never showed any sign of humour as he opened a small drawer in the desk and pulled out an orange covered booklet which he placed softly in front of me.

"This, Mr Stewart, is essentially an extensive and completely free guide to what exactly we do here. It's yours to keep of course, however it must not be taken off the premises, nor may there be any copies made of the materials inside. We don't want Mr 'Johnny Unawares' out there in the everyday world know our little secrets now, do we?"

He looked at me expectantly, clearly waiting for some kind of confirmation. Instead, I think he realised that I hadn't the bloodiest clue what he was on about, and slowly lowered himself back down into his vinyl-covered chair.

"I see that we may be having some kind of crossed wires." Teacher leaned forward and gently pushed my still-full glass toward me. "I understand, of course, lot to take in here, very overwhelming indeed. So how about I give you the Cliff Notes version, hmm? aha."

I lifted the glass and threw the whisky down my neck, before slumping back in my chair, "I'd appreciate that if you don't mind, seeing as how I came north for a funeral and ended up drinking expensive whisky alongside boogeymen and werewolves!"

Teacher raised a finger, "Wulver, actually. There is a clear distinction between the two." He smiled as he stood once more, picked up my glass and walked back over to the cabinet to refill it.

"You see, we have to be clear with our distinctions here at RUST, we want to be as inclusive as we can when it comes to the relationships between we humans and the others, last thing we need is a political powderkeg going off because we misgendered a fairy. Aha." His shoulders seemed to shake a little, making me think that the 'Aha' was actually a laugh, and not just an exclamation that he'd found something interesting in the bottom of my glass. Walking over he placed my overfilled glass back down in front of me and relaxed back into his seat.

"How do I start? Well, as a child I'm sure you've been entertained by stories of monsters under the bed, or vampires stalking the night. Perhaps you were fond of Frankenstein's monster! You'd maybe heard about legends like Bigfoot or Nessie, or been told tales round a boy scout campfire about bogeymen and ghosts that haunt little children if they don't brush their teeth at night, Aha." It was definitely a laugh, as he silently chuckled to himself at his own joke.

"A lot of these stories are based in some degree of fact. As you've witnessed tonight, there are things out there that do indeed go bump in the night. Not usually because they're scary, but generally they're just clumsy or short sighted, and it can be hard to navigate through the dark when you've got a hairy face or no eyes."

Teacher paused to take a tiny sip from his glass, wincing as the whisky made its way down. "However these are stories we encourage! The more tales about vampires wearing capes and biting young maidens in their undergarments through a lace curtain the better. The more these tales are fantasized, the less chance people will believe them. And that makes our job of keeping everyone safe much easier."

"But what is your job exactly!" I was getting frustrated, and a little sleepy if I was honest. It was maybe a mixture of the shock wearing off and the alcohol, but I was definitely eyeing up the stark leather sofa at the side of the room as a potential forty winks candidate.

Teacher sighed and took another sip from his glass. He looked momentarily annoyed, perhaps because I wasn't really giving him the option of spinning out a long and glorious tale of monsters and men.

"I am trying to keep it relatively short Mr Stewart, but it wouldn't hurt for you to know a little of our history. A little knowledge now only arms you more fully for what's ahead of you in the future." Pausing for a second, he readjusted his tie slowly then continued.

"A long number of years ago a group of academics formed a gathering of men and women to try and soothe tensions between our world and the others. Back then farmers mobs with burning torches and pickaxes would be banging at the door of anyone suspected of being, or consorting with the Others. Goodness, if you enjoyed a steak too bloody you were flogged and hanged as a suspected vampire in some towns! Aha."

Teacher was clearly trying to inject some humour into his story, but my blank and tired expression convinced him that he wasn't quite nailing the punchlines, before he cleared his throat and continued.

"These men and women were nicknamed the 'Wise Owls' by their peers, and came together from a variety of academical backgrounds. All with the same purpose, to work toward peace, cooperation and safety for all, no matter what their creed, race or species. Playing off the nickname they'd picked up from their colleagues and peers, these 'Owls' met in secrecy in a gathering place they called 'HRŌST', which translates from the Old English word to 'Roost'". He paused briefly, swirling the glass in his hand.

The dark liquid within licking its way along the rounded glass sides. He motioned toward my glass, encouraging me to drink some more.

"In this place they would negotiate with the leaders of the Others, Hoping through mutual understanding, learning and mediation that they could protect those on both sides from harming each other." He stood up, straightened his immaculate waistcoat and walked over to stand before the wall beside the inviting sofa. With a tap of his finger against the blank mahogany wall the room darkened, as the wall changed into a large blue screen showing several aged, sepia tinted drawings of people dressed in what looked like Anglo-Saxon style clothing.

"However hard these individuals worked, much of their endeavours had to remain secret, as a large majority of the human race couldn't see past the fangs, claws and slime to discover the truth of the soul that lay beneath. Yet through hatred, risk and little reward, they brokered peace deals that still stand to this day between the Humans and the Others."

Teacher once more tapped the screen and the image changed, showing what looked like an official-looking document with a variety of signatures at the bottom.

"However as the group moved forward and gained a degree of notoriety, prestige and influence amongst their peers who recognised their work, so did their own political ambitions. Many members now realising that their years working with the Owls had strengthened their own skills in diplomacy moved from the activities they'd performed at HRŌST into local and national governance, finding that their skills not only translated well into the public sector but also were proving to be far more rewarding, both financially and through recognition for their efforts."

The large screen shifted again, showing what looked like an ornate shield or crest design that looked vaguely like an owl, with wording I couldn't interpret along the bottom written along a flowing banner. Above the owl however stood a bold text that read, 'SONS OF THE OWL'.

Teacher continued. "As HRŌST slowly fell apart, with its membership splintered through debate or political ambition, the owls who had gathered themselves in the political sector decided that contact with The Others must not only be overseen by a more regulated body under their supervision, but also that they should have more power to control and police interactions between the two groups." Teachers' face flashed a hint of disgust as he turned to look at the large owl 'shield' that dominated the wall display beside him.

"Thus in their infinite 'wisdom', it was decided to set up a government body to oversee this seismic change in policy, creating huge divisions between themselves and the Owls who had chosen to remain with what was left of HRŌST. Many debates were lost, pleas ignored and friendships splintered as this new governmental body became more and more powerful, and pushed the remaining owls into either working alongside it, or to get out of the way entirely."

Teacher tapped the screen again and the image changed to a huge cathedral styled building under a dark grey sky, with the large golden 'SOTO' crest I'd seen in the previous image mounted in place over the huge oak doorway. It looked like someone had thrown money at a Stonemason and told them to make the place look as intimidating yet garishly rich as possible.

"Eventually HRŌST collapsed under it's diminishing membership, and the 'Sons' became the new power between the worlds, now more inclined to push advantage toward themselves than any semblance of fair balance between the seperate worlds it had deigned itself fit to govern."

The large screen switched again, a multitude of smaller windows opening all over the wall showing a sequence of disturbing scenes. Some images showed families weeping whilst around them creatures huddled together as they were herded into pens. In one picture, soldiers with gold 'SOTO' crests on their armoured shoulders raising weapons at 'things' that looked straight out of a kids fairy tale book. Below that, a drawing showed what looked like a family of human shaped birds huddled in a cellar, while shadows cast themselves through the gaps of the floorboards above their heads.

"What followed were dark times Mr Stewart. Times where the unity between worlds was shattered by the greed and power of men and women once held in the highest regard. Men and women who had previously dedicated their lives to the pursuit of peace with the Others, now corrupted by the money and power that government had given them." Teacher once more sat down in his chair and turned toward me.

At some point I'm sure while I was glued to the images on the wall beside us, he'd discreetly refilled both of our drinks. I wasn't going to argue as we both lifted our glasses and drank down some more of the whisky. I was finding myself grow wearier however, despite the fascinating story that was playing out in front of me. I didn't know if it was a mixture of the whisky, shock and Mr Biscuits nearly making me soil myself earlier in the night, but I knew that soon I'd lose the battle with my eyelids to keep them open.

"Once SOTO rose to its full power, the Others withdrew from the human world entirely. That's not to say they went anywhere off planet you understand, aha. No, instead they retired to their own hidden lairs, dens and communities away from the glare of the Son's administration." The screen changed again, pictures appearing of many different ghouls, monsters and beasties. I knew that these would probably not be the 'technical' terms for these different 'Others' that appeared on the wall, and I also knew that it was probably best not to repeat that terminology whilst still trapped potentially several hundred feet underground with people who probably ate other people.

"So you guys are all members of this 'Sons' thing? All of this, the fancy moving toilet cubicle, the wall that's actually a screen and the flippin' dog things that sang a song and made me hallucinate, 'Haggvar' I think they were called?"

"Ah yes! Wonderful, aren't they!" He tapped his desk and the wall-screen changed again now showing five images in a row, each showing a different Other, including one showing these 'Haggvar' things from earlier in the night.

"First of all may I stress that we are not 'SOTO' here.", He rose from his seat and walked back across to the wall, his cheeks noticeably flushed from the several large pours of amber nectar he'd already worked his way through.

"I can vehemently assure you that what we do here is in no way comparable to the actions of that group. If anything, the work we do here is directly opposed to the atrocities that they carried out in the alleged name of peace and control". He took a breath and slowly released his hands which had both curled up into tight fists by his sides. Leaning slightly against a small plain sideboard, he continued;

"The former Owls who had formed The Sons knew that some groups of Others had nowhere really to hide. Partly because they lived in huge areas untouched by the feet of humanity, or they had previously given full access to their lairs and homes to SOTO members back when they were still involved with HRŌST. Of course, that meant there were extensive written records that detailed exactly how to find them."All but three of the portraits on the screen melted away,

"Amongst these fae races, three of them had certain 'gifts' that could be harvested and abused by humanity." Teacher quickly pulled up his sleeve to look at his watch. It didn't seem that he was checking the time, more that he was reading a message as he swiped up on the screen with his finger. His hand dropped and he turned to look at me with a concerned look, before his clearly practised mask of calmness settled back into place.

"The Haggvar in particular were especially at risk, partly due to their trusting nature and partly due to the nature of their 'gift', which SOTO decided was a gift that they especially had every right to take for themselves."

I slumped further in my seat as the drowsiness threatened to swallow me. I was determined to take in everything that Teacher had to tell me about this place, but I was fighting a losing battle with the wave of fatigue that threatened to wash over me. Teacher clearly noticed my swift decline, as he set down his glass and once more tugged his waistcoat straight.

"Aha, I see that you are flagging young man! I hope I'm not boring you with all this, but it is important that you gain a somewhat deeper understanding about the situation that you find yourself in going forward." He glanced once more at his wristwatch.

"However time is short this evening! I think we will cover specific details about these gifts at a later date, but be assured that because of this they were in great danger, which forced the few remaining members of HRŌST to do what it could to protect them."

Once more the screen changed, the three portraits melting into the background to be replaced by a large circular badge. I recognised it straight away, it was the same one that was embroidered on the chest and sleeve of my uncles jacket.

"Not wanting to reform the HRŌST name due to its near destruction at the hands of its evil stepbrothers in 'The Sons', the remaining few Owls went on a secretive recruiting drive, bringing in people whose sympathies lay far more in tune with the original remit of the group and who wanted to bring peace and unity between the worlds of men and monsters." My eyes started to close despite my best efforts to remain focused. Teacher smiled briefly then continued; "Eventually they grew strong enough to re-introduce themselves to the world of the Others, hoping with all their might that they could rebuild bridges of trust that had been torn down by the manipulations of The Sons. No longer were they known as 'Owls' or 'HRŌST', instead becoming the 'Restitution & Unification of Supernaturals & Terrestrials." Teacher's arms flew wide as I slumped down into my chair, my eyes closing as he started walking toward me. "Or in short, we became R.U.S.T." I felt his hand touch my wrist as I started to fall into a deep sleep in the hard chair below me.

"And it seems that we are indeed, aha, out of time for the evening.. Sleep well Mr Stewart."

Chapter Nine

A Short Drive

 I slowly came awake, sweat coating me as I twisted free of the thin bed sheet that had wrapped itself around my arms and chest, I was still really groggy, in fact I could easily go back to sleep for a bit, but the small and suspicious animal part of my brain kept telling me that something was all wrong, and I needed to wake up and figure shit out.

 I climbed out out of the bed onto the obnoxiously decorated cheap carpet that covered the floor in my hotel room. I threw on the light and looked around for anyone that might be standing there in the dark, checking behind the shower curtain just in case I was in some kind of low budget horror film, but nobody else was here, it was probably just the police training making me twitchy.

 Huey's jacket lay folded over the back of the nearby chair and my shoes sat neatly together on the floor beside it. Other than that, apart from my tie which lay on top of the nearby desk, I'd clearly been laid to bed with all my clothes still on. I quickly changed out of my white shirt and black trousers, throwing them into my suitcase alongside my shoes and tie. I jumped into the shower and quickly washed, hoping that the hot water would help shake the head fuzz away and help me put together what had happened since I'd passed out in Teacher's office.

It was still dark outside as I dried off and put on my jeans, t-shirt and trainers. Looking at my phone I could see it was about half three in the morning, clearly I'd only been asleep for a few hours after having shared those drinks with the head of RUST. How the hell had I managed to get back to the hotel? I must have been helped back and put to bed by someone? I sat back on the bed and considered my next move. I really wanted to find out what had happened to me over the last few hours, I still needed questions answered about Huey's death, but I also couldn't help feel that this was all possibly too much for me to cope with.

I stared at myself at the mirror on the nightstand across from the bed. I could stay longer with a bit of luck if I played the 'emotional distress' card with work, but where do I start to process what I'd been through since I arrived back in Thurso? I'd seen some unbelievable shit, learned about a whole life that Huey, Maggie and others have had that I'd never guessed or suspected and found out that things that go bump in the night are not only real, but drive cars and have a love of Hob Nob biscuits.

Yet on the other hand, I couldn't help but feel like I needed to head back south before I got any deeper into this mess, get back to the Granite City and face this damned investigation, perhaps get that out of the way and cleared up and then maybe come back north and continue investigating Huey's passing on my own time? I couldn't run away from presenting my case any longer, I needed to get back to work before more disciplinary procedures were considered due to my prolonged absence.

Yep, I needed to get back south and refocus, try and get shit sorted and then maybe come back and face whatever this RUST stuff was, and if it was linked in any way to Huey's death.

I rubbed my face with my hands to try and clear away the last of the grogginess, deciding that if I was going I'd be as well going now while the roads are quiet and there would be less fuss having to visit family to say goodbye before I left.

Fuck it, it was decided. I pulled my bags onto the bed and started throwing things in, ramming in dirty clothes along with the clean stuff, hoping that I would maybe see Mary on the way out if she was working the night shift. If anyone was going to have their finger on the pulse of how I ended up back in bed, it would be her.

With both bags packed I threw on Huey's jacket, grabbed the box of belongings he'd left behind, locked up the room and headed downstairs to the reception area to hand back my key card. There was no sign of Mary, just some young man with a shaved head who grudgingly tore his eyes away from his mobile phone to grunt an acknowledgement that I'd placed the keycard under his nose, and that I was good to go. I dragged my bags through the back stairwell toward the car park at the rear of the building, pushed open the door and stepped out into the night.

I stopped dead. I could see a figure in the dim car park lighting half sitting on the bonnet of my car, one tartan-clad leg touching the floor as my wheel seemed to look a good deal flatter under his weight.

"That wasn't a long sleep laddie!" Boomed the wildly grinning Gunnar, "I'm no' one for being rude, but if ever someone could do with a bitty extra beauty sleep it's yersel!" He stood up from my car and walked over to take my bags from my hands.

"No no no man, we only just tucked you in all bonnie like a few hours ago. Get yersel' back to your bed and sleep til morning!" He winked at me as he moved toward the door back into the hotel, "Things are always much brighter and clearer in the mornings. Besides, you'll no' be wanting to upset your new best friend over there by running away in the middle of the night!"

Gunnar beckoned across to the other side of the car park, where the limo from earlier in the night sat in darkness. The interior light above the driver flicked on, and Mr Biscuits sprang into view, waving wildly with his face pressed forward against the windscreen.

"That there's a man who'll be proper broken-hearted if you take off before we can all catch up again in the bright light of day. No, you'll get yourself back to your bed before I have to call your aunty oot to come tuck you in!" He grinned as he held the door open back into the hotel, both my bags easily being gripped together in his free hand.

"Gunnar, it's been great getting to meet you, and Mr Biscuits" I could see the blank face almost light up in the windscreen across the car park, "But I need to head south, just for a while at least." I turned and pressed the fob on my keyring to open my car, turning on the interior lights as I walked across and opened the boot before dropping the box of Huey's belongings inside. "In the space of a few short hours I've been scared shitless by a blank-faced creature driving a fancy limo, had a plant pot give me the finger, I've watched these 'Haggvar' things singing pictures into my head, I've had a homosexual wolf hit on me and I'm not certain, but I'm pretty confident that I ended up getting drugged to sleep by an uptight man in a three-piece suit!"

I slammed the boot lid down and turned to face Gunnar, "Please, feel free to tell me exactly what part of tonight is supposed to encourage me to hang around for second helpings, while my career hangs in the balance back down south?"

I walked across to Gunnar and pulled my two bags out of his massive hand. Moving to turn away I stopped dead, my shoulders dropping as I let out a long sigh and turned back toward the sad face of the red-headed giant beside me.

"I'm sorry Gunnar. I'm truly sorry for being rude, that's just not me at all but I have had a lot happen to me these last few days." He nodded slowly as I continued, "I do in a strange way appreciate you all letting me see this hidden world of boogiemen and sea creatures, but I don't understand what my part is supposed to be in all of this, or why on earth you've all pulled me into this secret that it seems is supposed to be guarded against the regular people like me." I turned back toward my car and started to walk toward the rear doors to place my bags inside.

"I have my own life in Aberdeen now, my world isn't up here anymore. I have friends and commitments down there, and now that Huey is gone there's little left for me here in Caithness other than the odd visit now and again to see Maggie and Finn. I'm sorry, I need to leave here before I get drugged, eaten or have any more machinery jamming itself into my mouth."

Gunnar's face remained still, he almost seemed to shrink a little as he dug something out of an overly sequined pocket and walked toward me.

"Aye you're right, we maybe should have told you sooner, but things have a habit of jumping oot at ye' all o' a sudden". He gently grabbed my arm and pressed what looked like a small whisky miniature into my hand, closing my fingers over it as he moved back.

"We've got a situation lad, that's why things moved so fast. Huey leaving us has left us a bit in the shite if I'm honest, and that's why we needed you.

Needed to show you this world o' ours, hoping you'd have the same wee fire in your belly that your uncle did." His eyes seemed to glisten as he smiled at me, turned and walked slowly back toward the limo and Mr Biscuits. "We all miss Huey son, terribly. But unless I'm shite at reading people, I bet my neck that you've got questions too about how we lost him." Before I could answer he raised his hand to stop me.

"And we do have answers for you. But laddie, we also need your help to answer some of the other important questions too." Gunnar smiled and turned to walk toward the large black car behind him.

"Maybe that wee bottle o' the good stuff will help light that fire in your belly when you get back south. Just two drops in your tea mind!" He waved as he folded himself into the back of the large black car, Mr Biscuits slowly pulling on fitted black driving gloves in the front as Gunnar lowered his window and shouted out; "Any more than two drops and they'll be peeling you off of the bloody ceiling! Take care laddie, I sincerely hope we'll see you again awfa' soon." And with a slow, sad wave from a dejected Mr Biscuits, the limo backed out of the car park and disappeared into the night.

I stood for what felt like an age looking at the darkened street outside the car park, a part of me holding back to see if that limo would circle the block and come back to collect me. As I threw my bags into the back of my car and shut the door, part of me had to admit that I kind of hoped they would.

I climbed into the driver seat, started the engine and slowly made my way through the quiet town, crossing the road bridge that swept over Thurso River before making my way up past the cemetery. I slowed to a crawl as I drove past the darkened grounds full of memorial stones to my right, and with a short toot of the horn for Huey I pressed down on the accelerator and watched the lights of Thurso gradually grow smaller in my rear view mirror as I pointed the car south toward Aberdeen, hoping that Maggie, Finn and the rest of the clan would forgive me for disappearing quietly into the night.

For the next half hour I drove south, looking at almost every wide bit of road as I passed it thinking how easy it would be to U-Turn there and head back to the hotel. I fumbled with the stereo, flicking through the radio stations to get a clearer signal as I swept through the dark around me. What had Gunnar meant when he said they were in the shit? What exactly was the importance of showing me everything that they had, to convince me to stay and help? Was my being there in some way essential to them dealing with whatever crap they were going through?

What if Maggie was at threat, and me leaving so suddenly was making things worse for her.. I slowed the car to a crawl, the silent roads and hills around me bathed in moonlight as I stared in the rear view mirror, the lights of my hometown much too far behind me now to be seen.

Nope, I was being stupid. I had plenty of shit to work my way through down south, and if it was something serious then surely Maggie would have told me sooner than today.

The car accelerated through the dark as I set my mind to get as far as Inverness and hang around the industrial park until the supermarket there opened, so I could nip in for a piss, grab a coffee and sandwich and then give Maggie a phone to check in and make sure she understood why I had to leave.

I turned up the radio again, the station cutting in and out as I fiddled with the buttons to re-tune. These digital radios were all well and good in the cities, but when you try to tune in to your favourite Metal station as you're stuck in the arse end of nowhere, then they're as much use as a handbrake on a canoe. I focused on the road for a minute, stuck between arguing with myself about going back to Thurso, and why the hell car radios didn't have much in the way of spinny knobs anymore that were far easier to deal with. Ahead of me I could see the lights of Latheron, a small village where the road ahead split two ways. I could either turn left and head for Wick[6] or continue south toward Inverness and eventually Aberdeen.

I stopped at the junction for few minutes, staring toward the right turn that would lead me back home to Aberdeen, torn between my commitments down south and worry that me leaving would in some way put Maggie in danger.

Darkness covered the road to my left but it seemed clear, so I pulled out to turn right, in that second deciding that I was going back as I u-turned in the junction ready to head back to the hotel.

Right then the crackling sounds of 'I Want to Break Free' that had been blaring from my stereo for the last minute or so cut out, replaced with dead air. I leaned across and briefly considered punching the bloody thing for cutting out during a Mercury Masterpiece when blinding lights suddenly dazzled me through my passenger side window. I only had a moment to focus on what looked like a large truck barreling toward me with its full beam flicking on and blinding my vision, before smashing into the side of my car.

---

[6] There is a long standing rivalry between the two towns, and frankly nobody from Thurso would think of venturing into that dark land before they've had a full spectrum of anti-viral shots.

Chapter Ten

Thorne

I woke up and couldn't move. I was in a hard chair with my ankles tied to the wooden legs and my arms tied behind me to the backrest. My head thumped with pain and my left eye felt like it was glued shut as I struggled to open it. I couldn't see anything clearly around me, partly down to the concussion I was sure I was suffering from and partly because of the big bloody spotlight that someone had conveniently set up to shine directly into my face.

I turned my head to the sides slowly and tried looking around, hoping that if I stayed quiet then whoever had tied me up wouldn't suddenly appear and start swinging a heavy bit of rope like that bad guy who had Daniel Craig tied to a chair in the James Bond film. The light was too bright to make anything out clearly, but it looked like I was in a barn or large wooden shed of some kind, with large wooden boxes stacked at either side of the outbuilding beside smaller hessian sacks.

Just as I started to wriggle to feel if there was a conveniently cut hole beneath me where someone could swing a heavy metal item up into, a hand placed itself on my right shoulder.

"I'm not going to hurt you, stay quiet please while I try and clean you up a bit."

It was a woman's voice. Young, maybe in her mid to late twenties. It was hard to tell as I felt a cloth being gently rubbed down the left side of my face and over my eye. As the unknown woman's hand pulled it away from my head I could see it was heavily bloodstained.

"You've taken a bigger knock than was planned Mr Stewart." The hand appeared again in my peripheral vision, cloth rinsed out and pressed once more against my bloody head, "I promise you that the plan was for you to be unhurt during the extraction."

"The crash.. That was, planned? Why am I here, who are you and why the hell am I tied up to a BLOODY CHAIR?" As soon as I raised my voice I felt dizzy, as I tried to focus on the mysterious hand which stopped suddenly and disappeared behind me.

"Angus, please. Keep your voice down!" The woman stepped around in front of me, the harsh spotlight behind framed her in such a way that I couldn't see any detail in her appearance as she crouched down to look me in the face.

"Please understand, you're not in any danger here. Nobody is going to hurt you more than you've already been. Thorne was adamant about that. As was I." Her left hand came forward and rested itself on my strapped-down forearm,

"I am truly sorry for all you've been through, but we need you here for now. Please, don't make a fuss and I'm sure it'll all be over soon. He'll be here shortly, more will be explained then, I promise." With that she stood back up and moved again behind me, her perfume washing over me as she swept past. I wasn't enamored by it in some kind of 'falling for my captor' scenario, what with it smelling like it was bought from the middle aisle of a discount supermarket and the fact that I'd clearly been in a car crash and then strapped down to a fucking chair.

I heard some quiet splashing behind me, then once more felt the cloth being wiped across my face. Clearly I was bloodier than I thought as I squinted against the harsh light to see the rag as it was pulled away, still worryingly crimson in colour.

"So this trip home so far has been fantastic!" I spoke in hushed tones, but with enough grunt to let this woman know I was less than joyous about my current situation; "I've had the shit scared out of me, stale takeaway licked off me by a large dog and now here I am after a traumatic car accident. Concussed, bleeding and waiting for some stranger to arrive to rattle the hell out of my Gentleman's Sausage with a large bit of metal ended rope. Tell me mysterious stranger, exactly when do I get a pat on the arse and sent on my merry way out of here?" I kept details about my time spent at RUST quiet, as I was certain that whatever was happening here was linked to everything that had gone on the night before.

"You'll be let go as soon as I can talk them round." I could hear her squeeze out the cloth before wiping it around my neck and jaw. "You're here at the request of some very important people, some of whom you should be meeting soon enough. I ask that you please listen to what they have to say before you do or say anything stupid that might cause problems for you later on." I turned to ask exactly what problems when a heavy wooden door to my right crashed open. Through the haze of light still battering me from up front, I could just make out four men dressed in suits walking into the room, one of them being held back by two of his colleagues. He broke free from their grasp and ran toward me before stopping suddenly, then paused for a second before turning to walk quickly behind the spotlight instead. From what I could tell, the other men slowly glided round to three different positions around the room, all just behind the glare of the light in my face.

"How is he Silver, has he been badly hurt? Good god, look at the damn state of him!" The tense, deep voice came from directly behind the spotlight, it's owner was surely the man who had first burst open the doors. "I swear if anyone here", I heard his voice sweep around the room, "has any objection to me kicking the living shit out of Mr Early for his bullshit driving, I want to hear it now!" Silence answered him from the room.

"You're going to be alright Angus, you have my word. I'll not let a damned one of them touch another hair on your head."

I quietly breathed out a sigh of relief, my groin relaxing a bit now that it knew it wasn't getting the blunt end of the deal. I did however need to pee quite badly, and the way things were looking here I wasn't going to get the chance to let it out in the supermarket toilets in Inverness anytime soon.

"But speaking of heads, would you let Miss Silver here dress and stitch that cut you have there while we talk?" I heard something being scraped across the ground as, I assumed, this 'Thorne' character dragged a chair in front of the spotlight, spun it around and sat down with his arms folded across the backrest. I was about to answer that I just wanted to get the hell out of wherever I was when his voice boomed out again.

"You see Angus, if it were up to me you wouldn't even be here this evening, however recent events have forced our hand somewhat, and we've had to move our timetable a little bit forward after your uncle passed away so, abruptly." He paused for a few seconds, his silhouette slumping slightly forward against the backrest of his chair. I was blinded by the lights behind him, but I could see the blurry outline of Miss Silver move to step toward him from my left side before he lifted his hand, stopping her in her tracks.

"I'm fine, sorry. I have a bit of a chest cold, please forgive me." His arm moved down to his pocket, and I could just make out a handkerchief being pulled out before he raised it to his face. "Always the same at this time of year, isn't it?" He blew his nose hard into the hanky and stuffed it back into his pocket. I've always questioned the hygiene of people who think that's acceptable behaviour.

"Absolutely! I find though that the best way to get rid of a head cold is to have someone t-bone your car with a lorry while you're driving across a fucking remote Highland junction. Clears your head right out."

Mr Shadow Man sat bolt upright, the silhouette of his head turning sharply as he looked over his left shoulder to glare at someone behind that damn spotlight. Miss Silver meanwhile stopped dressing my head, laid a hand on my shoulder and spoke quietly into my ear;

"Angus, please. Mr Thorne isn't a man that you want to get angry."

"Mr Thorne? Is he called that because frankly, he seems like a massive prick?"

Thorne turned back toward me, "Witty as well as intelligent! I knew I liked you boy." He smiled and sat back down. "Now, we need you to use that brain of yours and tell us step by step exactly what happened after Maggie took you to the facility last night. And please, don't leave anything out, no matter how insignificant you think it may be."

So clearly whoever these people were, they knew about RUST and that Maggie had access. I needed to find a way out of here as soon as possible to warn her that she was being watched. I looked at the dark shape of Thornes' head in front of me as it leaned forward again on the backrest of the chair he sat spread-legged upon.

"Facility? I'm not quite sure what you mean. If you mean the public toilet facility that she took me too at the back of the church, then it was only because she has a key for the place and I was needing to go boom-boom. I think she's got a part-time job cleaning there." I was scrabbling for anyway I could look like I was willing to be helpful so that they would let me go, but also trying my best to give as little away as possible about what went on after we took the rocket toilet ride that those toilets provided, in case it put Maggie in any immediate danger.

The large man stood up slowly and spun the chair forward facing. Then after a few seconds of standing completely still, he took off his suit jacket and draped it over the backrest before sitting down again to face me. Framed by the bright light behind, he leaned forward until his elbows rested on his knees, bringing his head much closer to my own.

"Angus, please.." It almost sounded like there was concern in his voice, "I can see that Miss Silver there has nearly finished with her ministrations. This means we don't have a lot of time left to chat before we have to move on." He sat back slightly, and through the glare, I could see he was slowly rolling up each of his sleeves in turn.

"You must understand, I'm here for you. I'm here because I want to make sure that nothing untoward happens in your immediate future." He leaned further forward, his voice dropping low;

"But others in this organization are of a wholly different opinion. My position here allows me a certain amount of discretion in keeping you safe, but eventually others will take control of things. So again, please. What happened after you entered RUST with Maggie last night? And more importantly," His face remained in shadow as he moved closer to me and blocked out more of the light. "What 'exact' gift has been passed on to you from the Haggvar?"

I stared at the dark figure in front of me, trying not to give away that I was working on the knot that was binding my hands at the back of my chair.

"Look, I don't have a fucking clue what is going on here, or why you nearly killed me and then tied me up in this damned hot box" The knot behind me loosened as I kept talking, "But you need to know that I'm a serving police officer, and if I don't report in soon the armed police response is going to descend upon Caithness to find me, and it won't take them long to find this shitty warehouse." I could feel my left hand now loosening as the knot slackened against my tiring fingers.

"And all this-" I looked around the large metal-framed warehouse around me, "Bullshit you have going on here is going to come tumbling down in the most public and televised way possible." I swept my gaze around the other darkened figures I could make out behind the bright light that shone on my face, giving me room to move my fingers onto the section of the knot on my right hand. "You think that this secret little OWL group you have going on here will stay that way when you've got police and media helicopters hovering above us? Do you think that the 'others in your organization' are going to like that you've exposed their operation to the fucking world? My voice raised as I continued, anger now replacing the pain as I pulled harder against the loosened knot holding my hands, the rope coming undone as I tried to rise out of my seat,

"Do you think you're going to fucking walk away from this bin-fire of an operation unscathed? That kidnapping a police officer doesn't come without some consequences?" The rope binding my hands finally came free, allowing me to flex my hands and get some blood flowing back into them. I didn't know what I was going to do yet, but having my hands free was a great start to whatever fucking plan came to me. I relaxed back into the chair, pretending to calm down as I lowered my head and breathed deeply, clenching my fists behind me as Thorne stood up from his chair.

"You're fucked, you're all fucked unless you untie me and get me the hell out of here."

Thorne reached for the lamp and it grew brighter, forcing me to squint against the harsh glare in my face. He moved around the back of the lamp and came toward me, leaning his hands onto the armrests of my chair as his face came close to mine. In the reflected light I could see that he was wearing what looked like one of those wrestling masks that you see on television, like Rey Mysterio if he was over six foot tall and heavily muscled. The mask may have hidden his face, but I could see the cold blue eyes staring at me, pinching at their sides like he was grinning under the black mask.

"You know, it's funny that you think we don't know pretty much everything about you Angus. We've swept both you and what's left of your car for trackers, your phone won't connect to any network in this shielded building, and you've no other electronics with you apart from that electronic book reader thing you use to read those frankly quite smutty fairy books you seem so interested in." He suddenly leaned in close enough that I could feel his breath on my face. "Besides that, here's something else that interests me-" My hands were suddenly slammed flat against the back of the chair, what felt like a foot crushing against them as they were forcibly re-bound with the rope.

"-How did you know that we were Owls?"

Before I could reply, the wall to my left exploded inwards. Shattered lengths of wood flew all around us as the blinding lamp that had been torturing me for the last while fell and smashed, people all around scrambled for cover as the dust and debris settled across the body of the large, black limo which now sat sideways in the wreckage of the barn wall.

A few seconds passed and nobody moved. Only the sound of the splinters of wood falling to the ground could be heard as the limo's tinted rear window rolled down slowly to show the wildly grinning face of Gunnar.

"HULLO THERE!! Oooh, we've got ourselves intae a wee bit o' a pickle here! Awfa sorry I'm sure, my esteemed colleague isn't the best driver when he's angry.." Gunnar opened the door and unfolded his frame from the back of the car, "Anyway, let's see if we can resolve all this like bloody gentle fellows while my colleague digs oot the necessary insurance paperwork, shall we?"

Between the light having scorched my eyes for a good long while, the concussion, and the still blurry left eye, I couldn't quite see all around me too clearly. Ahead of me though I noticed at least two or three assault rifles being raised then aimed toward Gunnar and the now quiet limo behind him. And if my action movie-trained hearing was any indication, a good few guns behind me were also pointing in the exact same direction.

Gunnar raised his hands slowly, his lips pulling apart in a grimace showing off his pearly white teeth. "Ach, see now you've gone and bloody done it. Here was me, laying on the top-quality charm and happy enough to have a wee chat with ye all, maybe grab a coffee and exchange some light-hearted banter. But now that ye've pulled out the guns.. Well, now there's not much I can do to help you get out of this without a well-skelped arse." A short pause followed before a handful of the gunmen started to laugh, clearly wondering what this large red-headed peacock could do with his hands held up in the air.

"STOP! Everyone get the fuck out of here right now! You've NO idea what you've just bloody done!" Thorne was climbing to his feet from the floor in front of me, standing with his back to me as he shouted at the suited gunmen who seemed to line the walls around us, "PUT YOUR GUNS DOWN AND RUN!!"

I could feel the hair on the back of my neck stand on end. A shiver raced through me as I watched the darkened figure of Thorne sprint toward the large door he'd entered earlier, as a large crash to my left stole my attention away before I could get a better look at his face.

The limo door burst open, and from within the darkened cab out stepped a fully enraged Mr Biscuits.

"Ye see, he HATES guns. Absolutely despises the damned things." Gunnar seemed perfectly calm as Mr Biscuits suddenly sprinted around the room at an unnatural speed, ripping guns from the arms of the terrified collection of suited goons and launching them into a pile a few yards from my feet, his blank face radiated raw fury as he towered above each thug. His wide, evil-looking mouth screamed a silent note of rage that made me want to empty my bowels immediately into my trousers as he tore the last weapon from the arms of a terrified-looking woman who, judging by the look on her face and hastily crossed knees, clearly didn't have the same level of toilet control as I was currently praying wouldn't fail me.

"He's a big softy really!" Gunnar boomed across the room as Mr Biscuits sped across the floor on all fours, before standing atop the pile of confiscated weapons like a rabid guard dog, "But you've all pushed his buttons a wee bit I'm afraid. Ye point guns at us, AND steal his new bestest buddy?" He lifted a single box that hadn't broken from the wreckage by his feet, plonked it down on the floor and lowered himself onto it. "If I were you though, I'd maybe run as fast as you can before he realises that you're all responsible for that big bleedy looking wound on the side of the lads head.."

Mr Biscuits' head snapped round toward me just before he scuttled across the floor to loom over me. Through my abject fucking terror I watched as his hand gently swept along the side of my head, pulled back and turned palm up. Mr Biscuits looked down at the blood stain that ran along the pad of his hand before throwing his arms and head back to howl at the ceiling, a wild and horrifying sound that put shivers through every spine within earshot.

With that last booming roar still reverberating around the large warehouse, the full collection of suit-wearing halfwits made a mad dash for the door that Thorne had sprinted through earlier, many of whom ran as fast as they could from the knees down while Mr Biscuits raised himself to his full height and stared after them.

"AND TELL THORNE I SAW HIM TOO! SNEAKY SHIT-BALLOON SCURRYING OOT O' HERE WI' HIS TAIL BETWEEN HIS BASTARD LEGS!"

Gunnar turned and looked at me, his brow wrinkling as he sprinted over to check my head before scooping me up and carrying me back to the limo.

"That bastard will not get away with this, I can assure you." He laid me down along the large back seat of the car before climbing into the seat across from me. I didn't protest, my head was still ringing, and lying down on the big plush seat let the blood flow return to my numb hands and arms. I heard the driver's door of the limo close and the screen divider sliding back as Mr Biscuits leaned through, his blank face doing a magnificent job of looking worried sick, despite his lack of eyes, nose or ears.

"It's okay Biscuits, the boy's nae that bad. I'll just grab his stuff from his car then you get us back to RUST pronto though so that Dean can give him the once over."

Once Gunnar had loaded my bags into the boot and had jumped back into the car, Mr Biscuits spun around and started the engine before spinning the limo out of the debris and back into the slowly brightening skies around us. I lifted my arm to check my watch and noticed it was gone. Damn it, I liked that watch too, do you know how hard it is to find a Teenage Mutant Ninja Turtles watch these days in adult sizes?

I quickly patted my trousers and found I still had my phone at least. Like any man my age, losing your phone is like losing your masturbating hand in some farm machinery. My car didn't really come to mind at that point, it was a bucket of rust held together with sticky tape and good faith anyway and needed to be changed. Having it T-Boned by a large lorry probably was the best incentive I could have had to upgrade.

I checked for my wallet, which I found in its new home nestled in the inside pocket of Huey's old jacket. As I briefly acknowledged from my reclined position the sky around us flying by at an alarming rate, I pulled out my wallet and opened it up, to check the contents were all still where they should be.

My photo of Huey and I was still there peeking through the faded plastic screen that held my driver's license. My bank cards seemed untouched as did my cash, but as I closed the wallet I noticed a small, unfamiliar corner of paper peeking out of one of the folds of leather. I pulled it out and opened it up. It was a small handwritten note in red ink;

'I'm sorry. I know you have questions, I have answers. I'll be in touch soon, S,"

Had this note been in my wallet for a while? I'd never seen it before and couldn't think of any 'S' names that would leave me a note rather than text or talk to me. Wait, what was the girl's name again that had me tied up and was cleaning my head, Silver? I looked at it again, trying to determine whether or not I could make out a gender from the handwriting, but considering I can barely make out someone's gender these days even by having a wee peek in their undercrackers, my powers of deduction were hitting a brick wall on this one, so I folded it back up and stuck it back in my wallet. I'd wait until my brain stopped feeling like it was using the back of my eyes as punching bags before I tried to figure it out further.

Chapter Eleven

Rescued

It wasn't long before I felt the car swaying left and right as Mr Biscuits weaved through early morning traffic coming into the town, Gunnar sat opposite me doing his best to smile whilst anxiously wringing his hands together.

Were we back in Thurso already, how had the journey back taken so little time? I must have been dabbling with unconsciousness at some points of the trip back, as I lifted myself up to look out the window at the town ahead. The sun was just starting to peek out over the rooftops as we sped past the supermarket and across the toll bridge. I assumed we were heading toward the 'rocket-bogs' that had taken Maggie into RUST the day before, but instead the car veered right at the end of the bridge and drove down Riverside Road toward the harbour.

There were very few cars on the road, seeing as it was bastard o'clock in the morning. Mr Biscuits took full advantage of this as he raced along the riverside heading straight toward the large car park and public toilets that sat at the harbour mouth. I couldn't help but feel that maybe we were going a wee bit too fast as we shot into the car park, and I grew even more concerned as the car turned and aimed itself toward the small slip ramp which led down into the river mouth below.

"Uh, Gunnar! I don't mean to miscall Mr Biscuits driving skills here, but in about five seconds we're going to be a fucking submarine!"

He smiled through his big ginger beard and lifted his hand to show a small black square, looking a lot like one of those dongles you get to open your garage door. Sure enough, he pressed a button on it and a small red light blinked, and just as I was reaching for the door to attempt an emergency 'tuck and roll' procedure before we were sleeping with the fishes, the concrete slipway seemed to split in two, with both halves lifting up to show a concealed roadway leading steeply down a dimly lit tunnel.

As the limo suddenly lurched downward into this underwater passageway, my stomach lurched up into my throat as the wheels briefly left the ground. I couldn't protest this sudden injustice however, as my mouth was already busying itself screaming profanities at anyone that would listen while I hung precariously from the small handle you get above most passenger car doors[7].

The next minute or so was interspersed with Gunnar's laughter and Mr Biscuit's unnerving grin as he flew along the darkened tunnel ahead, before sliding the large black car sideways to a halt in a parking bay in front of a very plain-looking white entranceway, much like you would see in any generic shopping centre car park. As I climbed out of the battered black car with a little help from Gunnar, a large speaker above the door burst into life as HAMMER's voice boomed out across the parking area;

"DECLARATION: WELCOME BACK GUNNAR, MR BISCUITS AND ANGUS STEWART, NEPHEW OF IRRITABLE AUNT,

---

[7] Commonly referred to as the 'Jesus Fuck Strap' by most people in Scotland. Usually because when your distracted partner is about to drive you through the window of the local shop at thirty miles per hour while he checks social media on his phone, you grab that handle for dear life and shout "OH JESUS FUCK!!" right before you wake up in the dairy produce aisle covered in shattered glass and questionably dated cheeses.

MAGGIE STEWART. PLEASE WAIT FOR ASSISTANCE FROM MEDICAL PERSONNEL."

I wondered how big RUST must be, and how much of the area it covered below the town I used to call home. Just as I turned my aching head to ask Gunnar, the large wooden door at the front of the building swung open, and out jogged a man of average height with a dark, short beard and the biggest grin you've ever seen situated a good couple of hundred feet below the discarded condom filled waters of the Pentland Firth. Followed closely by a smaller woman wearing what looked like a leather armour. She wouldn't have looked out of place in a roleplaying fantasy game, except for the array of sharp and pointy looking tools strapped to different parts of her body.

As we walked toward the door, with Gunnar putting his massive hand under my armpit to help me, the smiling pair came to a stop beside us, the wheelchair the man was pushing rolling to a stop and bumping against the wonderfully sequined heel of Gunnars customised boot.

"Jeez mate, that's a beauty there!" He exclaimed in a broad, Australian accent, before rushing over and guiding me into the wheelchair whilst fussing around the cut on my head.

"Yeah, that's gonna need a bit of work for sure." The short Fantasy Fiction looking woman took charge of pushing the chair and fumbled round toward the entrance way into the facility and started toward the large doors ahead. "I can see someone's already had a stab at cleaning it? Not a bad job mate, not great but not bad for a highly trained bloody killer I'm sure." The Aussie fussed around my head, trying desperately to keep up with the wide-grinning elf that was, I suspected, slowing and speeding up randomly to make things a tad harder for her colleague.

I should have been wondering where the hell they were taking me, but considering that over the last twenty four hours I'd seen mythical creatures aplenty and been nearly wiped out by a man in a lorry with some kind of metal based name, having a cheery fighter-spec Elf pushing me in a wheelchair toward a darkened underwater warehouse seemed to be the most normal thing that had happened to me in my recent history.

The doors ahead opened as we approached, revealing what looked like a smaller airport departure gate, albeit with large portraits in massive gold frames hanging on every possible clear space of wall around us, lit by ornate gas lamps that hung from long cords that disappeared into the darkness of the high roof above.

The Elf-woman, (*I probably shouldn't be assuming her mythical species*) pushed me forward through the people who zig-zagged in front of us, some of whom seemed to be sliding, at least two of the paler ones looked like they were gliding and at least one hunchbacked individual was leaving a trail behind him that was being sucked up by what looked like some form of robotic floor cleaner.

I was clearly back at RUST, but a different part entirely from my first visit. As we wheeled through another doorway into what looked like a medical bay, we stopped at a toilet after I insisted that if they didn't, I was going to go off like a somewhat yellow-tinted garden sprinkler. Moments later, I was a few gallons lighter and back in the wheelchair flanked by Gunnar and a worried looking Mr Biscuits to my left as we moved further into the medical facility.

As we turned a corner I saw Maggie and Teacher standing beside a monitor next to one of the unoccupied hospital beds. The second she saw me Maggie threw aside her cane and dashed across the room, flung her arms around me then quickly pulled back, grabbing my head between her hands and turning it left and right to inspect the damage.

"Oh son, what the hell happened to you?" She spun round toward Gunnar and Mr Biscuits, who both visibly shrank back out of her striking range.

"Who did this to my boy Gunnar! You tell me now or I swear on the wee man, I'll plant my size six brogue so far up your back end you'll have 'Dr Marten' embossed on yer top palate." "Whoah bloody whoah!" Everyone froze as Dean stepped up to stand directly in front of my enraged aunt. I glanced around, and judging by the looks on everyone else's faces, I wasn't the only one here who was waiting for the bomb to drop.

"You need to calm down a bit here young lady, give the boy a bit of bloody space why don't ya?" Dean with the questionable beard stepped toward me and took my arm, leading me to the nearby bed and motioning that I should lay down while the pointy eared leather-lady took off with the wheelchair at a sprint with not even a backwards glance.

Maggie seemed to pause for a second before bowing her head briefly and stepping away. I was sure that Dean's masterful use of the term, 'Young lady' had probably saved him from the fiery wrath that we were all secretly looking forward to seeing unleashed.

"In fact, why don't you all bugger off out the room so I can get this boyband looking bugger all fixed up, alright?"

He leant over me and started to wipe down the cut on my head, the hint of an AC/DC t-shirt peeked out from the top of his light blue medical gown, and instantly I pegged him as a man of exquisite musical taste.

"Dean, if I may?" Teacher stepped forward, his hands clasped together behind his back as he paused and stared at me for a brief moment.

"If those of you who aren't involved in the immediate care and attention of young Officer Stewart could all follow me to the debriefing room, we can all hear in great detail exactly why Gunnar and Mr Biscuits went off gung-ho last night without authorization and almost destroyed a great deal of intensive infiltration work. Shall we?"

Teacher didn't wait for confirmation from those around the room, as he strode out the door and turned to the left and out of sight.

"Oh, and if someone could be gracious enough to ask Ms Fidget to stop using that wheelchair to aeroplane herself along the corridor and come join us, that would be appreciated."

Moments later Mr Biscuits walked out to follow, then stopped at the doorway before turning to give me an enthusiastic 'thumbs up'. I smiled and waved back as his grin spread across his entire face. He may make me want to fear piss all down the inside of my boxer shorts, but he pulled my neck out of the fire tonight back in that barn, and that made him alright with me.

He was quickly followed by Gunnar who flashed me a wink before disappearing out of sight, then after another quick hug Maggie quickly hobbled after them. As Dean dressed and cleaned my head I smiled to myself, knowing that despite itching to stay here with me, Maggie couldn't pass by the possibility of seeing someone get a thorough dressing down. It was too much for her nosey nature to ignore.

"So you're the lad they've been harping on about round here eh?" I felt a vibration on my scalp where the gash was, but Dean seemed unconcerned as he worked away. "Don't let the place worry you mate. I've only been here about eight months myself but the buggers treat me fair enough." More buzzing as Dean leaned over me, I could feel my eyes vibrating slightly as he continued talking;

"Lots of bloody stuff to take in for you too I'm sure! But stick around and go with it is what I advise. Don't let the bloody tentacles get you down eh!"

The buzzing paused as he leaned back, picked up a packet of sterile wipes from the metal tray beside us and unwrapped it.

"Kids love it here, get along bonzer with the Haggs so they do. Always having to chase the little furry buggers out the house though, can't stop themselves from mixing up my DVD's and I'm pretty sure one of 'em has been trying to romance the ruddy dog!" Another clunk at my head followed by a small jab of pain as he slapped on a good palm full of gel from a jar with no label told me he was pretty much done binding together the gash that I'd been rocking on my noggin.

"So what's your story Dean? What brings you under the sea here in this pretty fucked up version of Highland Atlantis?"

"Not very interesting story to be told mate if I'm honest" He leaned forward and lifted some wipes to my head, wiping away some of the blood that had dried on my face and scalp. I must have looked a right mess as I saw the state of the wipes when he pulled them away.

"Long story short here, came over on holiday, fell out with some of the furry locals, got rescued by a couple of these buggers, blah blah bloody blah, ended up taking a job here and moving the family over, the end." He stepped back and frowned, moving my head left and right as he checked out my scalp. After a bit of huffing and tutting, he stepped back and picked up a small mirror from a table that sat at the bed next to mine, and held it up to my face.

"Well mate, I can't cure ugly, but I can sure sort out a bloody head wound!

I was shocked. Apart from a little swelling around my eye and a thin, pink line where the gash had been, I looked a lot better than I assumed I had when I got wheeled in the place. My head felt clearer too, my thoughts not quite muddy as I stared wide eyed at the grinning Australian who walked over to a desk against the back wall of the room and poured two coffees from a small machine.

"Bloody amazing what the tech here can do eh?" He handed me a cup as he moved to sit on the end of the bed.

"I used to see head wounds like that back home in Adelaide, normally late at night when all the bloody drunks climbed into their cars to head home, and usually it would be fifty-fifty whether or not the buggers would walk out the front door of the hospital in anything less than a couple of months, if at all."

I took a drink from the cup while he talked, strong black coffee filling my mouth as I continued to check myself over in the mirror. If I'm honest, it was the most appreciated cup of coffee I'd ever had.

"Yet here we are, in the arse end of bloody nowhere in a secret facility under a town full of people that have to drive a hundred miles to have a ruddy baby, and I've just sealed up a messily stitched fractured skull with a ruddy 'Sci-Fi' tool that our little wood elf engineer Fidget dreamed up in a workshop about two hundred feet from here."

He drank down his coffee and stepped up off the bed, moving across to place his cup back on the table.

"Lovely girl too she is, a bit too quick with the kicks to the bollocks though if you piss her off. Bloody obsessed with pickled onions as well, smelled like an Italian restaurant's bucket at the Christmas party, put me right off the ruddy cheese board. Anyway! We better get a bloody move on and go see what the boss has found out about those bloody bastards that fair-dinged you up!"

I got up from the bed and wobbled briefly as I moved to follow Dean out the room. I was all fixed up it seemed, but I'd probably be best avoiding anything too stressful for a little while, like maybe being trapped in a secret facility with a bunch of monsters under several thousand gallons of murky Caithness ocean. I steadied myself and followed after the elf appreciating antipodean.

After a short walk, Dean pushed open the doors to a large conference room, where inside the very generic 'TV Police Drama' looking space I could see Gunnar and Maggie on one side of the table, sitting across from an athletic looking red headed woman and the Leather Lady I'd already met, who I assumed was the wood elf 'Fidget' that Dean had told me about. Dean plonked himself down on the chair beside her and threw his feet up on the side of the large desk, facing toward the head of the table where Teacher stood with his arms folded behind his back, talking in front of the largest digital screen I had seen outside of a Times Square billboard.

I pulled out a chair beside Maggie and sat down, her hand grabbing my leg as she turned to stare at my miraculously healed head. Satisfied that it was still in one piece, she slapped my knee and spun back round to face Teacher.

"Now that we've concluded the more, 'sensitive' issues of the day" Teacher looked straight at Gunnar, who for his part seemed to go a bit red about the massive cheeks. "I feel we should carry on with the business of explaining to Mr Stewart here a little bit more of what he's been going through these last twenty-four hours. Aha" The screen lit up with the same logo that sat on the chest of Huey's jacket,

"As you may remember Angus, I did try to discuss everything with you late last night in my office, however, and I apologise profusely for the inconvenience this caused you, I had to extricate you out of the building quickly due to.. 'Issues' that had cropped up in the bar. Unfortunately this meant slipping you a fast acting tranquilliser so we could manoeuvre you out and back to your hotel under the guise that you'd had too many drinks and had passed out." Teacher's arms clasped together behind his back as he circled around the large table.

"Again my apologies for putting you through that, and I take full responsibility for what happened to you in the early hours of this morning. I should have kept you here and discussed things with you further, rather than having you placed back in your room with no explanation."

Maggie's glare darkened as he paused briefly to look at her, his head lowering as he continued pacing.

"Still, what is done is done and thankfully you've come to no real harm."

"No real harm?" I leaned forward with my arms folded in front of me on the table top, glaring at Teacher as he stopped behind Dean. "So you call being almost wiped out by a truck smashing into me and leaving me with a hole in my head 'no real harm'? Mysterious warehouse-owning people nearly killed me, totalled my piece of shit car, tied me to a chair in a barn and tried to intimidate me into telling me about this place, and that's 'no real harm'?" I laughed as I stood up, my knuckles dug into the table as I glared at Teacher.

"I came home for a damned funeral Mr Cleaver. To bury my uncle and to find out what the hell actually happened to him, but instead of sitting with family reminiscing, I end up in the land of the fairies! So yes, please explain to me what the hell is happening to me right now, and who was that arsehole wearing the mask who tied me to a bloody chair last night, because if it wasn't out of respect for my aunt here I'd be tempted to jump this table and twat you with a table lamp."

The room went quiet, everyone taking sudden interest in the table's wood grain pattern rather than acknowledge the tension that now filled the air between myself and the well dressed man in front of me. I noticed the redhead move her seat back slowly, giving herself space to move in case things became more heated. But as she turned slowly I noticed that if anyone was getting tackled to the ground by this stern faced woman, it was absolutely going to be me.

Teacher looked at me with a serious look on his face; "Yes indeed Mr Stewart. Aha. You have been through somewhat of a traumatic time since you arrived here, I do understand this." He moved across to the large leather chair at the head of the table and sat down, his fingers steepled in front of him as he leaned forward onto the wooden top in front of him.

"You see, it's very easy to lose perspective working in this facility. I retired from field work many years ago and since then, I rarely find myself outside this 'land of the fairies' where our technical and somewhat magical achievements help me lose a degree of perspective. Now, if you'll be so kind as to accept my apologies and return to your seat, we can move forward here and debrief quickly what's happening around you, and why you're involved."

I sat down, noticing the red-headed woman relax back in her chair slowly before turning back toward where Teacher now sat waiting. Nodding my consent for him to continue, he once more stood and moved to the large screen.

"Firstly, that man who was involved in your kidnapping last night goes by the name of Thorne" I nodded as he continued. "Thorne is one of the leading operatives with the Scottish arm of the 'Fallen Sons', perhaps even one of their directors. More importantly, Thorne used to be a member of

RUST alongside your uncle Huey, before defecting to the American organisation."

I sat bolt upright, noticing Maggie flash a dark look toward Teacher, "So he knew my uncle? Could he have been involved with what happened to him?"

Teacher paused for a moment before continuing, "We don't know for sure Mr Stewart, we also have questions that we are still trying to find answers too. And with your help hopefully, we hope to find some very soon." Teacher moved toward the large screen and continued.

"Let me conclude this quick debrief of our situation here and then once we have all the facts, we can move forward with how we plan to further investigate Huey's passing with your help. May I?" I sat back and nodded my consent, allowing him to continue as the large screen came to life once again.

"So we covered some of our brief history with you during our last meeting Mr Stewart, about how we came to be here as RUST and briefly what our remit is. However, I didn't cover what happened to those members of 'The Sons' who found themselves suddenly on the back foot as the tide turned against them. Their numbers dwindling and their influence falling apart whilst RUST rebuilt links with the council of Others."

The large screen behind Teachers' chair blinked into life, and an image flashed up showing what looked like a scattered group of monks, or at least people going to great lengths to move through a crowd with their hoods pulled up completely over their faces.

"The more The Sons persecuted the fae and humans alike, the stronger RUST grew in opposition. Slowly rebuilding trust with the Others and turning the tide of opinion back against the members of SOTO, whose greed had transformed the group into little more than a nest of leeches who craved the prestige and wealth they had quickly lost as control slipped from their hands." He stood up and moved round the back of his chair toward the wall, tapping the large screen to show another image of those hooded figures moving through the crowd at a large harbour;

"Until they collapsed so completely that in fear of prosecution or retribution from either side, their remaining members scattered themselves and their riches toward America, where they settled themselves insidiously into the new world, reforming and scheming to rebuild all that they had lost here."

"Didn't RUST think it best to go after them and stop them doing over there exactly what they had already done here?" Everyone stared at me as I pointed toward the screen, "Surely if they were such a shower of bastards here, they'd be an even bigger collection of fuckwits over there?"

"Eloquent point Mr Stewart, However you have to remember that back then RUST was still rebuilding itself. They had neither the manpower nor the resources to mount such a trip to the New World to bring The Sons to justice. Instead our forefathers worked to rebuild their own structure, strengthen links with the Fae community and restore faith in a human led organisation that wasn't going to use its power to strip the fae of their profitable gifts. We simply hoped that they wouldn't pick up where they had left off here."

"Haha, aye, and that turned out bloody fine, didn't it!" Gunnar's laughter boomed over the table, and was suddenly cut short by the sudden glare of Teacher standing beside him. I'd never seen a big man shrink so suddenly as I did when Teacher calmly placed a hand softly on the technicolour giant's shoulder.

"As Mr Bjornsonn here says-" Gunnar noticeably winced at the use of what was clearly his real surname. I imagined that it was like when you heard your mother shout for you and used your full name along with heavily pronunciated punctuation, and you knew your arse was destined for a repeated meeting with the sole of a size six slipper. "-Things didn't quite work out as RUST had hoped, with the Sons soon finding a way to gain power and notoriety in this New World they had invaded. Aha" The screen switched again, showing a slideshow of small church buildings in that 'cowboy' style of decor I'd seen on tv whilst growing up watching Bonanaza and Clint Eastwood movies.

"Religion. Poured over the heads of the masses who had migrated across the ocean, it seeped its way into the hearts of all those who prayed that their crops wouldn't fail, or that bandits wouldn't come in the middle of the night and burn down their homes." Teacher motioned toward the screen as the image changed to show congregations of people in various different churches, all with their hands clenched together in prayer.

"Nothing gives you control over the masses faster than fear laced with a heavy dose of religious zeal sprinkled on top. The Catholic and Protestant churches had a firm foothold already throughout the States, but as the population grew and expanded into areas that had never before felt the foot of man, suddenly there were all new fae being discovered along with all new myths and tales."

Teacher once more touched the screen, changing the picture to show a slideshow of beasts and creatures, some of which looked familiar to things I'd seen in those conspiracy theory documentaries on the satellite channels that Stacey loved to watch all the time.

"Along with these new species being discovered came a whole new level of fear amongst the settlers in this new world, spurred on by the churches who labelled them demons and hellspawn, when in fact many of these fae had gentler hearts than the pitchfork wielding farmers who hunted them."

He poured himself a glass of water while the slideshow continued above his head.

"Recognising this, and seeing that the main churches were doing very little other than whip up fear amongst their congregations, the former Owls got together and formed 'The Church of the Fallen Sons', claiming to be followers of a holier power whilst protecting humanity from the scourge of demons that they claimed infested the god-forsaken land under their feet when in truth they were focused upon gathering wealth and discovering how to exploit the fae for their own gain"

"Aye, and the bloody eejit farmers raised their heids above the arse of their cattle for long enough to soak it all in as well-" Maggie was half out of her chair, waving her walking/combat stick at the digital church goers, "-Threw their hard earned money at the Sons too, lookin' for protection and a' that pish."

"Yes, quite" Teacher coughed as Maggie sat back down; "As the years wore on the 'Fallen Sons' grew in power and wealth, stripping the fae from the land, chasing whole communities into seclusion and almost wiping out other species completely, like the poor kinsfolk of our good friend Mr Biscuits." As he mentioned my limo driving saviour, an image of several 'Slenders' who looked identical to Mr Biscuits flashed up on screen, huddled in the corner of a room under a harsh, purple light whilst someone took the photograph we were looking at.

"What they couldn't barter from the fae, they took. What they couldn't religiously guilt out of their congregations, they made from selling 'protection from evil' to the gullible. As technology advanced they put preachers on TV on evangelical channels, who made millions from people at home watching them spout their anti-demon rhetoric. These 'Fallen Sons' flew around the world in private jets and helicopters, professing to be protectors of the people against the hordes of demons that lurked in the shadows, whilst those 'Demons' themselves were harvested like cattle for whatever resource they could provide."

The large screen above him changed to show the RUST logo;

"And we are the ones on the frontline, trying to protect those who fall under their malevolent gaze."

"Wow-" I leaned back with my hands on my head, the screen blinked off while Teacher sat back down in his chair. All eyes around the table stared at me as I tried to process all this fucking lunacy that had come at me over the last twenty four hours. "-That was dramatic as fuck.. Sorry Maggie." It was okay for her to swear clearly, but when I do it I get looked at like I've chucked a live wasps nest into a nursery class room.

"Truly, this is fucking.. Sorry! 'Feckin' amazing. Honestly, despite all the shit I've experienced, I'm thankful that you've all allowed me to see all of this." A few smiles cracked around the room, except for the red-head who still looked at me like she was planning on removing several of my teeth if I so much as farted in the wrong direction;

"But I still have no flippin' idea why the heck you've got me here telling me all this! It's fascinating, and it looks like you're doing a grand old job here too with your underground headquarters and your rocket powered toilets. But I'm just a low paid police officer in Aberdeen with a prematurely receding hairline, a bigger than is socially acceptable collection of He-Man toys and a whole lot of questions about my uncle's death that I would like some answers for." Everyone around the table looked at each other as I continued, "Oh, and the last time I ate, I think, was some kebab meat that was stuck to my face about twenty four hours ago, but I could be wrong since my brain got a little rattled during the ram-raid that wrote off my crappy car.. So excusing the fact that I'm somewhat delirious with hunger right now, why the hell am I here?!"

Teacher stood up, stood back from his chair and pushed it in toward his table. At this signal everyone else seated at the table followed suit, until we were now all standing watching the leader of RUST move around the table toward me.

"If you'll indulge us a little further Mr Stewart-" Both Gunnar and the red-headed woman stepped up to stand beside me; "-I'll pass you into the capable hands of both Mr Bjornsonn and Miss Simpson." Gunnar flashed me a wink, moving to tower over me as he was joined by the angry looking redheaded woman.

"They can show you why we've brought you into the facility, perhaps in a better way than just having me talk at you for a length of time, aha. If you'll excuse me?" And with that Teacher stepped out of the room, followed closely by the medic Dean and Fidget.

Maggie stood up, "Don't worry son, Gunnar and Crash will take good care of you! If ye need me, I'll be heading back to the reception to wait for ye, and helping mysel' to some of Joan's home bakes while I'm at it, so dinna rush!" Giving me a thumbs up as she set off for the door, she walked through after Teacher, Dean and Fidget. HAMMER's voice suddenly boomed out from overhead;

"OBSERVATION: PERHAPS MRS STEWART WOULD INSTEAD LIKE TO VISIT OUR FULLY STOCKED SALAD BAR? I CAN LIGHT THE WAY IF YOU FEEL YOUR EYES ARE FAILING YOU." As the door closed behind her I could hear a muffled rage scream, then a crash as her stick clearly rattled off something metallic.

"So uh.. Don't suppose either of you have a packet of crisps on you? Maybe some nuts?"

"Haha!" Gunnar slapped me on the shoulder, nearly knocking me over the table in the process; "Come with me loon, we'll pass the canteen on our way to the Haggvar, pick you up a sandwich or three eh?"

Chapter Twelve

Haggvar

I was well into my third bite of the Coronation Chicken baguette Gunnar had picked up for me as we made our way down the corridor trying to keep up with his massive strides. I was unsuccessfully trying to look cool with Crash walking beside me, whilst hammering yellow chicken mush into my mouth between gasps of breath trying to keep up with the sequined boots of 'Mr Bjornsson'.

"So, 'Crash' is a strange name Mrs Simpson? Sorry, should I call you Mrs Simpson while I'm here or can I use Crash?" I took another large bite of baguette as we rounded a corner, " I don't know much about rank or stuff here.. Want a bite of this? This here's some damned tasty chicken!"

Crash looked at the lump of soggy bread that suddenly appeared in front of her like I'd just tried to hand her my bogey handkerchief.

"Just.. Try and keep up with Gunnar for now, okay? And you can call me Crash, everyone else here does." She quickened her pace to catch up with the Man-Giant striding away majestically in front of us, jabbing him playfully with a finger in the ribs as she stopped at his side.

"Unlike you, you big lump of multicoloured brute. You can call me whenever the hell you like!" Crash planted her hands on her hips while

Gunnar's grinning face lit up like the bulb in an Amsterdam sex workers window, turning quickly to look at Crash and then me before chuckling to himself and hurrying back to the route he was leading us on.

"So are you guys together?" My headache was calming down as I packed more and more of the tasty carbs in my mouth. I wasn't sure if it was related to be perfectly honest, but I'm a firm believer that any ailment can be soothed with the internal application of marinaded hen boob.

"Who, me and the big boy?" Crash spun away from me and marched off after Gunnar;

"Well 'technically' you could say no. But I'm pretty sure I'm cracking my way through the big bastards shields one by one. It won't be long before I've worked my way into his oversized heart with my feminine prowess." As we quickened our pace to get closer to Gunnar his head cocked to the side slightly, clearly trying to overhear what we were discussing.

"He's basically like a giant Gobstopper. Even if it takes me bloody years to do it, I'll lick and sook my way through all those tasty layers to get to the chewy center!"

"OKAY WE'RE HERE HA HA SO LET'S ALL STOP TALKING AND DO THE THING THAT WE ARE HERE FOR OKAY!" Gunnar rushed forward and opened the large wooden doors ahead of us, leading into what looked like a large underground cave. Torches dotted along the walls on either side of us lit up what looked like small scaffolding running up sections of the rock to either side of me, with smaller tunnels leading off into the darkness from the scaffolding's wooden platforms.

I followed Gunnar and Crash into the room, suddenly remembering to swallow my mouthful of chicken before it choked me. The floor was covered in the small dog creatures we'd seen at the ceremony the day before, all running back and forth between tiny tables, all covered in a variety of electronic screens and lights.

"The wee buggers love their shiny things, pretty sure they're responsible for me losing a few Walkmans back in the day." Gunnar aimed a playful kick at one of the dog-things as it stepped in front of him. Leaping back out of his range, it made a rude gesture before blowing a raspberry and running off back toward one of the tables littered with pulled apart electronics.

"Haha! Little shit!" Gunnar turned toward us, "That's Dougie there, he's a right wee character. Always pissing about and getting under your bloody feet. Watch him near your mobile phone lad, he loves taking selfies, rude selfies."

"Maybe Big Red need stop complaining about photos on gadget. Maybe Big Red should appreciate Not-Dougie's artistic and beautiful body."

I looked around to see where the voice had come from. Neither Crash nor Gunnar seemed to react to it, but it sounded clear as hell to me. I looked down at 'Dougie' who was hunched over his table pulling apart what looked like an old VCR, and he looked like he was focused entirely on chewing on bits off of a circuit board.

Before I got a chance to ask either of my hosts who had spoken, Gunnar cut me off;

"These wee critters are the Haggvar[8], or as I like to call them, 'Shitebags'." This caused another flurry of rude gestures from the one he'd called Dougie. "They're pretty intelligent, but they canna talk like we can, mouth's are too wide and too many teeth, but they can sure as hell let you know when they want something off you."

---

[8] Haggvar comes from the Norske word 'hoggva' (sp) meaning to 'hack, hew' - When they were first discovered in Norway, they were believed to be spiteful spirits that would steal from your home and bring you bad luck in doing so, so they were hunted and killed as a rite of passage. Subsequently sending the species the same way as the Dodo or the musical career of Lily Allen.

Crash stepped forward, grabbing her phone back off one of the Haggvar who'd just slipped it out of her pocket;

"We call them 'Haggs' around here, there's only a few small colonies left and they're all based here in the Highlands. This group that live here in the cave systems are the friendly ones, the ones that let us interact with them and learn more about their abilities." Crash's voice suddenly dropped to a whisper as she moved close to me, "And their cousins who are less friendly, the 'Maulaggs' as we call them, live down along the river. Same species essentially, but they are darker in colour and paint their faces with a red stripe. Those fuckers aren't quite as pally, and if they decide to take your new tablet out of your backpack, they'll probably be taking a good chunk of your skin with it too. Nasty wee pricks" She stopped speaking as several furry heads turned in our direction and gave her a stern look.

"Aye, but we don't talk about them here in front of our friends now, do we Crash?" Gunnar's voice seemed to be pitched high enough so that it carried over the whole room. "No siree! Only pals I have here are these little shitebags!" Just then, one of the Haggs came out of one of the side tunnels carrying what looked like a flask, scampered down the scaffolding and ran across to Gunnar, chucking the flask up at his chest before flashing a quick wink, and scampering back the way he'd came.

"Aha! The good stuff!" He unscrewed the lid and took a big sniff, causing him to wobble for a second before sitting down on the floor with a thud.

"Ooocha, that'll put hairs on your pooping chute! You want another wee sip lad? That bit you had earlier nearly sent you into bloody hyperdrive!"

I motioned no as he wiggled the flask toward me. If it was the same stuff that he'd slipped into my tea at Maggie's house, then I thought it best to steer clear of it in such a confined, underground space as this in case my head rocketed off.

"Cracking stuff, purely scientifically you understand, nae good for a nightcap but good to get your motor started in the morning!"

Crash shook her head, "They brew the stuff in the caves down here, and use it to feed their young. Some brave human soul took a sip of it once and discovered that it has an alcoholic effect on us, even more so if you've been 'gifted' by the Haggs." She smirked, "And from what I heard of your reaction earlier, you're definitely in that category."

I added the question about what they meant by 'gifted' to the ever expanding list of messed up shit I was needing answers for as I looked around this 'Fraggle Rock' looking cave and the hairy little creatures that ran around it.

"How the hell have you managed to keep these guys hidden from the world? I mean, I'm no idiot, but I'm pretty sure growing up I would have noticed a bipedal dog rummaging through my backpack while I was swimming in the river and then making off with my calculator!" As I talked I looked around for somewhere to put the empty packaging of my chicken baguette, but seeing no bins I surreptitiously scrunched up the packaging and flung it into one of the nearby tunnels the Haggs were using.

"Ah, that's the clever part laddie!" Gunnar climbed to his feet, gently lifting off the small Hagg that had buried itself in his beard and started snoring, before placing it on one of the small benches by the tables. "You see, who's gonna believe a man when he comes staggering oot of the wilds claiming he saw a wee furry thing playing with a mobile phone? Especially when we're smothering the world with ridiculous folklore and made up stories about Haggis!"

It hit me then as I looked around at the mass of furry creatures running between tables fighting over random electronic bits. Why hadn't I made the connection before? Haggvar, 'Haggs' - Of course they were bloody Haggis!"

"And the more ridiculous you make them sound, the less people believe they exist! Think aboot it son." Gunnar walked over and slumped down beside me, "You convince people that Haggis are little furry, bagpipe-playing, porridge-eating lumps of short-legged nonsense with a trombone nose, wearing wee kilts while running around the hills and moors playing 'Auld Lang Syne' oot their blunderbuss shaped noses, you're covered!" He chuckled to himself as he continued;

"Then when a hillwalker ACTUALLY sees a furry wee thing raking through the boot of his car at two in the morning near his campsite, he'll run back to the nearest town to tell everyone, where his tales of finding a wee furry thing playing Candy Crush on his new mobile phone will have sniggering locals gently guide him to the nearest pub for a few medicinal brandies and a wee lie down."

"People believe what the hell you make them believe." Crash interjected, whilst kneeling down play-fighting with a large Hagg who was swinging what looked like a broken table leg at her, "And the more ridiculous you make it, the more people want to believe it, until every gift shop from John O'Groats to Gretna Green is packed with furry Haggis dolls and the occasional Innapropriate Gollywog."

"Lucky you a strong one lady! I even don't need stick to beat ya, cunning is me, Look! Here's ma left hand eh? And BOOM! Got ya with the right!"

"Who the hell said that!!" I stood up, prompting Gunnar, Crash and the large Haggvar to all stand up and stop what they were doing.

"Was that you talking?" I pointed at the Haggvar who looked at me with wide eyes, then turned to Gunnar. "Did you hear that thing speaking?

Can they speak? Because I didn't see it's bloody lips moving and I'm pretty sure I'm hearing voices in my head now and fuck, what if I have a concussion?"

"Oh shite- You not hear me big one, uh uh, we.. Uh, DOGS! WE DOGS NOT SPEAK YA HALFWIT! WOOF WOOF AND BARK AND STUFF! GIVE BISCUIT OR WILL SHITE IN YOUR SHOE!"

"Um, I'm not going mad here I don't think, but that Haggis is totally speaking directly into my fucking brain here." I backed up against the wall as both Gunnar and Crash looked at me with wide eyes, Crash lifting her arm before talking quietly into her sleeve.

"You're not a bloody dog, and this is not a concussion, you can flippin' talk, can't you?"

Gunnar raised his hands, "Now son, don't panic. All this can be explained, just come take a seat outside-"

"-Ronzo! Are stupid you?" Another Haggvar had run across now and was gesticulating wildly at the one that had spoken to me, *"You give game away! Keep doing dog pretend, maybe lick balls or pissing stick. NO I MEANING YOUR BALLS."*

"I can hear you too! You and 'Ronzo' there!" I pointed an accusatory finger at the new Hagg while out the corner of my eye I could see Ronzo trying to almost dislocate his hip to attempt to get his tongue anywhere near the same postcode as his genitals.

All Haggvar eyes were upon me now, as every furry faced critter nearby stopped to slowly turn and stare at me. That along with both Gunnar and Crash looking at me was freaking me the hell out, so I did the only rational thing I could think of; I turned and sprinted back to the safety of the hallway.

Once my feet hit the carpeted walkway of the hall I slumped to the ground and tried to catch my breath, unsure if I was hyperventilating because of the creepy brain voices I'd heard, or because I'd not long before inhaled a Coronation Chicken baguette that was as big as my thigh.

"Aha! It seems we have an answer then!" I spun round to find Teachers beaming face less than a foot from my own. I'm not embarrassed to admit that if it hadn't been for the near ten kilograms of baguette currently clogging up my pipework, I'd have undoubtedly made a mess of myself from more than one end.

The creepy bastard stood there calmly grinning as Gunnar and Crash bustled past him and raced across to make sure I was okay, helping me back to my feet as Teacher walked forward and offered me his hand.

"And it's an answer that also tells us why The Sons are so interested in you. Come, let's go and have some lunch in town shall we? It must be at least noon by now and I'm sure you'd appreciate some fresh air in more familiar surroundings. Oh, and you have my word there'll be no unexpected drugging this time! Aha.."

Not reassured at all, but surprisingly still hungry, I followed the three members of RUST as they turned and walked back down the corridor.

Chapter Thirteen

The Gift

We came back out the ramp leading to the harbour mouth, this time in a large 'Jurassic Park' looking 4x4 driven by Gunnar. The tiny door speakers rattling out some generic pop chart hit as we glided past the nearby cafe on our way toward the town centre.

"Perhaps some food and coffee back at your hotel-" Teacher twisted to look over his shoulder at me from the front passenger seat, "-and we can get you booked back in for a few more nights, just while we clear up all this dreadful mess we've managed to get you involved with, yes?"

"I'm not planning on being here long you know, I don't know what you're expecting of me yet. I just want to try and make sense of Huey's death, then I'm grabbing my shit and headi.. Ah dammit, everything was in the bloody car."

"Not to worry son-" Gunnar turned down the radio, "-Mr Biscuit's been away and recovered the stuff from your motor. It's all on your bed back in the hotel, same room as before."

We pulled into the hotel car park I'd just left the night before, climbed out and headed in through the back door, following in the wake of the oversized Gunnar who commandeered a table for us all to sit at before heading to the bar to collect some menus.

"My goodness-" Teacher wiped his handkerchief over the seat before sitting down, "-I haven't been in this hotel for a number of years now. Not since Huey and I.." He paused, briefly lost in thought. "Well, not for a very long time. Anyway, your aunt has asked that, rather firmly I hasten to add, we explain to you in a bit more detail why we had to sneak you out of RUST last night."

"Yep, great. Oh, can we also discuss maybe what happened with the Haggvar chatting away in my brain, like this is a perfectly normal thing that none of you seem overly concerned about?"

Teacher smiled, picking up the spoon from the table before rubbing it clean with his handkerchief. "Of course, yes. We shall get to that as soon as the soup of the day arrives! Always good to talk on a full stomach, don't you think? Makes one less irritable I feel. Aha"

Crash pulled her chair in beside me, picked up the butterknife from the table and started twirling it through her fingers, "You see pal, about the drugging thing.. Shit went a bit south in the bar while you were in yapping with Teacher last night. We discovered that some of our mourners had found out about the Sons interest in you, and were planning on cashing in by snatching you out of the building." The knife spun faster through her fingers, drawing some worried glances from the table of pensioners beside us.

"All this despite the fact they're Fae and have suffered PLENTY at the hands of the Sons in the past, AND disregarding the fact there are strict rules about violence on RUST grounds.. Still the greedy, shiny headed fuckers were willing to sell their souls to the devil for the sake of some pieces of gold."

"Aye, we left them a wee bit 'blue in the face' last night, if you catch my meaning lad!" Gunnar sat himself down with a thump that rocked at least a ten foot radius, causing one of the pensioners sat beside us to spit her false teeth into her chamomile tea before he dropped large glasses of whisky in front of each of us. Suspicious, I left mine sitting where it was for now, not wanting to wake up again randomly in my hotel room with my face glued to the pillow with drug induced drooling.

"The truth is Mr Stewart, we believe the Sons have had you under surveillance for quite a while, certainly during your entire time living down south. And when Gunnar tested you at your aunt's house, your reaction was not only far higher than we assumed it would be but enough that the Sons decided their interest in you was more than just observatory." Teachers' face took on a serious tone as he flashed a glance toward both Gunnar and Crash, "Quite how they knew about the test or its results continues to puzzle us. Your aunt's house had been subject to a full security sweep before the testing took place. I'm loathe to admit, but I fear we may have an information leak in our organisation." Both Crash and Gunnar frowned, the mood visibly darkening at the table.

"As you can then understand, we had to get you out of the building quickly and discreetly, whilst also setting a small surprise for those who planned you a mischief." Teacher sipped his whisky, grimaced and shot a sour look at Gunnar before continuing; "However, the only way we could get you out was with the help of the unique abilities of our friend Mr Biscuits."

Another taste, with a slightly smaller grimace this time; "In doing so, it is best that the, 'participant' is unconscious before they're inserted. Helps maintain one's sanity not being aware of what it's like in there."

I looked at the three faces all now staring at me and nervously smiling; "Wait.. Sorry, you'll have to forgive me but between the concussion, near death experience and being drugged then bundled into a dark hotel room-" this drew a few sharp looks from the table full of grey and blue headed pensioners nearby, "-I could have sworn you just said something about being 'inserted'?"

"It's totally safe wee man!" Gunnar grinned as he threw back his whisky, his wide eyes never looking away from me as he threw his head back and swallowed the cheap blend, motioning for me to do the same; "As long as you can't see or hear what's going on in there, there's only like a 10% chance of losing yer marbles when you come back oot!" His grin fell from his face as an exocet-teaspoon thrown by Crash caught him right between the eyes.

"Don't listen to that big fool, you were never in any danger at all. And listen, Biscuits was proud as punch being able to help and have you inside him until we could get you safely out of the facility.. And uh, him."

"Whoah.. Inside hi.. FUCKING INSIDE HIM? I WAS INSIDE HIM LAST NIGHT?"

Both Gunnar and Crash slammed a hand on my chest from either side of me to stop me launching out the seat, while Teacher smiled and waved his hand, trying to dismiss the worried stares from around as he turned back to me, leaning forward to talk in a hushed tone.

"Technically yes, but it was a matter of most urgency. Aha" He was now leaning into what I considered prime head-butting space, "Mr Biscuits' species used to be predators, and would capture subdued prey to take back to their spawn. In doing so, they would insert their catches.. Um, up into their abdomen, which by the way, interesting fact here, is mysteriously much bigger on the inside than it is on the outside, much like a TARDIS, aha!"

"He's no' got any visible genitalia you see-" Gunnar boomed a little too loudly, causing one of the old ladies next to us to drop her scone buttered side down on the carpet "-just one big hole for shoving things up into!"

"Wait-" I was teetering on the diving board of panic here, "-You're telling me that Mr Biscuits had me jammed up inside himself like some kind of HUMAN TAMPON?!?"

A crash from the table of pensioners momentarily distracted us, as one of the old ladies who had been leaning further and further in her seat to hear what we had been discussing lost balance, grabbing the tablecloth as she flew to the floor in a cascade of cutlery, buttered scones and the odd cream bun.

Mary, who'd clearly been hovering nearby monitoring our table for any snippets of gossip came running over to help the old lady back to her feet, while Teacher motioned for us to leave the bar area and to move through to the quieter reception area sofas where we could talk a bit more privately.

As we walked through I toyed with the idea of leaving the group and heading up to my room to climb into the shower with a bottle of bleach and some vodka, but I also needed answers to why I'd heard the Haggvar talking in my head when it seemed that nobody else had.

With the decision made, we sat down as Crash motioned to the reception desk that we'd like four soups of the day and a tray of coffees sent over, perhaps with a few whiskies as well, of the large variety please if they didn't mind too much.

"Let me reassure you Mr Stewart, this was a decision that didn't come lightly, but having Mr Biscuits snuggle- Um, excuse me, 'smuggle' you out of the building really was our only viable option. On the plus side however, we used a decoy out of our main entrance to trap your prospective kidnappers, who I believe are currently 'discussing their options' with the Selkie and her team of adjudicators."

As much as the thought of being shoved up a monster's pissing pipe made my skin crawl inside out, they did face off a bunch of armed men to save me from that barn full of Sons. Things could have been a lot worse for me if I'd been grabbed quietly earlier that night in RUST. I just wasn't sure I'd be able to not stare at Mr Biscuits crotch the next time I saw him.

"Right, okay, it's just been a hell of a lot to take in over a short period of time, especially learning I've basically been a living enema. Can we get to why you're so keen on me staying here longer, why these Sons are after me and why the hell the furry cast of Gremlins down there can speak directly into my skull?"

"To be brief, it's a gift Mr Stewart, a rare one. But also unfortunately one that is most prized by those who could abuse it." Teacher sniffed his whisky briefly before setting it back down on the table slowly like it was a live grenade. "A gift that was, uh, 'taken' by your grandfather a long time ago from the Haggvar, then inherited by both Huey and yourself."

"What about my father, did he have whatever this is?"

Teacher seemed to hesitate for a second. "This gift, or at least as you have it, passed your father by Mr Stewart. Or at least it didn't present itself in quite the same fashion for him." He quickly changed the subject.

"The Haggvar truly are an amazing species, Mr Stewart. Wholly under-appreciated by the Fae community as lower tier members of their society. However, the Haggvar and humanity have a unique relationship which has sadly led to them now becoming a heavily protected and endangered species." Teacher paused momentarily while Mary came by with the hoover, making sure to take extra care to attack the carpet around us as she made her rounds, which would have been a more convincing cover for trying to overhear gossip if she'd actually turned the thing on first.

"You see, Mankind discovered that if you built up a bond with one of the Haggvar, you would gain a 'gift' of some sort, be it increased strength, speed, wisdom or immunity to disease. And this gift would grow the closer you became to your Haggvar friend. But with humanity being the impatient and shallow beast that it is, people sought instant gratification and craved these gifts without the need to try and befriend something they saw as little more than a pet. Eventually, someone discovered that if you killed one of the Haggvar and ate its heart, you would gain whichever gift that they had to offer." His brow furrowed as he continued;

"Soon the Haggvar were hunted, tagged and killed as little more than livestock before their numbers took to the tunnels to escape the genocide of their species. After a few generations passed with the Haggvar hidden from the eyes of man, they fell into little more than folktales and stories to entertain children."

Crash leaned forward, "You ever wonder why there's still a pomp and ceremony to slicing up a haggis in front of a room full of braying guests? It used to be a moment of honour for men and women of supposed stature to have a live Haggvar sliced up in front of their family and friends, before eating the raw heart to gain whatever gift it came with, and even when the Haggvar disappeared the ceremonies continued, becoming little more than excuses to get drunk alongside your peers whilst some blowhard shouted a poem over an imitation haggis."

"In this respect Mr Stewart, you are unique." Teacher interrupted. "These gifts can be passed down through upwards of three generations. Your Grandfather took his gift through one of these ceremonies, and the gift was passed down the male bloodline to Huey and of course yourself, where it will presumably end. The difference however was the nature of the gift your grandfather took."

Teacher called over a nearby waitress and ordered some more whiskies, specifying that he would prefer something that was perhaps a relatively well aged single malt, and wouldn't leave his teeth feeling quite so furry.

"Your grandfather wasn't a 'good' man as such Mr Stewart. With all due respect, he had little regard for those he stepped on to raise his own fortunes, being both power hungry and determined. So when the time came for his ceremony, he wanted the rarest heart he could get. He spent a lot of money paying for the finest hunters throughout the Highlands, and after weeks of searching they managed to track down the nesting area of the largest clan of Haggvar in the region at that time. Your Grandfather took lead, and in turn managed to capture the grandest prize of them all, the Haggvar clan chief."

"They're a bit like bees you see. Or ants! Aye, ants might be a better description of the wee buggers, always stealing stuff to take back to the nest-" Gunnar had drunk his whisky, and after a surreptitious look around he quickly refilled the glass with the contents of the flask he'd picked up earlier from the Haggvar, "-With a wee queen or king coordinating them all through their song. 'Cept it's different wi' the Haggs pal, it's more like a wee army they run, with the boss hidden away while their captains run the troops, all based in different wee camps but still part of the same clan." He took a swig from the glass, and I could have sworn his eyes briefly glowed blue before he continued.

"Like the group you met at Rust. That's nae the whole clan ye understand, just a staging post of sorts that report back to the Heid'yin in the main camp."

Teacher butted in. "What our large friend here means by 'Heid'yin', is a term used by the Fae to refer to whichever Haggvar is the current ruler of the clan. Years ago, your grandfather by some miracle captured the Heid'yin of the largest, and possibly last clan we knew that still existed, throwing the Haggs into chaos and causing them to splinter into the smaller factions that we know today. The friendlier 'Haggvar' clans who you've already met some of, and their somewhat more aggressive cousins the Maulaggs, who have sworn off contact with humans at all after the actions of your grandfather and others like him."

"Your grandad ended up not only ripping apart an ancient clan of Haggvar, but almost destroyed any connection we had left with the suddenly leaderless groups. All because of a desire to be the most important knob in the collection of elitist penises he associated with." I could see the blade of the breadknife that Crash still clung to bending against the arm of her chair as she talked.

"According to the journals recovered by Huey after his father's passing, time went on and your grandfather noticed no physical change from the 'gift' he should have been granted from the Heid'yin's heart. His health didn't improve, his eyesight stayed blurry and his muscles showed no signs of renewed strength. He convinced himself he had been cheated out of what was in his mind rightfully his, and set himself to hunting down more Haggvar in private, so as not to alert his peers that no gift had as yet manifested itself."

Teacher looked around, cleared his throat and continued;

"After several weeks of late-night stalking through the moorland around the outskirts of Thurso, he finally cornered a young Hagg against a stone dyke. With no sign of escape for the undersized Hagg in front of him your Grandad moved in for the kill when he was stopped by a loud voice shouting in his head, pleading for him to stop."

"PLEASE DINNA KILL ME YE BIG, FAT BALDY FANNY!" Gunnar bellowed from his chair beside us, his arms waving in the air mimicking his surrender, "I'M JUST A WEE HAGGIS AND YOU'RE A LARGE SWEATY ARSEHOLE THAT COULD DO WITH SKIPPING A MEAL OR TWO!". He bellowed with laughter, until another precision strike between the eyes with a slightly bent breadknife encouraged him that maybe this wasn't the right time for him to interject.

Teacher stared a hole through Gunnar for a long few seconds before continuing;

"Despite our large friends pantomime here, we have no idea what the Haggvar said to your grandfather that night, he never wrote that down in his memoirs sadly. But we know that it caused him to stop dead in his tracks, allowing the small Haggvar to escape while he scanned the area for the source of the voice. As your panicked grandfather looked around for a possible attacker in this remote area of the moorland, he caught the eye of the small Hagg who had stopped higher up the nearby slope that ran alongside the wall he now leaned against. As he stared at the small creature, he saw it raise a defiant single claw in his direction before he heard it once again speak into his mind-" Teacher paused for a second, as both Gunnar and Crash hid smirks behind the lunch menus either side of me.

"-and your grandfather's memoirs were surprisingly specific about this conversation, and I only repeat this in the interests of historical accuracy you understand." He looked almost in pain as he looked toward me.

"The Haggvar in question, um, rather crudely I hasten to add, said to your grandfather, '*SOOK MY FURRY BALLS STINKSKIN!*' before running out of sight and into the darkness."

The twin menus either side of me were now jiggling furiously as Teacher glared a hole through each of his vibrating colleagues, "It was at this point that your grandfather discovered his gift. He'd been granted the gift of telepathy with the Haggvar. A gift that was passed down to your uncle Huey, and a gift that you also possess, judging by your interactions with our small friends earlier."

"This is just, just a lot to take in here. I can speak to these Haggs?"

"Aye pal, but then we can all do that-" Gunnar paused briefly as the waitress arrived, laying our soup on the table before heading back to the bar to collect some more coffee, "-These wee buggers can understand our patter fine, they just canna move their wee lips the right way to speak it. No, instead they yap back and forth wi' telepathy and song. It's pretty fancy if you think about it, they're chatting wi' words and pictures at the same time, like a Skype call wi' yer cousin in Australia!"

Teacher frowned, "Well, that's a somewhat simplified and frankly ridiculous example, but fundamentally yes. And now like your uncle and grandfather before you, you have the ability to hear their words. I can't tell you how exciting this is for all of us, we thought the gift was lost with your uncle!"

"Why exactly is this important? Why do you need to know what those things are saying?"

"It's quite a unique gift Mr Stewart, and frankly with investigations ongoing into your uncle's death, we hoped that perhaps our Haggvar friends might have some insight that they can't pass to us in song alone." Teacher looked toward the front doorway of the hotel for a moment before continuing, "If I'm frank, we too do not believe for a second that Huey was in a climbing accident. I fully believe that The Sons have a hand in this, in particular Thorne himself. But so far we've had nothing from the Haggvar that would suggest they know more than we do. Our hope is that if we can contact the Maulaggs safely, they might have information that could help us, but that's a difficult task in itself." Teacher downed the remains of his latest glass of whisky and leaned forward toward me as Gunnar stood to order more of the good stuff.

"Our concern also is that as time goes by your gift will develop with use. Like Huey, you'll soon be able to hear the thoughts of other creatures outside of just the Haggs, and with practice you'll be able to communicate back with them." His voice quietened, "And over time you'll find the gift develops to a point where not only will you be able to hear the thoughts of your fellow man, but with practice you'll be able to plant 'suggestions' of behaviour or thought that will influence their direct actions. A form of mind control if you will."

I'd been idly swirling my spoon around in the soup in front of me the whole time Teacher had been speaking, but when he said that I'd be possibly developing fucking mind control powers, the spoon fell from my hand and clattered into the bowl, splashing dabs of hot pea and ham soup onto my front. I stood up, brushing soup splashes off as I stepped back from the table;

"Listen, this has all been fun and all, meeting singing dogs, creepy guys in suits with caves for genitalia and being nearly killed by a group of people who sound like something out of a fucking Bond film-" I started walking toward the nearby staircase that led to the hotel rooms, "-But if you'll excuse me, this 'mind reading' piss really takes the biscuit. I need to go have a shower and lie down."

Teacher stood up behind me, "Mr Stewart, The Sons tried to recruit your grandfather when they learned of his talents, and he said no. He wanted this gift to benefit nobody but himself, and two days later he was found dead in his toilet having suffered a massive myocardial infarction through the night. Your uncle Huey hid his gift for many years whilst under the remit of RUST, nobody but a very small few of us knew what he could do until he was forced to use it to contact some Fae who'd been trapped in a tunnel collapse. Shortly after, he too was approached by The Sons who made him a very similar offer to the one they had made to your grandfather, to which Huey told them in no uncertain terms which area of their genitalia they could tightly pack their offer into."

I'd made it up to the first landing of the stairwell, Teacher following closely behind me;

"Mr Stewart, this happened just over a week ago. Six days later Huey suffered his seemingly accidental death."

I stopped dead in my tracks, turned round and faced Teacher. "Are you telling me that these 'Sons' killed my uncle?"

He paused; "I do not know for sure. But what I'm telling you Angus, is that the Sons will go to any length to have someone with your potential under their control. And if they can't have you, they surely will not want you under the protection of RUST where you can do them the most harm. Now if you'd please, come back to the table and we can have lunch, preferably before Gunnar makes his way through his own bowl and decides that ours should be saved from going to waste while we stand here chatting."

Chapter Fourteen

Guest at the Hotel

We finished our lunch and moved through to the bar area, where we spent the next few hours helping the hotel get rid of some of their rum, whisky and beer stock. Gunnar loudly regaled us with stories about some of the scrapes he and Huey had managed to -usually drunkenly- get themselves into, while Crash and Teacher sat and politely answered or deflected the multitude of questions I was throwing at them. However as I've learned through painful experience, I'm not the best drinker amongst my peers, and as the whisky and beer kept coming courtesy of the plastic card that Teacher intermittently waved over the bar, my line of questioning became a lot less probing.

"So.. Uh, So, what if like, a Haggis farts. Am I going to hear words?"

Gunnar leaned forward, "Aye possibly, but it'll probably be a load of shite! BWAH HAH HAH!!" His face went purple as laughter tore through him, forcing him to drop off his chair onto one knee whilst desperately clutching the armrest. His laughing stopped as he suddenly went wide eyed, jumped out of his chair and made a hasty shuffle toward the restrooms.

"AYE BIG CHAP! I DON'T THINK THAT'S THE ONLY THING THAT'S FULL OF SHITE EH?" Crash was out of her chair, pointing after the swiftly waddling Gunnar; "AND IF YOU'RE NEEDING A HAND POWDERING THAT TUSHIE AFTER YOU'VE CLEANED YOURSELF UP, I'M ONLY A HOLLER AWAY!"

The toilet door nearly slammed shut on the one-finger salute that poked out from it before disappearing into the darkness.

Teacher stood up slowly from his chair, doing his best to remain composed and dignified;

"I think Mr Stewart, that once our large friend emerges from the restrooms, I shall make my leave back to the facility, and allow you the rest of the day to do with as you will." Crash stood up beside him and passed something small into Teachers' hand, "And considering the increased threat we've already discussed, Crash and Gunnar have offered to take the rooms either side of you for the next few days until we can discuss your future plans and arrangements. Now, before I go please take this." Teacher reached out his open hand toward me, offering what looked like one of those small plastic button things you get for opening garage doors.

"This is for all intents and purposes, an alert button. I'd ask that for the foreseeable future, you carry this on your person so that if anything else 'unfortunate' happens, you can press this, allowing the inbuilt alarm and GPS tracker to lead us to you as quick as we can mobilise." I took the small device and placed it in the pocket of my trousers as Gunnar arrived back beside me.

"Now, if you'll excuse me, I believe the short walk in the fresh air up to the access point that Mr Stewart enjoyed during his first visit to our facility-" I shuddered a little remembering the rocket-bog that whizzed us underground toward RUST, "-will help me clear the head fog somewhat before I get back to an undoubted pile of paperwork and a scolding from Joan, aha. I will bid you all a good day!" With a quick brush down and straightening of his jacket, he walked through the rotating front door and out into the cold afternoon.

I finished off my drink and made the sensible option to head up to my room and climb under the shower, in the hope that I could wash away the fogginess of the whisky and perhaps some lingering mental images of being rammed up a tall, pale man's back passage. Both Gunnar and Crash followed suit as we carefully climbed the stairs to our rooms, both of them reminding me that they would only be a button press or loud scream away should I need them.

I opened the door to my room and stepped inside, the dying light creeping through the closed curtains showing a couple of boxes lying on the bed in which I assumed all my stuff lay in from my mangled car. I stripped off my clothes as I walked through the room, discarding them on the floor as I stepped into the bathroom and turned the shower on.

After quickly checking my head again in the mirror above the sink in case Dean's magical fixing machine had mistakenly given me horns or tentacles, I moved back through to the room and decided to crank the window open a little so that the steam wouldn't build up too much in the room, considering I was planning on staying in that shower until I looked like a Californian raisin.

I opened the curtains slightly, not wanting the world outside to see my nakedness as I crouched down and leaned through to crack the window open.

"I know it's late in the day, but I didn't expect to see a full moon quite this early!"

I spun around, accidently wrapping myself in the curtain and bouncing off the wall beside me. Sitting on my bed with a small smile on her face sat Silver, looking down at her lap whilst slowly flicking the pages of the magazine that sat there.

The alarm button Teacher had given me was about six feet away in the pocket of the trousers I'd kicked off onto the floor.

"WHAT THE, THE HELL ARE YOU *-ooh I've really rattled my knee on the bloody radiator there-* the HELL are you doing here!?" I painfully climbed to my feet, while trying desperately to maintain some decency with my new curtain toga which had pulled mostly off its runners and wrapped itself around me.

Silver looked over at me as a warm smile lit up her face. She set the magazine aside, stood up and smoothed out the spot she had been sitting on;

"I've been really worried about you, after what happened at the barn I had to make sure you were okay" She quickly stepped forward as I shrank back into the folds of my dusty curtain-shawl, cornering me against the wall and pushing my hair back with her hand to look at the area she'd been tending when we last met.

"Thank goodness you're alright! I've been worried sick, especially after the way things went down when your scary friends arrived. How do you feel?"

I scooted along the wall, trying to slowly edge my way around her and toward my trousers, but I was stopped in my tracks by two stubborn curtain rungs that blindly refused to abandon their post.

"How do I feel? You people nearly killed me for christ sake! How do you think I'm bloody doing 'Silver', or whatever your damned name is?" I was getting pissed off now that the shock had worn off, and a bit agitated that at least one curtain rung seemed to have embedded itself into my armpit;

"What the hell are you doing here?"

Her smile softened into a look of concern as she stepped back a few paces.

"I can't tell you how much I wish what happened didn't happen Angus. There should have been more formal introductions made than trying to grab you like we did-" She moved toward the bed and sat down, "-You've no idea how much I argued with them to approach this all more subtly, but I'm nothing but a tiny voice in a large choir."

"Okay, so are you here to take me back in so your pal Mr Thorne can strap me to another chair, shine some lights in my face, maybe try and cave my head in with another truck?"

I strode toward the bed now, all fear of having this stranger in my room gone as I demanded to get some answers. Silver sat and stared into my eyes as I stood beside her, clearly trying to avoid looking at the gaps falling open in my impromptu toga;

"What is it Miss Silver? Because frankly I haven't got all night and I REALLY want to get in that shower now because I'm sure there's things in this curtain that are starting to nibble on my knackers."

"I'm here through genuine concern Angus-" She stood up and glowered at me, "-I'm here because seeing you hurt in that barn really scared me, and I wanted to let you know I was a bloody friend if you needed, despite what you might have heard about the organisation I work for." She walked toward the door, unlocked it and paused;

"The Sons aren't all evil Angus, some of us want to do some good in the world. To help, and I want to help you." I picked up my trousers as she talked, fumbled into the pocket and pressed the alarm button. Instantly Silver's face fell;

"It seems our time is cut short. I have your number, I'll be in touch." She bolted out of the door just as the sound of Crash and Gunnar tumbling out of their rooms filled the hallway.

"I'll chase after the girl, you go see to Angus!" I watched Crash sprint past the door in the direction Silver had ran just before Gunnar came stumbling into the room.

"You okay there loon?" He ran into the bathroom and pulled back the shower curtain, looking for anyone else that might be hanging about before checking around the sides of the bed. Happy that nobody else was there he picked me up with both hands, forcing my curtain dress to fall to the floor and leave me dangling naked six inches off the floor.

"You're nae hurt are you? She's nae cut anything off you or anything-" He spun me around like I was nothing more than a toddler needing winded, checking me over for cuts or marks, "-Maggie will bloody cut bits off me if you're nae in one piece!"

"I'm fine! Let me down before.."

I was cut off by the sound of Crash returning.

"She bloody got away, sorry gu.. WHOAH! What have I interrupted here then!" I couldn't see her enter the room since Gunnar had me pretty much dangling upside down, but at the angle I was at I was pretty confident she was getting a direct view of my undercarriage.

"HOOO! Gunnar, if it takes me getting naked and tearing down the curtains to get you to handle me like that, I'll be next door kicking the shit out of the blinds!"

Gunnar reddened and dumped me on the bed like a bag of washing, where I quickly wrapped myself up in the bedsheet.

"Was that the wee lass I saw at the barn with the Sons?" Gunnar quickly sidetracked.

"The same, calls herself 'Silver'." I managed to fumble my trousers on under the folds of my bedsheet, "Maybe just a code name? I dunno.."

"I've seen her before-" Crash closed the door behind her as she came into the room, "-running around after some of the more senior Sons a few months back when we tracked them out past Dounreay. Pretty sure she's just an assistant to the higher ups. Wonder why she was here and not one of their operators instead?"

"I don't think she was here to grab me, she sounded like she wanted to help more than anything else, seemed pretty concerned about any damage I took from the kidnapping."

Crash stood to one side as Gunnar moved outside to the hallway with his phone pressed to his ear, no doubt updating Teacher about what had just happened.

"If that's true, she's the first Son I've met that has a bloody heart." Crash pushed the door shut and moved across to the bed where I still sat, "I'll need to speak to Teacher about this, but until then it might be worth listening to what this girl has to say. If we can get her onside, it may give us a way to find out more about what they're up to, or more importantly what they know about you and your new skill set." She patted me awkwardly on the shoulder, clearly trying very hard to look sympathetic;

"It might be best that you let us know about anything untoward as soon as it happens, so we can pass it directly to Teacher." She flashed a glance at the doorway before continuing, "Just so that the line of communication is as small as possible you understand, at least until we figure out if there is a mole passing information out to the Sons."

I nodded agreement as she stood and walked back to the door, stopping to smile and give me an awkward 'thumbs up' before stepping out and closing it behind her. I was too tired, drunk and overloaded with all this 'fantasy novel' nonsense to process any of what had happened over the past twenty four hours, so instead I threw aside my bedsheet toga, pulled back off my trousers and climbed into the shower, where I stayed until every last drop of hot water was sucked out of the hotel's pipework. I lazily dried myself off with the lime green bath towel that hung on the bathroom wall, and flicked off the light as I climbed onto the bed and passed out.

The next morning I woke up feeling surprisingly okay, despite the heavy drinking the night before, the near murder by speeding truck and learning that I had been little more than a glorified unconscious sex toy for a large skinny night terror. The large breakfast that Mary dropped in front of me as I sat down in the restaurant area of the hotel certainly helped, allowing me to avoid her snooping questions by way of my mouth being held captive by the five rashers of bacon that I'd stuffed in there while she orbited around me.

Just as I managed to dodge her questions long enough to fumble some black pudding into my face, I was joined by Gunnar and Crash who both ordered full breakfasts and as much coffee as Mary could safely carry without throwing her back out.

Since I finished my food first, I excused myself to the lobby where I opened my phone. After skipping past the multitude of missed calls and voicemails from Stacey, I dialled my work to check in and let them know I was still alive.

"Yeah, it's all cool bud. Your aunt already called and explained what was going on-" Steve was my shift partner, and had been in to cover my bereavement leave for coming north, "-everyone's asking for you pal, we're keeping our fingers crossed that the surgery goes fine and hopefully you'll be up and about soon, we're missing you down here! Oh, better go, that's someone just arrived to get checked in." Before I could get a word in edgewise the phone clicked and he was gone.

Surgery? I scrolled through my contacts to find Maggie's number, worried now about what kind of fictional surgery she'd told my work that I was suddenly needing. Just as I was about to press call, Gunnar's large 4x4 pulled up just outside the main door ahead of me and started blasting the horn.

I walked out to find Dean sitting behind the wheel, arm out the window waving for me to get in. Just as I stepped forward I was joined by both Gunnar and Crash, sprinting out of the hotel either side of me before diving into the back of the truck and pulling me in with them.

"What's going on-" I buckled myself in as Dean roared away from the hotel entrance, "-What's happening?"

"It's The Sons mate, they've found a nest and they've taken a bunch of Haggs." Dean was stoney faced as he weaved through traffic toward the harbour mouth entrance to RUST, "And from what we've learned so far, they've unwittingly hit bloody gold."

Just as I was about to ask more, Gunnar pulled me back into my seat and showed me his phone. On it was a message from Teacher,

'All teams return ASAP. Maulagg camp is being raided by SONS. They're after the Alpha.'

Chapter Fifteen

The Mighty Kah'Baj

It wasn't long before we slid to a halt back at RUST, where we followed Teacher back to his office for a 'debrief'[9]. However as we came close to the office our group suddenly veered left toward a large door near to where I'd met the Haggs the day before.

We walked into a large white room, clinical looking apart from all the Haggs scattered over the floor and chairs, ignoring us as they climbed over one another to press themselves against a large window at the back of the room, fighting to get a look into the well-lit space beyond the glass.

"How the devil did they find a way in?" Teacher stared at the floor around us. "I specifically remember CLEARLY STATING that I didn't want them to know what was in here. This just complicates matters as a whole. AND OH LOOK, ONE OF THEM IS VOMITING INTO A SHOE, HOW DELIGHTFUL!"

---

[9] *Or whatever it was these secret agent monster chasers liked to call it, My knowledge was limited to what I had seen on those late night American police dramas where they all wear shades and completely ignore safe working protocols.*

Teacher shoved his way into the bundle of fur that covered the floor, connecting the toe of his well-polished brogue with more than one furry rectum to encourage the Haggs to get out of his way as he made his way to the glass wall ahead. Led by a carefully stepping Gunnar, we followed as best we could through the hairy knee-high hubbub, several of whom taking the opportunity to punch or nip at our shins for daring to jump the queue.

I reached the large glass wall as Gunnar swung bunches of Haggs away from the glass with a massive sweep of his arms. There on the other side of the glass stood a solitary Hagg, a little stockier than the ones swarming around my ankles, with darker fur and a red paint-like smear across its face. And as it stared back at me, it was easy to see that it was a good bit more pissed off looking.

"Our honoured friend here has come visiting from the Maulaggs-" announced Teacher solemnly, "-From what we've managed to ascertain so far, It appears that shortly ago they suffered an attack from a large collection of humans, encircling their main encampment and more worryingly for us, probably aiming to take the High Heid'yin."

Gunnar gasped and Crash stepped slowly back toward the doorway white faced, opening the door just a crack as she leaned out and made a, 'tst, tst, tst' noise into the hallway. Seconds later, Gunnar's little 'mostly' furry friend 'C4' came swaggering into the room, looking like someone had become horribly drunk and tried building a cat out of burnt matchsticks. Surveying his kingdom, he eyed up the terrified looking Haggvar all now backing against the glass partition to get away from him. With determined and exaggerated swagger, Colin slunk across the side of the room toward Gunnar and rubbed himself briefly against the big man's leg as the tide of Haggvar slowly slid around the room toward the only exit door available, keeping as much distance as they could between them and what was, I'm pretty sure, a partially domesticated wildcat that had been interbred with one of those 'danger dogs' that you see being walked around council estates by men in ill fitting track suits.

C4 stared across at the swarm of Haggvar as they began edging toward the door, grinning as he squatted down into the pounce position ready to launch himself at the terrified Haggvar. The split second his arse left the floor on its forward trajectory, he was suddenly plucked out of the air by a large hand, Gunnar quickly clutching C4 to his chest as the swarm of Haggvar snatched the brief window of opportunity to get the fuck out of there before the cat-beast could escape his owner's clutches. A few vigorous strokes of the now incandescent cat followed before Gunnar, never taking his eyes off the defiant-looking Maulagg through the glass, stepped toward the door and shot-putted C4 out into the darkness, the sudden yell of a hell-demon being drowned out by the door being slammed behind it.

Teacher, who had been pointedly ignoring the whole event until the room was cleared of all beings that couldn't successfully tie a Windsor knot, straightened his suit jacket as his voice took on a sombre, more serious tone;

"Our most esteemed visitor has been nothing but accommodating about the unfortunate yet necessary isolation we've had to put in place to keep him from the 'pollution' of our resident Hagg population, and with respect, honour and dignity he has helped us as much as he can without a clear line of verbal communication."

Teacher was being as respectful as possible toward this Maulagg, who still stood staring at me through the glass. A large scar drove its way across its right eye, milking the lens slightly as it moved slowly toward me and pressed its small hand against the glass.

I jumped as Teacher suddenly placed a hand on my shoulder, turning me round gently to face him.

"However the Maulagg song is much more... 'Intricate' than the one sung by our resident Haggs, making it hard to decipher the images he obligingly tries to pass on to us. Which is where as luck would have it, I hoped you may be willing to help Mr Stewart."

"*YES, KAH'BAJ WILL TALK THIS ONE, YES?*" The Maulaggs words burst into my head, but not like the subtle whisper of the Haggs I'd already experienced. This was more like someone was kicking down the door in my head and stomping their shit-coated boots all over the freshly vacuumed frontal lobe.

"He.. Christ, he's loud... He says his name is 'Cabbage'? And that he will talk to me."

"*ACH! I AM MIGHTY KAH'BAJ. YOU NOT DISRESPECT MIGHTIEST KAH'BAJ*" His gaze swept across the room, staring at each person on the other side of the reinforced glass in turn, "*BUT YOU COME NOW, HELP KAH'BAJ, HELP CLAN YES?*"

I had to take a step back and ask for a chair when 'Cabbage' spoke. His voice felt like he was in my skull shouting out, like he was trying to use my ears as megaphones so that everyone could be told just how mighty he was.

Crash placed a chair under me as I sat back, and pulled one up for herself as Teacher moved across to a small table where he poured out some water into cups, "I know this is tough Angus, but your help here would be hugely helpful. The more we can learn from Mr 'Cabbage' here, the quicker we can start planning some kind of rescue of the Maulagg Heid'yin."

"*KAH'BAJ!*"

"She's quite correct-" Teacher handed me one of the cups before he too sat down beside us, "-I do understand your reticence when it comes to our operation here, we shan't stand in your way should you really wish to leave this all behind you, but bear in mind that it's not only this Maulagg's colony you would be helping here, but also you would be doing much to safeguard the population of Haggs that call this humble facility home. Plus of course the added safety we offer you against those who seek to harm you."

I knew he was talking about the shit-turds that had driven me off the road and damn near killed me. And as I looked at Cabbage behind the glass, who was now shaking his fist at a nearby potted plant, it must have been The Sons who had been responsible for the attack on the home of the Maulaggs.

"Okay look-" I stood up and walked back over toward the large window, "-I know you must be sick of me saying that I don't want to be a part of this world. I don't want to be shoved into the dimensional rift vagina of a large smiling ghoul in a suit again, I don't want to be run off the road by members of the periodic table and I sure as hell don't want angry little throw cushions using my head like the Sydney Opera House!" I felt a shake through the thick glass as Cabbage, clearly ignoring our conversation, tried to headbutt a fly that had landed on the other side of the screen.

"But if I'm really honest, what I DO want to do is get some kind of payback on those fuckers who smashed my car. I DO want to eat another one of those wonderful baguettes should it be offered any time about now, and I suppose I do want to help you stop the Sons from getting whatever fucked up 'gift' I have." I looked at Cabbage now sitting on the floor rubbing his forehead, "And I suppose more importantly, help however I can to protect this wee fella's family."

Teacher stood up from his chair and walked toward me, a large grin splitting his face while he held out his hand to shake mine. "I cannot thank you enough Mr Stewart, you will not regret this I can assure you!"

"KAH'BAJ THE MIGHTY NOT HAVE TIME. TAKE GREAT DISHONOUR COME HERE BUT YOU HELP, YES? MUST GO, NOW!."

An hour later we found ourselves back in the vehicle bay of the RUST facility, ready to again board the large off-road truck that had taken us there earlier. In the intervening time, we'd managed to debrief what information we could from the visiting 'Cabbage', during which I'd found that not only was it getting easier to communicate with the Maulagg, but I was able to better control the strength in which he broadcasted his voice between my ears.

It was agreed that while Teacher worked on finding more information about the Sons movements here at base, Gunnar, Crash, Dean and myself would head out with Cabbage and with him able to direct us through my gift of, 'brain-talkiness' or whatever the hell it was, we'd locate the nest and whatever was happening there that had him so enraged.

A short loading of equipment later, we were heading out past the old hospital at the edge of town with a decidedly unwashed Maulagg trying to stick his head out of the window like an excited Labrador.

The car turned at the junction toward Halkirk while I wriggled about in the back seat of the truck, trying to stop Cabbage from crushing my testicles while he was dancing around the window. Suddenly Gunnar's mobile phone started to ring. Watching this giant of a man trying to contort his already cramped body enough in the front passenger seat of the car to get his phone out of his pocket and to his ear entertained me for a good thirty seconds before his face turned serious and he motioned Dean to speed up.

"Right, wee update from the boss. Looks like our friendly eye in the sky says that we might have some company. A few more cars have been spotted pulling up in the area of what we believe is the Maulagg encampment, pretty safe to say we'll have Sons hanging all over the place."

I could see Crash and Dean straighten up as Gunnar hung up the phone, all three of them strapping various bits of equipment to themselves while Cabbage pulled his head out of the open window and moved to look through the gap in the seats toward the front windscreen.

"*WE CLOSE. KAH'BAJ LEAVE LOOKOUT HERE BUT NOT HERE NOW*" His shoulders seemed to stiffen slightly while I passed on what he'd said to the rest of the truck.

"Should I have something to protect myself with?" I said as I shuffled across to make space for Cabbage as he squatted down beside me, maybe a gun, some kind of taser thing in case they try to grab me again?"

The truck turned onto a rough farm track as Crash turned toward me.

"We can't give you a weapon yet Angus, not until we give you some training at the very least. The last thing we'd want is for you to tase your crotch by mistake while we're in the middle of a situation."

Gunnar chuckled from the front seat, "Although it would make a mighty fine distraction having you breakdance across the floor with your trousers soaked in piss."

Before long the truck pulled up behind two large black SUV's, parked in the middle of the single-track road ahead. Dean turned the engine off and we all climbed out, followed by Cabbage who leapt down and ran off ahead past the parked cars and the trees beyond.

"Stay between us for now Angus, best not go wandering off round here." Crash motioned for me to walk ahead of her and Dean as we followed behind Gunnar, making our way past the vehicle barrier and toward where Cabbage had raced ahead.

After a short walk along the hedge-lined road, we arrived at a small clearing between the trees, sunlight shining down through the overhead canopy onto a rough dug-out pit easily about a hundred feet wide, flanked by two large idle diggers and several men and women in dark clothing who all suddenly stopped what they were doing as we approached.

Suddenly Gunnar and Crash dashed forward to where they spotted Cabbage, frantically digging in the hole as two men in dark clothes moved down toward him from the opposite side of the pit.

"I'D ADVISE YOU STAY BACK!" Crash roared at the men as they scrambled down toward Cabbage, "YOU GO NEAR HIM, I GUARANTEE SHIT WON'T END WELL."

Gunnar made it down first, making a stand between Cabbage and the two black-clad men who now slid to a stop on the slope only ten feet away, only to then move cautiously toward him again as their hands moved slowly toward the inside of their jackets.

"STOP! HOLD POSITION! TEAMS DELTA AND CHARLIE SECURE PERIMETER." A loud male voice boomed over the pit whilst Gunnar and the two Sons faced off, Cabbage still digging furiously behind Gunnars' legs while we watched from the edge of the pit. Two duos of black suits suddenly appeared to our left and right and started to circle the upper lip of the pit, trying to cut off the road we'd just come in from. Crash tugged my arm as she started to move left whilst Dean moved out to the right, keeping their focus on the new Sons whilst Gunnar stood his ground in the middle of the pit.

I stumbled along behind Crash, all the while keeping my eyes on the team we were moving toward as they stopped and raised a hand to the inside of their coats. Everyone came to a stop, far enough away from each other that they couldn't be grabbed, but close enough that a hurried shot from a gun is sure to impact body mass of some kind.

"ONCE AGAIN IT SEEMS THAT RUST IS LATE TO THE PARTY!" The deep male voice boomed again, this time without the aid of what must have been a loudspeaker the first time we'd heard it. I recognised it instantly as its owner appeared from a large tent set up between the two diggers, it was Thorne, or as I liked to call him, 'Mr Shit-head who tied me to a fucking chair after hitting me with a truck'.

He strode down the hill into the pit, the arms of his long tan jacket spread wide as he made his way toward where Gunnar stood. He was still wearing a full-head mask, one of those Luchador-style ones you see on American wrestling shows. Fully black, with thin gold trim around the mouth and eyes. The twelve-year-old inside me couldn't help but think it was pretty cool looking, however the formerly concussed adult in me didn't know whether to laugh at what I was seeing or try and suplex the big arsehole as he came to a halt in front of Gunnar and Cabbage. His eyes turned to me for a moment and froze, his arms dropping to his sides as he stared at me for what felt like an age before turning his attention back toward Gunnar.

"Ah, big Bjornsonn! Good to see you old friend, keeping fine? Teacher's still treating you like his trained ape I see!" His eyes swept over to where Crash and I stood.

"And look! The always beautiful Miss Simpson there in tow with young Angus, who I hope has recovered well from the unfortunate accident?"

"ACCIDENT?" I roared at him as I moved toward him. Crash tried to grab my arm as I went to jump down the side of the pit, but I wriggled free and slid down the slope, coming to a stop just behind Gunnar and Cabbage.

"Hitting me with a lorry was an accident? And I suppose tying me to a chair in a warehouse while I was bleeding from the head was just an accident too, huh?" Gunnar's arm slammed into my chest as I moved forward. I may have slipped Crash's grasp, but my luck had run out if I thought I'd get past this massive paw.

I could see Thornes' eyes narrowing as he stared at me.

"I would ask that you show a little bit of respect boy, you don't know who you are speaking to here."

I was just about to reply with a poorly thought out wrestling based insult involving baby oil and latex when Gunnar cut me off;

"Do ye no' care what ye've done here Thorne?" He swept his hand around the pit, "You've ripped oot a whole nest. A WHOLE BLOODY NEST!" Gunnar's face was growing red as his anger rose, The large Luchador took a quick step back as the giant in front of him roared, before pulling out a gun from his pocket and quickly aiming it at Gunnars' chest.

"Whoah.. You need to calm down there big guy." He spoke calmly and slowly, as he looked across at both Dean and Crash on either side of the pit, "This is a legitimate dig site that we have approval to excavate. I can even show you the paperwork if that'll help diffuse this... Awkward situation."

Gunnar moved to stand in front of me but was stopped by Thorne lifting the gun toward his head.

"Oh, and while we're having this civil conversation, I will also have to request that Angus leave here with us." He looked toward me and smiled, "This is sadly non-negotiable."

Gunnar suddenly roared; "He's going nowhere with you or your lot. You're a danger to the lad Thorne, always have been and always will be.

You'll take the lad over my dead body." His deep growl of a voice rolled over the pit as Cabbage lifted his head from his furious digging to stare at Gunnar.

"I understand, I really do. But as much as it pains me, my old friend, I wish things could be different, honestly." Thornes' shoulders slumped slightly as he continued, the gun dipping slightly away from Gunnars' face, "But the lad will be coming with me. If it means putting you down first, I won't hesita.."

Suddenly I was pushed to the side as Cabbage leapt past me and landed on Thornes' chest, tearing and biting at his masked face. Before I could act, two large explosions of light erupted from either side of me, throwing the black-clad members of The Sons to the ground as Crash and Dean ran toward us. As I turned my attention back to Thorne, he'd managed to rip Cabbage off his face and had thrown him at Gunnar, knocking the big man to the side before pointing the gun at me.

"EVERYBODY FUCKING FREEZE!"

You always pretend in your head that if someone had a gun held against you, you'd pull off some quick grab-and-roll manoeuvre you'd seen someone perform in a movie before fending off the attacker with their weapon. But in reality, you just stand there frozen, trying not to fear-shit too heavily into your underpants until the bad man hopefully goes away.

The large man stared at me through the tattered shreds of his mask, blood dripping through some of the deeper gashes caused by Cabbage's attack.

"Heh... Okay, okay. I am fucking DONE being polite. You and I are going to take a nice walk back to the car-" He swung the gun around, motioning to the RUST members waiting to pounce, "-and we're going to leave here without any interference from anybody. DO I MAKE MYSELF

GOD-DAMN CLEAR?" As he yelled at us, he ripped off the shredded mask and threw it to the dusty ground beside him.

I knew his face. Through the cuts, the blood and the anger I recognised that face. I stumbled, unable to process just what I was seeing past the shaking gun barrel that pointed at me. The eyes that now stared furiously at me were the same shade of eyes that Uncle Huey had, the same shade of eyes that I had also inherited and the same shade of eyes that I had seen in countless photographs whilst growing up in Thurso.

"I can't go with you, I won't go with you. And I... I don't think you'd be willing to shoot me if I don't come along, would you?"

Thornes' eyes went dark and the gun lowered, he stepped backwards a couple of steps and ran a hand across his blood-covered face, lowering his head as if to regain his composure. Gunnar and Crash took this as a chance to try and rush him, but despite his injuries, Thorne was quicker and had the gun pointing back at me before they could take more than a step or two.

"I'm sorry Angus. Goddammit, I'm so very sorry, but we can't let RUST have the use of your gift. Come with me now, please, and I promise you nobody ends up getting hurt today."

I could feel my heart trying to hammer its way out of my chest as I looked up at the dark eyes staring along the length of the gun barrel pointing toward me. It felt like I couldn't open my mouth to speak, like my tongue was laying static against the bottom of my mouth. I slowly composed myself, and with my legs shaking I straightened Huey's jacket back across my shoulders.

"..I won't."

Thornes' expression didn't change.

"Then you have to understand this; Now that you're here I can't leave you with them, and I can't let them capture me. Do you understand what

I'm saying, Angus? Do you understand that you're asking me to make a choice that I swear to you I don't want to make? A choice that's out of my control, and that you will be fully responsible for?"

I could feel fresh anger rolling through me, how dare this man make demands of me, what right does he have? The only power he held over me was the barrel of that damned gun. The rage at his audacity raged through me, boiling over until I could feel my fingernails digging into my palms as I clenched my fists. The gun lowered slightly as Tho.. My father slowly moved closer.

"Angus, Son. I need you to underst-"

And that's when the rage exploded out of me, and I leapt at him.

There was a bright flash, and something slammed into my chest, throwing me backwards to land at the feet of Gunnar and Crash. I lay desperately trying to catch my breath, looking up at the bright sky as Dean suddenly leapt into view over my midriff. If only I could catch my damned breath If only I could tell what all the commotion and yelling was around me. If only I- Man, this was... This was uh. Shit, am I still wearing Huey's jacket? Hah, remember that time he stole eggs fro..

#

I just wanted to sleep. I felt like I had been for a while, but I kept hearing noises, kept feeling things grabbing me. Something lay heavy on my gut, wouldn't let me sleep and noise... A lot of noise, but muffled? It came and went though, I tried to open my eyes but only saw bright colours leaning over my face and then it all went dark again. Just wanted to sleep.

"Let me do my job dammit!"
"Gunnar, get us moving now!"

Never been so tired. Pain? Man, that weight on my chest was bad, someone needed to fix that. Could I fix that? Too tired, and I need to rest more.

"Are you wrong in the head? Get him the fuck off of there!"
"It's.. Something's working.."

I can't remember how long I've... Man, so tired. Caught a glimpse of... A dog? Am I at Finn's house? That beer, man... It.. Ugh, more pressure on my stom... Hot? God.. Burning. Please, stop the burni...

"This isn't working Dean, we're losing hi.."

Chapter Sixteen

A Fathers Betrayal

I woke up and tried to open my eyes. They'd never felt heavier, and when I tried to reach up to wipe away whatever gunk was glueing them together, my arm caught against a cable that seemed to be attached to my chest. I was shattered, my mouth was dry and I was having some trouble focusing on what was around me, and could only just make out a dark shape hurrying toward me from the right.

"Don't move about mate, you're doing alright but you're still not in the clear yet"

It was Dean's voice. So I must be back at RUST headquarters again. Things didn't seem right though; There wasn't the background noise of people and 'other things' rushing around, it seemed darker, with softer lighting showing off gold-rimmed paintings on the lavishly decorated burgundy walls and as my vision started to come back to me and I could get a better view of my surroundings, I was pretty sure that the hospital facilities at RUST didn't employ quite as many frills and throw pillows as part of their standard issue bedding sets.

"Where are we Dean? What's going on?" I leaned forward to look down at myself, almost naked apart from a small pair of pants that I was damned sure weren't the ones I had pulled on earlier that morning. Small pads with cables attached themselves to various parts of my torso, leading to a trolly of equipment that stood blinking at the side of my bed. My torso was heavily bandaged, but apart from some sharp, tear-inducing pain when I moved, I didn't seem to be in that bad of a state.

Dean didn't look up as he waved whatever Star Trek-inspired gadget this was over my head and torso, "You had a bad one there mate, not gonna lie to you. You need to rest up though okay? Still got a bit of healing to do before we can get you back home to RUST."

I grabbed his arm, the quick movement causing a jolt of pain to shoot from my stomach and across my chest. "Where am I Dean, what's happened now?"

He stopped and stared at me, closing the blinking device in his hand before setting it down on the bed.

"You got shot mate, pretty bad one too. We did all we could but we were losing you fast, we didn't have time to get you back to RUST for treatment, so we had to come to the nearest place we could get help-" He paused for a second, looking over his shoulder at the door in the far corner of the room that sat slightly ajar, his voice lowering as he continued, "-and the nearest place we could find it was here at the Selkie's Palace."

At that the door swung fully open, my breath catching in my throat as the Selkie walked into the room. Despite the pain, it was hard not to focus on her as she strode toward me, noticing that she was flanked by two tall thin and faceless men in dark suits, looking a lot like Mr Biscuits but without the fear-inducing aura that would make me want to go piss all in these clean tighty-whiteys. Both men glided toward the small bank of machines nearby, taking notes on clipboards as the Selkie swept toward me like a supermodel on a runway.

"AYE AYE LADS! How's the patient then?" She plonked down on the side of the bed hard enough that a jolt of pain shot up through my side, and a small machine on the cart beside the bed made a lot of angry beeping noises. "On the mend I bloody hope considering the fucking ton of work we had to do to keep your sweet little arse alive there!"

"He's doing much better, thank you. If you'd be so kind not to pull at that cable-" Dean seemed flustered as the Selkie tugged slowly at one of the monitors that had for some reason been glued pretty well to one of my nipples, "-But he does need a lot more rest before he's fit for questions."

"Ah yes, questions!" The Selkie rose off the bed in a wave of flowing silk and perfume so overpowering, that it caused more random machines to beep urgently as my blood supply seemingly relocated itself.

"So many horrible wee bloody questions needing to be asked and answered sadly, so many things needing to be... Sorted oot."

I tried to rise to my elbows to watch her as she moved around the bottom of the bed, only to be pushed back down again by Dean as he loomed over me again with that 'Captain Kirk Nokia' clutched in his hand.

Out of the corner of my eye, I noticed the two creature-men in suits glide toward the Selkie, one of whom subtly nodded at her as they moved to stand at her flanks.

"But there's plenty of time for having a fucking chinwag once you're healed up a bit pal!" The Selkie leaned forward, placing her hands on the bed as she stared at me, and I tried desperately to stare at her eyes and only her eyes as she leaned forward toward me.

"In fact, I insist that once you're fit to go home, you join me first for a private audience in my chambers so we can have a good chat about all this pish that you've gotten yourself into, eh?"

Her smile seemed sincere. Stunningly beautiful and doing nothing to stem the blood rush to my unmentionables, but with a hint of severity in there that made me think any refusal of the offer would not do well for my recuperation process.

I mumbled a quick "Yes" as she reached toward me, gently stroked my face and then strode out of the room flanked by her two skinny minions. I waited for the door to close before turning quickly toward Dean, another stab of pain reminding me why I probably shouldn't move so bloody fast right now.

"Dean, what the fuck is happening right now? My dad, he.. Shot me, didn't he? What about everyone else, Gunnar? Crash, Cabbage? Jesus, is everyone okay?"

Dean set down the Tricorder-style gadget on the small medical trolly and sat slowly on the side of the bed beside me; "Shit went south pretty quick mate. After Thorne.. Uh, shot you, Crash charged him and smashed the gun out of his hand, then Gunnar got his hands on him, and things took a much more smashy turn." Dean frowned at the screen of his tricorder before continuing, "He's in custody now, they managed to scrape up the bits that Gunnar hadn't stomped into mush and got him back to RUST, where I believe he's now staring at the bare four walls of a containment cell. If you hadn't jumped him and distracted the fucker, we'd never have been able to get him."

Dean pulled off his glasses, folded them up slowly and stuck them in his jacket pocket, "You however have had a rougher ride mate. We knew you'd bleed out before we got you to RUST and all my supplies were back in the truck. Before I could tell the big man you couldn't be moved, Gunnar had you scooped up like a baby and took off running back toward the road."

Dean stared at his hands, wringing them together in his lap slowly as he continued, "I'll be honest with you mate, things weren't good. Gunnar jumped in the driver's seat while I climbed in the back to take care of you, as much as I could given the bloody circumstances. We were just about to drive off when that 'Cabbage' fella dived in the back seat beside us right as Gunnar sunk the foot on the accelerator."

"Fuck.. Luckily we made it here to the Selkie in time then. Thank you Dean." I placed my hand on his shoulder, which he shrugged off before standing back up to fiddle with the machines beside me.

"Thing is mate, we didn't really make it here in time. I lost you Angus. I had my ruddy hands pressed against that hole the big fucker had put through you, and I lost you. I couldn't stop the bleeding, I couldn't stop you from slipping away... You were gone mate."

I lay back on the pillow, my head racing through what Dean was saying.

"Gone? You mean dead? Uh, PROPER DEAD? Like, 'tombstone over the head' dead? Right, oh, right, okay. That.. Seems to fit in with the rest of the fucking crazy I've gone through in the last 48 hours. So how am I now 'not' dead Dean, what the hell changed, and please don't tell me I'm some kind of immortal who now needs to chop off other immortals' heads with a sword or some shit."

"Nah mate, sadly Sean Connery couldn't be here wearing a ponytail to induct you into their ranks, so strictly a mortal you remain for now." He was wringing his hands again as he turned to me, "Like I said, we'd lost you. I tried... Everything I could mate, but you'd lost too much blood. I had to stop and let you go. And that's when Cabbage leapt onto you, grabbed you by the bloody face and touched his forehead against yours. I didn't know what in the blue fuck he was doing, I went to drag him off you in case he was trying to eat you or some shit, but the little fucker snapped at me, nearly took off my finger... And that's when your pulse came back."

Dean rubbed his face before continuing, "Mate, whatever the little bitey fucker was doing, it was keeping you alive. Your pulse was weak, but once we knew you were still there Gunnar drove like hell and got us here to

Selkie's palace. Cabbage hadn't moved, he stayed clung to you for dear bloody life the whole time, but he was failing badly as we wheeled you out of the truck and into the palace. By the time we got you to the palace medics, Cabbage had collapsed onto your chest unconscious, and I had no damned idea how to help him. A couple of Selkie's medics took him away. I haven't heard anything about him so far, but I've kept asking."

I lay back on the pillow, my tiredness suddenly washed away by the blast of pain that shot across my chest as Dean moved away to check the loudly bleeping machines. I had no idea how to go about processing everything that had just happened, let alone everything since I arrived back in Thurso. My own father! I hadn't seen him since I was a kid, my family always telling me that he just ran off and that I was better off without him, and yet here he was - a stereotypical 'bad guy' who had just shot his own abandoned son.

And hell, it wasn't even like he'd shot me to wound me, he'd shot me point-blank in the gut with the full intention of ending my life.

My throat swelled and I could feel tears starting to form, but they had no fucking right to! I didn't 'feel' anything for him, I mean yeah, I was shocked for sure that he had suddenly appeared back in my life in as dramatic a fashion as he had, and you're probably supposed to always love those who spawned you, but fuck - I felt nothing for the man, and knew that I hadn't done for a long time.

Although, as a few quick tears rolled down my cheeks, I thought that perhaps I wasn't being entirely truthful with myself. Maybe I did feel something for him. Maybe this burning knot in my chest wasn't entirely gunshot-related, maybe I did feel something. Something hot and painful and angry - something ready to explode out of me with a scream of rage...

I hated him. That was the only emotion I could find within me for Thorne. I hated the bastard, he was no kin of mine, and I was going to do whatever it took to make sure that bastard didn't see the light of day again.

"Dean, could you contact Teacher? Let him know I'm fit as soon as he needs me, whatever he needs I'm in."

Chapter Seventeen

Kiss From A Rose

I had no idea how long I had slept. The room was dark as I slowly opened my eyes, all of the wall lights had been dimmed and the blinds over the windows had all been pulled closed. I looked around and could see that Dean had passed out in another bed on my left-hand side, and as I looked over myself I could see that apart from one cable still attached to my arm, the rest had all been removed whilst I had been asleep. My chest wasn't as heavily bandaged as it had been before, and I was able to pull the dressing out slightly to get a look underneath.

It wasn't pretty, and I was pretty sure the shower I would be getting as soon as possible was going to look like the set of a low-budget slasher movie when I was done, but amazingly it didn't look at all like I had taken a bullet to the chest only shortly before.

I swung my legs over the edge of the bed, trying my best to ignore the dull ache spreading across my chest as I looked around for my clothes. Spotting a pile on a nearby chair topped with Hueys' jacket folded on top, I stumbled over and checked what was there, with the only thing missing being the t-shirt I had on earlier.

It wouldn't look quite as good now with a large calibre hole through the middle of it, however, it looked like whichever helpful soul that had taken the time to launder my clothes for me had replaced the holey shirt with one that read, "My dad shot me in the chest, and all I got was this lousy t-shirt".

I couldn't lie to myself, I kind of loved it.

I pulled the shirt over my head and quickly realised that when you suffer a recent chest trauma, raising your hands over your head to get arms through the sleeves of a fabulously insulting t-shirt is a damn near impossibility. Here I was, a grown man with his head now trapped in amongst some cheap cotton, unable to find the exit hole because my arms had slumped uselessly to my sides. I was just about to give up and just lay on the floor until Dean woke up and could help me, when two hands suddenly touched my sides, grabbing the shirt gently and pulling it down over my head. I gave out a sudden high-pitched yelp, realising I was face to face with the Selkie, standing about six inches away from me smiling as she guided my shirt down around my arms and chest.

"You shouldn't be up and about my boy-" she whispered as she straightened out the shoulders and sleeves of my new favourite t-shirt, "-The healing you've received was quite intensive, you need to give yourself time to recuperate."

Gone was the loud and jarring bark of a voice I'd heard her use before, replaced with a soft and reassuring tone. She helped me pull on Huey's jacket, moving behind me to hold it open to let me drop my arms into the sleeves. As I pulled the jacket up and onto myself, I suddenly felt her move close, her breath brushing against my ear as I struggled to remain calm.

"I'm sorry. I uh... I just wanted to find out what was happening with Cabbage. Wanted to make sure he was okay."

I whispered as the Selkie moved around me, her hand gliding across my shoulder as she moved across the room to look down at Dean, who was snoring peacefully on the other bed.

"Oh it's okay Angus, you don't have to talk so softly. Your friend here won't wake for another good few hours yet." I was right, her accent had completely gone. No longer did she sound like a 2am drunk in Glasgow angrily shouting at a dropped pakora, instead she now sounded like some kind of dignified elven queen.

"Ah, the voice." She smiled as she glided toward me, "I understand your look of confusion. The somewhat obnoxious voice is used for talking to the general population of fae or humans. For some reason being as brazen and loud as I can be seems to reassure others that they can trust me-" She placed her hand on my chest, a small smile crossing her face as she lifted her eyes to mine, "-and I find it makes people underestimate my intelligence when it comes to negotiating for things I want."

I could feel beads of sweat starting on my forehead as I tried to take a half step back to give myself a little bit of space between us,

"I just.. Please, I just want to make sure that Cabbage is okay. I don't know what he did, but he saved my life from what I understand. I need to make sure he's alright."

The Selkie stiffened slightly, her hands dropping slowly to clasp together in front of her.

"That's where we have a problem Angus, a problem of... Definition. If we define Kah'Baj as being physically alright, then yes, he's recovering well and should be able to head hom-" She paused briefly, "-Oh. Of course. He should be able to leave soon, to wherever he chooses to go. Mentally, and more importantly culturally however, he's going to experience some serious difficulties moving forward."

The Selkie sat down in one of the ornate chairs that were dotted around the large room and motioned that I should join her in the seat across.

"Haggvar culture is an overly complicated affair you see-" She crossed her legs toward me and laid her hands on her knee, "-I'm sure you've only really experienced the much friendlier herd that have managed to ingratiate themselves amongst the halls of RUST. The Maulaggs however are far different than their friendlier cousins, with a deeper and somewhat darker sense of 'code' that they expect their kin to adhere to."

Selkie raised a hand, and one of the suited man-things came bustling into the room with a tray, laying two glasses and a decanter down on a table beside us before making a swift exit.

"One of their strongest tenets is that interaction with humanity as a whole is strictly forbidden, punishable by expulsion from the clan and nest. This in itself is unthinkable for any Maulagg to suffer, however Kah'Baj broke this law to seek help with RUST after the attack on their home by the Sons." She paused briefly to pour the dark liquid from the decanter into the two glasses before continuing,

"Possibly, he would be allowed to defend himself with the other Maulagg tribes out there, considering the extent of destruction to his home nest, maybe even earn himself a reprieve. But alas, Kah'baj has sinned far worse than simply interacting with humanity-" Her expression saddened as she slowly looked up at me from her glass, "-He created a bond with a human, with you Angus. And in doing so, he is now facing the death penalty."

I was stunned. "Cabbage has... 'Bonded' with me? Do you mean like the bond where they supposedly gift you something? But I thought I already had a gift from my grandfather, what reason could Cabbage have to bond me?" I didn't feel any different and was pretty sure I didn't suddenly have any form of super-powered laser eyes or super strength. I tried to discreetly crush the arm of the chair with my hand to double-check and barely creased the plush reddened leather in the attempt.

"To save your life, he had to create a bond with you so that he could give you his energy, it was the only way of keeping you alive." She passed me one of the glasses, "Kah'Baj has done what we all assumed was unthinkable for a Maulagg; He's thrown away his life, his clan and his future all for the sake of making sure you stayed alive." The Selkie leaned forward, staring at me, "For some reason he deemed you worth more than his own life. What is it about you Angus that is so.. 'special'? What secrets do you have locked inside?"

I took a big drink from the glass just for the chance to break the serious bout of eye contact that was boring through me.

"I. I don't know what he was thinking, I'm just glad that he considered me worthy of saving at all. Can I please see him? I just want to make sure he's doing okay." I wondered if the whole 'Haggis telepathy' thing I had going now was in some way linked to why Cabbage had saved me, but I didn't think it wise to mention it to the Selkie. Probably best that I don't broadcast that I'm turning into some kind of mind reader, especially to the leader of a horde of literal monsters.

The Selkie stared at me a moment longer before a smile spread back across her face and she leaned back in her chair.

"Of course, we'll make sure you're the first person he sees when he regains consciousness." She stood quickly before gently stroking her hand down my shoulder. "Now, let's focus on your recovery, shall we?" She stood up from her chair, picking up the decanter in one hand and our two glasses in the pinched-together fingers of her other.

"I shan't have you recuperating in this, 'broom cupboard'-" Her eyes swept over the massive room covered in gold-rimmed paintings, "-I've had the staff prepare you a guest room with a bit more luxury. Come, I'll show you the way and make sure you're comfortably settled."

I stood from the chair and made to say it was probably best I stuck around with Dean until he woke up, but she was already gliding out of the open door at the far end of the room. I checked the pockets of my jacket to see if there was at least a pen and paper I could write a note with so that Dean didn't think I'd been kidnapped or something when he woke up, but finding nothing I could use I set off to follow my host through the darkened doorway.

We climbed two or three sets of stairs, passing by large, imposing figures in paintings, staring down at me with judging looks as I found it hard not to focus on the sway of the Selkie's body through the sheer nightdress that glided ahead of me. Despite everything that had happened over the last while, it was hard to focus on the shit show that had been my last couple of days as she swept along the corridor ahead of us, finally stopping at a large red door before motioning me to join her.

"Here we are, somewhere a bit more suited to your recuperation". She threw open the doors, showing a room filled with far more throw pillows and lace than is probably mentally healthy. I walked in following the Selkie, stepping over cushions that had clearly come wholesale from the 'Frills R Us' store as we made our way over to the large bed on the opposite side of the room. The place put me in mind of an upper market, Wild West boudoir, except more prone to shiny furnishings and a horrendous amount of scented potpourri.

"I'm sure you'll be more comfortable here" the Selkie sat down gently on the side of the bed, turning sideways toward me so that the material of her dress pulled tight against her. I couldn't help staring, and judging by the smile on her face she was having exactly the effect on me that she'd intended. "Please, come sit and let me take a good look at that injured chest of yours." She patted the bed beside her, and completely involuntarily my legs stumbled forward and plonked my incoherent self down on the mattress.

"I. Uh.. Huh, hahah, um I like what you've done with the place! Very cushiony!"

Fuck my life, 'Very cushiony'. What the hell? I'd clearly lost control of any semblance of rational thought, my brain turning to jelly under the shadow of the wonderfully heaving bosom gliding slowly toward me.

"Before you get settled for the evening, let's just have a quick look and see how you're healing, shall we?" The Selkies' hand slipped under my t-shirt and tried to lift it over my head seductively, but since the upper half of my body still was healing from the gunshot I'd suffered, I got stuck halfway out of the shirt and was left stumbling around like a half wrapped burrito, trying desperately to look cool whilst wriggling out of my cotton tortilla.

With one final tug I was free, throwing the shirt defiantly on the floor before turning toward the bed triumphant. The Selkie however was also on her feet, heading toward a doorway in the corner of the room.

"If you'll excuse me for a moment, I'm just going to slip into something a bit more... Comfortable."

I had no idea what on earth could be more comfortable than the almost transparent nightgown she was currently sporting, but I sure as hell was all for finding out. I lay down on the bed as she closed the door behind her, and spent the next few minutes trying out different poses to see which would be my most seductive. I settled for the classic, 'lean on the elbow, rest head on palm, raise one knee, lay other arm over the aforementioned knee, present crotch' approach that always seems to work on the telly and waited for the most beautiful woman I'd ever seen to walk back into the room.

I had no idea what the fuck was happening, or how the hell I'd gone from being shot by an absent father to now laying in bed waiting for a supermodel to hopefully come ravish me, but right now this was the bloody best thing that had happened to me since I arrived back in Thurso. Hell, this was perhaps the best thing to happen to me ever, and nothing was going to stop me from enjoying every bloody second of it, ghosties and bogeymen be damned.

I was just in the middle of having a deep, motivational talk with my manhood when a loud crashing sound came from the bathroom, followed by what sounded like two deep barks. I jumped off the bed and ran across to the door, deciding it probably wasn't wise to run in first to check, in case the Selkie was in the middle of a troublesome bowel movement.

"Is uh, everything okay in there? I thought I heard a dog maybe?" Whatever was fumbling around noisily in the bathroom suddenly stopped, before a shuffling sound could be heard behind the door.

"EVERYTHING'S FINE! NO NEED TO WORRY! *And the lesson here Selkie is to take off the fucking nightie before you change, goddamnit that cost me a fortune too, right through the lace and everything..*"

I moved slowly back to the bed, obviously concerned that she'd maybe hurt herself, but also praying that whatever had happened could be sorted with a quick antiseptic wipe and a plaster, so we could get back to the sexy-flirty stuff as soon as possible. Hey, I'm not ashamed to say that despite adversity and a near-miss with infanticide, I was still a young man whose movements were primarily dictated by how soon I can get my penis touched by a hand less well-known than my own.

"You sure I can't help at all, maybe come hold something for you? OH.. UH, I DON'T MEAN LIKE THAT, *shit*, I MEANT LIKE A JACKET

OR SOMETHING NOT ANYTHING BOOB, *shut the fuck up Angus! AGH!* I DIDN'T MEAN BOOB I MEANT JUST GENERAL THINGS LIKE SOAP OR TOILET ROLL *soap or fucking toilet roll? Kill me now* UH I'LL JUST BE WAITING HERE BY THE BED YOU TAKE YOUR TIME HAHA!"

I sat back on the bed and pulled a lavender-scented pillow over my face, hoping that I might smother myself enough that I'd suffer some short-term memory loss of perhaps the last twenty seconds or so.

Another minute passed, and I was just in the middle of trying to convince my manhood that everything was still very much sexy and that he should stick around and see how this all played out when the bathroom door crashed open, a wave of perfume-infused air flowing out from the darkened washroom beyond. The lights seemed to dim around me, and soft music started playing from all around the room. I stared across at the bathroom, quickly remembering to jump into my sexy pose as I waited for the Selkie to make her dramatic reappearance.

'FLOMP. FLOMP. "I hope that you've made yourself comfortable enough." FLOMP. FLOMP. "I have to admit to being a little bit-" FLOMP. "-Nervous.".

I like to think I'm somewhat adventurous when presented with alternative sexual experiences. I understand some people like to shove things in their pooping chutes, and all respect to them but the only thing that goes in my rear end is the occasional stray fingertip when the double-ply paper isn't up to the task. Or those people who like to get dressed up as a horse and then get repeatedly kicked in the genitals by a woman in a PVC suit. It's not for me, but if you want to have your hairy eggs smashed up by an angry size 6 Louboutin shoe, then you do you brother.

However, I have to admit that as I lay there frozen in terror whilst a large, mostly white-coloured seal with black patches flopped across the floor trying to get one of its front flippers wriggled free from the torn and formerly enticing negligee that trailed along beside it, my previous 'pep-talk' to my manhood had been for nothing, as my entire genitalia inverted itself and flew back up inside my body.

"HO! WHAT IN THE NAME OF FUCK!" I leapt backwards across the bed, grabbing a pillow on the way to clutch to my naked chest as way of protection from the large whiskered sea creature that was now staring at me, cocking its head like a dog does when it thinks it heard someone say 'Walkies'.
"JUST STAY THERE GOOD.. Uh... GOOD SEAL. I'm just going to walk slowly back toward the exit here, no reason to try and kill me or anything.."
The seal lowered its head, its shoulders slumped as it seemed to sink toward the floor. I was now pinned against the far wall, still clutching an ineffectual pillow as the large seal turned itself back toward the bathroom door.
"Are.. Are you okay?" I was still willing the molecules of my arse to somehow phase through the wall behind me so I could escape, but also I couldn't help but be a little concerned about the creature slightly entangled in the remains of an expensive nightie in front of me.
The seal turned toward me and lifted itself to its full height, its large, wet eyes staring at me as its mouth fell open into what looked like a large yawn.
"BWAH HAH HAHA!!" OH YOU SHOULD SEE THE LOOK ON YOUR FACE RIGHT NOW!" The seal keeled over onto its side, shaking with laughter as it pointed at me with one of its fin-arm things,

"Oh honey, the look on your face right now! You, my friend, are 'seal-liously' cute!" The seal continued laughing, presumably at its crap attempt at a pun while I slid along the wall toward my discarded shirt, struggling to pull it over myself whilst the Seal seemed to climb up into its hind... 'Fins' in front of me.

I'd like to think I'd seen my fair share if insanity over the last short days, but as I stood there while the seal's body started to bulge and shrink, bones poking out randomly against the skin as everything seemed to pop and click around inside the sack of seal skin that was also now changing colour, I was now considering that this indeed had taken the biscuit.

Within moments I was no longer faced with a large sea creature, but instead a fully naked Selkie, standing in front of me with her hands on her hips and a wicked smirk on her face. I tried to find words to express the horror I'd just witnessed, but between the shock of seeing, (what, a were-seal?) change in front of me into a fully naked version of the woman I'd been laying 'legs akimbo' for moments before, I could only mumble a collection of incoherent swear words as she twirled away from me and made her way back into the bathroom.

"I'm so sorry sweetie, I could NOT resist teasing you so!" I could hear the smile in her voice from the bathroom while I tried desperately to figure out where the key was for this damned bedroom door, "It's just that I feel it's important to show you my full self before we carried on getting to know one another." She swept back into the room wearing a new dressing gown, not quite as revealing sadly as the previous torn nightdress had been.

"So you're a.. Seal then?" I had quite the talent for stating the obvious, as she sat down on the bed and patted the mattress beside her. I walked over slowly and sat on the corner of the bed, balancing on one buttock in case I had to make a swift dash toward the window.

"It's a little more complicated than that I'm afraid, but in basic terms yes, that is indeed one aspect of who I am." Her hand landed gently on my leg, "You must have realised that for me to be the leader of the Fae, I too would be of a similar nature to those I rule?"

It made complete sense of course. I hadn't considered her true nature before this, doing most of my thinking with the smaller, feral brain residing below my belly button.

"Uh, yes. Of course. I'm sorry Selkie, I wasn't thinking straight it seemed. I apologise if I offended you with my reaction."

She stared at me for what felt like a long time, a small smile drawing over her face as she gave my leg a small squeeze.

"To be honest Angus, I'm quite impressed that your reaction is as calm as it is. I know that much of humanity has never been exposed to this world before, other than films featuring glittery vampires or goat-footed Scotsmen." She stood up and moved toward the door leading out to the hallway, pulling a key from an unseen pocket before opening the lock, "Alas though I will need to show you back to your former bed this evening, I have much to deal with tomorrow with this whole Maulagg affair." I followed her out the door and along the hallways toward the room I had been resting in before, before bumping into her as she stopped suddenly ahead of me.

"But on a personal note, I do hope despite the 'shock' you experienced we can perhaps further explore this, 'friendship' we're developing here?"

"I would... Like that very much Selikie." She smiled, taking my hand in hers before planting a small kiss on my cheek that made my face suddenly flush with heat.

"Then I will bid you goodnight Angus. You'll find your friend will be waking shortly from his short nap, I'll arrange communication with your colleagues at RUST and I'll leave word that you are both to be given full access to Kah'Baj when he becomes conscious." She swirled away down the hallway, "I look forward to our next meeting, perhaps you could join me for dinner tomorrow evening? Yes, I'll make the arrangements now." Then she turned a corner and was gone.

I entered the room where I had woken up before to find Dean still fast asleep, so rather than wake him I decided to try and grab myself a shower. It wasn't until I was stripped down in front of the massive seal had I realised that I still looked like I had done the back stroke over a butcher's floor. I stepped out of the room quietly to let Dean sleep and tried a couple of doors along the hallway before I found what looked like a simple shower room. I found an old bottle of shower gel in a cupboard and stripped off before stepping into the hot stream of water.

One shower later and I was feeling much better. The pain in my chest had lessened dramatically, and I had almost a full range of motion again in both arms. I stared at myself in the small mirror attached to the front of the shower room cabinet. Apart from a small flower pattern of scars, my gut looked surprisingly good considering it had accommodated a bullet only a short while earlier. I was just wondering if it would be inappropriate to ask the Selkie if I could have the bullet back as a keepsake when the door to the shower room burst open.

"There you are!" Dean seemed in a panic, "Quick, get your knickers on and let's get a move on. I don't want to hang about here any longer than is needed." He threw a clean shirt that he'd rustled up from somewhere onto the pile of clothes I'd left on the floor. I ignored it and instead grabbed my now blood-stained, 'My father shot me..' t-shirt. It was indeed now my favourite t-shirt in the world, the blood only added authenticity to it.

"We can't leave yet Dean, I need to find out what's happened to Cabbage first, make sure he's okay and what exactly he's done for me."

Dean stared at me for a long moment, "Pal, we might be wise to leave Cabbage alone for a while. What he's done... Well, it's ruddy unheard of. He's probably not going to be in the best humour for visitors for a good while."

"That's the thing Dean, I don't understand what he's done! The Selkie mentioned something about him bonding to me and giving me 'life', but I don't understand." I dressed quickly as he stood in the doorway in front of me, "I have no idea why I've survived a damned bullet to the chest, and walked away with little more than a pretty cool-looking scar. What exactly did he do Dean? What's happening here?"

Dean paused for a second before motioning me back to the large room where we'd first been taken. Closing the door behind us, he walked across the room and flopped into one of the large, cushioned chairs.

"So you've learned about the Haggvar and their gifts, yeah? How they can be gifted or taken by force?" I nodded as he continued, "Well, Cabbage has bloody given you something else entirely mate, something far more serious if what we understand from the old texts we have in the RUST archives is true. Essentially mate, he's shared his life force with you, and in doing so the two of you are now bloody linked to each other."

I was confused, "What do you mean his 'life force'? Like some kind of 'Obi-Wan Kenobi' bullshit?"

Dean suddenly glared at me as I slowly realised I'd just offended someone who was balls-deep in the Star Wars fandom. No rage matches that of a nerd who's just had their entire life's obsession questioned by someone who used to think Gandalf sat on the Jedi Council beside Yoda and Jean-Luc Picard.

"No, nothing like 'The Force' you ignorant swine! When you were laying there dying, he jumped on you and essentially poured his essence into you." Dean sat forward in his chair, "He's given you life pal, his life, or at least a share of it. It means that Cabbage has not only shortened his life span dramatically, but more importantly because of this connection he's made, you fellas are now somewhat inseparable."

I sat dumbstruck for a second. My life had not only been saved by the small angry 'haggis' that had been ripping at my father's face the last time I saw him, but he'd also given up part of his own life to extend mine. I had no way of understanding this, nor any idea how long he had given me, but I knew that I had to see him, to let him know that the sacrifice he had made meant everything to me.

I jumped up and made for the door, followed closely by Dean. "Whoah fella, where do you think you're going? We need to get the hell out of here. I don't want to be hanging around when the Selkie comes knocking looking for the debt to be repaid!"

I looked back at him as I pushed through the door to the hallway, "I uh... I think I paid some of that debt shortly ago Dean. Now let's go find Cabbage."

Dean stopped briefly before shooting me a 'you dirty dog' look, nodded and followed me out of the room into the brightly lit hallway I'd travelled along earlier with the Selkie, I opened the first door we came to and sure enough there was Cabbage, laying in what looked like an incubator surrounded by three of those tall faceless creatures in the suits.

The moment they saw us they stepped back, one of them made for the rear of the room and picked up a telephone, clearly calling for help dealing with our unexpected arrival.

I ran over to the side of the incubator-style box that held Cabbage inside. I could see that he was breathing, but he'd lost a lot of colour from his fur and face, the red streak now standing out even more noticeably against his flesh than it had before."

"*Cabbage? CABBAGE? Can you hear me?*" I could see Dean diverting the attention of the tall creatures around us, distracting them from asking why to their eyes I was just standing staring at the Haggvar lying prone in the transparent box, saying not a word.

"*Cabbage, please. I need to know that you're okay.*"

He remained motionless, the rise and fall of his chest being the only indication that he was still alive as I stood there waiting. I could see that the tall men with Dean were getting restless, pointing emphatically toward the exit door and trying their best to shove their way past my relentless antipodean friend as I stood by Cabbage's bed.

"*Kah.. Baj. My Name.. is KAH'BAJ!*" His eyes shot open, swinging round to stare at me angrily as he stirred awake within the chamber. "*You... You am alive? Mighty Kah'Baj save stinkskin from going in rotting hole?*"

It took me a second, but I figured he meant a grave rather than me being reinserted into Mr Biscuits expansive pooping chute, "*You did! I.. I can't thank you enough. I owe you my life! Why Cabbage, why would you do this for me?*"

He slumped down once more onto his bed, clearly still drained from whatever he'd done to keep me alive.

"*Not like you I do... But see you I do.*" He coughed, his whole body shaking as it racked through him, "*I.. See you and what you are. What you become with time, what other should have before cover-face hurt.*" I was confused, what othe.. Did he mean Huey? Did he.. Wait, 'cover-face'? The mask, my father...

"*Oh mighty Kah'baj*" I gave it my best effort to pronounce his name correctly, trying not to upset him as I continued, "*The other who was hurt, he was hurt by cover-face? Same cover face who hurt me?*"

His eyes were closing as he looked at me, rolling back slightly as he fell back into unconsciousness before he could answer.

I held myself back from slamming my fists into the incubator, Dean grabbed me and pulled me back toward the doorway as the tall men gathered in front of Cabbage, we exited out of the room and made our way back into the bright hallway.

"Dean, Cabbage knows something about Huey's death, I'm sure of it. I just need more time!" He stared at me with a concerned look on his face, looking around before pulling me over toward the wall and away from the doorway we'd just come from.

"What could he know mate? I don't think any Haggvar was there when he died, surely we'd have heard something by now if there had been?"

Before I could ask him about how secret the Maulaggs were, we were stopped by a crash from the room we'd just left, followed immediately by a loud alarm ringing throughout the building. Lights flashed as the noise rang through the hallway where suddenly two of those tall, suited creatures came rushing around the corner toward us.

"Please return to your room for safety, we are in a full building lockdown." the suited creatures ushered us back to the room we'd just left.

"What's going on?" I planted my feet, refusing to move against their insistence.

"Escape from quarantine facility, you must be isolated for own good." said one of the entities that kept moving slowly toward us.

"What's escaped? Is Cabbage okay? The Haggvar, is he okay?."

The entities continued to push forward. "The Haggvar. The Haggvar has escaped quarantine. The facility is on lockdown."

Dean and I stopped dead in our room, as the two suited ghouls closed and locked the door in front of us.

"Well, fuck."

After around a half hour of searching for any vents, unsecured windows or plain old holes we could escape through in our palatial jail cell, the main door swung open and the Selkie swept into the room, my attention momentarily snatched by the very low cut, light purple gown flowing around her fluidly as she walked toward us, her arms held open wide as she glided across the carpet.

"Ach, I'm awfa sorry for having your wee arses briefly locked up-" Stepping forward, she took a hand each from Dean and I, "-Please dinna think the worse of me! Just a wee security thingy to deal with, but all sorted now, and my two pals here that look like oversized thumbs will happily show you the way oot to your impatient pals in the car ootside."

The two thumb-heads in suits seemed to slump for a second before recomposing themselves to step forward and usher us toward the door, despite their lack of faces they gave off a vibe that they were a bit done with her shit if we were all perfectly honest with each other.

"NOW DINNA BE STRANGERS!" Selkie waved at us as we were shuffled out of the room, "And Angus, I'll be hoping to 'seal' you again real soon eh?"

The sound of her laughter as the door closed behind us somewhat distracted me from the questioning look I was getting from Dean while we were guided outside to the main courtyard, the doors unceremoniously slamming behind us as we stepped out into the sunlight.

Sitting in the courtyard ahead of us was the RUST 4x4 we'd used earlier, with a large ginger mountain trying to unfold himself from the driver's seat as he saw us. Out of the back seat jumped Crash, a huge smile on her face as she ran over and gave me a crushing hug.

"Fuck sake lad, never do that to us again-" She squeezed tighter, "-I was sure we'd lost you there." She shoved me back and stared at me with a hard look on her face, only softening when she saw I was wearing the best t-shirt in the whole fucking world.

"You are NOT allowed to play 'bullet sponge' ever again, do I make myself fucking clear?"

"Uh yeah, sure. Of course, I'll do my best to avoid getting shot in the chest again by any other relatives."

Her face softened briefly, a sad edge creeping into her eyes before she softly punched me on the shoulder and took off back to the truck. I was just about to follow her when suddenly I was lifted off my feet from behind and spun around in a full circle.

"Laddie! Ach hell, do ye understand the shite I'm going to get from Maggie over all this? She's going to break another bloody walking stick over my legs, I can bloody tell!" Gunnar boomed with laughter before setting me down hard on the ground, and walking me back to the car where I climbed into the seat beside Crash.

"We need to find Cabbage as soon as we can, I think he has information about what happened to Huey." The cab went quiet as everyone looked at me, Crash grabbed my hand and I turned to face her.

"You sure? You've been through a lot buddy, Cabbage too. Did he tell you this? Maybe you confused things?"

"I'm pretty confident he knows something, and I think it's linked to my da... Thorne. I think Thorne was involved in Huey's death." Everyone went quiet for a few seconds before Gunnar broke the mood.

"You best drive Dean-" Gunnar bellowed as he folded himself into the shotgun seat, "-I'm pretty sure my hands are seized up from gripping that bastarding steering wheel for the last however many hours of waiting we've had."

With that, Dean jumped into the driver's seat and we took off, heading back to RUST where I expected an unwanted family reunion awaited me.

"Should we have the red-bloods followed Mistress?" The Selkie's diminutive assistant looked out the window at the vehicle now pulling away from the Selkie's grounds.

"No need Mister Clutch, we know where they're going for now-" the Selkie poured herself a large drink from a nearby decanter, turning to look out the window at the retreating vehicle, "-And all other assets are in play."

Selkie turned away from the large window and moved back into the quiet room, sitting herself down in a large chair.

"Keep me updated on that Haggvars movements for now. Otherwise, let's just sit back and witness everything hopefully coming together in a 'beneficial' resolution, shall we?"

Chapter Eighteen

An Old Friend For Dinner

We'd been back at RUST for a short while now and had debriefed everything that had happened to Teacher before I was man-handled by Gunnar and Dean over to the nearby medical wing, where Fidget was waiting with a variety of sticky, wired pads that seemed needed to be attached to my hairiest places. There was a brief disturbance when the heart monitor I was attached to started going apeshit, but I wrote that off to the fact that C4 had unexpectedly jumped onto my crotch, stared at me malevolently for a second, slowly gathered three of the cables in his mouth then 'brain-shouted', "*MINE!*" before leaping across the room at full sprint, ripping the sticky pads off my chest and removing a good clump of hair and at least one nipple in the process.

Once I was all wired up again and they had every machine they could find that had an annoying recurring beep powered on, I was told to try and get some rest while they ran some more tests, but there was as much chance of that happening as there was that potted plant by the door getting away with giving me the finger whilst dry-humping the door frame. Was that the same bloody plant from when I first came here? I climbed off the bed to go investigate, maybe pour some hot coffee on the fucker when the door opened and in walked Crash.

"You out that bed already lad?" She bustled over and pushed me backwards toward the mattress, "If Dean catches you up and about, it's me that's going to get it in the neck from him for the foreseeable future!". I grabbed her forearm and stopped her, her hand lowering as I stared at her.

"C'mon Crash, I'm fit. Whatever the Selkie and her people did.. Hell, whatever Cabbage did has me fighting fit again. I need to... I think I need to see him." I sat on the edge of the bed, shuffling across to let Crash sit right beside me. She placed a hand on my knee and smiled, sighing as she looked toward the doorway ahead. Suddenly she was on her feet and darted over toward the potted plant that was giving her the double finger, booting it hard enough that it lifted and flew through the doorway and out into the hallway beyond.

"You sure about that Angus? You've gone through hell pal, not just physically but you must be pretty mentally fucked up too. At least let Dean and Fidget give you a good look over first, see if the Selkie's team missed anything, maybe they missed something important that they don't know about human physiology for all we know?"

I looked over at the jacket slung over a chair beside the bed. "I need answers. I need to know what happened to Huey, and if my... If Thorne was involved in some way." I stood up and moved to grab my new favouritest shirt in the whole world, pulling off the sticky diagnostic pads and trying not to yelp as I continued, "Cabbage said something strange before he passed out at the Selkie's palace, something about what I was to become, what the 'other' was to become before 'cover-face' hurt him? I think he meant Huey, and that he was hurt by someone with a covered face. That can only be Thorne, right?"

Crash seemed to lose colour in her face. Standing up quickly, she moved to the door, turning to face me before she ducked out of the room.

"I'll go and investigate, this could be a great lead Angus. I'll go run some checks through the computer and speak to Teacher. In the meantime, please get back into bed. Dean will already be on his way since you unplugged those pads." And as if it had been coordinated beforehand, Dean came barging into the room demanding to know what the hell was going on, just as Crash smiled at me and left.

A half-hour later after being reprimanded by a very insistent Australian and a somewhat heavily weaponized wood-elf to stay in my bed, Gunnar came into the room and plonked himself down in the chair, wearing what can only be described as the most rainbow-coloured tartan trews I'd ever seen in my life, accompanied by a very sparkly cuban heeled pair of shoes.

"You know this? I've never seen such a bloody hubbub in this place since you first showed your bloody face! If you're going to stick about lad, I'm going to invest in some more extensive life insurance!" He bellowed laughing, enough that I'm pretty sure that at least one of the machines attached to me registered some form of seismic activity taking place.

"So it seems that Crash has talked to Teacher and told him that you want to talk to Thorne, aye?"

"I do Gunnar. I think I really do. I need some answers."

"Right!" The massive ginger man climbed out of his chair and motioned for me to get up, pulling clumps of wires, (and a good few chest hairs too), off of me as I climbed off the bed.

"Boss-man says it's okay as long as you take it easy, and don't give away too much about how our investigations have played out so far, and to make sure of that I'll be coming as your chaperone!" He picked up my t-shirt jacket from the chair that he'd just sat on and threw them over to me, "And Dean seems confident that you've got nothing immediately wrong with you apart from your god-awful haircut that would force you to stay here, so it's me and you pal, off to see the wonderful Wizard of Oz!"

I paused, a lump forming in my throat as I pulled on my clothes. Did I want this? Did I want to see him after all this time, and after what he had done to me? I finished getting dressed and followed Gunnar out the door, the inner police officer shouting at me that I needed to follow this through, to put my personal feelings aside and find the answers to what happened to Huey. And while I was at it, to find out why that fucking potted plant seems to be moving through the facility just to keep insulting me.

Before long we arrived at a large metal door, Gunnar placed his hand on a large tablet device to the left of the doorway before a loud beep sounded and HAMMER's voice came out from the nearby wall speaker;

"GUNNAR BJORNSONN IDENTIFIED, ALONG WITH NEW AGENT, CUB STEWART" Gunnar rolled his eyes as the large door slowly opened ahead of us.

"He's not a 'cub' hammer, this isn't the 'Scouts'. He's a trainee field agent, which I suppose is a Scout of sorts." I couldn't help but wonder if HAMMER was opening the door slowly enough that it would annoy Gunnar, but also to give him more time to insult us.

"INDEED. AND MAY I SAY YOU MAKE A LOVELY COUPLE. MIGHT I SUGGEST SOMEWHERE MORE ROMANTIC FOR YOUR FIRST DATE THAN AN UNDERGROUND HOLDING CELL? PERHAPS A CAFE?"

Gunnar laughed as the door finally opened enough for us to squeeze through. "Ignore the electronic bastard, he's just trying to get a rise out of us. Come on lad, let's go and get this over with."

We made it through the door just as the theme song from the 70's tv show, 'The Love Boat' started playing through the speaker. Gunnar gave the overheard camera the finger and we moved on deeper into the holding area.

I couldn't help but be reminded of the movie, 'The Silence of the Lambs' as we moved along the dark bricked walls, clear glass-fronted cells lined up on either side much like the one that housed Hannibal Lecter in the film. All these cells were empty apart from the one at the far end on the left, Thorne coming into view as we stepped in front of the perspex-style door and wall keeping him contained within.

He was sitting on a bench at the back of the small room, hunched over holding the remains of the mask he'd been wearing before Cabbage had shredded it during his attack, his head bowed down in darkness as we approached. Gunnar grabbed two chairs from a stack nearby so that we could sit and face the man who'd tried to kill me earlier. We sat down and stared through the glass, all of us in silence for a few long minutes before Thorne raised his head and looked back at me, his eyes wide as he quickly got to his feet and stepped up to stand at the glass partition that divided us.

"I'm glad you're okay Angus. You being hurt was not my intention, but when you leapt at me... Well, it was self defence and nothing more. I hope you can understand." He placed his hand against the glass between us.

I sat forward in my chair, crossing my arms over my lap as I stared at my father, the overheard lights throwing shade over his face as he looked down at me. "Truthfully? No, I don't. I really don't." I tucked my hands between my thighs, trying to hide the slight shaking. "I do have questions though. So if you don't mind, can we at least try and be adults here and talk?"

He lowered his head for a second, a small smirk spreading across his face. "Talking seems to be the only thing I can do in this god-forsaken place. Do you know they won't even give me a phone call?" He turned quickly, raising his hands and throwing his head up to face the overheard light, "I NEED TO SPEAK TO MY LAWYER THIS INSTANT!" Turning his attention back to me I could see he was quietly laughing, the smile on his face widening like this was all some kind of joke to him, that all if this meant nothing.

I leaned back as he returned to the wooden bench in his cell. "I can't help but be curious, why the name 'Thorne'? What was wrong with plain old Liam Stewart, does it not sound 'cool' enough? Do you need some kind of nickname when you take up a career in murdering people?"

He looked up, staring at me with cold eyes as he replied, "My boy, you rea-"

"I'm NOT your boy." my fists clenched as I tried with all my might to remain calm, "You have no right. Simply 'Angus' or I'll settle for 'Mr Stewart', but not 'My Boy'. Understood?"

I saw a momentary flash of anger in his eyes before the cold smile returned, "Understood. My apologies of course, 'Mr Stewart'." He sat upright, leaning his head back against the wall behind him as he spoke.

"You know, you really should learn more about your family history Angus-" He spread his arms out wide as he spoke, "-Our past is a rich tapestry that defines who we are! My mother, your grandmother, took great lengths to make sure Huey and I knew where we came from."

"I know enough Thorne. Like that name, It took me a minute to figure it out, it came from my grandmother, didn't it?"

Thorne smiled, "Indeed! Her surname was originally Thorne before she married into that fool Stewart Clan. She was the daughter of the great Edison Thorne, the man who is responsible for the damned 'gift' you and my brother were unfairly given." He stood up, moving slowly to stand before the cell door between us.

"I am my maternal grandfather's descendant, I have no loyalty to the Stewarts nor their theft of what should have been mine by rights." Before I could speak he continued, "By what natural right does the gift pass me only to present in you and Huey? What did I do to deserve this, what did I do wrong as a child that nature deemed it necessary to punish me and reward my brother and my damned offspring before me?" His fist slammed against the glass separating us.

"BY WHAT RIGHT SHOULD I BE DENIED TAKING WHAT IS OWED ME? Hell, if that means ripping a nest of these, 'vermin' you seem to hold in such high regard out of the ground, then that seems only fair in my eyes." He spun to look at the security cameras that pointed down from the ceiling, "But not to those you surround yourself with!" Thorne pressed his finger against the glass, pointing toward Gunnar as he spun away and moved back to the bench at the back of the cell. "And if it means punishing those who took from me what by rights is mine, then I feel fully justified to do so."

I was out of my seat now, standing as close to the glass as I could, staring at the spiteful prick in front of me as he stood and moved to stand inches away on the other side of the glass wall. "You blame me and Huey for you not being gifted?" I tore open my new favourite shirt to show him the scarring that remained from the shooting, "You try to kill your only son because you didn't get whatever the FUCK I have? Don't you care at all, even a small part for the loss of your brother or for what you've done to me? Your son?"

He lifted his head and smiled again, staring at me with his darkened eyes. "You assume I don't care, because I haven't been around?" Boy, you have no idea the resources I've put in place to keep you safe from these RUST goons until I could ascertain how exactly your gift was going to present itself." He returned to his seat, slumping back against the brick wall behind him as he continued, "Have you heard much from your girlfriend, sorry, 'ex-girlfriend' Stacey since you came north? Has she been acting somewhat, irrational at all?" My eyes widened, thinking back to the multiple missed calls and the trouble she had caused about me leaving for Thurso, "Son, I placed Stacey... Sorry, 'Agent Crawford' with you. Her job was to monitor your movements, keep an 'intimate' eye on any changes you may exhibit as the gift manifested itself and ultimately, do what she could to discourage you from coming north where RUST could get its hands on you."

I sat back dumbstruck, thinking back to how she had sobbed and screamed at me to not be selfish and leave her alone when I planned to come north for the funeral. All that had been an act? Because hell, the things she did to me in private leading up to this trip should earn her some kind of Academy Award in the secret agent circles, or at least a financially rewarding career on the internets favourite 'Hub'.

"And what about your work partner Keith? You think he caused all that shit with your work by mistake? You think that the sleaze investigation into the pair of you has come about purely by unluckly chance?" Thorne stood again and walked up to the glass, staring down at me as I sat in my chair shocked, "He's one of ours boy, he's been kicking up shit so that you'd get bogged down in paperwork and investigations, all designed to keep you where you bloody were!" He spun around with his arms in the air, his face raised to the roof as he continued, "You could have stayed where the hell you were, safe and sound and under my watch until such time that we saw what you were becoming. But no, you had to come north against EVERYTHING we'd done to keep you there, and end up getting tangled up with these... Bastards." His gaze swung toward Gunnar, sitting completely still beside me, refusing to respond to the deliberate provocation from Thorne.

I stood up and stared directly at the man now staring at me from the other side of the glass, "This is ridiculous. You can't expect me to believe that you care enough about my movements to have put bloody spies in my life! Stacey, how the hell.. And Keith! There's no bloody way you've manipulated one of your 'Sons' into the police force just to control me, or to stop me finding out more about Huey's death." I glared at him, trying my best to control the anger that swept through me, "There's no way damned way you care that much about me Thorne."

He stepped back from the glass and returned to his seat, once more leaning forward to stare at the floor beneath his now clenched fists. "If I didn't care son, I wouldn't have put all of this in place to keep you safe and secured. Good god, you're just like your mother, you can't help but pick and pick the scab until the damned blood is flowing again."

Rage burst through me as I slammed my fist against the glass, "You do NOT get to talk about my mother!"

He stood once more, walking over to the glass so that he was mere inches from me, "Your mother was just like you boy. She loved to question everything, dig her nose into places it shouldn't go. She couldn't just be happy with the life I had given her, couldn't stop asking bloody questions about my work and why I had to keep it so secretive." A smile crawled its way slowly across his face as he stared at me, "And look where all that curiosity got her eh? She lost her husband, lost her mind and lost herself into the bottom of a vodka bottle."

I launched myself at the glass, punching as hard as I could to smash that gloating face that stared back at me. Gunnar grabbed me from behind, pulling me out toward the exit door that had already opened for us. I screamed with rage as I was dragged away, fighting against the giant hands that gripped me so that I could get back and smash the smile off that bastard's face.

"Your scream, where have I heard that before I wonder... " Thorne smiled as he stared along the corridor toward me. "Ah yes, I heard a scream much like it out on the hills a week back. Terribly dangerous to be climbing when you're out by yourself.. Never know what horrible fate may befall you."

I stared at him as Gunnar dragged me out of the room and the door slammed closed behind us. He killed Huey, I was sure of it now. Hearing the faint laughter coming from Thorne through the heavy door, I knew then and there that I would do everything in my power to make him pay, even if it was just making sure he saw only the inside of a dark cell for the rest of his fucking days. I reached my hand out to touch the large door just as Gunnar spun me around and crouched down to face me.

"Son, let's concentrate on saving the Maulaggs first, then we'll have plenty of time to make sure Thorne sees justice." I glared over his shoulder at the jail door as HAMMER confirmed that full lockdown was back in place. I stood for a few moments clenching my fists, trying to get my breathing and heart rate back under control, before we finally turned away back toward the main facility and headed toward Teacher's office to discuss what was going to happen next.

#

After a while talking with the facilities chief, Gunnar and I headed out and made our way to the bar, where Koba placed two large coffees down on the bar top in front of us. 'The Rusty Cog'[10] was quiet today so Gunnar and I had pretty much his full attention the moment we'd walked in and took a seat together, which meant that the moment one cup was emptied it was soon magically replaced with a full one with very little pause in between.

"So you lads had a bit of a shit show I hear!" Koba tried vainly to cram his massive hand into a pint glass with a drying towel as he stared at us both with those slightly too far-apart eyes of his. "Word has it that one of you lads got pegged by Thorne?"

I was just about to blurt out the whole tale when Gunnar placed a hand gently on my leg, clearly cautioning me to watch what I said.

"I don't know what pish you've been hearing Koba, does it look like either of us has a hole in us? I swear this place is like a bloody hen house!"

Koba smiled as he spat in the glass and continued to ineffectively wipe it with the towel, making me put my coffee cup back on the bar top wondering how it had been cleaned before I had drank from it.

"Yeah Gunnar, maybe just the hens clucking mate, nothing to see here hey?" He smirked as he turned his attention back to us from the saliva-coated glass in his hand, "Funny though when the hens clucking are ones from the Selkie's private roost though.." Koba winked at me and

---

[10] Gunnar had taken great delight earlier that day regaling the story about why the bar was called 'The Rusty Cog'. Turns out the place had never really had an official name for long enough, until one day the barman Koba had bent over to pick up a box of Prawn Cocktail crisps that had fallen to the floor, causing the back end of his ill fitting trousers to rip open and expose his 'Gentleman's Passage' to two off-duty admin staff who had each been enjoying a small Strawberry Daiquiri at the other side of the bar. 'The Rusty Cog' was one of the more polite descriptions of the anatomical horror that had faced them both that evening.

turned away to serve a couple of RUST staff who'd just walked in, leaving Gunnar and me a moment away from his ever-hovering ear.

"Don't mind him laddie, that's a critter that loves a bit of gossip." Gunnar took a big swig from his frothy latte, leaving a nice foam moustache on top of his normal moustache. "He means no harm, and he's a handy man to know too. Got his hefty sausage fingers in a lot o' pies does auld Koba. Need any information in a hurry, then he's usually the one you come get a gossip with."

"So what happens next to him, my father? Does he just stay here locked up?"

"No lad, he'll be shipped south to the holding facility where we keep all the uh, 'beastie' related bad things, probably be locked away for a long while whilst they try and dig oot whatever they can from his heid." Gunnar finished off his coffee and placed the empty cup back on the bar. "It's not far from where you live actually, a wee village called Oldmeldrum, nae too far from Aberdeen. There's a distillery there that's been around since the 1700s, lovely dram if I may say so too, especially the twelve-year-old."

He waved at Koba who nodded briefly before pulling out two new cups, "But the building itself is only a cover for a holding facility that's about the same age. Buried under their warehouses is a secure unit. It's officially called 'SCAR-T11', but that disnae roll of the tongue now, does it?" Gunnar smiled before turning his attention back to the cup in his hands. "We just call it 'The SCAR' or 'Warehouse Five', seems right with it being a distillery and all."

I finished off my coffee and waved away Koba when he offered me another. I wanted to know more about what was going to happen to Thorne. Did I want to see him again before he was shipped out, could I hold my temper? My stomach knotted at the thought. Well, that or the gunshot wound that had mysteriously healed up was giving me gyp. There were so many more things I wanted to ask him, and with him being locked up in this place, this was probably my best chance to do it before he was locked away in a secret prison under a bloody whisky distillery. But frankly after what had happened the first time we'd tried face to face, I wasn't sure I could maintain the 'professional calm front' that my training had given me in Aberdeen.

I wondered if maybe I could go for another coffee as I looked across the bar toward Koba before something over at the far side of the bar caught my eye. Staring in amazement, I watched as the potted plant by the far door awkwardly wiggled itself round to face me before throwing up the fingers in a botanically violent fashion. I was just about to run over and punt it against the wall when the room suddenly and violently shook all around us, throwing me to the ground as glasses and bottles spilt from the shelves and smashed on the floor. The screens around the bar that acted as windows showing scenic views of the Highlands suddenly switched to solid red, flashing 'Emergency Lockdown' as the main doors leading into the bar slammed shut.

Gunnar stumbled to his feet, grabbing onto the stool as he climbed back to his feet and raced to a computer panel near the main bar door.

"It's shut down, I canna override from here." His face darkened as he continued to work with the panel. "It's got to be the holding cells, they're only two rooms away from here". Gunnar slammed his fist into the panel before moving to the door to try and pry them apart with his hands.

"Don't waste your time man-" Koba was back on his feet and leaping over the bar, "-That door is going nowhere fast. Quick, follow me."

I could hear shouting and what sounded like gunshots as I ran after Gunnar, following Koba through a large swinging door into the still flickering lights of the kitchen area. Ducking down behind the large steel ovens, he pulled open a hatch door and led us down into the cellar below. I looked up to see Gunnar scowling slightly as he looked around at some of the boxes stacked up against the walls around us, Koba doing his best to hurry us forward.

He grinned at Gunnar as we made our way to the back of the room, "A lot of our customers have very, 'specific' tastes that RUST regulations don't approve coming through the delivery doors" Koba moved aside a large stack of boxes revealing a brick wall, "So we've had to get a bit creative on getting things in and out of here. I'm sure I can count on your discretion gents?"

Gunnar reluctantly nodded, bringing a small grin to Koba's face as he tapped the brickwork behind him. Several of the bricks suddenly slid back and then upwards, revealing a tunnel leading into darkness.

"Follow this tunnel and take the first left and then the first right, and this is important; Take no other turns than those. You'll eventually come to a dead-end wall with a single red brick. Tap the brick and a door will open out to the parking garage." Koba stepped in front of us as we moved forward to the tunnel, staring up at the large red-haired man ahead of me. "You will not take any other turns, are we clear?"

"Deadly," muttered Gunnar, before pulling out a small torch from one of his pockets and motioning me to follow him into the tunnel. We made it a few steps before the sounds of the brickwork shifting behind us made it clear that we had no going back the way we came.

The tunnel was barely wide enough for Gunnar to fit, so we didn't make very fast time as we navigated the first left turn before arriving at the next right turn. Gunnar seemed to hesitate, looking ahead down the tunnel toward a distant light source, seemingly blinking intermittently as we stared down at it. Gunnar moved a half step forward, clearly eager to head straight on and investigate what Koba was so keen on hiding. With a grunt, he turned right and we made our way toward the dead-end wall ahead.

Sure enough, a single red block stood out from the brickwork wall, and moments after Gunnar pressed it into a recess, the bricks started to shift and an opening appeared leading out to the carport.

We rushed out into a gap behind two black vans, running around the vehicles just as ahead of us Thorne swung a RUST security officer into the wall beside him, the man instantly crumpling to the floor.

"STOP! DON'T FUCKING MOVE!" Gunnar's voice bellowed around the walls of the large vehicle bay. Thorne froze briefly, turning his head slightly to smile before jumping into the passenger seat of an idling black SUV, the wheels spinning on the painted floors as it sped off up the ramp leading out toward the exit at Thurso Harbour.

Gunnar and I ran across toward the two security guards, checking they were still breathing before Gunnar grabbed a set of keys and sprinted over to one of the nearby RUST vehicles.

I ran across and dived into the passenger seat beside him, buckling myself in as he jammed the keys in the ignition and twisted. Nothing happened. Gunnar cursed and twisted the keys again, but still no response from the engine. We quickly unbuckled and ran to the next truck in line, where Gunnar fumbled with the set of keys before jamming them into the ignition, but again there was no response from the engine as Gunnar furiously twisted the key over and over.

We popped open the bonnet of the truck and tore it open, straight away noticing the sheared cables running through the engine bay. Checking the first vehicle also had the same results, somebody had taken the time to disable all the vehicles in the motor bay.

Gunnar smashed his fists down on the bonnet of the car, causing two large dents as he roared with rage. I stepped back as he continued to pound on the truck, confused as to why he'd suddenly snapped so dramatically, his fists crumpling the metal below as he raged on.

Finally, his anger seemed to exhaust itself. He slumped down to the ground with his back against the now destroyed engine bay, his fists dripping dark red blood onto the grey-painted floor below him.

"Did you see who was driving Angus? Did you see her?"

"I... I didn't. Who was it?

Gunnar pushed himself to his feet and stared toward the exit ramp, his shoulders slumping as he turned away and moved toward the now-open security doors.

"It was Crash, she's in league with the Owls."

I froze in place. "Crash? It can't be her, it must just be someone who looks like her!"

"She stared at me before they sped off lad, it's Crash for sure. Come on, let's go find the others."

Scott Taylor

Chapter Nineteen

Hammer & Nails

Engineers were still working on getting the power back to full capacity as we sat around the large table in the meeting room, Dean administering to Gunnar's hands to my left while Teacher moved to the flickering wall monitor at the front of the room.

"It looks like this was a very well pre-planned attack on our facility. From what we can tell all security systems have been taken offline and more importantly, the HAMMER system is down, so we're still awaiting a full report of all that's happened."

"What was Crash's involvement Teacher, did you know that she was involved with these bastards?" Gunnar grunted as Dean stitched a large cut on his left hand. "How the hell could we not know?"

Teacher paused, staring at Gunnar for a long second before dropping his eyes to the table in front of him. "Gunnar, I'm as much in the dark as you are about her involvement in all this. Perhaps she's being forced, or has been taken prisoner by Thorne, we just don't know." Gunnar was about to interrupt before Teacher cut him off, "But I shall not allow us to speculate until more details are available. As it stands, we give her the benefit of the doubt and work under the assumption she's being manipulated or controlled somehow."

Gunnar started to rise from his chair, his face burning red as he glared at Teacher. I jumped as Teacher's fists suddenly slammed the table, making Gunnar freeze where he stood,

"AM I MAKING MYSELF CLEAR?"

Despite the clear fury in his eyes, Gunnar lowered himself back into his seat, letting Dean continue his ministrations while he stared back at the stern-faced administrator.

Teacher recomposed himself, "Initial reports show that there were explosive charges set at different structural points around the holding cells, security control, and the data processing and AI facility." Teacher turned and clicked on the large screen behind him, showing four camera feeds from what I assumed were different parts of the facility.

"Luckily as a security precaution, our cameras record all data into a server in a remote location, which means that all footage was immune from this attack". Teacher tapped out something on the keyboard in front of him, changing the camera feeds to different time stamps. As the footage rolled, each camera taking its turn to play out its chosen section of footage, we watched as Crash appeared in the shot each time, spending time pulling a section of wall panel open and then fastening something behind before resealing the panel."

It appears that these explosive charges were planted over the space of three months, however, the system hadn't flagged anything suspicious due to there being a logged work pass in place each time." Teacher looked at us all in turn. "Crash knew that the system wouldn't flag her, but she must have also known that when all was said and done, we would know it was her that planted the explosives."

"How the hell did she get explosives into RUST? Surely we'd notice her taking blocks of C4 out of her lunch box!"

"She didn't" Teacher clicked a button and the screens switched again, showing the blue-headed men I'd seen before at Huey's ceremony. "The Blues took them in under their ceremonial robes during the funeral gathering. Diplomacy forbids us to search our Fae guests if they come under a banner of mourning, and considering we have little to no idea of how they look under those large shawls, they could have smuggled in any assortment of contraband into the facility right under our noses." The cameras switched angles again, showing a darkened corridor which I recognised from when I first met Cabbage, "They met with someone, presumably Crash in a bit of a camera dark zone that she knew of. We can only assume that she took delivery of whichever explosive they had, and hid it before attending the ceremony shortly after.

The only sound from the room was the tap of keys as Teacher pulled up a new camera feed. Footage from the detention cells appeared, showing the room shaking dramatically, dust flying around as Crash ran into the scene, quickly taking a small handheld device to Thornes' cell door moments before it sprang open. He grabbed her by the shoulder in what looked like a familiar gesture before they both turned and ran toward the camera and the exit door below it. Crash stopped briefly and stared directly into the camera. It felt almost like she was staring at us as we all sat watching the large screen before a hand appeared and pulled her out of sight of the camera as the screen went blank.

Gunnar leaned forward and pointed at Teacher, "So if they went to all this hassle to get explodey shit in place for him being arrested, then him being arrested must have been part of their plan. But why? What the hell was the purpose of it?"

Teacher tapped his keyboard once more and a new camera popped up on the screen showing what looked like a server room. Papers were scattered all over the floor, desks were overturned and more importantly, a large metal door at the rear of the room was hanging loose on one hinge.

"The data centre backs onto the holding area, and all security doors between the two allowed access to Crash's identity card. It seems their main target was our servers, and more importantly the theft of our H.A.M.M.E.R. AI System." Teacher sat down at the chair and leaned back, steepling his fingers in front of him as his chair spun slowly to look at the screen behind him.

"Access to the HAMMER systems needs two people, Crash needed an accomplice to help with the data core removal. With the evidence in front of us, it seems that the capture of Thorne and his subsequent detention here was all part of their plan."

"Wait, so shooting me was part of a damned plan to get locked up here?" Teacher lifted his hand to stop me,

"No, I don't believe it was at all. I believe that Thorne intended to be taken into custody, hence the very public, daytime extraction of the nest to get us out there. I do however believe that the gunshot you received was purely reactionary, and not part of his plan whatsoever."

Teacher continued, "Either way, we now have somewhat of a dilemma. With access to HAMMER, the Sons now have all RUST data on personnel, procedures and more importantly, all of our data on every Fae species we've encountered. Information they've craved for a long time now."

"How bad is that?" I asked, wondering why everyone else in the room seemed so concerned, "What can they use that information for?"

"With this information Mr Stewart, they can not only find every nest, encampment and burrow of every species of Fae that we've documented in Scotland so far, but also how to control, destroy or abuse them for profit." Teacher pressed the keyboard and the large screen went dark, "Basically gentlemen, they've taken the keys to the kingdom."

I spent the next few days back at the hotel while RUST worked on rebuilding their systems and repairing the damage caused by my so-called father and Crash. I had occasional lunch visits from Dean, who told me that Gunnar had pretty much taken to his quarters and was ignoring everyone. I spent some time with the family who, thanks to Maggie, all had been given a suitable explanation for why I was hanging around the town for longer than they expected, and checked in with everything down south, where it seems RUST had also been at work securing my rented flat, smoothing the paperwork and questions with the senior management at the Police Headquarters and redirecting my ex-girlfriends plans to jump in a car to travel north and give me a solid piece of her mind.

It was a wonderful sunny day, and I had just left Finn's house after trying some of his new 'alcohol-free' recipe for beers. Despite feeling like I needed to shave my tongue, I didn't come out of it too badly I thought. I'd also managed to strike up a deal for Finn to supply stock of his more popular lagers to be stocked and sold at The Rusty Cog. In particular, Koba had been almost literally knocked over by the 'Mazarooni IPA' that Finn had been producing, and straight away had placed a recurring order of upwards of fifteen cases. With a little bit of Administrative help from Teacher, Finn thought he was selling the ale to a new artisanal pop-up bar that had just opened down in Inverness, and had been delighted with the photo I'd shown him of the beer stocked behind the bar of the Rusty Cog, with as many 'mostly' human passing patrons around so that it looked like a regular pub.

I was just passing the new franchise monstrosity of a hotel recently built in the town as I walked down the hill from Finn's when I stopped and quickly pulled my wallet out of my back pocket. Fumbling with the clasp, I opened the tattered leather partition inside and there it was, the card that Silver had left for me the night she appeared in my hotel room. If anyone could give us some insight into Thorne's movements and where Cabbage had ended up, she could be our best option. I didn't… Couldn't trust her, but the police officer inside me was screaming out that this could be a great lead. I typed out her number and then started writing a message.

'Silver - We need to talk. I need answers about Thorne and the Maulaggs. Can you help?' I pressed send and then instantly regretted it. What was I doing? Why the hell didn't I run it past Teacher first? I was sort of working for him now, what would he say if this led to me getting into trouble again?

I was just about to call him when my phone beeped, a red '1' sat blinking on the thumbnail of my messaging app. I opened it and saw it was from Silver.

'We can. Will arrange a safe place to meet. Wait for details. -S'

Suddenly the phone that Teacher had given me started vibrating in my pocket. I quickly shut down my phone, shoved it in my pocket and pulled out the Rust phone, placing it to my ear as I walked down Ormlie Road back toward the centre of town.

"Mr Stewart! Would you mind popping in by RUST as soon as possible? We have a plan in place that might help us track down where the Owls have taken the Maulaggs. However, we need your help to enact it."

I was just about to reply that I was on my way downtown, and could use the toilet block that I'd used with Maggie the first time I'd visited when suddenly a large black car screeched to a halt beside me. A shiver ran the length of my spine as I turned and saw Mr Biscuits waving enthusiastically from the driver's seat, fake eyeglasses and nose wobbling squint on his face as he grinned from fake ear to fake ear.

"Transportation should be with you now-" I could almost hear the grin in Teacher's voice, "-Please make your way to the meeting room when you get here."

A short and somewhat terrifying drive later and we were back at RUST HQ, Mr Biscuits pulling the car into the same parking bay that Gunnar and I had rushed into to find Crash taking off with Thorne a few short days before.

Unfolding myself from the rear of the car, I walked off toward the swinging doors leading into the facility, when I heard a loud 'honk' behind me. I turned to see Mr Biscuits leaning uncomfortably far out of the car window, fake glasses and moustache askew on his face with his hand held up in the air toward me. I stood still for a second, wondering what the hell he wanted as he pointed with his other hand to the open one, then made a 'high-five' motion.

Now, I'd become quite fond of Mr Biscuits as time had passed and owed him my skin from at least two occasions, but as I walked toward him with a terrified grin on my face, I won't lie that it didn't take all of my willpower not to fear-piss myself a little when my hand slapped quickly against his before I hurried off and ran through the doors into the facility beyond.

I made my way to the meeting room past work crews repairing walls, cables and electronics all around me. As I turned the corner to pass the data facility, I could see that not only was the door wide open, but Dean was inside with Georgie the wolfm... Sorry, 'Wulver', and Fidget the wood-elf, the three of them working on fitting a large electronic panel to a wall. I was going to pass by quietly and not disturb them when Dean spotted me.

"Oi Dingo-breath! Get over here and help us with this will ya? Wee Fidget here is as much use as a chocolate jockstrap!"

With one of the swiftest and most finely tuned kicks to the knackers I'd ever seen, The small woman dropped Dean to the floor clutching his man bits before she turned to me with a big smile on her face and extended her hands.

"Alrighty Angus! Glad to see you up and about pal. Settling in fine with the new job then? Deano here says that you've fitted in like you've always been here." A groan from the floor and a shaky 'thumbs up' seemingly confirmed this. She continued talking as she turned back to the panel, motioning me to help by grabbing the side that a now incapacitated Dean had been dealing with, "I'm pretty much the chief engineer in this shitehole. Deano here is kinda my apprentice."

"I'm fucking not.." Dean climbed slowly back to his feet with the help of a giggling Georgie, "I know more about this bloody AI system than you d-Fuuuck me, that hurt. I thought all you Wood Elves were supposed to be all huggy lovely bastards? All about love, peace and understanding?"

"Understand this pal, the clue is in the name. Do you think we're called Wood Elves because we hug trees?" She quickly drilled two of the wall-mounted unit brackets into place, "We're called wood elves because we're masters of booting people in the dick."

I thought it best to quickly change the subject before she once again decided to show off her specific skill set, "So what are you folks working on here, isn't this where HAMMER was housed?"

"Yeah", Fidget finished fixing the unit to the wall and moved off to open the next box with Georgie, "We're having to install our secondary backup AI unit for now until Teacher decides what we're doing going forward." She heaved another large, electronic panel out of the box, lifting what looked easily like a ninety-plus kilogram unit up like it was nothing at all, "This one is gonna have access to a lot of the archived knowledge that HAMMER gained that had been copied to different locations. Once up and running, 'NAILS' should be able to do most of the technical heavy work around here that HAMMER used to. Where did that bloody screwdriver go?"

"*MINE.*" The voice boomed in my head as I spun around to see C4 walking out of the room with the large screwdriver in his mouth, looking back smugly before the end of the tool caught against the door and made him stumble out into the hall, right into the arms of the suddenly delighted Mr Biscuits. The look of resigned indignation on C4's face as he was quickly carried away was compensation enough I felt for the nipple and collection of chest hairs the little ginger fucker had cost me just days before.

I picked up the screwdriver and passed it back to Fidget as she and Georgie heaved another large unit into place, and began fixing cabling into various awkward-looking sockets, "So the last unit was called HAMMER, and then you've called this one, 'NAILS'?"

"Yep, stands for, 'Neuro-Analytical Intelligence Logistics System'. Pretty state of the art too, but not quite as extensive a knowledge set as HAMMER had." Dean cracked open three cans of Cola and passed them between us, "But it'll do pretty much everything we need to be done for now until we can recover HAMMER."

"So wait, the plan is to rescue the first AI?"

"Indeed" Teacher appeared at the door behind us, "I was hoping to give you more details in the meeting room Mr Stewart, but it seems you've been... Distracted." Fidget, Georgie and Dean began working a little bit harder on the panel they had just put in place, acting like they had no idea what Teacher was on about.

"Despite the Sons group now controlling HAMMER, they have very little way of copying his information." Teacher pulled up a chair, conveniently in the way of Dean, Georgie and Fidget as the three of them scurried around the data centre room pulling various parts out of boxes, "The data has extensive data copy protection installed, so even if they pulled him apart to the last data chip, that information remains secure from digital copying. However, they still can access his entire database. The more time we give them to make HAMMER operational again, the more time we allow them to access that data and if need be, set a team down with keyboards and data pads to write down and copy the data presented to them." Teacher leaned forward as he continued,

"First, we find their facility, then our priorities are simple; We rescue the captured Maulaggs, in turn hopefully finding Kah'Baj and getting more details on what he knows about Huey's death. Then, we rescue HAMMER before they can get any more information out of him."

Georgie interrupted, "Sorry to butt-in boss, but wouldn't it just be easier to destroy the AI so that they can't use it? Gonna be a nightmare heaving that unit out of there potentially under fire."

Teacher glared at Georgie as he continued, "HAMMER is not only an important part of our facility, but he's a valuable team member too." He raised a finger just as Georgie motioned to speak, stopping the Wulver in his steps as he continued, "You may see HAMMER as little more than an AI, but he's proven more than once that some form of, 'soul' resides in those data cables. He's one of us, and we will afford him the same respect and urgency of rescue as we would any of our human or fae members of RUST. Do I make myself clear?" Everyone nodded while Teachers gaze swept over us.

"So we go tackle the buggers!" Dean seemed a bit more 'chipper' after his meeting with Fidget's steel toe-capped safety boot, "Only problem is we don't know where their bloody 'nest' is."

"And this, Mr Mayes, is exactly why I had a full presentation arranged and ready to go in the meeting room." Teacher rose from his chair and wiped away some imaginary dust from the shoulder of his jacket, "So if it's not too much of an imposition, would you all kindly follow me there so we can go over some of the finer details of our retaliation plan?"

Chapter Twenty

You Can't Say No

Three days had passed since the meeting at RUST. Plans were now in place to find a way in, and I'd been tasked with trying to use whatever mental, psychic or bloody witchcraft-related connection I'd been given to Cabbage to try and track his location, and hopefully that of the Sons facility. I tried sitting on the floor of my hotel room with my legs crossed making 'umm' sounds, but that just made my knee sore and gave me pins and needles in my toes. I tried laying in a sensory deprivation tank that RUST had installed in their crew facilities, but all that happened there was I could hear the blood rushing in my ears which made me want to pee a lot. That, plus the newly installed NAILS AI shouting at me every ten minutes through the pod's in-built speakers, "ARE YOU FULLY RELAXED YET BOY? I CAN'T DETECT NOISE MIGHT I SUGGEST RELAXING MORE - THINK ABOUT BOATS'. [11]

---

[11] It was fair to say there were still some 'kinks' left to sort out with NAILS' installation. The AI had already made a toaster attack someone the previous night trying to warm a seeded bagel, and earlier that day had spent fifteen minutes blaring 'We Like to Party' by the Vengaboys over the facilities PA system, because it felt that everyone was being a bit too uptight.

I decided to take a break from trying to commune with the now non-communicative Haggvar who had saved my life and instead decided to grab my laptop and head out for some lunch. RUST was picking up the bill for all my food, and despite the hotel food being quite nice, I just couldn't face another meal with auld Mary sitting grinning at me, then only asking me questions once I had a mouth full of mince and tatties. Instead, I threw on Huey's jacket and headed out for a short walk along to the Cafe on the corner of the main street. I walked in, went up to the counter and ordered a large latte and a large slab of cake. Don't judge me, I've nearly died a couple of times these past couple of weeks AND been jammed up the supernatural rectum of a glorified taxi driver, so at the very least I deserve some sugary goodness in my life.

The cafe was packed, but the lady behind the counter pointed out a table that had just come free at the back of the room which I dashed over to claim before the two or three people who were hovering around before me noticed it. I got myself seated and had a look around the room to see if there were any familiar faces I knew. I was kind of hoping there wasn't, as I prefer to sit alone when I'm eating and not have someone recognize me and then spend the next twenty minutes talking about shit I should remember from our school days. It seemed I was in luck though, as my coffee and cake arrived I realised there wasn't a single face I recognized in the place. With me having lived away south for several years, and the increase in tourists now that the NC500[12] route had become so popular, it

---

[12] The 'North Coast 500' is a road route around the Highlands of Scotland, promoted by the government as the nations very own 'Route 66', however the roads themselves are not designed for the kind of heavy traffic it subsequently faced as a barrage of caravans, people carriers and middle aged men on spluttering motorbikes descended upon the route looking for excitement. Instead, all they found were passing places filled with illegally parked motor homes, and bins overflowing with disposable barbecues and dog excrement.

wasn't too surprising that I was surrounded by a mixture of unfamiliar faces.

I opened my laptop while my coffee chilled a bit, and piggybacked onto the free wi-fi that the cafe supplied. I'd neglected my social media for a while now, and I had a shit ton of notifications to dig through when I suddenly heard a voice beside me.

"Mind if I sit here? All the other tables are taken." I raised my head from the screen to say yes and froze. Silver stared down at me as she moved round to the other side of the table, highlighted by the light from the doorway behind her as she sat down and smiled at me.

I closed the lid of the laptop slowly, looking around to see if anyone else was watching us or moving to grab me, but no, everyone else in the cafe carried on with their conversations oblivious to what was going on at our table.

"Um, hi you."

As an opener, I've fared much better, but in my defence, I was expecting to have a burlap sack thrown over my head any second. Silver smiled and leaned back in her chair as a waitress appeared and laid down a small espresso cup in front of her.

"I hope you don't mind me imposing-" The smile never leaving her face as she picked up the small cup, "-I've been wanting to catch up with you for a little while now but you never seem to be free for visitors. I'd kind of given up hope until you got in touch the other day."

"Yeah that's true," I kept my eyes trained on the entrance door behind her, "But being hijacked off the road and locked up in a warehouse, then being shot in the chest by your boss will naturally make someone a bit wary, as I'm sure you can imagine."

The smile on her face dropped briefly, the cup pausing as it made its way down to the table.

"Have I been anything but honest with you since our first meeting Angus? Have I personally not tried to help you and check on you as much as I can?"

I could feel my temper rising, but I didn't want Silver to think she was getting under my skin, so I smiled and scooped up a large fork full of cake, taking time to chew it down before replying to her.

"Well, you haven't done anything directly, but you also haven't been entirely truthful with me either, have you? That day in the hotel when Crash chased you as you ran. She helped you get away, didn't she? You knew that you were safe under her watch yet you didn't tell me that she was one of you, did you?" She made to answer but I cut in, "So why on earth should I trust anything you say now? When Thorne had me tied up in that goddamned warehouse after my head was almost smashed in by a truck, you never thought to tell me then that it was my bloody father who was running your whole shit show?" Despite my best efforts, my voice had risen which prompted a few shitty looks from some of the other customers sitting around us.

She looked crestfallen as I continued, "So no, I don't trust you Silver. All I can think is that you're trying to play 'Good Cop' here, and I'm now kind of wishing I hadn't got in touch with you, so if you'll excuse me I'll bid you a good day and be on my way." I pushed back my chair and made to leave. Suddenly every single other person in the cafe did the same, all standing up out of their chairs and turning to stare at me.

"Please Angus, sit back down. Everyone here wants you to be safe, I'm here to offer you an easier way of doing things, a way that can benefit us both and let you get back to your life down in Aberdeen and away from this dead-end of a town."

I sat back down slowly, my ass barely touching the seat before every other person in the cafe also sat back down and continued their conversations like nothing had happened.

"Wow, so everyone here is here with you? All this was a trap?" I leaned back in my chair, laughing as the front door of the cafe opened and in walked Crash, refusing to look at me as she locked the cafe door behind her and turned the sign to closed before standing and blocking the exit. Nobody within the cafe seemed concerned.

"Please don't try and communicate with your RUST friends, we have electronic dampeners running so there's no phone or wireless signals travelling in or out while we talk. Can we talk? I just want to run a scenario past you that I think might benefit us all, without any need for trouble." I was only half listening now as I stared at Crash, still standing guarding the doorway and refusing to look in my direction. I wanted to run over and demand to know what the hell she thought she was doing, why she had betrayed her friends and mostly, did she at least care that she had crushed Gunnar?

I turned back toward Silver and took a drink from my coffee, "What makes you think I'd be inclined to help you? In case you'd forgotten, you and your friends have tried to kidnap or kill me now more than once."

Silver smiled as she crossed her legs and sat back in her chair, hands crossed together over her knee, "A series of events out of my control Angus. I know you don't believe me, and you have no reason to either, but I genuinely have nothing but your wellbeing in mind." She uncrossed her legs and sat forward, leaning down to pull a tablet from the shoulder bag beside her, "You have a gift that you don't understand fully, a gift that if fully developed could make you a very powerful person indeed." She pressed the screen on her tablet and brought up what looked like a live stream of the police station I worked at down south, not subtly showing me that they had access to the closed CCTV system that had been installed earlier in the year.

"We know that your partner has put you in a bit of a pickle, and we know that part of this is down to your partner stealing." I was about to interject that Thorne had already told me that Keith was a Sons plant when she flicked the screen again and brought up screenshots and names that also should be securely locked down in the PNC (Police National Computer) system back south, "I can show you step by step how he's been playing dirty, extorting money and turning blind eyes to drug runners with heavy handshakes. Without our help Angus, you face a lot of very tough questions about why you've done nothing when this portfolio of evidence we've put together lands on your supervisor's desk tomorrow morning."

I smiled, drank some more coffee and was about to talk when she raised her hand and cut me off, "I know, you are innocent of all charges. But without help proving that you've had no knowledge of his behaviour, you could face criminal prosecution as well." She grinned as she leaned forward, touching the back of my hand with hers, "Let me help sort all this mess down south out. Let me help you develop your gift, and over time you'll see that working alongside us can make you more powerful than you ever dreamed."

I sat back in my chair and motioned for her to keep talking, hiding that I knew Keith was a plant. I decided instead to play dumb and see how this all played out.

Silver placed her tablet back in her bag before continuing, "I am truly sorry about the way you've been treated so far by my colleagues Angus. If I could change what you've been through I would in an instant, but you have to understand that we're not quite the bad guys that RUST have made us out to be."

I laughed as the waiter refilled my coffee, "Really? Because despite what you've all put me through-" I pointed directly at Crash, "Your 'associate' here injured countless people stealing technology from RUST while betraying everyone around her. Hell, if I can't even trust someone who hugged me as a friend shortly before that raid, how am I supposed to believe a word that comes out of your mouth Silver?"

Silver moved to speak but I cut her off, "You and your people have done nothing but cause harm to me, my friends and my family. You've almost outright killed me twice, and she-" I stared at Crash, who at least had the decency to look downcast, "-has taught me a valuable lesson in who I place my trust in."

I quickly stood up from the table as the waiter turned and came running toward me, reaching out as I launched the full cup of hot coffee into his face. As he fell to the floor screaming I kicked the table, slamming it into another three customers who were suddenly moving to grab me. The commotion caused enough space for me to squeeze past Silver and sprint for the door and Crash. I picked up a chair and threw it toward her, hoping she would move out of the way and it would smash the glass behind her, but she stood still, casually swatting the chair to one side as her other arm raised toward me holding what looked like a gun. I froze, in my head once again facing down Thorne before he shot me. I felt something jab me in my left side, Silver's mouth suddenly against my ear as I started to lose consciousness.

"I'm sorry Angus, but I must insist."

Scott Taylor

Chapter Twenty One

Infiltration

You know that feeling the morning after you've been out on a real bender with your pals, probably ended up getting groped by a random woman in the kebab shop with miscellaneous yellowed teeth, all while you're trying to dislocate your jaw to consume the whole tray of chips, cheese and donner you've undoubtedly half spilt over yourself? That was the exact feeling I was getting waking up in this random, white-walled room I'd found myself in. My head was thumping and my tongue felt like I'd licked a carpet, but otherwise after a quick check, I was all in one piece.

I was getting bloody sick of waking up in random places after being put to sleep against my will. At least this room had a sink and a selection of toiletries so I could wash my face and swill my mouth out. So clearly I'd been stunned, drugged or knocked unconscious before waking up here. But where was here? My room was pretty sparse, with only the bed, toilet and sink along with a small desk and chair on the other side of the small room. Everything was white, from the walls to the bed linen, and the lighting was just the wrong side of bright, which I'm sure over an extended period was going to give me a headache. There was only a small, barred window that I had to pull a chair over from the desk to look out of, and the view was pretty much the brickwork of whatever building sat across from this one.

I tried the handle on the door and sure enough, it was locked. I hammered on the door until a voice to my side suddenly barked, "What is it?"

I did that half-yodel thing you do sometimes when you get a sudden fright, looked round and noticed that the mirror above the sink had changed to a screen showing a man in some kind of uniform sitting at a desk glowering at me.

"Uh.. Hi there, unhappy-looking mirror man! Hey, quick question, where the fuck am I?"

He stared at me for a few seconds before answering, "You're currently a guest of Commander Thorne. Meals will be served three times daily for the foreseeable, clean laundry and clothes will also be supplied daily until such time you leave our accommodations." with that, the video feed cut off and the screen turned back to what appeared to be a normal mirror.

I gave the mirror the fingers in the slim hope that 'Captain Happy Pants' was still watching, then went over to the desk where it looked like all the stuff I'd been carrying on me had been laid out. My laptop was missing, but it seemed that everything else was present. I quickly put my watch back on and gathered together all the contents of my wallet that had been pulled out and searched before being laid out on the table.

I grabbed the bottle of water that had been left for me on the desk, sat on the bed and assessed my situation. I was locked in an admittedly plush cell, this wasn't a surprise. My head was starting to clear and the cold water was helping my tongue and throat feel less furry. After a few drinks of water, I started to feel more like myself, stretched out some of the stiffness in my side and back for a bit and then after some contemplation of my navel, decided that there was no time like the bloody present to get on with things.

Hopping off the bed I moved across to the sink, put in the plug and then turned on both taps fully. Once everything started to overflow, I turned and grabbed the big fluffy towel my captors had kindly left for me and jammed it down into the bowl of the toilet, using the heel of my foot to really jam it in there before pressing the flusher. Sure enough, the toilet started to overflow onto the hard floor below me, and a few flushes later along with the overflowing sink, the majority of the floor was now covered in water.

I didn't have long before it would start to flow out under the cell door, so I jumped up on the bed and pulled my belt free of the loops of my trousers. Pulling the fastening pin from the buckle like I'd been shown by Teacher, the pin came loose and was followed by a long length of metal cable that unfurled itself from inside the belt. Once I'd pulled out the full length, I threw down the cable so it lay across the water now covering the floor, twisted the small crest on the metal buckle so that it popped out like a small button, and then waited with my feet folded up on the bed waiting for the ever-increasing water flow to be noticed.

It didn't take long. I could hear someone swear from the other side of the doorway and then what sounded like a keypad being rapidly tapped directly outside. The door burst open and in walked the guard I had seen shortly before on the bathroom mirror, his eyes wide as he stared at the overflowing sink and toilet to his left.

I pressed hard on the raised crest on the belt buckle and sparks flew along the water as the guard shook violently, falling quite dramatically backwards into the hallway outside with a splash. I made sure that the buckle was deactivated and jumped off the bed, running across to check on the guard. Teacher had assured me that the jolt from the belt device would knock someone unconscious but not permanently harm them. The guard showed no signs of injury that I could see, his breathing was strong and his pulse was fine. Feeling sure that he'd be okay as I pulled him clear of the wet part of the floor, I grabbed the key card from his belt and ran to the door at the far end of the hallway.

The card reader beeped as I waved the guard's access card over it and the door slid open. I moved quickly through into another corridor with what looked like the guard's office on the left, and a main exit door at the far end. I looked quickly in the office to see if any visible alarms were activated but all looked clear. Spotting what looked like a police-style baton hanging by the door I grabbed it, and sprinted down to the exit door at the far end of the hallway. A quick flash of the card and I was through into what looked like a reception area. Luckily nobody seemed to be around, so I headed straight for the large glass doors which led outside. It was dark and raining, so clearly I'd been out cold for a few hours at least. Pushing open the exit door I stepped out into the cold wet night and looked around to get my bearings.

It looked like a large military courtyard, with off-road style vehicles all around and armed guards milling around between them, ringed by a large fence all around with spotlights beaming down into the grounds of the facility. I ducked behind a large crate down the entrance steps to my left and searched for any sign of where they might be keeping the Maulaggs from the nest they had raided, and possibly Cabbage too if he'd been caught trying to rescue his kin.

Just as his name came to my thoughts his voice suddenly boomed in my head.

"*SMELLY MAN-PIG! WHY ARE YOU HERE IN THIS PLACE AND WHY ARE YOU NOT HELPING THE GREAT KAH'BAJ IMMEDIATELY!*"

"*I don't know where you are! Are you with the other Maulaggs? What can you see around you that might give me a bearing?*" I ducked down as a two-man patrol walked right past my hiding spot, stopping briefly to light up a cigarette before moving on with their patrol. I was just about to try and contact Cabbage again when suddenly a sharp, searing pain in my head threw me down onto my ass.

Coming to my senses quickly, I panicked and looked around for whoever must have attacked me, but there was nobody there. I started to check my head for any wounds when suddenly I could feel my focus being pulled behind me on the left side. It was strange, almost like I was being gently but insistently pulled toward an unknown point.

"*YOU COME HELP KAH'BAJ TRIBE NOW YES? I PULL BUT VERY DANGEROUS TO ME SO COME NOW INSIST NOW.*"

Whatever he had done, I now at least had a rough idea of where he was. I looked out from behind the crate and saw that the foot patrols all seemed to have moved on from my position, and if I stayed low and moved along the hedgerow that flanked the front of the building I'd come out of, I could move around to the back of the facility and toward wherever Cabbage and the rest of the Maulaggs where.

It took me a good fifteen minutes to slowly work my way around the building, keeping out the sight of any guards wandering around or the one woman in the lab coat who had suddenly opened a window above me and leaned out, only to hack up a huge mound of chest-butter that she then launched a good fifteen feet over my head with one of the most impressive spits I'd ever seen, before she ducked away and slammed the window closed behind her.

It wasn't long before I could see the pens that contained the Maulaggs. As I moved toward the large cage that was holding them I could tell that their focus wasn't on me or my movements, instead facing inward toward something else. As I moved closer the sounds of snarling and growling grew louder, as did the occasional shout appear in my mind.

"TRAITOR FILTH!"

"YOU PAY FOR BETRAY!"

All different Maulaggs shouting, more hostile than Cabbage and too angry to mask their words from my ears.

"YOU BETRAY ALL TO THE EATERS!"

"Cabbage! Are you in there, are you okay?" Suddenly all motion in the pen stopped. The Maulaggs all turned slowly round to face me, their faces contorted in anger. In a heartbeat they smashed up against the bars toward me, snarling and baring teeth in rage as I took a quick step back in shock. I steadied myself, reassured that they couldn't get to me through the thick bars, and I moved slowly closer, scanning the mass of hair and fangs to try and spot Cabbage.

Almost as one, the Maulaggs stopped their thrashing and snarling. Never taking their eyes off me, they moved back from the bars and slowly parted down the middle. As I looked between them I could see one Maulagg lying by himself at the back of the pen, its hair matted with dirt and blood, its face swollen and still. I moved closer, the Maulaggs to either side staring a hole through me as I stared open-mouthed at Cabbage, broken and beaten on the floor of the cold and wet cell.

I sprinted around the outside of the cell, looking desperately for a way to open the holding pen and let the Maulaggs free so I could help Cabbage. I spotted the key card scanner to open the gates and scrabbled in my pocket to dig out the card I'd taken from the guard, but before I could lift it to open the door, something quickly wrapped around my legs and pulled, slamming me against the bars of the Maulagg pen and then to the floor. Before I could react, I was being dragged across the ground away from the pens and toward Crash, holding the handle of the whip she'd used to grab me.

"You did well Angus, better than we thought you would. I didn't expect you to break free for at least another day." Crash smiled as she moved forward, placing a foot on my chest and pinning me down as she pulled out what looked like a tazer from the holster by her left side.

"I see Teach gave you the belt. Handy that one, it's got me out of a couple of close shaves in the past." The smile left her face as she looked me up and down, still pointing the tazer at me while her eyes fell on the watch on my left wrist.

Her foot left my chest as she quickly tried to pin down my arm, but she was too late. I raised my arm quickly and slammed it back down onto the wet concrete below me, shattering the glass screen of the sturdy-looking watch. Crash paused, her face falling as she quickly pointed the tazer back toward me. She pulled a radio from her hip and clicked down the broadcast button.

"Sector three command to all teams, code red protocols. Reinforce and secure all entry points. We're about to have some unexpected visitors show up."

She motioned for me to roll onto my front and place my arms behind my back before cable-tying my wrists together and dragging me to my feet.

"I forgot about the fucking watch.." She pushed me gently from behind, "Come on Angus, someone wants to see you before everything starts getting loud and shouty around here."

"Why did you do it Crash? Why did you betray everyone?" We moved along a brightly lit corridor before entering a lift, Crash pushing me to the back of the small space while she pressed the button for the roof, her hand pausing and slowly curling into a fist before dropping to her side.

"I should have known about the watch Angus, a common tool too, just haven't used one in a while is all. A tracker hidden inside a Faraday cage-type housing, activated by breaking the seal. I take it Teacher told you to smash it outside the facility?"

I wasn't going to let her change the subject, "Please, Crash. Why all of this?" She at least had the decency to look upset.

"I didn't want this to happen, I swear. I never wanted to hurt anyone." I could see her eyes well up as she spoke, "But they got their hooks into me a couple of years ago. I was weak, in a bad place and they got me when I was at my lowest." She paused for a second, staring at me before slowly sliding her weapon back into its holster. Before I could say anything, she quickly pressed the 'stop' button on the elevator before turning to look at me.

"My... Father used to work with RUST. He was one of the best ambassadors they had between our world and the Fae. Back then, things weren't quite as friendly between the two worlds, and my dad helped broker the peace treaty that stands today." She leaned back against the mirrored carriage wall behind her as she continued,

"I was fifteen years old when he was attacked. He'd worked all his days to make peace with the Fae, only to have one of the bastards tear him open as he walked home from RUST in the early hours of the morning."

"Jesus, Crash. I'm so sorry." She pressed the button to restart the lift climbing toward the roof of the facility, her hands clenching once more into fists as they returned to her sides.

"Turned out the Sons had been tracking him, so when he was attacked they were the first ones on the scene. They managed to get him stabilised and into a cryo-stasis chamber when they realised that his injuries were too severe. He's technically alive, and when they pulled me in to talk about his situation they told me over and over again that if I helped them, they would help him. I had to lie to Teacher and the rest and say that my father was missing and I had no knowledge of where he was, but in reality the Sons kept pushing me for more, and in my naivety I gave and I gave until I was in too deep to stop." Crash rubbed her hands together as she continued, tears fell down her cheeks and splashed onto the elevator floor. "Over and over again they pushed, dangling the carrot that my father was slowly getting better, but they needed me to do more to help them expand their knowledge so they could apply it to helping him." She looked crestfallen as she continued, "I had to steal more from RUST to feed to the Sons, all the time betraying those I loved in the belief that they were using this information to help give my father his life back. But they never have."

She stared at me, tears streaming down her cheeks, "And what has it got me? We never found out who or what attacked my dad, they've never done anything more than hide him away in stasis somewhere and they've made me betray those who put their faith in me. I'm in too deep Angus, and I can't see a way out." She grabbed my shoulder, gripping tightly as the lift started to slow. "They got me, and they made it so that I was theirs forever. No matter what happens or what they may promise, I can't see a way out of this shit without my father. Don't let them get you too."

Just at that, the lift came to a halt and the doors slid open onto a dark flat rooftop, slick with rain soaking the rooftop under a lone figure, standing at the far edge looking down on the compound, their profile highlighted by the occasional flash of light from somewhere below.

Crash quickly wiped her face with her sleeve, her jaw tightening as she pushed me forward out of the lift and toward the broad-shouldered figure ahead. As we stepped closer my heart began to sink as I recognised who it was I was being taken to see. The figure turned toward me, the light below briefly showing the new luchador-style mask pulled over his face as his eyes met mine.

"Hello son. You're just in time for the show. Care to join me?"

Chapter Twenty Two

Unrepentant

Crash prodded me forward, causing me to stumble toward where Thorne stood looking down from the edge of the rooftop. I moved beside him, determined to show him no fear, but internally I was crippled, flashing back to that gun barrel pointing at my chest before the sudden flash.

"I need you to understand what we're doing here son."

"You DO NOT get to call me son!" I flared at him, rage suddenly pouring through me. "You're no father to me, and you've no right to stand there and call me son. I am Angus Stewart, nothing else to you."

I could see Crash step back as Thorne turned and towered over me, his dark eyes shining through the holes in his mask as he looked me up and down.

"You know, you're absolutely right. I do not claim you whatsoever. But I do require you to listen." He walked slowly around me, all the while glaring down at me mere inches from my face as he circled like a predator.

"You've been given chances Angus. Chances to join us and lend your gift to our cause. With our training, you could become even more powerful than your Uncle Huey!" He laughed, "Hell, look at you standing there in a dead man's jacket. Maybe unlike him, you might even become powerful enough to see the shove coming before you plummet off the cliff edge."

I froze in place, staring at this man who shared my blood, Huey's blood, as he circled me grinning, waiting for my reaction.

"Did you... Kill your brother? You killed Huey?

Thorne suddenly charged toward me and grabbed me by the lapels of my uncle's jacket, pushing me backwards until the rear of my legs hit against the small wall that lined the edge of the rooftop. He shoved me until the top half of my body leaned dangerously over the edge, my hands scrabbling against his chest as he pulled my face close to his. I clung desperately to his wrist as his hand gripped my shirt and jacket in a ball under my chin, his other hand reaching into his jacket and pulling out a gun.

"Of course I killed him. He took everything from me! That power, your power BY RIGHTS SHOULD BE MINE! And what did he do with it? He used it to speak to those fucking ANIMALS that RUST seems to value so much!" The gun was jammed under my chin, as inch by slow inch I was being pushed further and further out over the ledge, Thorne's face mere centimetres from mine. "His misguided belief that our brotherly bond could be redeemed led him to meet me on those cliffs, to think that we had a chance to be, 'family' again" His face was mere inches away from mine, his smile widening as he glared at me, "I still remember his face as he fell, the disbelief mixed with horror as he disappeared into the low lying mist below us. He killed himself Angus, by taking what was MINE!" He stood up straight and raised his face into the air, the rain bouncing off that stupid mask as he roared into the darkened sky above.

"But now that I have the Haggvar, all that has changed!" His large hand let go, and I had to scrabble against the ledge to stop from falling over toward the sheer drop below. Thorne walked around Crash, all the while staring at me, his mask stretching to show off the huge smile splashed across his face as the rain peppered us from above. He reached into his large jacket with his free hand and pulled out what looked like a small glass bottle full of a dark purple liquid, giving it a little shake as he held it up to examine it against the light from one of the nearby spotlights that shone down into the courtyard below.

"It's amazing how much of a leap the study of the fae has come thanks to The Sons you know. Why, it used to be the case that eating one 'Haggis' heart would give you a gift, It was all they knew! One gift! Whereas now-" Popping the cork out of the end of the bottle, he smiled at me again before lifting his head and drinking down its contents, wiping his mouth afterwards with his sleeve, "-Well now, our scientists can gather the hearts of multiples of these creatures, condense the 'essence' from them and combine it all into one solution, potentially granting multiple benefits! Purely hypothetical you understand, it's still to be tested on humans. Haha.."

I stared at him in horror, realising what he was talking about. I could do nothing but watch as the smile left his face, his body doubling over as he clutched his stomach and stumbled forward to lean with one hand against the small wall at the edge of the rooftop, the gun leaving his grip and sliding across the wet ground beside him.

"Haha! Ungh.. You know boy, I spent all this time hating you and your uncle for what you stole from me, and I apologise! Why envy such a meagre thing, such... 'Meagre' people, when greatness is... Agghh.." His fist thumped against the wall as his legs gave out, doubling over he screamed briefly as his hands raised to the mask and started tearing it off. "I.. GREATNESS BOY, IS GIVEN TO THOSE WHO FIGHT FOR IT!"

I was frozen in place until I felt a hand grab my shoulder and pull me backwards, Crash dragging me toward the lift as Thorne writhed and howled on the ground in front of us, his body seeming to twist and grow in unnatural ways in the darkened light bathing the rain-soaked rooftop. Thorne's mask landed in front of us as he climbed back to his feet and threw it in our direction. It was hard to see him with the light from the courtyard shining behind him, but he looked... Larger, more beast-like. He threw his head to the heavens, his arms spread out wide and let out a terrifying roar that caused both Crash and I to stumble backwards.

"YES! I CAN FEEEEL IT! Such power, coursing through me.." Thorne, or whatever he was now, flexed his large hands, his forearms threatening to break through the jacket that now clung tightly to him, "This, THIS IS WHAT I DESERVE! Such power, such... I can think so clearly! Hah! What other skills have I acquired I wonder!" He stopped suddenly, his head snapping round to stare at both myself and Crash, bright yellow 'cats' eyes glaring at us as the smile once more returned to his face. Before I could react, he ran across and grabbed me, faster than any human should be able to move, picking me up before walking casually over to the edge of the building where he dangled me over the long drop into the courtyard.

"So, you know what 'Angus'? On second thoughts I don't think I will need your services moving forward, please consider this me terminating my offer." He stared at me with those horrific, beastly eyes, smirking through a mouthful of bleeding gums as his face continued to twist and grow, "Give Huey my regards, won't you?"

I was suddenly yanked to my left as Thorne casually let go. Crash ran up beside us and grabbed my arm, pulling me as I toppled over the edge of the building.

I swung over the sheer drop while Crash cried out with the strain of holding me, my body scraping against the side of the building as she swung me back toward the ledge where I grabbed on with my free hand and scrambled for some purchase, finally getting the tip of my boot to catch against an extended piece of brickwork, allowing me to get my other hand onto the ledge and pull myself up quickly,

Crash's grip on my arm suddenly loosened as I watched her spin around and level her weapon at Thorne's chest, stopping him in his tracks as he powered forward toward us. I flopped over the roof's edge to the safety of the rooftop and tried to catch my breath, watching Thorne move slowly toward Crash who was edging backwards toward the edge of the roof.

"Come on now Claire-" He looked monstrous now as he ripped off what was left of his jacket and threw it down to his side. I followed its trajectory and saw it land next to the gun he'd dropped shortly before, "-Do you think that little zap gun is going to have any effect on me now? LOOK AT ME!" He roared, his mouth opening unnaturally wide as I crawled over to where his large calibre pistol lay on the ground. "Nothing is stopping me now. Not you, not the Sons or those sanctimonious fuckers at RUST."

"Please, don't do this Thorne. You have what you need, just let us go, please." Her arm trembled as it raised slightly, aiming the taser gun now directly at Thorne's face. He kept moving forward, raising his huge arms with palms raised, his bloody smile becoming wider as he moved within feet of Crash's weapon. I reached out as far as I could, my fingers just touching the hilt of the large weapon, scrabbling to pull it into my grip.

A second later Thorne shot forward, faster than I could believe as he ripped the weapon from Crash's hand and backhanded her across the face, her body flying to the left and smashing against a large air conditioning unit before crumpling to the floor. Before she could recover he was on top of her, picking her up like she weighed next to nothing and hoisting her body over his head, turning once more to walk toward the edge of the rooftop.

"THORNE!" I held the gun steady as I aimed at his head, tracking him as he turned slowly toward me, dropping Crash to the ground where she scurried away to lean against the small wall beside her. He held his arms out wide as he slowly walked toward me.

"Son! Don't be stupid now. Put that weapon down before I take it from you and feeeeed it to you.." His voice was much deeper now, more animal-like as he turned his full focus on me. Blood ran from his eyes and mouth, the yellow slits of his eyes fixed on mine as he moved forward.

I cocked the large handgun and steadied my feet, watching as Thorne braced himself to lunge as he edged forward. I sucked in a deep breath and focused on my aim.

"When you meet Huey, I hope he forgives you for everything you've done, to him and our family. Goodbye Thorne."

"HAHA!! You think I ca-" The sound of the gunshot boomed around the rooftop, the kickback knocking me back a foot as the bullet tore through Thornes's body and exploded out of his back, a mist of blood and bone showering the air behind him as he stumbled backwards against the small wall behind him. I froze at what I'd done, horrified as he tipped backwards and toppled over the edge of the roof, tumbling down to land with a loud thump in the courtyard below.

I ran to the edge of the roof, staring down at what remained of Thorne lying broken in the courtyard below. I was numb as I looked down. This was my father, but also the man who had now tried to kill me twice. Is this how it all comes to an end, and why didn't I feel worse about it? It was then that Crash grabbed my arm and spun me to face her.

"I don't know what to say to you about all this, but RUST is going to be here any second, we need to get you somewhere safe before all of this goes down."

Almost like she had timed that statement to the very second, an explosion rocked the main gates leading into the courtyard below, smoke billowing in as guards took cover around the vehicles and crates around the yard, waiting for what was going to come through the wreckage. Crash and I stood transfixed as the smoke spread around the wreckage of the gate, before slowly starting to settle. Everything seemed to go quiet as through the dust settling, a lone tall figure in a black suit stood alone in the middle of the yard, a large horrific grin spreading over his featureless face.

It was Mr Biscuits.

Gunfire ripped through the dust as the Owl security forces opened fire, but Mr Biscuits had already launched himself full speed at the nearest truck to his left, tipping the vehicle over and scattering the four armed men who had been taking shelter behind it. Before they could recompose themselves, Biscuits had already torn the weapons from their hands and launched them out and over the wreckage of the destroyed gateway. The tall faceless ghoul was already moving onto the next vehicle when Crash motioned that we should get moving. I looked down for one last look at the man I had just killed, but he was gone. I frantically looked around the courtyard below me, maybe someone had moved his body while we were distracted. No, he was simply gone. I could see the bloody patch where his body had been, and what from this distance looked like a single set of footprints moving away from it. Had someone carried him away? There was no possible chance he had survived the bullet and the fall...

"We can't stay here Angus, we need to get you out of this place" she took my hand and dragged me along to the elevator, my head still foggy from everything that had just happened as she slammed the button to call the carriage.

Just then, the spotlights that covered the courtyard below plunged into darkness. Before we could figure out what had happened, they powered back on again, but instead of the bright white lights they had shown before, this time the lights were a strange purple colour. I ran over to the edge of the roof as we waited for the lift to arrive and looked down below. The air felt strange, almost electrified as down below, Mr Biscuits appeared to be frozen in place, vibrating as his wide mouth opened wide to howl silently into the sky.

"These lights, they're counter measures against his species. The Sons are prepared for almost anything" Crash explained as the elevator doors suddenly opened. Down below, Biscuits seemed to be in horrible pain. His skin seemed to blister, and smoke was rising from his body as he sunk onto his knees.

"We need to help him! Please Crash, how can we kill those lights?" I looked down to see Gunnar, Dean and Fidget all running into the courtyard, setting up a perimeter around Mr Biscuits to protect him, "I know you don't want to see them get hurt, please Crash!" But she had already raised her weapon and had begun firing at the large, purple lights that bathed the courtyard. I raised Thornes's gun and aimed at the nearest light to me, but before I could get a shot off one of the other spotlights exploded in a fountain of sparks, then another. I dropped the gun and stared out across the tops of the solid metal fence, catching sight of a dark shape leaping between the lights, smashing its fist into each light in turn and causing them to explode. For a brief second, I saw the figure illuminated against the harsh light before it was smashed. It was Georgie, the Wulver. Before long he had made his way around each of the powerful lights, destroying them one by one in turn and bathing the yard below in darkness.

Vehicle headlights and torches slowly clicked on throughout the rain-soaked courtyard, bathing the space in light. Mr Biscuits twitched, his body still smouldering as he slowly stood bathed by a solitary headlight pointed in his direction. His head jerked and twisted, looking all around him as his mouth took on a more sinister grin, and in a moment he was once again sprinting into action against the terrified security forces. We watched as Gunnar, Dean and Fidget all ran toward the main door of the building and into the facility, whilst Mr Biscuits ran amok throughout the armed figures below, shooting wildly as they tried to fend off the faceless demon attacking them.

The elevator door dinged behind us as Crash and I ran in.

"You need to let me go. I need to get those Maulaggs free before something terrible happens to them, to Cabbage." She ignored me as she hit the button leading to the server floor. I grabbed her arm, pulling her to look at me. "Crash, please. You know they're heading to rescue the AI. If you want to make it up to Gunnar, this is your chance. Just let me go and free the Maulaggs and save Cabbage. I can't let him suffer after everything he's been through."

Crash stared at me as the elevator came to a stop, the doors opening into the sterile-looking facility that held HAMMER.

"Here, take this-" She handed me her key card and took the one I had taken from the guard earlier, "-This card will grant you access to all areas of the site, including the Maulagg pens. This card here will grant me enough access to help Gunnar do what he needs to do."

She pressed the button for the ground level before stepping out backwards into the server centre,

"Head for the exit marked 'Animal Holding', that card will get you out there. Good luck" As the doors started to slide closed she stuck her foot against it to stop it.

"And Angus, I'm sorry. Truly, for everything." The doors slid closed on her smiling at me, I stared at the polished steel of the now sealed entrance as the lift carried on downward toward the bottom floor.

Chapter Twenty Three

Crash

Crash stood staring at the elevator doors for what felt like ages, her head slowly rising as her fists balled up by her sides, turned and set off toward the server centre. Walking up to the large, frosted glass doors she punched her access code into the grey keypad, striding through as they opened up in front of her.

The inside of the server area was chaotic as facility staff ran around securing computers and gathering up sheaves of paper into unruly bundles that were then being hurriedly fed into nearby shredders. Nobody seemed to notice Crash as she walked into the middle of the large room and unholstered her firearm, running through quick visual checks as people ran around her, oblivious as she checked the chamber and then raised the weapon toward the roof.

The firearm discharged, the boom echoing violently around the room as people screamed, others falling to the floor or diving behind the desks they were working on.

"EVERYONE IS TO LEAVE THIS AREA RIGHT NOW." Crash boomed as her gaze swept across the room, "STOP WHAT YOU ARE DOING, LEAVE THIS FACILITY AND NO HARM WILL COME

TO YOU." The white-coated workers around her didn't need to be told more than once, as they realised their lives weren't at risk and instead a good walk out into the dark night as far away from this place was exactly what they needed right then to clear their heads.

Crash moved around the perimeter of the room checking for anyone hiding, securing windows as she passed them before moving on to the back of the large room and the isolation chamber attached to the rear wall. Crash placed her hand on the strengthened window looking into the chamber. There inside lay HAMMER, the metal casing of his housing laying on a table in the centre of the room with various cables attached to him, leading to the larger computer racks that surrounded him within the sterile room. Punching a code into the keypad swung the door open with a hiss and Crash ducked inside, hurrying over to where HAMMER was. A small speaker had been retrofitted to his body, and as she approached the tinny voice of the AI boomed out,

"WHO IS THERE? I CAN SENSE YOUR VIBRATIONS, WHO ARE YOU? PLEASE, YOU MUST LET ME GO." Crash had never heard HAMMER sound so nervous, he'd always been the cocky smart-ass who made fun of her whenever she came out of the gym at RUST looking like she was fit to pass out. She realised though that not only was he scared after everything that had happened, but he had no connection to any visuals whatsoever. By isolating him here in this room they had blinded the AI, ensuring that he couldn't identify anyone who worked on him. Stepping toward him slowly, she placed a hand carefully on his housing. "It's okay Ham, it's me, Crash. I'm here to help you."

"HELP ME? YOU TOOK ME! YOU ARE WITH THEM CRASH, WHY?" His voice rattled from the small speaker, "WHY DO THIS, I THOUGHT WE WERE FRIENDS." small lights flickered on HAMMER'S housing unit. "I'M.. I'M VERY SCARED CRASH."

A single tear rolled down her cheek as she ran her hand over his metal casing. "I can't begin to tell you how sorry I am Ham. Please, I know you can't forgive me, but at least let me help you."

The lights on HAMMERS' dented casing blinked slowly, long seconds passing before his voice once more came from the attached small speaker.

"I'M BLIND AND I CANNOT SEE THE WORLD. YOU... THEY CUT ME OFF FROM EVERYTHING AND HURT ME, TAKEN FROM ME, I AM DIMINISHED AND I AM SCARED. I AM... SCARED OF YOU CLAIRE."

A gasp burst from Crash, her hands clutched the table where HAMMER lay as tears rolled down onto the polished surface below. "We haven't got much time Ham, please don't worry." And before he could reply, she unplugged his speaker and began pulling out the cables that plugged in throughout his systems. Once he was clear and she had checked his internal power systems were fine, she picked up his housing and carried him out of the isolation chamber, through the control room she'd cleared before and out toward the stairwell and lift shaft beyond. Setting him down on the ground, she stepped back into the control room, locked the door and waited.

It felt like only seconds passed before the stairwell door burst open as Gunnar, Dean and Fidget came running in, stopping dead when they saw Crash beyond the reinforced glass ahead holding her weapon by her side. Gunnar stared at Crash while Dean and Fidget spotted HAMMER and started preparing him for transport.

"Why Crash-" Gunnar's gaze swept around the room behind her, "Why all this? Why throw away your life for this? Why.. Why betray us?" Tears began to run down the giant's face, mirroring his counterpart on the other side of the reinforced door. "You can come with us! Come with us and we'll talk to Teacher, get this all sorted out and fix it."

Crash smiled, placing her gun back into its holster as she stepped forward and placed the flat of her hand against the glass dividing them both. Gunnar lifted his hand and did the same, his massive palm only separated from hers by the cold glass between.

"I can't tell you how sorry I am Gunny, I never meant for any of this. Please believe me." Gunnar was about to reply when a large explosion rocked the building, the lights went off above for a second before the room that Crash was in was bathed in red light, smoke starting to slowly roll over the roof behind her. She stepped back from the door, looking around before quickly turning back to the door.

"It's the safety systems, they're blowing up the servers throughout the building to prevent RUST from getting access." As she spoke, the server stacks in the isolation chamber that had housed HAMMER started to spark and smoke. Gunnar hammered at the keypad to open the door, smashing his massive fists against the pad desperately trying to get the door open.

"It's no use Gunny, the door's sealed." Crash smiled at him as she spoke, looking across to Dean and Fidget who had finished getting HAMMER ready for removal. "You all need go now before this place goes up in flames." Gunnar was about to protest when Crash raised her hand to stop him. "Speak to Angus, he can tell you more about why I've done what I have. Now, you need to get the hell out of here big guy!" Crash stepped back as smoke filled the room, flames from the servers behind her illuminating the fire gases now billowing around her. "Don't worry about me, I'll find my way out. NOW GO!" She suddenly stepped back into the smoke, and as Gunnar hammered against the door, she was gone.

"Gunnar, we need to get the hell out of here!" Dean pulled on the big man's arm, "Don't worry about her, she's a resourceful bugger, she'll be fine."

Gunnar took one last look into the now smoke-filled room, red lights and fire lighting up the fire gases, but he could see no sign of her silhouette anywhere. Without a word, Gunnar heaved the backpack holding HAMMER onto his back and set off down the stairs with Dean and Fidget.

Chapter Twenty Four

We Are Lost

The doors opened onto chaos. Bright flashes and screams could be seen and heard through the windows looking out into the courtyard, people shoving against each other to escape whatever disaster Mr Biscuits was visiting upon them out in the open courtyard. Through the commotion of bodies around me all looking for some guidance, I snuck along the back wall of the room and came to the exit for the holding pens just like Crash had told me. A quick swipe of the keycard and I was through the door and back out into the rain-soaked night.

I had to hide briefly as Sons Security Officers came charging around the corner, running toward the front of the building and the terrifying Mr Biscuits. Once clear, I moved toward the Maulaggs pen and again was faced by a wall of glowering eyes and teeth, most of which I was pretty sure would not be too friendly with me once I used this card to open their pen. I caught sight of Cabbage still lying at the back, and called out to him.

"*Cabbage, please! Are you you okay? I want to come in to help you, but your family are probably going to tear me apart the second I open this gate.*"

No answer. Cabbage was either unconscious or.. No time to think about that right now, I had to get this cage open and get to him as quickly as I could. My hand hovered inches away from the card scanner, scared to move forward and beep the system as I watched the Maulaggs immediately at the gate move back slightly and duck down, almost like sprinters getting ready for the gun to go off for the 100m sprint, all the while their dark eyes glued to me, grinning and waiting for that lock to click open.

I couldn't wait, I had to get to Cabbage. I raised my hand again when an explosion behind me spun me round, wondering what new bullshit I was going to have to face. A rectangular section of the perimeter steel fence collapsed flat toward me, and through the space it had made walked Teacher, hands raised and motioning for me to stop.

"Hold please Mr Stewart! I wouldn't be so hasty opening that door if I were you, not when our 'friends' on the other side seem so ungrateful for our help, aha" Before he could say anymore, another explosion blew out two windows on the building a few floors up, two ropes were thrown out of them followed by Gunnar, Dean and Fidget all rappelling down to where Teacher and I were now standing.

"We've got HAMMER back boss-" Gunnar pulled off the large backpack and set it down by his feet, "-We also met an old friend, said that Angus here can fill us all in on some details"

"I can, there's a shit-ton to tell you, but can we focus first on getting this pen open and getting the Maulaggs out of here without them killing us?"

Teacher raised a hand as the sounds of gunfire and explosions seemed to get further apart from around the SONS facility, clearly Mr Biscuits and Georgie were getting close to finishing off their part of the mission.

"Mr Stewart is right, and that's why after expecting some resistance, I called in some friends to help."

Seconds later, a swarm of Haggvar came pouring through the hole Teacher had made, and over the top of the fence, covering the ground around us the yard filled with them, all jumping around excitedly and peering into the holding pen, now containing a pack of Maulaggs that didn't seem as keen to tear us apart.

"Everyone please move back and give the Maulaggs plenty of space. Mr Stewart, if you could please communicate to our friends that they are about to be released, and are welcome to make their escape out through the compromised fence behind them."

It seemed that the Maulaggs didn't need me to translate or 'broadcast' anything to them, their response was instantaneous,

"WE GO NOWHERE WITHOUT HEID'YIN! BIG EATERS TAKE HEID'YIN INTO TALL HOUSE, WE TAKE BACK!!"

I passed this back to Teacher, as the Haggvar around us chorused agreement with their Maulagg cousins.

"Sir, they won't go without the Heid'yin, and we can't let them, can we help?"

Teacher hesitated, looking around at Gunnar and the rest of the team before turning toward the Maulagg and addressing them directly,

"Our friends, we will not stand in the way of you recovering your Heid'yin, and if you will allow it, we would offer our help in recovering him from the Sons."

The Maulaggs didn't need me to translate Teachers' words it seemed. They all stepped back from the gate and seemed to relax, no longer tensed like coiled springs ready to launch themselves at the exit once it opened.

"*We agree to your help Eater. Now open the trap and let us free now.*"

With a nod to Teacher, I stepped forward and beeped the card against the lock, moving back out of the way quickly as the door of the pen slid fully open. I'd barely taken two steps back before the Maulaggs came pouring out. There weren't nearly as many as there were Haggvar, but that didn't stop them from immediately lining up to face off with their friendlier cousins.

"Nobody reacts, everyone stays still, this doesn't need to escalate any more than it has already. We all want the same thing, to rescu-" Teacher was cut off by the Maulaggs all suddenly dropping to the floor, lifting their heads towards the sky and screaming with all of the strength in their lungs. I had no idea what was happening as moments later, the Haggvar also seemed to stagger before dropping to their knees and lowering their heads onto the floor in front of the screaming Maulaggs, now rolling about the floor clutching their chests as if in pain.

"What the hell is going on?" Shouted Gunnar, stepping carefully through the prone Haggvar to stand alongside Teacher. "Have we missed something here?"

"It is... Pain... Heid'yin is gone. Taken... Ended. We are lost!" That was Cabbage, I was sure of it as my gaze tore away from the screaming Maulaggs and back to the pen. I saw him still on the floor of the pen, dragging himself toward the open door, his legs seemingly unable to carry him.

Hoping the Maulaggs wouldn't notice me as they mourned, I moved slowly toward the cage door before jumping inside and using the key card to close it behind me, just in case any of the Maulaggs decided that I shouldn't be near their injured brother. Running across the pen I sank onto the ground beside Cabbage and checked him over. He was covered in cuts and bruises, his fur was matted with blood and one of his eyes was closed over. Worst of all, he didn't seem to have much mobility in his rear legs.

"Cabbage! What's happened to you? Is there anything I can do to help?"

He coughed, blood splattering his face as he spat out a mouthful of blood onto the floor,

"I followed brothers here, come to save but ended up catched. Big man with mask get me. I thought I had killed mask but was wrong." He paused as more coughing racked through him,

"Clan not happy to see proud Kah'Baj it seems. Angry with Kah'Baj for bonding with human to save human. Angry with Kah'Baj for not being with them when taken, and angry with Kah'Baj for not being here for father now gone."

Father now gone? Did he mean my father?

"My father is dead Cabbage, he was shot and killed shortly ago. He fell from the rooftop... He.. He can't hurt you anymore."

Cabbage stared at me, his small hand grabbing mine and gripping hard onto my fingers,

Not your father stupid pink-skin. Kah'baj father. Heid'yin was Kah'baj father. Now he gone, that why my kin howl, we feel his sudden gone. Kah'baj now... Heid'yin."

I sat back and turned to look at Teacher, now looking at me through the bars of the pen with what looked like concern on his face. I looked around to see what was causing him to worry, only to notice that the Maulaggs had stopped their screaming and had now moved to surround the cell, all staring at me as I tended to their leader's son. I moved round so that Cabbage was now between me and his angry brethren, in the hope that they would see I was trying to help, but it was no use. Slowly they moved ever closer, their teeth baring as their darkened eyes all focused on me. I looked around for the Haggvar to see if they could help, but their horrified attention seemed focused off to my right at something sprinting through the gap in the fence. I looked over my shoulder to get a better look, and a second later I was knocked face down to the ground as something small, ginger and furious launched into the air and then landed on my back.

"*MINE!*"

The Maulaggs fell back in terror as the full might of an angry C4 roared from between my shoulders, both his heckles and tail fully raised in anger at the two different tribes of Haggvar around him. I took the opportunity to talk to Cabbage while Gunnar's cat fended off the swarm of dangerous haggis with the power of pure will from my shoulders.

"*Cabbage, you gave part of yourself to me to keep me alive after I was shot. Is there any way for me to give back to you now to help you heal? Can you take back what was given?*"

He opened his one good eye to stare at me, relaxing his grip on my fingers as he spoke.

"*Kah'baj can take, but it not be good for you if do. I cannot.*"

I grabbed his hand this time, pulling his focus on to me.

"*Oh Mighty Cabbage-*" I 'shouted' loud, in the hope that all the Haggvar around me could hear my words, "*-I demand that you take from me what was given, that you take from me what you need to recover. My honour demands it, and my debt to the Maulagg shall be paid.*"

I was winging it with the dramatic flair there, but I guessed that Cabbage and his clan were suckers for that stuff, so I was keeping my fingers crossed that it would work.

I noticed from the corner of my eye, and the hairs on the back of my neck, that both Mr Biscuits and Georgie had arrived, clearly having finished whatever mop-up duties they'd been working on. Seeing me laying in the pen surrounded by Maulaggs disturbed Mr Biscuits, who in the blink of an eye had charged to the side of the pen, throwing a few Maulaggs aside before bending apart two of the thick, steel bars like they were nothing more than thin strips of plastic. I raised a hand and motioned for him to stop, smiling at this monster who had become a friend and protector to me, and shaking my head that he need not rescue me this time.

Mr Biscuits seemed to understand, seeing C4 standing on my shoulders probably helped as he carefully bent the solid steel bars back to as close to their original configuration as he could, before wiping his hands down the front of his suit, giving me a double thumbs up then slowly moving back to stand beside Gunnar and Georgie.

I turned my attention back to Cabbage, who had managed to pull himself up to an almost sitting position in front of me. I nodded at him, and I noticed a small smile cross his face briefly as he nodded, before he suddenly fell onto my lap and the world burst into thunder and darkness.

#

I came too and everything was pain. I opened my eyes carefully and noticed straight away I was laying on my side, and I had next to no power to move myself. My chest ached and my legs trembled below me, every part of me aching or throbbing as I tried to sit up, falling back to the ground as pain racked through my body. My chest in particular was killing me, and as I painfully pulled open the Huey's jacket, I could see blood very slowly starting to spread through my shirt over my chest.

I closed my jacket, lay back and tried to breathe slowly. Turning my head to the side, I noticed through blurry eyes that Mr Biscuits was trying to tear his way into the cell, only stopping when Teacher pulled his arm and showed him that they had managed to get the cell door unlocked. As my friends burst into the pen I noticed that the Maulaggs were all standing well back from the bars, their attention focused on Cabbage who was standing in front of them pounding his chest and roaring. Despite the mess of his fur, he seemed mostly healthy.

I tried to call to him, but either my brain 'walkie-talkie' thing wasn't working, or I was too beat up to find the energy to do it. Gunnar and Mr Biscuits appeared at either side of me, judging by the look on the big Highlander's face as he opened my jacket I probably looked as healthy as I felt. Dean shot me a reassuring smile as he ran some kind of tricorder nonsense over me that made lots of alarming beeping noises.

"Don't worry fella, I can deal with this. It's uh, it's a ruddy tough one, but I've got ya." He motioned to Fidget, who immediately ran off back through the gap in the fence and came back moments later carrying one of those rescue boards you see firefighters use to lift people out of car crashes. Within a short time I was strapped to the board, and was being carried by Dean, Gunnar and Mr Biscuits away to safety with C4 riding along sitting on my crotch to make sure that every Haggis within a fifty foot radius knew that I was not to be touched.

I motioned for them to stop, as I used all my strength to turn around and face Cabbage, who along with his brethren was watching me be carried away. I nodded my head at him, (almost passing out in the process) and lifted my arm to my chest to mimic the movement he had been making before. This must have been the right thing to do, as he copied the movement before shouting loud enough to nearly blow out my mental earwax,

"I Kah'baj, Heid'yin of Maulaggs say that this eater is good eater. He remains SAFE from all kin, aye?"

And with little more than a quick glance over his shoulder, The Mighty Cabbage took off toward the perimeter wall hole along with his kin, dashing through the gap and disappearing into the thick trees beyond.

I caught Teachers attention, trying hard to speak through the pain in my chest, "Their Heid'yin is dead, Cabbage is now in charge." I pointed back at the building beside us, "But it happened moments ago when they all started howling. Whoever killed Cabbage's father must be still inside."

With just a nod to Gunnar, the big man and Mr Biscuits lowered my board to the ground, dropped the large bag carrying HAMMER and raced off back inside the building, followed by Fidget as they left Dean behind to tend to me, Mr Biscuits also it seemed refusing to leave my side for now.

I slumped back down, Teacher shouting to some of the other operatives who'd followed him through the gap to go and organise urgent transport for me back to medical. Mr Biscuits sat on the ground beside me, and with the most gentle grip he could muster, lifted my head and laid it back down across his slim leg as I lay looking up at the umbrella he'd opened above me.

I don't know if he'd somehow managed to subdue his fear pheromones or I was too beat up to register them, but for the first time in a while I felt the safest I'd felt in a long time as his long, grey fingers ran across my brow.

The calm was broken by the sound of rotor blades above. I pushed aside the umbrella to see a dark shape swoop in to hover over the top of the building. It was a sleek looking helicopter with all of its running lights off, a rope ladder dropping from the open door on its side. It soon lifted away from the roof, and I could see a figure clinging onto the ladder with one hand, the other holding tight to a small metal box, looking down at me as the helicopter swung out and swept away across the yard and then the nearby canopy.

It was hard to tell through the rain and pain, but I was sure that it had been Silver escaping into the darkness.

Scott Taylor

Chapter Twenty Five

Equilibrium

It had been a month since the attack on the Son's Facility. I'd spent most of the time recovering from whatever Cabbage had done when he had drained from me whatever he needed to heal himself. I had no physical marks or changes as such, but internally I felt like I sucked out fruit pouch, feeling weak as a kitten and for a good couple of weeks afterwards was still sporadically spitting up flecks of blood. Dean was confident that internally I was doing much better, and that whatever was ailing me would soon pass and I'd be back to normal soon enough. Sure enough, it wasn't long I was up and moving about the facility, spending time at the gym and making calls to check up on my life down south.

On the night of the attack on the Owl facility, Gunnar along with a support team had swept through the building to find the Heid'yin and any remaining Sons that might be still stuck in the building. Despite finding the remains of the dead Maulagg leader, The building had been pretty much evacuated by anyone of importance, and all that remained were some IT staff, security officers, engineers and medics.

Everyone had been interviewed and vetted, and the majority of Owl employees had either faced criminal charges or had been released. The I.T. staff had been held and interrogated longer, as RUST needed to find out exactly what information had been taken from HAMMER before he had been rescued by Gunnar, Dean and Fidget. It seems that at least eighteen percent of data had been compromised and copied according to best estimates. Knowing which eighteen percent though was another story entirely. Unfortunately despite a successful re-integration with the RUST mainframes, (*and a very brief power struggle with NAILS who was adamant that Hammer could 'just fuck right off' and leave her to it*) there was no way to ascertain what had been copied since HAMMERS short term information buffers had been compromised in the rescue.

After the facility had been cleared, I had told Teacher what had happened to my father. However a search for his body proved fruitless, he was nowhere to be found.

As for Silver, nobody had heard or seen from her since the attack on the Owl facility. We knew by the Maulagg's reaction that the Heid'yin had died moments before her escape, and secretly I hoped that the two weren't linked, but seeing her on that rope ladder with the large metal case, I couldn't help but suspect that she'd taken the heart.

Speaking of the Maulaggs we had learned from a Haggvar scout that they had set up a new nest in Westerdale, about fourteen miles outside of Thurso. Apart from a few reports that RUST had to investigate of 'shiny things' going missing from tourists camping throughout the county, they seemed to have settled quietly into their new home. I drove out there recently as my grandparents used to have a cottage there, hoping that my abilities would let me hear them, and to make sure they were okay.

Either they were quiet, absent or deliberately shielding their thoughts from me, but either way I didn't hear a thing from the Maulaggs or Cabbage. I spent some time looking around for anything I might find different from my memories of the place I had from my time spent there as kid, but like most of the county very little had changed over the decade or so that had passed.

I hopped back into the car loaned to me by RUST and set off back to Thurso. As I turned at the junction beside Corner Cottage, I saw a small face with a red stripe over it pull swiftly back into the hedge that lined the property. I smiled and set off for home, hoping the wee furry bastards were doing okay.

I'd officially accepted Teachers offer of a job with RUST, knowing that my future belonged with this world I'd been unceremoniously dumped into. This past while had been one of the toughest chapters of my life. You know, what with people trying to kill me and getting shot in the chest once. Oh, and did I mention I nearly had a sexual liaison with a large seal in a negligee?

Despite all this, I'd never felt more.. 'Needed'. Like I'd finally found a purpose, or something that I was good at. It felt like the right place to be, where I could finally rest and call home, albeit I was currently still living in the hotel which RUST were graciously covering the costs for.

In fact, I was about to get a bigger suite all to myself in the hotel. It seemed that RUST had a long standing agreement with the owner of the place that it could be used as semi-permanent accommodation for whoever they deemed needed it. I was given essentially my own bedsit in the old building, and was still eligible to have my laundry and meals cooked as part of my tenure with RUST.

This was going to help me to set aside a lot more of my wages and savings, and gave me the security to finally hand in my notice to the police force. I'd miss the city and the job, and while packing up my old rented flat in Tillydrone, (an area of Aberdeen well known for its eagle sized seagull attacks and local, sexually explicit Butcher shop), I'd learned that I'd been absolved of any charges in the ongoing investigation of Keith, my former shift-partner. He however had been hit with new charges of sexually inappropriate behaviour, after being caught whacking one out with the help of a 'lady of the night' in his old Ford Focus down outside the old 'Peep-Peeps' pub by the harbour in Aberdeen. Damned shame.

I was going to really miss this city. I'd lived here long enough to lay down some roots, some memories and some regrets, but as I closed the doors on the haulage van I'd hired to transport my stuff north and watched it pull away, I realised that this had never truly been the place for me. I never belonged in a city, surrounded by granite bricks and the faint smell of second hand weed. I needed to be somewhere where I could truly live. And as it turns out, that place was covered in scary biscuit eaters and superpower-giving Haggis.

I walked up to the Broadsword pub that lay on Hayton Road, only a short walk from my old flat and where I'd parked the car I'd borrowed from RUST. I took a deep breath and shouted out loud, "GOODBYE ABERDEEN!!" to which a random voice could be heard from a street away replying, "FUCK OFF, PRICK!"

Good times.

RUST: Harvest of the Hidden

My training with RUST had begun in earnest, Gunnar being in charge of getting me up to speed and Dean charged with patching me up when Gunnar was a bit too 'enthusiastic' with the dangerous parts of it.

The Haggvar in the facility took great delight in having me around. Not only could I translate for them their urgent need for cheese and biscuits whenever it was desired, but also they had someone they could use as a taste tester for their special brand of home brew, someone who could tell them quite how far into space they had launched after two or three sips of the vicious bloody concoction.

I'd also learned that when picking up a sandwich from the canteen, it was best to also pick up an extra one that you had no intention of eating. This was essentially the sacrificial sandwich that you would set beside you for C4 to inevitably steal, leaving you a free second or so to munch down your real sandwich before his interest returned to you.

I'd even met up with the Selkie a couple of times for coffee. Not sure if I could call them 'dates' as such, but whatever they were they were fully encouraged by Teacher since I could be an unofficial liaison with her while her interests still lay with me, and also he felt that relationships between Humanity and the Fae needed interactions like this to mend any wounds that the Sons had recently caused with their treatment of the Maulaggs. She seemed really interested in what had happened at the Sons facility, and I told her everything I was allowed to by Teacher, between bouts of spitting out coffee when she suddenly played footsie with my crotch under the table, or when she suggested we head back to her place to 'knock out some of the cobwebs'.

Despite everything that had happened, I was happy. Possibly for the first time I could remember. Life had found a purpose for me, albeit involving bitey dog creatures, wulvers and blue-faced bald men who looked like they should be performing in some kind of band.

Pulling on Huey's jacket I headed out of the hotel, getting a quick pat on the arse from auld Mary as I left, and walked over to the waiting car with the maniacally waving driver wearing his fake nose and glasses, who along with myself had a date with two other grown men, (technically one of whom was part wolf) in a shed on Oldfield Terrace that had just been allegedly visited by the whisky fairy.

Epilogue

Silver knocked on the large, ornate door and waited anxiously for an answer. Soon, the door was opened by a small man in a dark suit, who without a word beckoned her in and motioned for her to walk ahead toward the figure sitting in darkness in the middle of the room.

A voice suddenly echoed through the large, darkened room,

"So little one, things seemed to have become a little.. Messy?"

Silver winced, a small bead of sweat ran down her forehead as she dropped to one knee, her head bowing low as she answered,

"Not all was lost. We recovered some valuable data from the AI that Thorne captured, and we learned much during the capture of the Maulaggs."

The figure quickly rose from the chair, "Indeed, much was learned from the Maulaggs. I believe a prototype solution was created, which was then subsequently stolen by Thorne?" Silver moved to interject, but the figure cut her off,

"YOU LOST THEM, DID YOU NOT? BOTH THE MAULAGGS AND THE PROTOTYPE?"

Silver lowered her head even further, her forehead almost touching the floor beneath her,

"The attack by RUST was unforseen! We did the best that we could and recovered much before we had to abandon the facility! And Thorne's actions were unexpected!"

The dark figure stepped forward, suddenly bathed in the harsh spotlight that shone from above. Her golden hair shimmering as she glowered down at the prone young woman in front of her.

"I expect more, especially from you of all people." Her tone softened as she leaned down and pulled Silver to her feet, "But do not worry child, you are not entirely to blame. And besides, if anything it's shown us how the strengths of our enemies lie, and the capabilities of their new, 'ally'. She turned and returned to her chair, the little man in the dark suit moving to her side with a large glass on a silver tray.

"I trust that you have looked over the plans for the new facility, and how I wish the Owls to focus their talons moving forward?"

"I have, extensively. And I assure you that no more mistakes will happen."

The golden haired woman lifted her glass, taking a long drink before returning it to the tray beside her.

"And how are you developing with your newfound powers?"

Silver froze where she stood. Lifting her head slowly toward the golden-haired woman she smiled, *"Things go well, I am finding it easier to use the more I work with it."* Silver bowed once more, *"I thank you again for allowing me the opportunity to take this gift. I will honour it."*

Silver hesitated before continuing, *Also, if I may be so bold, can I ask what your ongoing intentions are with Angus?"*

The woman in the chair smiled, *"He amuses me and I enjoy his company! Plus, this gift he shares with you now, it is best if it's kept under my scrutiny for the foreseeable, don't you agree?"*

Silver's smile dropped for a second before she recovered, *"Of course. But does it not trouble you that he and I are.. Siblings?"*

The Selkie rose up from her seat to her full height, her shoulders squared as she looked down upon Silver who had dropped to her knees once more on the floor before her. "*Why should I be troubled that you and he share a father? The boy has no blood link to me.*" the Selkie kneeled down, taking Silver's hands and raising her back to her feet before pulling her into an embrace, "*I'm sure you have no issue with me having a pet for a while, do you child?*"

Silver stepped back from the golden haired woman in front of her, "*Not at all your highness.*" she replied, before bowing then turning to walk to the large ornate doors leading out of the chamber. As she stepped through, she turned and smiled at the woman in the chair,

"*And I will continue as always to honour you, dear mother.*"

The doors closed.

The End.

Scott Taylor

Acknowledgements

Rust: Harvest of the Hidden would not be the book it is today without the incredible support and encouragement of many wonderful people.

First and foremost, I would like to express my deepest gratitude to my wife, Claire 'Roobs' Taylor. Her unwavering belief in my abilities, her insightful feedback, and her patience throughout the writing process have been invaluable. I am eternally grateful for her love and support.

I am also indebted to my dear friend, Alex 'Tiny' Gauntt. His keen eye for detail, his honest critiques, and his enthusiasm for the story have significantly improved the quality of this book. His contributions have been instrumental in shaping the final product.

A special thanks goes to Dean Mayes. His friendship, his advice as a fellow author, and his thoughtful edits have been a constant source of inspiration and encouragement.

I would also like to acknowledge Stephen Early for his relentless teasing and unwavering belief that I would never actually finish this book. His constant prodding served as a healthy dose of motivation.

Finally, I want to thank my family and friends for their love, support, and encouragement. Your belief in me has meant the world. To everyone who has expressed interest in reading my work, thank you so much for your support.

Scott Taylor

Find out more about my other projects over at scotttaylor.uk

Printed in Great Britain
by Amazon